PENGUIN BOOKS
THE FEAST OF ROSES

Indu Sundaresan, born and raised in India, came to the United States for graduate school. In addition to her first novel, *The Twentieth Wife*, which was published in 2002, her short fiction has also appeared in *The Vincent Brothers Review* and on iVillage.com. She lives in the Seattle, Washington, area.

Praise for *The Twentieth Wife*

'Rich and realistic... A delicious story.'

—*The Seattle Times*

'Indu Sundaresan has written a fascinating novel about a fascinating time, and has brought it alive with characters that are at once human and legendary, that move with grace and panache across the brilliant stage she has reconstructed for them.'

—Chitra Divakaruni, author of
Mistress of Spices and *Unknown Errors of Our Lives*

'Good, old-fashioned historical fiction... Full of jewelled beauties and crumbling ruins, [*The Twentieth Wife*] satisfies every craving for the pomp and mystery of India's past.'

—*Chicago Tribune*

'...a wonderful tale of love, hate and deceit, all woven into one magnificent Mughal tapestry.'

—*Indian Express*, Chennai

'Sundaresan is a gifted storyteller with an obvious passion for history.'

—*USA Today*

'The epic tale... is informative, convincing, and madly entertaining.'

—Marilyn Yalom, author of
A History of the Wife and *A History of the Breast*

ALSO BY INDU SUNDARESAN

The Twentieth Wife

The Feast of Roses

INDU SUNDARESAN

PENGUIN BOOKS

Penguin Books India (P) Ltd., 11 Community Centre, Panchsheel Park,
New Delhi 110 017, India
Penguin Books Ltd., 80 Strand, London WC2R 0RL, UK
Penguin Group Inc., 375 Hudson Street, New York, NY 10014, USA
Penguin Books Australia Ltd., 250 Camberwell Road, Camberwell,
Victoria 3124, Australia
Penguin Books Canada Ltd., 10 Alcorn Avenue, Suite 300, Toronto,
Ontario, M4V 3B2,Canada
Penguin Books (NZ) Ltd., Cnr Rosedale and Airborne Roads, Albany,
Auckland, New Zealand
Penguin Books (South Africa) (Pty) Ltd, 24 Sturdee Avenue,
Rosebank 2196, South Africa

First published by Atria Books 2003
First published in India by Penguin Books India 2004

Copyright © Indu Sundaresan 2004

Typeset in *Perpetua* by SÜRYA, New Delhi
Printed at Pauls Press, New Delhi

For my husband Uday,
for, quite simply, everything

The mask is off—the charm is wrought—
And Selim to his heart has caught,
His Nourmahal, his Haram's Light!
And well do vanish'd frowns enhance
The charm of every brighten'd glance;
And dearer seems each dawning smile
For having lost its light awhile:
And, happier now, for all her sighs,
As on his arm her head reposes,
She whispers him, with laughing eyes,
'Remember, love, the Feast of Roses.'

—THOMAS MOORE, *Lalla Rookh*

Selected Members of Mehrunnisa's Family

Selected Members of the Mughal Imperial Family

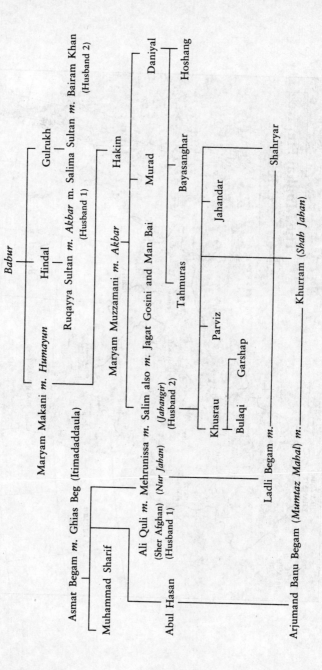

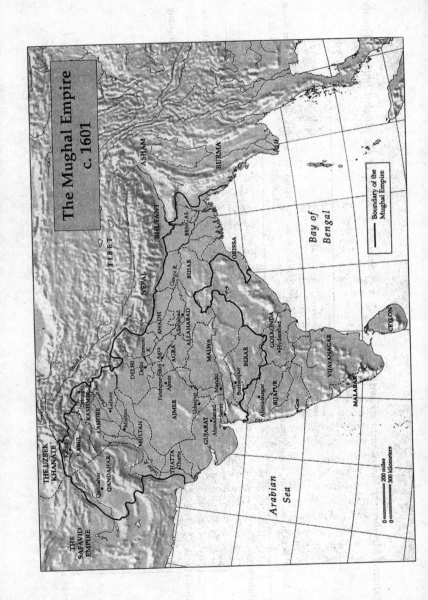

The Mughal Empire
c. 1601

THE SAFAVID EMPIRE

THE UZBEK KHANATE

Qandahar

QANDAHAR

KABUL

Kabul

Khyber

Multan

MULTAN

LAHORE

Lahore

Srinagar

KASHMIR

TIBET

NEPAL

BHUTAN

ASHAM

BURMA

DELHI

Delhi

Fatehpur-Sikri

Agra

AGRA

Jumna R.

AWADH

Allahabad

ALLAHABAD

Ganges R.

BIHAR

BENGAL

ORISSA

AJMER

Ajmer

Udaipur

MALWA

Mandu

BERAR

GOLKONDA

Hyderabad

GUJARAT

Ahmadabad

Surat

THATTA

Thatta

Burhanpur

Ahmadnagar

BIJAPUR

Goa

VIJAYANAGAR

MALABAR

CEYLON

Arabian
Sea

Bay of
Bengal

0   200 miles
0   300 kilometers

Boundary of the
Mughal Empire

Principal Characters

(in alphabetical order)

Abdur Rahim — The Khan-i-khanan, Commander-in-chief of the Imperial Army

Abul Hasan — Mehrunnisa's brother

Akbar — Third Emperor of Mughal India

Ali Quli Khan Istajlu — Mehrunnisa's first husband

Arjumand Banu — Mehrunnisa's niece and Abul's daughter, later Empress Mumtaz Mahal

Ghias Beg — Mehrunnisa's father

Hoshiyar Khan — Chief eunuch of Jahangir's harem

Jagat Gosini — Jahangir's second wife

Jahangir — Akbar's son and fourth Emperor of Mughal India

Khurram — Jahangir's third son, born of Jagat Gosini

Khusrau — Jahangir's first son, born of Man Bai

Ladli — Mehrunnisa's daughter by Ali Quli

Mahabat Khan — Jahangir's childhood cohort and minister

Mehrunnisa — Ghias's daughter, later titled Nur Jahan

Muhammad Sharif — Jahangir's childhood cohort, now Grand Vizier of the empire

Nur Jahan — Mehrunnisa's title upon becoming Empress

Parviz — Jahangir's second son

Ruqayya Sultan Begam — Akbar's chief queen, or Padshah Begam, now a Dowager Empress

Shahryar — Jahangir's fourth son

Thomas Roe — First official ambassador from England and the court of James I

Chapter One

Nature had endowed her with a quick understanding, a piercing intellect, a versatile temper, sound common sense. Education had developed the gifts of nature in no common degree. She was versed in Persian literature and composed verses, limpid and flowing, which assisted her in capturing the heart of her husband.

—BENI PRASAD, *History of Jahangir*

THE MONTHS OF JUNE AND JULY PASSED. THE MONSOONS WERE TARDY THIS year—the nights hinted rain constantly with an aroma in the air, a cooling on the skin, soundless lightning across skies. But when morning came, the sun rose strong again, mocking Agra and its inhabitants. And the days crawled by, brazenly hot, when every breath was an effort, every movement a struggle, every night sweat-stewed. In temples, incantations were offered, the muezzins called the faithful to prayers, their voices melodious and pleading, and the bells of the Jesuit churches chimed. But the gods seemed indifferent. The rice paddies lay plowed after the pre-monsoon rains, awaiting the seedlings; too long a wait and the ground would grow hard again.

A few people moved torpidly in the streets of Agra; only the direst of emergencies had called them from their cool, stone-flagged homes. Even the normally frantic pariah dogs lay panting on doorsteps, too exhausted to yelp when passing urchins pelted them with stones.

The bazaars were barren too, shopfronts pulled down, shopkeepers too tired to haggle with buyers. Custom could wait for cooler times. The whole city seemed to have slowed to a halt.

The imperial palaces and courtyards were hushed in the night, the corridors empty of footsteps. Slaves and eunuchs plied iridescent peacock feather fans, wiping their perspiring faces with one hand. The ladies of the harem slept under the intermittent breeze of the fans, goblets of cold sherbets flavoured with khus and ginger resting by their sides. Every now and then, a slave would refresh the goblet, bringing in another one filled with new shards of ice. When her mistress awoke, and wake she would many times during the night, her drink would be ready. The ice, carved in huge chunks from the Himalayan mountains, covered with gunnysacks and brought down to the plains in bullock carts, was a blessing for everyone, nobles and commoners alike. But in this heat, ice melted all too soon, disappearing into a puddle of warm water under sawdust and jute.

In Emperor Jahangir's apartments, music floated through the courtyard, stopping and tripping in the still night air as the musicians' slick fingers slipped on the strings of the sitar.

The courtyard was square, built with Mughal and Persian precision in sharp-cut lines. An arched, cusped verandah filled one side; along the others were trees and bushes, smudged and indistinct in the darkness. In the centre was a square pool, its waters silent and calm. The sandstone steps of the verandah led down to a marble platform that thrust into the pool like a missing tooth in a gaping smile. Two figures lay here in sleep under the benign gaze of the night sky. The music drifted down from the screened balcony over the verandah's arches.

When Mehrunnisa opened her eyes, she first saw the sky above her, packed with stars. Every inch of her vision was filled with them, a ceiling of diamonds on black velvet. Emperor Jahangir slept by her side, his forehead resting on her shoulder. His breath, warm on her skin, was steady. Mehrunnisa could not see her husband's face, just the top of his head. His hair lay flattened against his skull with a ring around where the imperial turban sat during the day. She touched his face lightly, her fingers resting against his cheekbones, then swirling down his chin, where a stubble scratched at the pads of her fingers. She did this without waking him, feeling his face, searching through familiarity, although her memory was flooded with every contour and line.

When Mehrunnisa had gone to sleep, she had been alone. She had waited for Jahangir, reading by the light of an oil lamp, but soon, exhausted by the heat, the words blurring before her eyes, she had slept, the book by her side. He must have come to her later, taken the book away, covered her with a weightless cotton sheet. Her fingers stilled on the Emperor's face and moved to lie on his chest.

For the first time in many, many years, Mehrunnisa woke to an absence of feeling. There was no fear, no apprehension, no sense that something was amiss in her life. For the first time, too, she had not put out a hand blindly, half-asleep, for Ladli. She knew that Ladli was safe, in a nearby apartment. She knew, without thinking about it, that before he slept, the Emperor would have glanced in at Ladli, so he could tell her when she woke that her daughter was fine.

She rested her face on his head, the dull essence of sandalwood filling her nostrils. It was a scent she associated with Jahangir, with comfort, with love. Love. Yes, this was love. A different kind, one she had not known existed, did not think she could have. For many years she had wanted a child, then she had had Ladli. For all those years she had wanted Jahangir too, not really knowing why.

Because he made her smile inside, because he lightened her life, gave it meaning, a fullness, a purpose. It surprised her, this force of feeling. It frightened her—this possibility that her self would be so engrossed by him once they were married that she could have no control over the life she had so carefully built.

And now it was two months after the wedding, two languorous months, when time seemed to pass in a slow circle around them. Even the empire and its concerns stepped away, hovering somewhere in the periphery. But last night, for the first time, Jahangir had been called away as they had gone to bed. The empire would wait no longer.

She moved Jahangir's head gently onto a silk-covered pillow, shifted his arm from where it lay on her stomach and sat up. To her left, along the arches of the verandah, the eunuchs on guard stiffened. She sat there looking at them, these half-men who had care of the Emperor's person. There were fifteen eunuchs, one in each sandstone arch. They stood with their feet apart, hands behind their backs, gazes fixed past the pool into the deep shadows of the garden. The guard around Jahangir changed every twelve hours, and in different combinations so no two men would have the opportunity to concoct a conspiracy.

As she sat there, looking at them, being pointedly ignored by them, sweat began to pool damply under the weight of her hair, on her neck, soaking through the thin cotton of the kurta she wore. She rubbed her back and unwound her hair from its plait until it lay about her shoulders in a dense blanket. Stepping past the sleeping Emperor, Mehrunnisa went to the edge of the platform and sat down, letting her legs dangle in the water. A breeze swept through the courtyard, and she raised her face to it, lifting her arms so it could ruffle the long sleeves of her tunic. It brought the scent of smouldering neem leaves from braziers in the verandah, unpleasant enough to keep away the mosquitoes.

The water around her was afloat with banyan leaf lanterns, stitched together with little sticks to form cups that held sesame oil with a cotton thread wick. At one end of the pool, in full night bloom, a *parijat* tree swooned over, slowly drifting its tiny white flowers into the water. The stars were captured on the pool's surface too, intermittently, where the light of the lanterns did not reach. Pushing herself off the edge of the marble platform, Mehrunnisa melted into the pool.

The water was warm as honey and heavy around her, but cooler than the air. Mehrunnisa dipped her head in, letting her hair swirl wet about her face. She said her new name out loud. 'Nur Jahan.' Her voice fractured in the denseness of the water, little air bubbles blossomed and escaped to the top, tickling around her cheeks.

She was Nur Jahan. 'Light of the World'. In her reposed the brilliance of the heavens. Or so Jahangir had said when he had given her the title the day they were married. *From today my beloved Empress will be called Nur Jahan.* No longer just Mehrunnisa, the name her father had given her at birth. Nur Jahan was a name for the world, for other people to call her. It was a name that commanded, that inspired respect and demanded attention. All useful qualities for a name to have. The Emperor was telling the court, the empire, and the other women of the imperial harem that Mehrunnisa was no trifling love.

She kicked away from the platform and swam. When she reached the parijat, she rested against the wall, watching the white flowers coast down like flakes of snow. She did not turn to her left to look at the hazy figures in the verandah, and if they were watching her, they did not betray it by any movement. Yet, had she stayed too long with her head under the water, some hand would have come to lift her out of it. For to them, she was Jahangir's most prized possession now. Mehrunnisa pedalled her feet in the water, restless, longing for some movement, something the eunuchs could not see, something that the whole imperial *zenana* would not know by tomorrow.

This watching bothered her, tired her out, always wondering if she was doing the right thing. Jahangir never worried about the people around him—he had grown up with them, understood they were necessary. He thought so little of them that in his mind they were as divans or the cushions or the goblets of wine.

She turned away and cleared the parijat flowers from the stone edge of the pool with a wet hand. Then, picking up the flowers one by one, she laid them in a row. Then another row, petals turned inward towards her. This was the courtyard of the *Diwan-i-am*, the Hall of Public Audience. Here were the war elephants at the back, the commoners ahead of them, the merchants, the nobles, and, in the very front, the throne where Jahangir sat. To the side, she put two more flowers, behind and to the right of the Emperor. Pulling off the petals of the parijat flowers, she laid the orange stems, edge to edge, around the last two flowers. This was the harem balcony at court; the stems were the marble latticework screen that hid the imperial zenana. Unseen by the men below. Unheard by them.

Jahangir had just begun his daily routine of darbars, public audiences, meetings with courtiers. Mehrunnisa sat behind him in the zenana balcony, watching as the Emperor dealt with the day's business. Sometimes, she almost spoke out loud, when a thought occurred to her, when an idea came, then she stopped, knowing that the screen put her in a different place. That it made her a woman. One without a voice, void of opinion.

But what if... she picked up one of the harem flowers and laid it in centre court, in front of the throne. For many years, when she had been married to Ali Quli, when Jahangir had been just a distant dream, Mehrunnisa had chafed against the restrictions on her life. She had wanted to be in the imperial balcony, not merely an onlooker but a member of the imperial harem—not just a lady-in-waiting but an Empress. She moved the flower back within the orange-stem confines of the balcony screen. It was not enough. Could she ask for more? But how much more, and how to ask for it? Would Jahangir give to her what she asked? Would he defy these unsaid rules that fettered her life as his Empress, as his wife, as a woman?

Her hand trembling, she picked up the flower again and put it next to Jahangir. There they sat, two parijat flowers, fragrant with bloom, side by side on the imperial throne. Mehrunnisa laid her chin on the edge of the stone and closed her eyes. All her life she had wanted the life of a man, with the freedom to go where she wished, to do what she wanted, to say what came to her mind without worry for consequences. She had been a watcher in her own life, unable to change the direction it took. Until now...

With a gentle finger, she moved her flower back a little, just behind Jahangir, but still in open view of the court.

In an inner street, the night chowkidar called out the hour as he went by, his stick tapping on the ground, 'Two o'clock and all is well.' Mehrunnisa heard a muffled cough and saw a eunuch's hand move to cover his mouth. A small frown gathered on her forehead. In time, only she would be exempt from the prying eyes of the zenana servants and spies—when she was the Padshah Begam, the chief lady of the realm. Empress Jagat Gosini held that title now.

She swam back to the platform through the warm water, and when she reached it, she put her elbows on the marble and rested her head in her hands, looking at Jahangir. She traced a finger over his brow, then put it in her mouth, tasting his skin. He stirred.

'Can't you sleep?'

He woke like this always, not needing to shake off dreams. Once she had asked him why. And he had replied that when she wanted him, he would give up sleep.

'It is too warm, your Majesty.'

Jahangir smoothed her wet hair from her forehead, his hand lingering on the curve of her cheek. 'Sometimes I cannot believe you are here with me.' He looked intently at her face, then reached into the water for a leaf lamp. Holding it close to her, he said, 'What is it?'

'Nothing. The heat. Nothing.'

The Emperor laid the lamp back in the water and pushed it on its way. Clasping her hand, he pulled her out of the pool. A eunuch slid into view, holding out silk towels. Mehrunnisa knelt at the edge of the platform, lifted her arms, and allowed the Emperor to peel off the kurta she was wearing. He wiped the water from her body slowly, bending to inhale the musk scent of her skin. Then he dried her hair, rubbing the strands with a towel until it lay damp around her shoulders. He did all this with great deliberation. She waited obediently until he was finished, the warm night air on her shoulders, her waist, her legs.

'Come here.' Jahangir pulled her onto his lap, and she wrapped her legs around him. He framed her face with his hands and pulled it close to his own. 'It is never nothing with you, Mehrunnisa. What do you want? A necklace? A jagir?'

'I want them out of here.'

'They are gone,' he replied, knowing what she meant. Jahangir did not look back as one of his hands left her face to signal the eunuchs in dismissal, but Mehrunnisa clasped it and pulled it back.

'I want to do this, your Majesty.'

'You have as much right as I do, my dear.'

Still looking into his shadowed face, she raised her hand. Out of the corner of her eye she could see the eunuchs tense, hold still, then glance at each other. They had strict orders not to leave the Emperor's presence unless commanded by him... and only by him. No wife, no concubine, no mother had that power. But this wife, she was different. So they waited for a sign from Jahangir. But he did not move, did not nod his head in assent. A minute passed thus, then one of the eunuchs stepped out of line, bowed to the royal couple, and shuffled out of the verandah. The others followed, hearts suddenly wild with fear—afraid of obeying, yet more afraid of disobeying. Mehrunnisa dropped her hand.

'They have gone, your Majesty,' she said, wonder in her voice.

'When you command, Mehrunnisa,' Jahangir said, 'do so with authority. Never think you will be ignored, and you will not be ignored.'

'Thank you.'

The Emperor's teeth flashed. 'If I were to thank you for all you have brought to me, I would be doing so for the rest of my life.' His voice echoed near her ear. 'What is it you want? Tell me or you will fret for it.'

She was silent, not knowing how to ask, not really knowing what to ask for. She wanted to be more of a presence in his life, and not just here, within the walls of the zenana.

'I wish to…,' she said slowly, 'I wish to come with you to the *jharoka* tomorrow.'

Early on in his reign, Jahangir had instituted twelve rules of conduct for the empire. Among those rules were many he did not obey himself—prohibiting consumption of alcohol was one. But these, he thought, would provide a framework for the empire, not for himself. He was above those rules. Wanting to be fair and equitable to his subjects, he imposed the ritual of the jharoka, something his father, Emperor Akbar, had not done, something that was exclusively Jahangir's.

He called it thus—a jharoka—a glimpse, for it was to be, for the first time since the Mughal conquest of India around a hundred years ago, a personal viewing of the Emperor by any subject in the empire.

The jharoka was a special balcony, built into the outer bulwark of the Agra fort, where Jahangir gave audience to the people three times a day. In the early morning, with the rising of the sun, he presented himself at the balcony on the eastern side of the fort, at noon on the south side, and at five o'clock in the evening as the sun descended into the west sky, on the western side. Jahangir considered this his most important responsibility. It was here the commoners came to petition him, here he listened to their appeals, important or not. And in the balcony he stood alone, his ministers and the commoners below him. It cut away the pomp surrounding his crown, made him less of a figurehead on a faraway throne.

'But you do come to the jharoka with me, Mehrunnisa,' Jahangir said. Something more was coming. He was wary, watchful now. For the past few weeks, Mehrunnisa had stood behind the balcony arch, along with the eunuchs who guarded his back, listening, talking with him later about the petitions.

'I want to be with you in the balcony, standing in front of the nobles and commoners.' She said this softly, but without hesitation. Ask with authority and she would not be ignored, he had said.

Clouds began to move across the skies, blanketing the stars. Lightning flashed behind them, branches of silver light blotted by grey. She sat in his arms, unclothed, covered only by her now-dry hair that tumbled over her shoulders down to her hips.

'It has never been done before,' Jahangir said finally. And it had not. The women of his zenana, whatever their relationship to him, had always stayed behind the brick walls of the harem. They were *heard* outside, in the orders they gave through stewards and slaves and eunuchs, heard also when he did something they wanted. 'Why do you want this?'

She asked a question in response. 'Why not?'

The Emperor smiled. 'I can see that you are going to cause trouble for me, Mehrunnisa. Look,' he raised his eyes to the sky, and she followed his gaze, 'do you think rain will come?'

'If it does...' She paused. 'If it does, can I come to the jharoka tomorrow?'

The clouds had now covered the skies above their heads. They looked like the others had, fat and thick with rain, sometimes pelting drops of water on the city of Agra. And then, some errant wind would come to carry them away, clearing the skies for the Sun God to ride his chariot again. Mehrunnisa was commanding the monsoon rains. She smiled to herself. And why not? First the eunuchs, now the night sky.

He said, 'Close your eyes.'

She did. With his eyes shut too, with her aroma to lead him, Jahangir bent to the curve of her neck. She wrapped her hair around them. She did not open her eyes, just felt the warmth of his breath, sensed him tasting a line of sweat that escaped from her hairline down her face to lodge itself against her shoulder blade, shivered as the rough of his fingertips scraped against the sides of her breasts. They did not speak again.

And afterwards, they slept.

The sun, a flat line of gold behind purple clouds against the horizon, woke them the next morning. Mehrunnisa lay with her head against a velvet pillow looking up at the play of light against the sky. The clouds hung dense above her. But there was no rain. Moisture in the air, but no rain.

The eunuchs were back in their positions in the verandah arches, slave girls moved in on noiseless feet carrying brass vessels of water. Mehrunnisa and Jahangir brushed their teeth with a twig from the neem tree, and when the muezzin's voice called for prayer from the mosque, they knelt side by side on prayer rugs and lifted their hands towards the west, towards Mecca.

And then, as they had all these days past, the Emperor and his new wife left their apartments to wend through the palace corridors for the first jharoka of the day.

They walked in silence, hand in hand, not looking at each other. The servants behind them padded on soft bare feet, Mehrunnisa's ghagara swished over the smooth marble floors. She could not talk, could not bring herself to ask again—would she be standing behind the arch of the balcony or with the Emperor? In a sudden flight of superstition, she looked again at the sky as they passed, but no, the clouds lay massive and unwilling. A weight settled over her and her feet dragged.

They reached the entrance to the balcony, where the eunuchs of the imperial zenana spread out from the doorway in two lines. When Jahangir entered the balcony, they would close ranks behind him.

Hoshiyar Khan stood in front, taller than most of the other men around him. He was dressed, even this early in the morning, as immaculately as a king. His hair was smoothed down below his turban, his face grave with responsibility, his manner impeccable. Hoshiyar had been head eunuch of Emperor Jahangir's harem for twenty-five years now. For a long time, almost all that time, Hoshiyar had been Empress Jagat Gosini's shadow, by her side, advising her, lending her his support. A month before her wedding, Mehrunnisa, greatly daring, asked for him to be her personal eunuch. So Hoshiyar had come to her side, and willingly, for had he not wanted to be here, he would have found a way to disregard even Jahangir's orders.

He bowed. 'I trust your Majesties had a good night?'

He would know of all that passed, know also that Mehrunnisa had dismissed his men from the verandah, know that they had left at her command and why. It seemed to Mehrunnisa that he nodded briefly, just a flicker of an eyelash, with a smile more on his countenance than on his lips before he turned to the Emperor.

Hoshiyar leaned out of the arch and raised his hand. The royal orchestra started to play, announcing the Emperor's arrival. The shehnai trilled, the drums were beaten, and in the distance, a cannon let out a harmless boom.

Mehrunnisa almost spoke again, opened her mouth, and then closed it. With the noise of the orchestra echoing around them, the Emperor reached behind her head. Her indigo veil lay shawl-like over her shoulders, and he raised one end and brought it over her face. As Jahangir stepped out into the balcony to the glow of the lightening eastern sky, he tightened his grip on Mehrunnisa's hand and pulled her with him.

Almost the first sensation she experienced, one utterly irrelevant, was that the marble ledge of the balcony, carved with thin vines of jasmine flowers, came up to her waist. It hid their hands, still linked together. Then Mehrunnisa looked down at the expanse of inclined backs, clad in thin cottons embroidered with gold zari, bowed in unison. The nobles and the commoners, the orchestra itself to one side, the slaves and guards armed with spears and muskets—not one eye was raised to them.

Even the Mir Tozak, the Master of Ceremonies, had his head bent. His was the first to raise though, the first to see the Emperor and the lady by his side. His voice, when he found it, came in an uneasy quaver, 'All hail Jahangir Padshah!'

The nobles straightened up and saw the veiled figure at Jahangir's side. Involuntarily, most of the men drew in breaths of astonishment. In the silent courtyard, stilled of drums and trumpets, the noise was like a rush of wind, gone in an instant.

Mehrunnisa held on tight to Jahangir's hand. Unsaid between them was that Jahangir was granting her a privilege, and Mehrunnisa acknowledged it in silence. It was not a privilege she would misuse. It filled her heart that he would take her into the jharoka despite the chaos it would cause.

Mehrunnisa watched the men below, knowing no one could see her face This life of hers, behind a veil, had its advantages. Her hands were cold. It was the first time a woman from the imperial harem had appeared in public, veiled from view, but boldly present. Jahangir stepped ahead of her, holding his back straight, his shoulders thrown back, his imperial turban sitting squarely on his head. For these minutes of the jharoka, he was the Emperor, no longer the man who slept with such comfort in her arms. These were lessons she was fast learning, on how to have a private face and a public one.

'My good people,' Jahangir began, his voice strong with authority, 'as you can see, I am well and have had a good night's sleep.' He turned to the Mir Arz, the Officer in Charge of Petitions. 'Bring forward the petitioners.'

For the next thirty minutes, the Mir Arz called out the names of the nobles gathered in the courtyard to present petitions to the Emperor. They came forward, performed the *taslim* thrice, and then presented the Emperor with a gift. Depending upon the gift's value or uniqueness, Jahangir would signal his consent for them to speak. As for the common people, he chose his petitioners based on their looks, or perhaps the colour of a turban or where they stood in the courtyard or whether they faced east or west. This whimsical culling out of the supplicants was the only way to hear as many petitions as possible in the limited time allowed. Given the sheer numbers, most were turned away, and they would return day after day, hoping that eventually the familiarity of their faces would catch the Emperor's eye.

Mehrunnisa was silent, watching the two men on the right side of the jharoka. Mahabat Khan and Muhammad Sharif were the two main players at court. They were powerful, in both position and influence over the Emperor. Mahabat Khan was an intelligent man, grasping and cunning. It was said he had refused the rank Sharif now held, that of Amir-ul-umra—Prime Minister and Grand Vizier—preferring to rule without a title.

A petitioner came forward. Mehrunnisa listened to what he had to say, thinking all the while that his name was familiar. Ah, he was Mahabat Khan's cousin. And so it had been during the daily darbar also. Cousins, friends, brothers, all had been granted honours, estates and contracts while others had been turned away.

Unable to restrain herself, Mehrunnisa put a hand on Jahangir's arm. 'Your Majesty.'

The Emperor turned to her.

'Perhaps it would be best if this matter was decided later on. There are others, more needy. This man already has a *mansab* of six hundred horses, raising it now would do little good,' she said. She spoke softly. Jahangir hesitated, then allowed his gaze to fall back on the Mir Tozak. This was the Mir Tozak's cue to dismiss the petitioner.

In the courtyard below, anger lit Mahabat Khan's face, and he whipped around to Mehrunnisa. From under her veil, Mehrunnisa held his gaze, forcing herself to keep from flinching.

When the jharoka was over, Mehrunnisa and Jahangir left together, the audience quiet, cautious. She went back to her apartments immersed in thought. She had raised her voice against Mahabat Khan. It was not something he would easily forget, this public denial of a request. Mahabat would be a dangerous enemy, one to be regarded with care.

Her step faltered. Why had she spoken at the jharoka? It was a small thing—this touch on Jahangir's arm, this murmur in his ear, but played out under frighteningly huge circumstances. Mahabat's flare of wrath at her, as though he could see through and beyond the cover of her veil, proved this. But to Mehrunnisa, standing there alone, among those powerful men of the empire, *above* those men, this blatant demonstration of her power had been irresistible. Mahabat would never forget this morning's jharoka. And neither would she, Mehrunnisa thought.

She went through the wide doors of her apartments and stood with the docility of a tame fawn as the slave girls undressed her for a bath.

Hoshiyar had told her once that Mahabat had tried to stop the Emperor from marrying her. Why? What did Mahabat care about the women of the imperial harem? He had no enmity against her father or her brother... yet he had spoken against her. Why?

It was almost as though Mahabat was the Emperor, not Jahangir. He held no special title. Yet there had been times when he had cleverly overruled Jahangir's intentions. One word from Mahabat, and the empire stopped in its tracks, righting itself in whatever direction he pointed. This Mehrunnisa had forgotten in her haste to speak during the jharoka. It did not matter, she told herself. It *could* not matter. If she were to be supreme in the zenana and at the court, she would make enemies. That she had always known.

Coolness flitted over her skin and she turned to the window. One of the slave girls, about Ladli's age, ran excitedly to the balcony. Clouds blotted out the weak morning sun, enraged and black. They seemed to suck out the heat from the palaces. When Mehrunnisa stepped into her bath, it started to rain. No mere sprinkling—this was a violent, war-filled rain, thronging with the sound of a thousand drums.

As she lay there, listening to and watching the rain outside, Mehrunnisa's heart became light. It would not be easy to break the hold Mahabat had over the Emperor. Theirs was a connection that went back many years. But, Mehrunnisa thought, so did her understanding with Jahangir. All things could be broken in the end.

Before the jharoka was over, the whole zenana knew of Mehrunnisa's presence at the balcony. The eunuchs and attendants had been very busy. Even as the new Empress left the balcony, word fled throughout the palaces of this unprecedented occurrence.

The palaces of the imperial harem were many and scattered, connected by a maze of exquisitely wrought brick courtyards and lushly verdant gardens, all inside the Red Fort at Agra. Within the harem lived the three hundred women connected with the Emperor.

The hierarchy was simple. The reigning Emperor's wives took precedence over all the other women in the zenana. Of them there would be one dominant one—the Padshah Begam. With that title came supremacy over the entire zenana, the power to watch, to weave intrigues into the women's lives, to control their finances, their very lives.

Empress Jagat Gosini, Jahangir's second wife, had married him twenty-five years earlier, when he had still been a prince. Then, Jagat Gosini had been a young girl with classic features and a haughty countenance. Emperor Akbar's ruling Padshah Begam, Ruqayya, had seen the stiffness in Jagat Gosini's spine as she bent to perform the taslim in front of her, the raising of an eyebrow when something disgusted her, and she had viewed this arrogance with wariness.

And so a feud had started between the two women. They never fought openly; instead, they waged a subtle campaign for supremacy, tormenting each other with sarcastic, hurtful comments delivered on the sly. As long as Emperor Akbar had been alive, Ruqayya had been absolute in the zenana, but once Jahangir ascended the throne, she had to give up her place to Jagat Gosini. For though Jahangir had married many wives by the time he became Emperor, Jagat Gosini, a princess in her own right, born to a mighty king, easily established herself paramount in his harem.

The evening of the momentous jharoka, Mehrunnisa went to visit the Dowager Empress in her palace. There were six palaces fronting the Yamuna River at Agra within the walls of the fort, and each had a unique style reflective of its occupants. Some had marble balconies and verandahs built into the battlements of the fort, and some were made of the same red sandstone that graced the fort's walls. Mehrunnisa did not have one yet; but when the time came, she wanted it to be hers, with her voice directing the laying of each stone, and supervising the polishing of the marble floors.

Among the symbols of imperial esteem, this mansion of brick, sandstone, marble, enamel and mirrorwork was paramount in the zenana's world. The abodes, though, were merely loans during the Emperor's lifetime; sometimes, if a woman was stupid enough to lose favour, for less than the Emperor's lifetime. And as the crown moved to the heir, his harem would chase out the current occupants.

Yet Dowager Empress Ruqayya—a woman who was not even Jahangir's mother, but merely his father's favourite wife—had a palace.

When Mehrunnisa entered, Ruqayya was lounging in her usual pose on her divan, puffing at a hukkah and watching the antics of a Chinese lapdog someone had presented her. The water pipe gurgled as she drew on it, and smoke swirled blue around the room, laced with the sweet smell of opium.

Ruqayya saw Mehrunnisa at the doorway—it was hard to ignore her presence, for all the maids had risen to bow and there was a general bustle. But Ruqayya turned her attention to the dog, putting down the hukkah to clap with the delight of a child, then calling the ugly little animal to her to pet it. A few minutes passed thus, with Mehrunnisa standing at the door, waiting, and Ruqayya busy with the dog as it pranced around her, filling the now-silent room with little yips of barks.

Finally the Dowager Empress turned to one of her eunuchs. 'Well, here she comes, after all this time. One would think she grew horns of pride when she married the Emperor. Some people forget I have been Empress for a long time, longer than them.'

Mehrunnisa laughed and bent in front of Ruqayya in a well-executed taslim, touching her right hand to her forehead and bending from the waist. 'How could I forget, your Majesty? Even if I were to do so, you would not let me.'

She straightened and watched Ruqayya try to maintain the frown on her face. Then she gave up and laughed in return, her plump face creasing into well-run lines. 'Ah, Mehrunnisa, it is good to see you. Does it take two months to visit an old friend? Has the Emperor enamoured you this much?'

Mehrunnisa sat down next to her. 'Only a little. I hear it is said in the zenana that I am the one who has enamoured him. Not just enamoured him, but used sorcery to cast a spell on him, to keep him by my side. I am a simple woman, your Majesty. Where would I have access to such guiles?'

Ruqayya laughed again, a rich, deep laugh from inside her throat. 'You simple? Nothing has ever been simple about you, Mehrunnisa. Not since you were nine and refused to cry when the concubine slapped you.'

'And you saved me then by scolding her.'

'True.' Ruqayya's beady eyes took on a shrewd look. 'That was a small thing, but this, your becoming an Empress, was also due to me. Remember that always, Mehrunnisa.'

Mehrunnisa shook her head. 'I will not forget, your Majesty. There are few things I forget, this is certainly not one of them.'

A servant brought a copper and silver hukkah and set it near Mehrunnisa. Ruqayya leaned forward on her divan, balancing her weight on one elbow. 'Will you not smoke some opium?'

'No, your Majesty. I am here to talk. Did you hear of the jharoka this morning?'

Ruqayya nodded. 'Everyone knows of it. Wait.' She snapped her fingers, and the slaves and eunuchs bowed and left the room, taking the dog with them. When they had gone she continued,

'Was that wise? A woman's place is in the harem, behind the zenana walls. Even I never asked Emperor Akbar for such a favour.'

'But you asked for other things, your Majesty,' Mehrunnisa said softly. 'Khurram, for one.'

Prince Khurram was Empress Jagat Gosini's son. When he was a year old, Ruqayya, who had no children of her own, demanded custody of the prince from Jagat Gosini and got it, for Emperor Akbar rarely refused her anything. So Khurram had grown up with Ruqayya, thinking her to be his mother and Jagat Gosini some subordinate princess. The transposition in power in the harem had not changed Khurram's affections, though he was now twenty and knew Jagat Gosini to be his mother and Ruqayya his step-grandmother; he still called Ruqayya 'Ma.' So Jagat Gosini would not forgive Ruqayya.

The Dowager Empress stared unblinking at Mehrunnisa, then her face cracked into a smile. 'You are wicked, Mehrunnisa. But no matter, I think I taught you to be wicked. Here is another debt you owe me. And be wary of Jagat Gosini; she is still the Padshah Begam.'

'I know that, your Majesty. Today, I went to the jharoka. Tomorrow, who knows, perhaps even that title will be mine. Only time will tell.' Mehrunnisa picked two cashews from a silver bowl from the Dowager Empress's side and popped them into her mouth. 'But this is what you have always wished for, isn't it?'

Mehrunnisa watched as Ruqayya leaned back and drew on the hukkah, spinning lazy circles of smoke in the air above her. This was what Ruqayya had recently wanted. But once, the Dowager Empress had supported Emperor Akbar's decision to give Mehrunnisa to Ali Quli, even though Jahangir, then a prince, sought after her. One word from Ruqayya might have changed the shape of things... but there was a streak of cruelty in the Dowager

Empress that made her sometimes turn even on those she loved.

But when Mehrunnisa had come back to the capital, widowed after Ali Quli's death, Ruqayya had taken her into the zenana as a lady-in-waiting, against Jagat Gosini's wishes. And it was Ruqayya who had engineered the meeting between Jahangir and Mehrunnisa at the Mina Bazaar. This was what the Dowager Empress wanted her to remember. She was saying, in effect, *Don't forget who put that crown on your head, Mehrunnisa—if it wasn't for me, you would still be a maid in the imperial zenana.*

Which was why Ruqayya called her by her old name, Mehrunnisa.

But she was here for another reason.

'Your Majesty, tell me Mirza Mahabat Khan's story,' Mehrunnisa said.

Ruqayya sat up. 'Ah, you angered him at the jharoka.'

Mehrunnisa nodded. 'Why is he against me? I can be no threat to his position. Yet I hear he was opposed to my marriage to the Emperor. Why?'

'I am not sure,' Ruqayya said slowly, chewing on the tip of her hukkah. 'But I have heard it comes from Jagat Gosini. She has never wanted you in the zenana, this you must know. I wonder if it is possible she enlisted his support in the matter. But what argument did she use to convince him? That she was apprehensive of your intelligence? Of your beauty? Would a powerful minister listen to such reasoning? Hmmm...'

And so the two women sat and talked late into the night. The Dowager Empress's memory was almost perfect. She recalled for Mehrunnisa incidents from the Emperor's childhood when Mahabat had said or done something unusual. She told her of his hold over Jahangir, of the deep affection the Emperor had for Mahabat that sometimes blinded him to his faults. Mehrunnisa listened, wanting to know everything about him.

As the night lengthened and the palace slept around them, Ruqayya suddenly said, 'It is late, why are you not by the Emperor?'

'He needs his sleep, your Majesty.'

Ruqayya grinned. It was a knowing grin. She reached out to touch Mehrunnisa's face. 'You know this will not last.'

Mehrunnisa moved away. 'My face, or my relationship with the Emperor?'

'Both, my dear. You have to have much more. So be wary. Watch your face for signs of aging, watch your mouth too. Emperor Jahangir does not like a woman who is too witty or too intelligent.'

Jahangir's Empress kept her expression immobile, but inside a sharp anger flared to life at Ruqayya's words. She could have said much to Ruqayya about the Emperor, much she did not know or willfully ignored. The Dowager Empress was prejudiced for many reasons, most of which hinged on Jahangir's rebellion against his father when he was a prince—a rebellion that in Ruqayya's mind, had hastened Emperor Akbar's death. Mehrunnisa did not say anything, because she was fearful also that perhaps, just perhaps, what Ruqayya said was true. No other woman in the zenana had enjoyed such favour from Jahangir... And so came the little pestering doubts Mehrunnisa tried to keep at bay, as they always did when she talked with Ruqayya.

The Dowager Empress was again lying back on the divan, watching Mehrunnisa with cunning eyes. 'Go now,' she said. 'Go back to your apartments and to bed. You need to sleep.'

As Mehrunnisa kissed Ruqayya's hand and rose to leave, she said, 'It was good to be with you again, Mehrunnisa.'

Mehrunnisa bowed to the Dowager Empress. At the door she turned. 'I now have a new title, your Majesty, I am no longer Mehrunnisa.'

'Be careful, Mehrunnisa. Be careful of how you talk to me.

Remember what I have done for you.'

Jahangir's newest Empress shook her head. Two months ago, Ruqayya's words would have cowed her, but things were no longer as they once were. 'I will never forget the debt I owe you. But I am now Nur Jahan. Perhaps I will allow you to call me by my old name. But I am no longer Mehrunnisa. *You* must not forget that.'

Chapter Two

*But there was one fatal flaw in her. She was a woman...
And in the prejudice of the age, women had no public
role, and ambition was the prerogative of men.*

—ABRAHAM ERALY, *The Last Spring: The
Lives and Times of the Great Mughals*

EVEN AS MEHRUNNISA AND RUQAYYA SAT TALKING THROUGH THE NIGHT, A
man neared the inside doorway of the Hathi Pol, the Elephant Gate
on the western side of the Agra Fort. He stood for a moment
watching the two guards leaning in sleep against spears dug into the
hard ground—stringless puppets silhouetted against the looming
sandstone walls. The man coughed and the guards sprang awake.
One stumbled back to level his spear at the man's chest, the honed
tip a few inches from the zari-embroidered front of his coat.
'Identify yourself.'

The man raised both his hands. His well-oiled hair, long to his
nape, caught a midnight glint in the light of the lamps. 'Mahabat
Khan,' he said simply, letting his voice and his name do the rest.

The guard let his spear fall, then bowed deeply. 'Mirza
Mahabat Khan, I beg your pardon, I did not recognize you,' he
said, tripping over his words in distress. 'But how... I would have
thought you had left the fort by now...'

Mahabat shook his head gently, with the indulgence of a man

not accustomed to interrogation. 'Such solicitousness on behalf of the Emperor is commendable. But you must know whom you question. Open the door for me.'

'Of course, of course, Mirza Khan. I beg your pardon. I only meant...' He rushed to the side door near the huge gates and pushed it open. The rest of the guard's explanation was lost as Mahabat Khan let himself out of the fort. He walked away with carefully measured steps, the soles of his leather boots crunching on the dirt path.

Mahabat's hand rested lightly on the dagger tucked into his cummerbund. His eyes wove through the shadows in the streets, skimming over the snoring drunks in the corners, waiting for a twitch that signalled danger. The stench of arrack and old wine ambushed him. As Mahabat passed, the pariah dogs sniffed and growled, nostrils quivering. But no one, man or beast, came to threaten him. No voice raised itself in intimidation, no hand commanded the thick string of pearls around his neck or the marble-sized ruby in his turban. It was as though they all knew that Mahabat Khan was Emperor Jahangir's favourite minister, his trusted confidant. Mahabat walked through the streets, his steps leading him to Muhammad Sharif's house.

The mansion lay well back from the main street in Agra, along the Yamuna, in the shade of ancient mango trees. Its roof was flat, the front surrounded by a deep verandah of peach-coloured limewashed pillars. Mahabat climbed the front steps and knocked on the heavy wooden door, plated with embellished silver leaf. A servant boy, who usually slept on the floor with his back against the door, opened the latches and peered around the door. He bowed when he saw the minister.

'Please come in, *huzoor*.' He lurched back to allow Mahabat in. 'I will inform the master that you are here.'

'No need to do that,' Mahabat said. 'Tell me where he is.' As he spoke, the low dull throb of a tabla came to him from within the house. There was no music in accompaniment, just the sound of the drums.

'The inner courtyard,' the boy replied.

'Asleep?'

'No, sire.'

So Sharif could not sleep either. Mahabat slipped off his boots and found his way through the maze of corridors and courtyards to the private sanctum. Sharif's wives were not there with him, or the slave boy would have mentioned this, and Sharif would have come out to meet Mahabat. He entered the courtyard, stopped, and then leaned against a pillar looking at Sharif.

The Grand Vizier of the Mughal Empire was lying back on a divan, head pillowed on a cushion, arms resting on his chest. His short, stocky legs barely reached the end of the divan. Everything in his posture suggested repose and ease, even sloth. His eyelids were hooded, he looked indolent, but Mahabat knew that this was merely a pose with Sharif.

A slave girl, clad in thin muslin skirts, bodice, and veil, swayed to the rhythm of the tabla's beat. The tabla player sat behind one of the courtyard pillars, out of sight, the sound of his drums filling the heavy air. Slow, insistent, compelling. The girl was slim, not particularly pretty, her nose spread over her face. But what nature denied her, cosmetics embellished to something akin to beauty. Her eyes were outlined with kohl, giving them depth and breadth, her lips were reddened with carmine, henna flowers tattooed her hands and feet. Her body hardly seemed to move, yet the cadence of the drums filled her gestures. The sound surged around Mahabat. His breath wedged in his chest as her hand touched the front of her bodice, her fingers undoing one wood button, then another, then a third, sliding against raw blue silk. She turned away from the Grand Vizier, and as she did, she saw Mahabat.

She stilled, then, her hips still swaying lightly, her gaze holding his, she pulled off the flimsy piece of muslin that covered her breasts, slipping her arms out of the sleeves. Young as she was, she had been taught her skills well. Mahabat laughed out loud, his voice hoarse with relief from the building tension. Under the bodice, the girl wore yet another piece of muslin barely covering her breasts. He could see it; Sharif, more intent on watching the girl's baring back, could not. Mahabat clapped his hands. 'Well done! You had me wondering too.' He looked at Sharif. Sweat dotted his forehead and shone on his upper lip, drenching the quill-thin line of hair he liked to call a moustache. Sharif's nostrils flared at the interruption, and when his eyes swung to the cause of it, they were already glazed with the anger that was quick to come to him. Then he saw Mahabat, and his face settled into smooth lines.

'Mahabat,' Sharif's tone was reproachful. 'In another minute—'

'You would have seen nothing, my friend,' Mahabat said. He went up to the girl and turned her around, his hand warm on her shoulder.

Then he dug into his cummerbund and flipped her three gold mohurs, the coins arcing through the air. Her hands flew, swift with practise, palms enclosing the coins, one after another. She bowed to the two men.

Muhammad Sharif waved her away. 'Do not go too far.' He turned to his friend. 'And what brings you here?'

Mahabat Khan crossed over the marble tiles of the courtyard and sat down on the divan next to Sharif. A goblet of wine appeared at his elbow. He dismissed the attendant with a hand, then nodded in the direction of the tabla player. The music stopped as the servants bowed their way out on soft feet. Mahabat picked up the goblet and stared into the wine.

'Is this new Empress cause for concern, Sharif?'

Surprise and amusement lit in quick succession over Sharif's face. 'A woman? Cause for concern? Surely you jest, Mahabat.'

'You saw what happened at this morning's jharoka. She stood in front of us, brazenly, like a woman of the streets. You saw this, and you do not think we need to worry?'

Muhammad Sharif lifted himself on an elbow. 'Ah, you are upset because her Majesty denied one of your petitioners. Her presence at the jharoka was surprising, that is all, most likely the result of a night of pleasure for the Emperor, Mahabat. It will not happen again.'

'I am not upset about anything, Sharif,' the minister said, bitterness in his voice, though, for he was uneasy. If not for that low, soft word in Jahangir's ear, Mahabat would not be thinking thus. 'What you do not see is that this marriage is different. Emperor Jahangir married her for love.' His mouth twisted. Women had their uses for Mahabat, true, but love was not an emotion he would bestow upon them. 'This Empress has no royal blood in her.'

'She is the daughter of the *diwan* of the empire, Mahabat. Ghias Beg is responsible for even *our* salaries as part of his duties as a treasurer. He is well liked, and for the most part, known to be an honourable man.'

What Sharif said was true. Ghias Beg had come to India as a penniless noble fleeing his Persian homeland. Emperor Akbar had taken him into his court, and when Akbar died, Jahangir made him treasurer of the empire. The Emperor's new wife was Ghias Beg's fourth child, born on his journey from Persia to India thirty-four years ago. To Mahabat, she was an old woman; he barely glanced at any woman over thirty. It was like marrying a mother, or an aunt. Yet the Emperor was enamoured.

'What *is* her attraction?' Sharif asked, echoing Mahabat's thoughts.

In reply the minister reached into an inner pocket of his *qaba* and pulled out a scroll of paper. Untying the red satin thread that held it together, he unrolled it and laid it in front of Sharif, watching as the Grand Vizier caught his breath and expelled it audibly. The portrait was done in watercolours. The background was of shimmering gold, real gold flakes. The woman in the picture sat with her head turned in half-profile, looking into a jewelled mirror held high in hands as delicate as closed lily buds. Her wrists were slung with jade bangles. She wore a small choli covering her breasts and a full-skirted ghagara, her waist bare between the two. Her bare back was swathed with the cascading darkness of her hair. But it was her face, her expression, that caught their attention. Her eyes were a lovely blue in the mirror's reflection, deepening to almost indigo.

She had not, however, a beauty classic of their time. She was too thin, her arms too slender, and not voluptuous enough. And her face was too strong, her cheekbones too pronounced. It was, Mahabat thought, almost a man's face in its intensity, in its concentration of energy. It lacked softness. Yet something made their gazes linger.

Sharif slowly traced the curve of her face, his finger tarrying longer than necessary over her shoulder. His touch was light, as though the picture was newly finished, the paint not yet dry.

'This is the new Empress? Is it a true rendition?'

'I think so. Yes, it must be. This is how she looks under the veil,' Mahabat replied, watching his friend. Now things made some sense to him, why the Emperor had married her, what her physical charms were. The rumours of her beauty, almost elevating her to a goddess-like stature, had been based on truth. If this portrait was to be believed.

Sharif's voice was quiet. 'How did you get this?'

Mahabat did not look at his friend. 'The less you know the

better. Emperor Jahangir would not forgive me for... er... borrowing this portrait. But I wanted you to know, Sharif. I wanted you to see what she looked like.'

'You stole this portrait?'

Mahabat nodded. 'Just now. I went to the painters' atelier in the fort. I wanted to see too.'

Sharif watched as Mahabat rolled the portrait carefully and slipped it inside his qaba. 'She is still just a woman.'

'I wonder,' Mahabat said, exhaustion crumpling his sun-browned face. The stubble of his unshaven beard was flecked with white. Age had come to Mahabat too, in the greying of his hair, in the lines on his face, only it did not matter so much. For he was a man, and his importance was not based on his physical appearance or the ability to bear children. Mahabat had the advantage of Emperor Jahangir's ear. Now Mehrunnisa, Jahangir's twentieth wife, had it too. He leaned back onto the divan. 'Do you remember that Empress Jagat Gosini did not want her in the imperial harem?'

They were silent, looking up at a low crescent moon still hanging over the horizon, stubbornly refusing to fade. Empress Jagat Gosini, Jahangir's second wife, had met with Mahabat in secret, several times over, in the past few years, flaunting the rule that she not be seen by any man from the outside world. Mahabat had not actually seen her, although he had been close enough to touch her, to smell the essence of camellias in which she bathed, to see the flash of a smile under her veil. Every single meeting had been about Mehrunnisa.

'How many years have passed since the Emperor first saw her?' Sharif asked.

'The *first* time? Seventeen, I think,' Mahabat said. 'She was seventeen then, not yet married to Ali Quli, although her betrothal had been finalized.'

Sharif rubbed his chin thoughtfully. 'The Emperor tried to

dissolve that betrothal. And did not succeed.'

'And years later, he tried to invalidate her marriage.'

And that was when Empress Jagat Gosini had come to Mahabat Khan for help. Mahabat, curious and intrigued at the summons, had responded. He had needed an ally in the imperial harem, for he knew that in fatigue or moments of weakness, a woman could get anything she wanted from a man. So Mahabat had gone to see what the Empress had had to say.

The command had been a simple one. *Make sure the Emperor forgets Mehrunnisa. He must not bring her into the royal harem.* Mahabat had almost smiled that first time, thinking Jagat Gosini absurd, thinking himself half-witted to have agreed to meet her, risking disfavour from Jahangir. And all this over a romantic alliance; Mahabat had thought he was being commanded for some other reason—a political one, or something related to court matters—something in which he could be of use. Then he had paid heed as grants of land had been bestowed on Ghias Beg, for he was Mehrunnisa's father. He had seen Jahangir's unwavering resolve to marry Mehrunnisa even after her husband had killed Koka.

Mahabat, Sharif and Koka had grown up with Jahangir, brought into the imperial zenana to provide the young prince with male companionship. They had played together, slept in the same room, shared food from the same plate, untiring of this constant intimacy as only children can be. They were Jahangir's closest friends, and when he had become Emperor, he had rewarded them for their loyalty with governorships and ministries. Koka had wanted to go to Bengal as governor, and there, he had died at the hands of Mehrunnisa's husband. To Sharif and Mahabat's astonishment, it had only seemed to make Jahangir more determined to have her.

Sharif, his eyes shut, asked softly, 'Empress Jagat Gosini was right in not wanting her in the imperial harem?'

'She said Mehrunnisa would be a threat even to us.'

'Yet the Empress allowed this marriage to take place.'

'Four years after her husband died, who could have foreseen that the Emperor would see Mehrunnisa in the palace bazaar and that he would marry her?' Mahabat smiled, though with a touch of cynicism. 'His Majesty is not known for constancy, Sharif... so we grew slack too.'

Sharif touched Mahabat's chest with light fingers where the picture lay in the inner pocket. 'She is beautiful. Beautiful women are too impressed by themselves, spend too much time impressing others. They can easily be stupid.'

'I wonder,' Mahabat said. Then he shook his head. 'No, her presence at the jharoka was not foolishness, Sharif. Even if she were inclined to stupidity, she has a father and a brother who thirst for wealth and power.' He rubbed his cheek, feeling the rasp of unshaven skin against his fingers. 'I see trouble ahead. In what shape, I do not know.' He rose from the divan and stood looking down at his friend. Over the years they had been together, he had always been the one who saw the dangers, who made plans to demolish them, who goaded Muhammad Sharif to greatness. Sharif viewed things differently, of course, thinking of himself as the voice of reason, and Mahabat the willful, impulsive one. 'I must go home now. It would be better if you gave this matter some thought too, Sharif, instead of lolling around with a slave in your courtyard.'

Muhammad Sharif's eyes gleamed. Very few people in the empire would dare to talk to him like this, and Mahabat was one of them. They were both intrinsically fearless men, born to cruelty. It was simply a mishap of nature that they had no royal blood. Even in early childhood they had known their alliance with Emperor Jahangir would bring them prosperity, so they subdued their instincts, willing to wait for successes they thought were rightfully theirs. Now that they were two of the most powerful men in the empire, a woman would not, could not, take that away. So Sharif would not bother to give Mehrunnisa much thought.

Mahabat knew this. He shook his head again and turned away. Sharif snapped his fingers. The slave girl, who had been sitting leaning against a pillar in the courtyard, beyond comprehension of their voices, came up to the Amir-ul-umra. When he patted the divan cover, she sat down next to him.

'This history of wanting, Mahabat,' Sharif said slowly. 'I have learned this much. It is better to want than to have a desire fulfilled. Once it is... it has little importance. So it will be for the Emperor.'

'Perhaps,' Mahabat said, walking away. 'And, if not... what then, Sharif?'

Sharif pulled at the skirts of the slave's blue silk ghagara, fanning them around her with gentle hands, as though she were a child.

Mahabat had reached the outer door to the courtyard when Sharif's voice came floating to him. 'She is but a woman, Mahabat. Remember that. There is little they are good for.'

Mahabat turned again to see Sharif strip the girl's bodice off her shoulders. His meaty hand lightly touched the slope of her breast, one stubby finger trailing against a rouged nipple, his eyes intent on her. She did not look at him. All her earlier bravado seemed to have fled—the dancing, the gestures, the glances from eyes languorous with seduction, these she had been taught. For this, the ultimate result of those lessons, there had been no advice, no teaching. Her lower lip trembled, tears filled her eyes, her face drooped. Still, she did not flinch as Sharif loosened the tie of her ghagara. The bow broke easily, knotted for a lover's hand.

Mahabat left Sharif's house, his heart lightened somewhat at being able to share his thoughts with his friend. But worry still lingered. In their world, Jahangir was omnipotent. *Their* power came through him. So why not Mehrunnisa's? If Sharif was wrong, if the Emperor did not tire of this latest wife. If Jahangir allowed her power. If she came to hear of his—Mahabat's—own involvement in Jagat Gosini's attempts to stop the marriage. This last point gave Mahabat the most pause, for there were no secrets in the imperial zenana; sooner or later, everything was revealed. If Mehrunnisa wanted, if she was vindictive...

Mahabat knew what Sharif would say, languid and dismissing, 'There are too many "ifs", my friend.' And yes, there were too many uncertainties. But there *were* times, rare enough, when they all came to pass. And if they did... Mahabat shuddered. If they did, the new Empress could very well decimate Mahabat's and Sharif's standing at court.

Empress Jagat Gosini paced the rich Persian carpet in her palace in short, quick strides.

She had waited patiently these last two months for Jahangir to visit her. Each day the reception room of her palace was swept clean, the rugs taken out and dusted, the shades drawn over windows by ten in the morning to keep in the night's cool. Each day her eunuch went to the royal kitchens to command the Emperor's favourite dishes made afresh—*kheers* with new milk, coconut burfis flaked with thin foils of silver, or rice biryanis cooked in mutton broth. Wines waited in gold flasks, and the hukkahs grew warm with live coals. The Empress knew Jahangir's desires to the littlest detail. And until this marriage, he had never failed her yet. Within a week of his other marriages, Emperor Jahangir had come to her palace to pay a visit, acknowledging her place in his zenana. It had been years since Jahangir had spent a night in her palace, slept by her side, years since she had woken to the sight of him first. But this total lack of attention was unprecedented.

Besides, the other wives also called upon Jagat Gosini. She

made sure that they knew, even as they stepped into the harem, in whose hands the real power in the zenana was vested. It was easy to do. A word dropped in their ear by the slaves. Or if they would not heed the servants, a visit from an aunt or a cousin. But Mehrunnisa had ignored her. She had deliberately stayed away. This much Jagat Gosini knew for sure.

The Empress stopped at the window and looked out. The monsoons were here. Since yesterday, rain had battered the city of Agra, coming down in thick sheets, until the Yamuna River outside her palace was a roiling sea of water. Jagat Gosini would have been happy at this break in the heat, happy that she could breathe again without drawing dust into her lungs, but now she leaned against the windowsill, shaking with anger. She had heard about the jharoka. Who had not in the empire? Mehrunnisa had actually dared to stand by the Emperor during his morning audience. Did he not know, did she not have any sense of how highly unbecoming it was to the dignity of a Mughal woman to show herself thus in public? How could Jahangir allow this?

Jagat Gosini wrapped her hands around herself and with both hands pinched the soft underside of her arms, just below the sleeve edge of her choli, until the pain brought tears to her eyes. Why had she not thought of asking Jahangir to let her stand beside him at the jharoka? Why had she not even *thought* of this? Because this she had not been taught. How could she have dared to think that it was even possible? And why was it Mehrunnisa who had claimed this privilege, and not another woman in the zenana, one she hated less?

Jagat Gosini had not wanted Mehrunnisa in the harem ever since she had first met her in Ruqayya's gardens that summer afternoon in Lahore. Then, Mehrunnisa must have been only sixteen or seventeen. Jagat Gosini had gone to visit Khurram during Ruqayya's afternoon siesta. With the Empress napping, she had thought she could spend some time with her son. He had been alone, with only Mehrunnisa to look after him. And she had sent her, Jagat Gosini, away with a sly, 'The Empress will soon awaken, your Highness, and ask for the prince. You must go.' Then she had let her hand fall possessively to Khurram's curly head. As though he had belonged to her.

All the rage she had not dared direct at Ruqayya had gone to Mehrunnisa. A few days later Jahangir had been mooning about Mehrunnisa like Majnu, as if she, Jagat Gosini, had been nothing. As though she had not borne him Khurram. She had tried to step back from this rage. As a princess should. As a daughter of one king, and the wife of another, should.

So Jagat Gosini had bided her time. Years passed, and she consolidated her position as Padshah Begam, during which time her spies kept her informed of Mehrunnisa's activities. *She embroiders, reads to her child, weeds the imperial gardens.* Harmless activities, she had thought. Let her spend time in the sun, it will age her.

But it had not aged Mehrunnisa. If anything, now that she was older, there was a certain loveliness about her that time brought to only some. Jahangir remained entranced, talked of bringing her into the imperial harem. Jagat Gosini suggested he take her as a concubine, thinking that if Mehrunnisa was going to have a place in Jahangir's life, at least it would be a lowly one. The Emperor simply said this, 'She will be my wife, nothing else.'

At those words, after fighting against it for many years, a deep sadness came over Jagat Gosini. She was defeated.

Jagat Gosini had always known she would be Padshah Begam of Jahangir's zenana. She had worked hard for the position, kowtowing to senior princesses, learning of their power so she might have it one day. She studied with the mullas so she could talk intelligently with Jahangir. She learned to shoot and use the bow and arrow, for he was fond of hunting. Most importantly, she had given him Khurram. Beautiful, bright-eyed Khurram, who would one day wear his father's crown. And as his mother, she would rule too. But she had kept her power in the zenana, not interfering too much in court politics or appointments. How could she have foreseen that this commoner would nudge her, Jagat Gosini, daughter of a raja, from her position?

Shaista Khan, her new eunuch, coughed at the door to attract her attention. She turned from the window, rubbing her arms. She could already feel pits in the flesh where her nails had pinched. She pulled the sleeves of her choli down her arms.

'What news?' she asked sharply.

'Your Majesty,' he hesitated, 'it is not good.'

'Go on.'

'The Empress was not a silent spectator at the jharoka. The Emperor turned to her for advice on decisions regarding the petitions and the gifts. True, she did not speak aloud in public, but her influence was visible. And your Majesty, Mirza Mahabat Khan begs an audience.'

The Empress bowed her head, only half-listening to Shaista as she fought not to let anger overcome her. Matters had gone too far out of hand. Mehrunnisa had to be stopped somehow. 'You may go now.'

Shaista Khan bowed and left the apartments, tripping over the edge of the rug on his way out. Jagat Gosini clicked her tongue in irritation. Shaista was a new eunuch, and she was unused to his ways. She missed Hoshiyar Khan, head eunuch of the harem, who had been at her side for twenty-five years. Hoshiyar was an extremely intelligent man, gentle in his ways, smooth in his talk, cruel when necessary. Jagat Gosini remembered when Hoshiyar had knifed a dog. The dog had barked half the night, and she had sent him out to silence it. The Empress had only meant for Hoshiyar to take the dog away to another location. Instead, he had calmly held its diamond collar and sliced its neck, stepping fastidiously out of the way when the blood spurted out. The next morning, the princess who owned the dog had cried out for justice, but when she had found it was Hoshiyar who was responsible, she had kept quiet. The Emperor never heard of the incident. In this harem of women, Hoshiyar Khan was the silently acknowledged master.

There was only one woman he had listened to, one woman he had respected almost as much as he respected himself. Empress Jagat Gosini. Together, they had been powerful, for Hoshiyar could go where she could not go, see things she was not privy to. And then, a week before Jahangir's twentieth marriage, he had slipped out of her apartments with a small apology. 'The new Empress commands me, your Majesty.'

He had gone to Mehrunnisa and left her with the idiot Shaista Khan.

Jagat Gosini had let him go, knowing it would be useless to complain to Jahangir. Hoshiyar was powerful in the harem, true, but she would show them both who was more powerful.

She clapped her hands lightly. Shaista Khan, never too far from his mistress, immediately came to the door.

'When does the Emperor go hunting next?'

'In three days, your Majesty. He is going to take the new Empress with him.'

Jagat Gosini spoke slowly, enunciating each word, for the eunuch was sure to mistake her command if she did not do so. 'Take a request to the Emperor asking if I may be allowed to join the royal hunting party.'

'At once, your Majesty.'

Jagat Gosini watched him leave with a small smile. The Emperor was excessively fond of hunting. Jagat Gosini was an excellent shot. In fact, she was the best in the zenana. There was little possibility that Mehrunnisa could have her skill with the musket.

She had not forgotten Shaista's other message. So Mirza Mahabat Khan wanted to see her? She would meet him. Now more than ever, she needed Mahabat Khan, but of course, he would never fully know that.

It was mid-afternoon, and Jahangir was taking a nap when the message came to him from Jagat Gosini.

Shaista Khan was stopped at the entrance to the royal apartments by the guards. They were two hefty women of Kashmiri origin, known to be extremely brave and fiercely loyal to the Emperor. For years, the women of Kashmir had guarded the inner apartments of the Emperors of Mughal India, for no men were allowed into the zenana except for the eunuchs.

One of them stepped forward, towering over Shaista, and pointed a spear at the eunuch's chest. 'What is your business here?'

'I come with a message from the Empress Jagat Gosini.'

The guard looked at her companion and she nodded. She recognized Shaista Khan.

'The Emperor is asleep and is not to be disturbed,' the guard said. 'Come back in two hours.'

'Surely his Majesty will take a message from his chief Empress?' Shaista asked.

The guards snickered. 'Take the message to the new Empress's palace. She will answer it.'

Shaista backed away. 'No... it is better I relay it to the Emperor personally.'

One of the guards backed him against a wall and pinned him down with her spear. 'Go to Empress Nur Jahan's apartments if you are fond of your life, you fool,' she hissed in an undertone. 'Go!' She pushed him away.

A troubled Shaista Khan presented himself at Mehrunnisa's palace. His mind worked slowly, but methodically. If he disobeyed the guards, the Emperor's new favourite would wreak vengeance upon him, but if his mistress came to know... he shuddered. He had no wish to be caught between the two women, but even he knew who was fast gaining ascendancy in the harem.

Besides, Shaista was curious. There had been much gossip about Mehrunnisa. She was beautiful, she was cunning and sly, she had a charm no woman could match. How could that be, he thought. She was thirty-four. There were many younger women in the zenana, slim of figure, lithe of feet, with a rippling laughter that even made his toes curl. How could the Emperor love this woman, who had a child by another man? It was incomprehensible to him. But he would find out for himself.

The Empress was taking her bath when Shaista Khan was announced. The *hammam* was a room set high in the palace on the top floor, with open verandahs on one end decorated with arches and sandstone screens. A gentle breeze whistled through the chamber, picking up coolness from the Yamuna below. The room was bare with white marble floors polished to a dull shine. In the centre was a black slate tub, carved out of one piece of stone.

When Shaista entered, the room was silent except for a child's little voice. She was seated at the edge of the tub, fully clad, her ghagara gathered around her knees. Her feet were in the water, and she had a book of poems open on her lap. He stood to one side and watched as the girl turned a page and said, 'Here is one by Hafiz. Shall I read it?' Then not waiting for an answer she went on, 'Harvest. In the green sky I saw the new moon reaping,/And minded was I of my own life's field: What harvest wilt thou to the sickle yield/When through thy field the moon-shaped knife goes sweeping?'

It was read in a breathless voice, with no pause for effect. The girl looked at the woman in the tub and said, 'This is too hard. What does it mean? What is a moon-shaped knife? A knife is a knife, the moon the moon. What does he mean by putting them together? Finish your bath, Mama, let's go play outside. I am tired of reading.'

Shaista looked at the child again. So this was her daughter. She was small, with bony arms and legs and a thick head of hair plaited down her back, swinging over the edge of the tub. She sat like a queen, back straight, an imperious look on her face. What an ugly little thing she was, Shaista thought. He had never liked children, thankfully they grew into passable adults. How old was she? Six? Seven? Something like that. And the lady in the tub, she must be the Empress. Just then, his arm was seized by a tall eunuch.

'What are you doing here?' the eunuch hissed. 'This is the Empress's private sanctuary. How did you get past the guards?'

Shaista backed away and bowed hurriedly. This was the great Hoshiyar Khan. In the zenana, Hoshiyar's reputation had taken on almost mythical proportions. Shaista had not seen him before, only heard of him. He wanted to be what Hoshiyar was to the Emperor, to Jahangir's favourite, whoever she may be, and to the zenana. They all, all the eunuchs, aspired to be Hoshiyar. Shaista spoke with gravity, with the right amount of respect. 'I beg pardon, huzoor. I come from Empress Jagat Gosini with a message for the Emperor.'

The grip on his arm loosened just a little as Hoshiyar glared at him. Then he let him go. 'You may approach the Empress.'

Mehrunnisa looked up and watched as Shaista, still aware of Hoshiyar and hoping he was watching, performed the taslim.

'Why is he here?' she asked.

'Your Majesty, Shaista is Empress Jagat Gosini's eunuch. He has a message for the Emperor.'

Mehrunnisa raised an eyebrow.

'Your Majesty—' Shaista stammered. 'The Empress wishes permission to be present at the hunt.'

Mehrunnisa dipped her hand in the cool water and let it run

through her fingers, her diamond rings glittering bright in the afternoon light. Rose petals, freshly picked that morning with the kiss of dew still upon them, floated in the scented water. Ladli turned her bright eyes on Shaista briefly, then she turned away, already losing interest.

But Shaista Khan was watching the Empress in fascination. He had never before been close to her; he could see why Jahangir was so enraptured. She lay back in the tub, eyes closed, head resting against a jewelled cushion. Her hair streamed behind her, tumbling to the floor in a single ebony sheet. The water lapped gently above her breasts, and her skin shone like pearls. One graceful foot, toenails painted red with henna, peeped out from under the water.

He held his breath as Mehrunnisa lifted her head and smiled at him. Where were the lines painted by the hand of time? Her face was almost perfect. Her eyes were undimmed by age, the clear blue of a washed monsoon sky. A gift from her Persian ancestors.

'The Emperor will be glad to have Empress Jagat Gosini at the hunt.' Her voice was low. 'It will also give me an opportunity to meet my sister. Give my compliments to the Empress.' She waved a hand in languid dismissal.

Shaista bowed.

As he was leaving the room, Mehrunnisa's voice stopped him. 'You have done well in coming to me with this message. Remember, the Emperor cannot be bothered with trivialities, it will perhaps be better if you come to me from now on.'

'I understand, your Majesty.'

'Hoshiyar, give the man fifty rupees. He is a good servant.'

Fifty rupees! That was five times his month's salary. Shaista performed the taslim four times, in gratitude for many things—for having been able to see her, for being brought to Hoshiyar Khan's notice—before he backed out the door.

Mehrunnisa lay back and closed her eyes again. So Jagat Gosini wished to be at the hunt. Why? What had she planned? It would have been churlish to refuse the request, and there was no good reason to do so. Yet she couldn't help the sudden flood of apprehension. So far they had not met. But that could not continue. As a new wife, she should have paid her respects to the reigning Padshah Begam, but Mehrunnisa had not cared to do this. At first it was because of the Emperor, because so much time was spent with him. And then it was because she recognized the summons for what it was—a command and not a request. An order for obedience from a woman who had not wanted her within the zenana walls.

If she was to arrange for her presence to be felt in the empire, it had to start from here, from the inside. As long as Jagat Gosini was considered Jahangir's most important wife, as long as she had possession of the Emperor's seal, Mehrunnisa would be inconsequential, no matter how much time Jahangir spent with her. The title of Padshah Begam, the seal that was so powerful that even the Emperor's word could not revoke its orders—these were the real bastions of authority in the harem.

Mehrunnisa had gone to the jharoka again this morning. Today she had said nothing, merely watched. There had been more men in the courtyard below than yesterday, some eyes had been curious, some guarded and wondering if this was to be a common practice from now on. As much as they had been unaccepting and disbelieving of her presence yesterday, today they had at least been resigned. Tomorrow, in a few days, a few months, they would welcome her.

'Mama!'

Mehrunnisa opened her eyes and looked at her daughter. 'What is it, *beta*?'

'Don't fall asleep, Mama. Finish your bath and come out to play.'

A pout decorated Ladli's face. Mehrunnisa picked up her hand and kissed the little palm. At one time, she had thought there would be no children from her marriage to Ali Quli. It had hurt, dreadfully, for the longest time, subsiding into a dull ache that flared up when she saw some other woman's face light up at the sight of her child. Questions were asked constantly, prying, intimate questions about her childlessness. How did one reply to them? That slave girls in the house gave birth to children who were possibly sired by her husband? That he visited her at night yet there was no sign of a child? Then eight years into the marriage came Ladli, the night they reached Bengal, sent into near exile by Jahangir. It had not mattered that she was a girl child, that after eight years of being barren she had had only a girl. Ali Quli had been disappointed, but not Mehrunnisa. Hence her name. Ladli. One who was loved.

Ladli pulled her hand out of Mehrunnisa's grasp and said again, 'Let's go, Mama. Hoshiyar, help Mama out.'

Mehrunnisa smiled. She already acted like a princess, ordering Hoshiyar around. 'I have something to do now, beta. Go to your quarters, Dai will play with you there.'

'But—' Ladli's face screwed up, as if to cry.

'No buts, beta.' Mehrunnisa smoothed the hair from her face. 'Go now. Mama has to do something. I will come to you in the evening.' She nodded to Hoshiyar and he came and lifted Ladli out of the tub, her feet dripping water. Then he wiped her legs and handed her to another eunuch. Ladli squirmed out of the eunuch's arms to the floor. At the door she turned and asked in a small voice, 'Will you come, Mama?'

'Yes,' Mehrunnisa said, but her thoughts had already escaped elsewhere.

When Ladli left, Mehrunnisa sat up and snapped her fingers. Hoshiyar Khan came up and pulled the plug on the tub. Mehrunnisa watched the water whirlpool from the tub, rose petals rushing to clog the drain. A slave girl brought her a robe. As she rose to slip into it, she looked at Hoshiyar Khan. He had his eyes averted.

Here was one man who could tell her about Jagat Gosini. So far Hoshiyar had been useful in telling her of the Emperor, of his moods, what pleased him. Yet she would not ask him about the Empress. That would be revealing a weakness. She would not ask. One day, he would tell her.

'How much time until the Emperor rises, Hoshiyar?' she asked.

'Another hour, your Majesty.'

Mehrunnisa allowed herself to be led to a cotton mattress on the floor. The slave girls poured out musk oil on their palms and gently massaged her body. When they were finished, they oiled her long, black hair and coiled it around her head like a crown. Little white jasmine flowers, her trademark, were woven into her hair, contrasting its darkness.

Next came the makeup. Kohl was used to rim her blue eyes and darken her eyebrows. Carmine was painted on her lips. Her hands and feet were already decorated with delicate patterns in henna.

The Mistress of the Wardrobe entered with five slave girls, each carrying an outfit. Mehrunnisa considered for some time and finally decided on a ghagara and choli made of flimsy muslin, the green of unripe limes, so transparent that her legs were visible as she walked. She had already made up her mind about what to wear even as the slaves came into the hammam. But the appearance of deliberation—this Mehrunnisa had learned from watching Ruqayya—was important, to emphasize that she had a choice, the right to exert her will. The Mistress of the Wardrobe then put out a veil to match the outfit and went out of the room as the slaves helped the Empress dress.

She came back presently with three eunuchs. The eunuchs opened the caskets they bore, and jewels of every colour spilled out. Mehrunnisa carefully chose a set of sunset-pink pearls. A broad belt studded with hundreds of pearls went around her slender waist. Armlets were tied at the ends of her sleeves. A round gold disc, encrusted with pearls hanging from a slender gold chain, was pinned to her hair, the disc dangling in the centre of her forehead. Ten pearl bangles went on each wrist, and finally a small, beautiful, perfect pearl was put in her pierced nose.

A eunuch silently brought in a gold tray bearing paan. Mehrunnisa slipped it into her mouth and chewed. The entire operation had taken over an hour, and all the while, without Ladii there to distract her, Mehrunnisa had been thinking. The hunt would be important, even decisive.

For it was time to meet her biggest rival in the imperial zenana.

Chapter Three

Once Jahangir went ahunting accompanied by both Jagat Gosain and Noor Jahan... Both the ladies sat by his side... Suddenly a lion came in roaring.

—MOHAMMAD & RAZIA SHUJAUDDIN,
The Life and Times of Noorjahan

THE IMPERIAL HUNTING GROUNDS WERE VIGILANTLY GUARDED ALL THROUGH the year, and except for partridges, quails and hares, which were caught by nets, no one was allowed to disturb the wildlife within the grounds. Consequently game abounded; antelopes, *nilgai*, and lions roamed freely. The land encompassed forests with tall grasses, sometimes reaching eight feet in height, which would conceal even a man seated on a horse.

For two weeks, the keepers had stalked out a lion for the Emperor. They followed the animal to its favourite resting spot, a clearing in the forest under a patchwork of sunlight. They did this for a few days, blending into the undergrowth with clothes of green cotton, river mud smeared over their skins to keep their smell from the lion's nostrils. When the lion left the spot, the men brought a donkey into the clearing and tied it to a stake in the ground. Then they waited, pendant on branches of the trees, upwind from the lion. The first day, the lion stood at the edge of the clearing, suspicious of this meal that came so easily. And for the first few hours, the donkey brayed, twisting its neck this way and that, almost strangling itself when it saw the lion. Then the lion approached, carefully, skirting around the donkey. It neared. It swiped at a haunch, ripping through flesh and drawing blood. By this time, the donkey was silent, its brays abandoned in fear and trembling, knowing it was to die.

This happened day after day, and the lion turned too slothful to stalk its prey. It came leaping out of the undergrowth in one bound to fall upon the donkey, which had no time to even let out a sound, and no chance to even lose courage before it died.

The day of the hunt came bright and clear. The clouds had broken for a brief respite, leaving an earth lavish with green after just a few days of rain. The palaces of the fort at Agra stirred well before sunrise, as the hunt had to begin before the day became too hot.

On the morning of the hunt, the donkey was led to the stake as usual. But today its throat was forced open, and two handfuls of opium were shoved into its stomach by the keepers. The lion would come again for its free meal, and again it would pounce on the hapless donkey, slashing through the soft flesh of its belly first, eating the undigested opium. An opium-drugged lion was easier to hunt.

At sunrise, three thousand soldiers beating drums formed a circle around the forest. They were carrying large nets made of a thick jute fibre. As they walked inward, all the game within the forest fled towards the centre. Once the circle had been narrowed to a few miles in diameter, the royal party would enter the forest and there find the game waiting to be slaughtered.

Mehrunnisa was in her apartments, getting ready for the hunt. There was a hush in the room as the slave girls moved around on bare feet, straightening the sheets, laying out her clothes, talking in whispers. She stood in front of a long mirror, looking at her reflection. A sudden gust of early morning breeze swept through the room, sending the oil lamps wavering, bringing goose bumps up her arms. Jahangir had not been hunting since their wedding, but it was one of his favourite occupations. She did not want to disappoint him today.

For most of the night, Mehrunnisa had lain sleepless, rising to stand at the windows of her apartments. In the inner streets of the forts, the night guards had appeared and ebbed into shadows, clad in soft-soled boots so as not to disturb the palaces. In the early dawn, before the first light escaped from the horizon, she had been in the balcony of her apartments, leaning over the edge. On the farther bank of the Yamuna was the *dhobi ghat*, where the *dhobis* washed the laundry. Little pinpoints of light from their lamps had bobbed in a line as they had picked their way to the edge of the water, and then there had been the rhythmic slap of cloth against stone. And just as she had been able to make out their figures, hunched over, hands busy, the slave girls had come in to wake her for the hunt.

Hoshiyar Khan entered, carrying a musket bagged in red velvet, its snout poking out of the wrapping.

'With his Majesty's compliments. He wishes for you to shoot with his favourite musket.'

Mehrunnisa reached for it. The weight took her by surprise, and for a moment her hands fell and then settled around the iron barrel. She read the Persian verses engraved over the barrel, etched into the metal. This was a hunting musket, not a war musket—the verses lauded the chase. She held it up to her shoulder, as Ali Quli had once taught her, and put a finger in the trigger. The musket was not loaded, and the trigger pulled back smoothly with a well-oiled click. She handed the musket back to Hoshiyar and wiped damp palms on the silk of her pyjamas.

'It is a sign of great favour, your Majesty.'

She turned to the eunuch. 'I know.'

His face was bland. Mehrunnisa opened her mouth, then closed it. No, this was not the time to betray her fears. There was never a time to betray her fears. Not even to Hoshiyar. With him especially, she must be careful.

Hoshiyar said quietly, 'It is time to go, your Majesty.'

The sun rose in the eastern sky as the royal party assembled in the main courtyard of the fort. As Mehrunnisa came into the courtyard, she saw Jahangir and Jagat Gosini standing close to each other, conversing in low voices. It had been many years since Mehrunnisa had seen Jagat Gosini in anything other than passing glimpses. The Empress was only a few years older than Mehrunnisa, but she had more to show her age—the rule of Jahangir's zenana for six years, a child who was now a twenty-year-old man, a marriage that had lasted even longer. And yet, when she smiled at the Emperor, she became youthful, flirting, her hair brilliantly black in the morning glow, her eyes the same shining ebony as black slate.

They talked and then did not. When Jahangir turned to instruct one of the grooms, pointing to the jewelled blinders of an Arabian horse, she turned too, said something, and Jahangir nodded. It was all done in comfort, without hesitation, talk that flowed from twenty-five years of togetherness. Mehrunnisa's toe jammed against a paving stone and she stumbled, clutching Hoshiyar's arm to steady herself. How could she compete with this, what they had? It would come with time, but no matter what, Jagat Gosini would always have had more time with him.

The Empress said something, and Jahangir put back his head and laughed. Mehrunnisa stopped at the sound of that laugh, a hundred questions in her mind. How long had they been here? Where had the Emperor spent the night? With the Empress? For he had not been with Mehrunnisa. She knew she did not have claim to all of Jahangir's waking hours, or even his sleeping ones. This she had known before she had agreed to be Jahangir's wife—that she would have to share him. No Emperor could devote himself to just one wife, when there were courtiers, diplomats, wives, concubines, sisters, aunts, and mothers, all wanting a slice of his attention.

A warm hand touched the skin of her back, between her short choli blouse and the start of her pleated pyjamas. 'Come, your Majesty. The Emperor will wish to start on the hunt soon. He will be happy if you are content too,' Hoshiyar said softly, bending to catch her ear. Mehrunnisa nodded. She started to walk towards them again.

The Emperor turned at the sound of Mehrunnisa's footsteps. 'There you are. I was wondering what happened to you.'

Mehrunnisa gracefully performed the *konish* in greeting; her right hand went up to her forehead and she bowed. 'I took some time getting ready, your Majesty.' She indicated the musket in Hoshiyar Khan's hands. 'Thank you for the gift.'

'It gives me pleasure, my love.'

Mehrunnisa then took a deep breath and turned to Jagat Gosini. They were meeting for the first time as equals. All these years, Jagat Gosini had always been a notch above her. Her position made her so. But even so, at one time, when she had had the care of Khurram, Mehrunnisa had had an upper hand. It must have hurt, she could not imagine giving up Ladli to anyone. But Jagat Gosini was still powerful, still an Empress, still, in this zenana world of theirs, the Padshah Begam. Silence settled thickly around them as they stood watching each other carefully.

Eunuchs and slave girls froze in their places. The grooms, who had been busily adjusting the saddles on the royal horses, stopped and stared. And they waited for some movement, some speech, something other than the breeze that lifted the edges of the two Empresses' veils with gentle fingers.

Mehrunnisa bowed to Jagat Gosini, but she did so stiffly, her head barely bending, her eyes not leaving the Empress's gaze. 'Please accept my compliments.'

A flush bloomed on Jagat Gosini's face. It was a simple statement, but an insult. In the first place, Mehrunnisa should have performed the konish or the taslim; secondly, it was not her place to speak first, and then to speak without respect... it was a slap on the face.

'And mine,' Jagat Gosini replied, enunciating carefully, the weight of her anger underlining each word.

Mehrunnisa turned to Jahangir. He stood watching, giving away nothing of his thoughts. The Emperor did not have a tremendous amount of affection for Jagat Gosini, but he would not countenance a public display of disrespect. Although he had never explicitly said anything, he did not like fights within his zenana. This much Mehrunnisa had understood from her years of living within the walls of the harem. She could have been more polite, but she had not wanted to be.

'We should leave,' Jahangir said. He spoke in a low voice, but at his words the activity in the courtyard resumed in a frenzy, as though the pause had not occurred. Every person there had heard the exchange between the two women, knew that etiquette had been ruffled, and saw that Jahangir had done nothing in retaliation. Glances stole at the new Empress with admiration—in so few words she had diminished Empress Jagat Gosini. How brave she was, how proud, what a noble bearing for a woman born to a Persian refugee. There would be much to talk about after the hunt.

The mahout brought the imperial elephant forward. He caught hold of one of its ears and slithered off its neck, pendant for a moment like an earring, before he fell on his feet. He then knocked his stick against the elephant's trunk and commanded it to kneel.

The imperial howdah had been strapped onto the elephant's back. It was a canopied seat made of wood plated with gold. A thick mattress covered with satin reposed on the howdah. Cushions, buttoned with rubies, were strewn around for comfort. Four thin gold pillars held up the silver cloth canopy fringed with pearls and diamonds.

Jahangir climbed into the howdah first, and Mehrunnisa followed. None of the eunuchs present had dared to assist Jagat Gosini in after the Emperor. In a small way, the hierarchy was being broken. The muskets were handed in, and the mahout jumped on top of the elephant's neck. It lifted to its feet slowly, forelegs rising first, the howdah tilting back and then forward. As the elephant lumbered out of the courtyard, the two ladies pulled their veils over their heads.

Outside, the Emperor was joined by five hundred Ahadis. They took up positions on the sides, in front, and behind, forming a tight net around the royal elephant. The rest of the court rode behind with their soldiers, all heavily armed with muskets and spears.

The sky grew pink as the imperial party progressed through the streets of Agra. As usual, almost the whole city had turned out to watch the Emperor. The crowd stretched their necks to catch a glimpse of the two women in the howdah. People shouted praises as they passed, and Jahangir threw silver rupees into the crowd, pleased with their adulation.

Suddenly a child yelled out, 'Which one is the beautiful Empress Nur Jahan?'

Mehrunnisa smiled under her veil and waved a graceful hand at the little girl. The crowd roared its pleasure, and Jagat Gosini became more furious. The people had never commanded her in such a manner.

Jahangir handed Mehrunnisa the gold brocade bag. 'Throw some silver rupees to the little girl, my dear.'

Mehrunnisa dipped her hand in the bag and threw the coins

into the crowd. The crowd roared even louder. They certainly approved of the Empress now. The elephant moved slowly through Agra, stopping at places while the guards cleared the roads.

Finally, the imperial party left the city and proceeded towards the hunting grounds. The keepers had by this time beaten the lion into its retreat in the centre of the forest. As the Emperor approached, the Mir Shikar, Master of the Hunt, came running up to the royal elephant and fell to his knees in salutation.

'The lion awaits, your Majesty.'

Jahangir threw the man some rupees, showering silver over his head. He scrambled in the dust for the coins and counted them surreptitiously. Fifteen rupees! It would feed his family for a few months.

The elephant carried the Emperor and his wives into the forest. When they had reached the soldiers guarding the enclosure with their nets, the Emperor signalled them to move on inward.

The forest was thick and dense with vegetation, overhead the trees formed an awning from the rising sun. It was cool and damp in the shade, redolent of rotting leaves. All was quiet except for the sound of twigs and grass crackling under the feet of the soldiers as they moved forward. A quail flew out of the grass, squawking, a group of gazelles flew nimbly across an open expanse. Muskets rose to shoulders and then fell. The lion was the prey.

Jahangir leaned back on his cushion and closed his eyes. He would normally be alert, watching for a sign of the lion, a flash of a golden mane in the green of the forest. But today, the two women who sat ahead of him, their backs rigid, leaning over the edge of the howdah, were the hunters. Since Mehrunnisa had come to him, he had been filled with happiness. If he could rub her shoulders now, take away the tension, he would do it. But there were other women in his harem who had a claim on him, as Jagat Gosini was demonstrating. He knew that Mehrunnisa wanted the royal seal, and the title of Padshah Begam, but she would have to earn it. Jahangir would not interfere in the matters of the zenana, even though he had the power to give Mehrunnisa anything in the world.

Mehrunnisa swayed with the rhythm of the howdah. She breathed in the smells of the forest, listened in the unnatural stillness for sounds of game. Her palms became clammy, and the musket slipped from her hand. She wiped her hands on her pyjamas and picked up the gun again. She did not look at Empress Jagat Gosini. They had not talked since their greeting. Words were useless, for they each knew what they wanted. And only one of them would get it.

By her side, Jagat Gosini sat forward, her eyes moving through the shadowed and lit undergrowth with practised ease. Her hands gripped her gun, right finger loosely curled around the trigger.

The breeze shifted direction imperceptibly; the women did not notice it. But the elephant twitched its long trunk, moving it up and to one side, then the next. It stopped, and the mahout said over his shoulder, 'It senses the lion, your Majesties.'

The two women tensed, bringing up their muskets. But the grasses lay still, unruffled, nothing to indicate that an animal moved within them. The elephant started to quiver, and they felt the vibrations that shuddered through its large body. The lion was close, that was for sure, but where? And they waited, the soldiers quiet behind them, the elephant trembling, the Emperor watching them.

Then they heard the voice of the lion, to the right of the royal elephant, there, at the rear of a large rock. It was not a loud roar but a questing one, yet it fractured through the silence in the forest. Drugged, its senses dull, the lion had not seen them yet, or heard them, or smelled the scent of their skins. It came around the rock and froze where it stood. It saw the elephant, the humans atop it, the humans around it. All the soldiers had their muskets raised by this time, sighted steadily on the lion.

Mehrunnisa flinched. She had seen a lion once, in the royal zoo. Then it had looked so scrawny, so pallid, pacing its cage. This one was three times the size of the royal lion, gold-tufted and heavily muscled. This was a lion in the wild? She watched, mesmerized, as the lion shook its head to clear its drugged brain, then leaped through the air, going for the royal elephant.

The elephant immediately reared back, trumpeting in fear, lifting its forelegs and almost displacing the howdah. As the howdah tilted, Mehrunnisa jammed her shoulder against one of the posts and willed her hands to lift the musket to aim it at the lion.

A shot reverberated through the forest, coming fast at the edge of the lion's roar and the elephant's cry. The lion lay at the feet of the elephant. The shot had caught it in mid-leap, through its heart. its head was askew, neck snapped in the fall. A small round hole blossomed under its ribs, trickling blood on the dusty ground.

The soldiers let out a cry. 'The Empress has shot the lion!'

The drummers beat their drums loudly, and the silent forest echoed with the noise of human voices and laughter.

Mehrunnisa sat still, her hands trembling around the musket, her finger still pulling the trigger back. Jagat Gosini pulled herself upright; the elephant's rearing had thrown her to the back, against Jahangir. Lying thus, half across her husband, her musket pulled up to her, the metal lodged under her chin, she had fired. Mehrunnisa's gun lay cold, Jagat Gosini's smoked in wisps and whorls. Her face, her hands, and even Jahangir's hands, for he had held her as she had shot, were peppered with black flakes of gunpowder. The Emperor rubbed Jagat Gosini's face free of the gunpowder, and she smiled at him, a little smile showing she was grateful for the action.

'You have done well, my dear wife. The lion could have killed us. You are indeed an excellent shot.'

He then turned to Mehrunnisa. She put her musket down, its weight suddenly heavy on her shoulder. It had all happened so fast, without warning. One moment the lion was in front of them, flushed out of its hiding place, the next it was dead. And not because she had shot it.

'See how brave Jagat Gosini is,' Jahangir said. 'I am very proud of her. What other king can claim such a markswoman in his harem?'

'You are right, your Majesty. The Empress has done us all proud,' Mehrunnisa replied. Still she did not look at Jagat Gosini. As the acrid smell of freshly burned gunpowder bittered the air, she sensed a brief smile on the Empress's face.

The hunt went on. Antelopes and nilgai were flushed out of the tall grass and killed expertly by the accompanying nobles. At noon, the royal party returned to the fort, dragging behind them the carcasses from the hunt.

Mehrunnisa sat hunched in her place in the howdah. All morning, Jahangir had praised Jagat Gosini for her skill, her valour, and her bravery in the face of danger. It was all true. Not one of her own shots had found its mark. The nobles had laughed openly when she had missed. Even the Emperor had smiled, showing her how to hold the musket, how to pull back on the trigger, how to cushion the recoil against her shoulder. And he had pointed out Jagat Gosini's skill. Watch her, my dear, see how she takes aim.

When they came back to the fort, dusty and tired, Jahangir left them without a word. Before he did, even as they descended from the howdah, needing the aid of eunuchs now, a slave girl stood near with a silver tray in her hands. Jahangir lifted the satin cloth covering the tray. On it, on a bed of velvet cloth, lay an exquisite necklace of gold and pearls. The Emperor lifted the necklace and clasped it around Empress Jagat Gosini's bent neck, over her veil. The ends of the necklace captured her veil around her head, the pearls glowing like the moon in the afternoon sun. Then, as they all bowed, Jahangir left. He had said little during the hunt, now he walked away without even looking at Mehrunnisa. Jagat Gosini's entourage settled around her like a flock of pigeons, exclaiming at the necklace, praising her, and they moved out together. She did not speak to Mehrunnisa either.

Mehrunnisa stood alone in the courtyard watching her husband leave, listening to Jagat Gosini's unsaid words. *What else could you expect of woman not born to royalty? Not aware of royal etiquette or pastimes? You are common, Mehrunnisa. Nothing but common.* Mehrunnisa was wearied from the hunt. She was hot, her skin blistered from the sun. Her lips were cracked, and wetting them with her tongue had only made them more dry. She felt her hold on the Emperor slipping.

'Come, your Majesty,' Hoshiyar Khan said at her ear. He led her away, and she let him, leaning on his arm as though she was suddenly very, very old.

There were to be celebrations all evening in Empress Jagat Gosini's apartments. Preparations had started even before the royal party returned from the hunt, even as the bullet left the Empress's musket and fled in search of the lion. For among the soldiers behind the elephant were Jagat Gosini's stewards. They waited only to see who fired the shot, and then ran back to the palaces in the fort with the news. Twenty minutes behind them were the imperial runners, sent on to the treasury in search of the pearl necklace, for it had to be waiting for the royal party when they returned.

So the whole zenana knew of the hunt, knew who had killed the prey, who was to be lauded upon her return and who to be ignored. The harem was aflutter with gossip. Mouths worked busily. Those envious of Mehrunnisa and predicting the demise of Jahangir's affections for her, those in Jagat Gosini's camp, those hateful of Dowager Empress Ruqayya—and these last went to her as she woke to tell her the news. *So unfortunate. You have put so much faith in Mehrunnisa, your Majesty, and it seemed as though that faith was to be justified. But the Emperor*—and here there was a sigh, long and theatrical—*he enjoys women who are brave, who can shoot.*

And so it happened that when Mehrunnisa returned from the hunt, she found Ruqayya in her apartments, waiting for her, the ever-present hukkah against her mouth. Mehrunnisa was surprised at this visit; Ruqayya never went to anyone, people came to her. They talked for some time as Mehrunnisa's bath was prepared, and then Mehrunnisa went to bed to sleep away the afternoon. In the evening, Ruqayya said, with Hoshiyar Khan by their side, they would really talk.

As Mehrunnisa slept, so did Empress Jagat Gosini. But she did so after having given orders for the night's feast. In the royal kitchens, fifteen cooks were commandeered for the Empress. They went by foot to the outskirts of the city to the slaughterhouse. There they picked out a goat, chickens and ducks, and watched as they were slaughtered, washed and put into sacks. In the kitchens, water-carriers poured river water out of leather bags into earthenware jars, which were sealed with white cloth until the cooks were ready to use the water. Every single ritual was supervised by the Mir Bakawal, the Master of the Kitchen.

The rice for the pulav was rinsed three times and let to soak for twenty minutes, until it plumped up to a pearl softness just like the Empress's new necklace. Cardamom, cinnamon, cloves, coriander seeds, fenugreek, anise—all sorts of spices and herbs were ground, wet and dry. When the cooks were ready to put the dishes together, they washed their hands well, and wore thin white muslin masks over their noses and mouths, and white cloth caps over their hair. Not a drop of sweat could sully the Emperor's meal. In one corner, the Mir Bakawal watched, and if a cook sneezed he was sent out, the food he was cooking thrown away, and another cook would take his place. Jahangir's favourite foods were prepared—he had many—and that afternoon, fifty-one different dishes simmered, stewed, steamed, roasted and boiled over the wood fires of the kitchens. The Emperor could not possibly eat every one of the dishes, perhaps he would not even taste all of them, but if he wanted something special, it would be there.

When the food was ready, it was packed into gold and silver vessels, porcelain and earthenware vessels, brought out every day from a storage stronghold. The dishes in gold and silver vessels were wrapped with red cloth, the others in white cloth. They were then sealed with the imprint of the imperial kitchens, and in his neat hand, the Mir Bakawal spent one hour detailing the contents of each dish and attaching it with a piece of paper to the top of the seal. When the Emperor and Empress Jagat Gosini were ready to eat, the Mir Bakawal would break the seals himself and stand aside, waiting to be commended for his work.

And so the afternoon passed into evening. The sun escaped into the flat lines in the west, leaving the gathering monsoon clouds edged with shimmering gold. With the clouds came the humidity, and fans swished furiously in all the palaces of the fort. Lamps were lit, some in sconces on the walls, some in little earthenware saucers filled with sesame seed oil, the flames standing steady and upright in the still air, as though pulled skyward by an invisible hand. Outside the zenana, lined against the walls, jostling for positions of the most visibility, the dancing girls waited with their madams. They were all young, all pretty with a sameness of beauty, eyes pronounced with kohl, faces powdered white, sequins glittering on their short cholis and embroidered ghagaras. They were accompanied by singers and musicians, both male and female, and these were the only men allowed into the harem. They took stories of the zenana ladies to the outside world, embellishing those tales with many sprinklings of lies, for there was no one to deny the truth of what they spoke. The Ahadis stood guard outside too, regulating the crowd, keeping down the noise until Shaista Khan came to the door to choose the troupe for his mistress.

Emperor Jahangir walked slowly to Empress Jagat Gosini's apartments. The slaves following behind were silent, but some had already rushed to the Empress's palace to announce his arrival. He passed through corridors and courtyards, nodding when a bow captured his eye, smiling to bestow favour upon a concubine who caught his attention. It was a familiar route, the one he was taking, one he had taken many times before his marriage to Mehrunnisa. One he should have taken earlier in these past two months. This the Emperor knew, that Jagat Gosini's position should have been acknowledged by him; it was an unsaid rule of his zenana, of all zenanas. Yet, he had not been able to leave Mehrunnisa. She had never deliberately kept him, never said not to go, but she smiled and he fell in love with her again, she laughed and he took root by her side. Even now... he did not want to be here, but he had to.

He reached the outer door of Jagat Gosini's palace and she stood there, a silver thali in her hands, on which was a gold lamp and small mountain of vermilion. He bent so she could swirl the flame from the lamp around his head three times to take away the evil eye. Then the Empress put a streak of vermilion on his forehead.

'Welcome, your Majesty,' she said.

Jahangir smiled to himself. She greeted him as if he were preparing for a campaign, invoking her Hindu gods to protect him.

Empress Jagat Gosini ushered Jahangir into her reception hall, standing back to allow him to enter. She had outdone herself. The room was sweetly perfumed with civet from incense censers and coal braziers smoking with tiny slivers of sandalwood. Carpets lay thick across the floors, edge to edge, until there was no glimpse of the marble underneath. Divans lay piled in a semicircle on the farther end, and slave girls waited, demure, eyes cast down, their veils of thin muslins in green and blue, holding softly luminous peacock feather fans.

And so the evening passed, wine appearing at his elbow without request, Jagat Gosini by his side, playful and pleasing. The Empress wore her new pearl necklace, and Jahangir reached out to touch it against her throat.

'It becomes you, Jagat,' he said.

'Thank you, your Majesty,' she replied, her eyes glowing.

After dinner she turned to him. 'May I request something, your Majesty?'

'Of course,' he said. Inside he was guarded. What could she want? He remembered that early in their marriage she had always asked for things. Not jewellery, or grants of land, or a palace, or a swimming tank in her apartments, but other, little things. These came in the guise of helping him, according to her notion of what her duties were. *Allow me to choose the woman who will most please you tonight, your Majesty.* Or, *a man of your ancestry, descended of Timur the Lame himself, could not possibly like the guavas from this orchard, but that one will do very well indeed.* These were strange requests, taking from Jahangir the will to make his own decisions. He had let her, for they had seemed like simple requests. They had showed an affection, a liking for him that he had not expected from a wife, only a mother. But he had realized over the years that there was no real affection. They did not fight; she always acquiesced at everything he said, her voice at times too soothing. When his father, Emperor Akbar, had commanded their son be taken from Jagat Gosini and given to the care of Ruqayya, she had said nothing. Not one word. Jahangir had known she was upset, but she had been taught, and too well, not to show it to him.

'What is it you want, Jagat?' the Emperor asked.

'Our son, Prince Khurram, begs an audience, your Majesty,' she said, rising from the divan to clap her hands.

'Bid him in,' Jahangir said, but she had already done so. The wooden carved doors to the reception hall swung open, and Khurram came in eagerly. He almost ran the length of the room, came up to his father, and, dipping his right hand to the ground, he bowed from the waist. As his back straightened, his hand came up to touch his forehead in the konish.

'Bapa, your Majesty, I trust you are well.'

Jahangir rose to embrace his son, kissing his smooth forehead. He drew back to look at him. He was a handsome boy, no, now a handsome man, already married, with a child born two months ago. His eyes were a clear black, glittering like the depths of an inkwell; they were his mother's eyes. He had Jagat Gosini's eyebrows as well, and her chin. Khurram had grown up with Emperor Akbar. In the years that Jahangir had spent away from court, either on campaign in Mewar or rebelling against Akbar by establishing his own 'throne' at Allahabad, Khurram had stayed with Ruqayya. Jahangir did not know Khurram very well, but he was an endearing boy, always ready with a smile, always respectful and courteous.

Khurram turned to his mother and bowed. 'Your Majesty, thank you for allowing me to pay my respects to my father.'

She nodded, her face grim, but her hand went involuntarily to ruffle his hair, and he moved away. This was done very imperceptibly—Khurram moved his head to turn his eyes to his father, but Jagat Gosini stiffened. When he entered, Khurram had flown to Jahangir, as a boy child must to his father first, but Jahangir had been 'Bapa', and she was 'your Majesty', not 'ma'.

Khurram still called Ruqayya 'ma'. Jagat Gosini had asked him once, when he was eight or ten, to call *her* ma instead and he had replied with a great deal of seriousness and some surprise, 'But I already have a ma, your Highness.' After that, she had said no more, could not bring herself to ask again. Could not shout that *she* was his mother.

And so the evening passed into night. The music played, the girls danced, inviting and pouting. The three of them sat on the divans in an uneasy triangle, full of thoughts, smiling at each other until Jahangir rose to leave for his apartments.

'Will you stay the night here, your Majesty?' Jagat Gosini asked, her hand on Khurram's arm, stopping him from leaving with his father.

'Not tonight, Jagat,' Jahangir said. He walked away rapidly, before she could say more.

The Empress said nothing; she let him go. Her fingers tightened on Prince Khurram's arm, and he gently pulled them away. 'Your Majesty.'

Jagat Gosini looked away. 'I apologize, Khurram. You must go if you need to also.'

He stayed, though. For just a few more minutes. Prince Khurram talked about his daughter, Jagat Gosini's granddaughter, that she was feeding well, that his wife was pleased with her progress, that they had found a reliable wet nurse for her. Jagat Gosini nodded, not listening to him. In her mind, she watched Jahangir walking to Mehrunnisa's apartments. She saw her welcoming him. It had been a frightful evening, full of silences and some feeble conversation. Through all this, Jagat Gosini was aware that the Emperor had been thinking about Mehrunnisa. Nothing she had done had taken his attention from her, not even bringing Khurram into his presence, not even showing him the son they had made together, the son who would be Emperor next.

When Jahangir left her, he went not to Mehrunnisa but to his own apartments. He was tired, his head ached from the wine and the smoke of incense and the hukkah, and he had eaten too much at dinner.

The Emperor had spent five hours with Jagat Gosini, five hours during which she had not reproached him even once for not coming to her earlier. And the evening was the same as all their evenings had been——with music and dance and a general noise and chatter to drown out all other conversation. Seeing Khurram there had made his heart lighten with affection. He was delightful, awkward in movement still, like a young foal, but his very bumbling, his calling him 'Bapa', had been charming. Khurram was open, easily deciphered, like Mehrunnisa. And so, as they always did, his thoughts turned to the woman he loved—not because she was his wife or his concubine but simply because he had wanted her for seventeen years before he married her. And having married her, he wanted her still.

In Mehrunnisa there was no deceit. None that he could find, anyway. When she wanted something, she asked for it, not afraid of seeming selfish or grasping. When she was reading, she did not want him to disturb her, and he liked that concentration in her. She did not treat him as a child. She loved him, and she showed it. And if she disliked what he did, if she did not tell him so plainly, she found a way to tell him without words. There was no subterfuge in her.

He undressed for bed slowly, slipping out of his embroidered qaba and pyjamas, replacing them with a crisp cotton kurta and pyjamas. Jahangir rubbed his hand over the cotton thread embroidery over the front. Was this the kurta Mehrunnisa liked to wear? He held the cloth up to his face, but he could not smell her essence; the dhobis had washed it too well, and instead it smelled of the Yamuna River, of soapnuts, of the sun that had dried it. Jahangir lay back on his bed, watching as the punkah on the ceiling swung back and forth in a dark, rectangular shadow. Mehrunnisa wanted what Jagat Gosini had. She wanted to be Padshah Begam. She wanted to possess the royal seal. His giving her the title of Nur Jahan, one that no other woman in his zenana possessed, was a public declaration of his love for her. And he could give her this too.

His word was never questioned, and if he wished for Mehrunnisa to be supreme in his harem, he could make her so. But before he gave her what she wanted, she had to earn it. To prove she was worthy.

Chapter Four

...Jahangir, disregarding his own person and position, has surrendered himself to a crafty wife of humble lineage, as a result either of her arts or of her persuasive tongue. She has taken, and still continues increasingly to take, such advantage of this opportunity, that she has gradually enriched herself with superabundant treasures, and has secured a more than royal position.

—W.H. MORELAND AND P. GEYL, TRANS.,
Jahangir's India

WHEN EMPEROR AKBAR FIRST CAME TO AGRA, HE FOUND AT THE BANKS OF the Yamuna River a small fort with crumbling walls, indifferently and haphazardly built. The fort was destroyed, and in its place, for its situation was excellent, a new fort was built with three gateways. At its longest, along the river, the fort stretched one and a half miles. The walls, made of red sandstone from local quarries, rose seventy feet from the banks of the river. Akbar had intended, in demolishing the previous fort, to build one instead whose very appearance would speak of the might of the Mughal Empire. And he succeeded. From the outside, the walls rose sheerly vertical, topped with pointed merlons, awesome in their grace, frightening in their majesty. A moat curved around the fort on the land side, almost as deep as the walls were high, and it was dry—water was a luxury not to be misused, even by great Emperors. But scrub and hardy bushes filled the moat, subsisting on rain, giving shelter to snakes and the occasional tiger. At night, jackals, greatly daring and with a courage they did not have in the light of the day, would howl at the moon, sending their voices bouncing off the walls of Agra Fort. The guards along the top, mostly to keep awake, would send arrows whizzing into the darkness in the direction of the howls—target practise for the blind.

The zenana quarters, Emperor Jahangir's palace, and various other palaces and pavilions fronted the Yamuna, their filigreed screens greeting the morning sun as it woke to first touch the waters of the Yamuna, then to send fingers of light through the marble latticework of royal bedchambers. The waters of the Yamuna cooled during the months of harshest sunshine, and even in years of capricious monsoons, the river glowed blue, a giver of life along its banks, a symbol of stability.

On the western side, away from the Yamuna, was the main entrance to the fort, the Hathi Pol—the public doorway to the Red Fort. It stood high above the ramparts, ablaze in sandstone inlaid with white marble and blue tile. An open gallery of arched verandahs decorated the top, and this was the Naqqar Khana, the drum house that seated an imperial orchestra. The Hathi Pol was visible from miles away, almost the first glimmer of Agra itself, but as a traveller neared, he would see that it was not as welcoming as it seemed. All three gateways of the fort had false facades—a tiny gate in front, dwarfed into inconsequence by its more magnificent cousin, or a series of gates with steep ramps, bordered by high walls, herding pens to slaughter unwelcome visitors.

Just outside the Hathi Pol, stretching into the vast bareness of the Indo-Gangetic plains, were the shooting ranges of the imperial palaces. The ranges were in an enclosed maidan, blighted of vegetation and rocks. The earth was baked mud here, dust rising at the slightest breeze to thicken the air. At its edge, the lifeless circle gave way to forests of stunted trees that tenaciously clung to life, their roots plunging into the ground in search of water. Within the maidan itself, and in its periphery, no birds roosted in the trees, no animals wandered into the patch of bare earth, for fear that a marksman might use them as shooting practise.

Mehrunnisa stood at one end of the grounds, matchlock loaded and raised to her shoulder, waiting for a signal from the Mir Shikar.

'Now!' he yelled.

At the far end, a servant flipped a clay pigeon into the air. It arced over the trees, catching a glint from the perishing sun. Mehrunnisa swung with her shoulder, carrying the six-foot length of the matchlock with her body rather than her arms. Her eyes were on the sight, following the path of the pigeon. The wick of the matchlock, dipped in saltpetre, smouldered on top of the barrel, acrid smoke from it filling her nostrils. Then her finger pressed the trigger. The wick bent into the barrel and ignited the gunpowder. The matchlock boomed, slamming against her, as the explosion sped the bullet out of the barrel and on its way. The clay pigeon flew harmlessly as the bullet shot past it, falling on the ground with a dull thud, kicking up dust.

Mehrunnisa sighed and gratefully let the musket fall. Another shot missed. Just as she had missed time and again during the hunt. She rubbed her shoulder. She knew that tiny pinpricks of blood clots would already be forming under her skin, like the skin of a freshly plucked chicken; she had seen this after the hunt when she had taken off her clothes and stood in front of the mirror. Her muscles flared with pain. Her right arm was numb, fingers nerveless, the ache riding up her shoulder to her neck and down her back.

'Beta.'

She turned around. Ghias Beg stood there, his hand raised to shade his eyes from the sun.

'Bapa,' she said. Mehrunnisa's father came near and put his

arm around her. He drew her in for a kiss on the forehead.

'You are tired. Come and sit for awhile.'

'All right, Bapa. But only until the Mir Shikar reloads the musket.' She handed the gun to the man and followed her father to the shade of a jamun tree. Purple fruit hung in bunches from the tree, their smell heightened in the heat of the sun. A carpet had been laid under the branches. While she had been shooting, a servant had climbed the tree to pick the fruit and pile it in a silver bowl. Mehrunnisa sat down on the carpet with Ghias Beg and offered him the bowl. They ate in silence, biting into the flesh of the fruit, letting the indigo juice slide down their arms.

Ghias reached over to rub Mehrunnisa's neck. She leaned against him, resting her head on his shoulder.

'Why tire yourself so much, Mehrunnisa? Is it worth it? Your Maji tells me you have been at the shooting ranges every morning for the last week. Look at you.' He pulled her hands forward, palms decorated with angry red blisters. 'Are these the hands of a queen? An Empress?'

'Bapa,' she said, 'did you hear what happened at the hunt? I wake at night, every night, with the lion plunging through the air at the imperial elephant. The howdah tilts... I fall from it...' She pressed closer into him, and he held her tight, as he had when she was a child.

'Why dwell on what did not happen?'

'I try, but I cannot help it. These are dreams, Bapa, they do not obey me.' Mehrunnisa pulled away and looked at her father. When had those worry lines come to pattern his face? And his eyebrows were winged with white too. Ghias Beg took off his turban and laid it on the carpet. She reached for his forehead with a light touch.

'You are losing your hair, Bapa.'

'Signs of wisdom, beta. The white hair, well, no hair even.

The wrinkled skin. All these show I am an old married man, father of an Empress, a grandfather many times over, diwan of the Mughal Empire. I could not, with all these accomplishments behind me, show to people an unlined face and hair as dark as these jamuns. They would laugh at me. They would not take me seriously.' Ghias Beg's eyes sparkled.

Mehrunnisa turned away and looked into the distance at the figures on the other end of the maidan. The sun had set, and the grounds were awash with the smudged blue haze of twilight. 'I did badly at the hunt, Bapa. The Emperor is pleased with Empress Jagat Gosini.' Her voice dipped. 'He has not come to see me, not in some time.'

'Look at me, Mehrunnisa.' When she turned to him again, her eyes filling, one tear rolling slowly down her cheek, he reached to wipe it with the back of his hand. 'Is this what I have taught you? To flee from obstacles? To give up even before the fight has started? Yet you are here, have been here at the shooting ranges practising your shooting for the last week.'

'And I am no better than I was a week ago. You saw me miss the shot just now. So it has been almost every day. I stand here, the gun raised to my shoulder, following the path of the pigeon, missing most times. If I cannot hit a clay pigeon, what chance do I have against a live one?'

'One day you will hit the clay pigeon, Mehrunnisa. The day after that the live one. But it won't happen unless you try. Unless you keep trying. Think of how much we have gone through these last few years, when every day was an effort, when we fell into disfavour with the Emperor, when it seemed we would never rise again to our former positions of glory. Today, we are much more. You are an Empress, married to the most powerful man in the empire. A man on whose life our lives depend. I did not think this would happen when I came to India from Persia. All I had expected was notice from Emperor Akbar, perhaps a small position at court. Mostly, an opportunity to feed my family.'

'And everything has come through you, Bapa. I had hoped that once I became Empress I could do more for our family. But you were diwan before I married the Emperor. I have done nothing.'

Ghias laughed and picked up another jamun. 'Nothing? A new title for your brother Abul. A larger mansab for me. These are nothing? I have seen the Emperor after his other marriages. With no other wife has he been so enticed, so much in love.' This time his laugh bordered on the edge of embarrassment. 'Look, I speak to you of the Emperor's love, such talk as a father should not have with his daughter. I must know of this and that is enough. You must know too, Mehrunnisa. Do you not know that Emperor Jahangir loves you?'

'Yes,' she said. 'But... he has not come to me... I am lonely, Bapa.'

Her words hung in the air, as forlorn as what they said, and a deep ache came over Ghias.

The cicadas chirped, first one, then all of them, in a grand cacophony of an orchestra. Ghias wanted to reach out to Mehrunnisa again, to tell her everything was going to be all right, to tell her she could come home so she would no longer be alone. But he hesitated, knowing that she was now a grown woman, and his love, her mother's love, was no longer enough for her. In the four years that Mehrunnisa had been a widow, a thin skin of hardness had come over her. He had wanted, had insisted, that she come to live with him—where else would his child live but with her father? But she had gone to the imperial zenana to serve Dowager Empress Ruqayya. She had earned money sewing and designing clothes; she had kept away from them, and he had let her be. For it was what he had taught her, not to beg favours of anyone with an open palm. Mehrunnisa would not come home now, *this* was her home, here, by the side of the Emperor. It was just a quarrel, surely, a simple mistaking of intents. Surely. Yes, this had to be so. He brought her to him then, let her cry into his shoulder, and her tears soaked into his cotton qaba.

He said quietly, 'You may never be as good as Empress Jagat Gosini at the hunt, but you will be almost as good as her. I know you can do this. You must not think otherwise. Even when I almost abandoned you as a baby, you yelled loud enough to be found again. Do you remember that story?'

After a long while, Mehrunnisa said, 'Tell me again.'

So he did, reliving the winter sandstorm at Qandahar when Asmat had lain down to have Mehrunnisa. He remembered how he had sat in the shelter of a rock, the sand whirling around him, laced with cold, how the wind had stopped for a moment and he had heard her first cry. A few weeks later, even as they had been on their way to India, he had thought it best to give her away. She had been feeble, not taking to the goat's milk, Asmat could not feed her, and a wet nurse cost money they did not have... problems had come to ambush him. So he had left her wrapped in his shawl under a tree, a village in sight, praying with all his heart. *Allah, let someone find my daughter and give her a good home. Let them be kind, Allah.* Someone had found her and brought her back to him. It had not happened that simply, but it had happened.

When Ghias Beg finished the story, Mehrunnisa picked up his hand and kissed it. She asked, 'How do you know it was your daughter who was returned to you, Bapa? Maybe it was another baby, born to some poor peasant in the countryside.'

The diwan shook his head vigorously. 'But you have your grandfather's blue eyes. You have his smile. You have your brother Abul's stubborn spine.'

'And of you, do I have nothing of you?'

'My wisdom.'

She laughed then, the sound spilling over the silence of the shikar grounds. 'And of Maji?'

Ghias thought of his wife. 'Maji gave you her gentleness, her soft speech, her kindness.'

'Do I have anything of me, Bapa?' They played this game each time he told her the story. Of late he seemed to tell her the story more often, marvelling at how far they had come. He would say that he had had four gold mohurs tucked into his cummerbund the day she was born. The day he gave her away, his cummerbund was empty. The moment she came back, their hearts were full, their lives brimming with wealth.

'You have in you the ability to be anything you want, beta.'

She drew back to glance at her father. Ghias had never ended the story this way before. For the first time, he told her she could do what she wanted.

'Your Majesty,' the Mir Shikar said. They both turned to see him standing there, holding a loaded matchlock.

Mehrunnisa rose from the carpet. Her tears were gone, and in the halflight from the torches dug into the ground, she knew her face would show nothing. 'I must practise now, Bapa.'

'Do so,' he said. He put out a hand to her. She clasped his elbow and helped him up. 'But in moderation. Don't tire yourself out too much, Mehrunnisa.'

Suddenly, by his saying so, she was tired. A wave of nausea came to slap her in the stomach, and she felt the jamuns rise up her throat. Her limbs were loose and heavy, moving with slowness. She took the matchlock from the Mir Shikar and hauled it up to her shoulder again. When the Mir Shikar shouted out his order, the servant set fire to the round wedge of *palas* wood used for night practise. She watched as he moved his arm, first below his waist, then above his head, clutching the burning pigeon in his mail-clad hand. The pigeon shot out into the night, smearing the darkness with a streak of gold. It spun in circles. Mehrunnisa traced its path, and as it went downward, she pressed the trigger. The shot bolted from the matchlock, the recoil almost knocking her off her feet, but she kept her eye on the ball of fire. It seemed to be suspended for a moment, and then it exploded, sending shards of burning wood in all directions—a thousand pieces of gold.

Mehrunnisa looked back with a delighted smile to see if Ghias Beg had been watching. He had. She saw him raise his hand in a wave, and his voice came across the dusty grounds. 'Now hit ten more in a row, beta. Then you will truly have reason to celebrate.'

The next day, as court matters were being wrapped up in the Diwan-i-am, Ghias Beg came forward and performed the taslim in front of the Emperor. He did this four times, not lifting his gaze until the last.

'Mirza Ghias Beg?' Jahangir said from his throne.

'Your Majesty,' Ghias said, 'I beg pardon, but may I beg a private audience? It is not a court matter.' He was uncomfortably aware of the curious glances from the other nobles in the hall. Mahabat Khan and Muhammad Sharif were a few feet from him. They too were attentive, clad in the etiquette of the court, but their eyes questioned. Ghias had spoken in a low voice, as near to the throne as he dared to be. He had not known how else to approach Jahangir other than at court. He was the Emperor's father-in-law, but so new at his position that he did not realize he could have sent a message directly to Jahangir.

'Of course,' the Emperor said immediately, rising as he spoke. 'You can accompany me to the zenana and talk as we walk.'

They went back through the arched corridors leading to the harem quarters. Ghias Beg walked a few steps behind Jahangir; the servants were ordered a few more paces away. They walked in silence for a while, Ghias worrying with the words in his head.

How was he to say what he wanted to say? Suddenly, Jahangir stopped and turned to his minister.

'How is Mehrunnisa? I hear you visited her at the shooting ranges yesterday. Does she keep well? She looked tired after the hunt.'

'She is well, your Majesty. But...'

'But what? Tell me, Ghias Beg, does something ail her? Do the servants bother her?'

'It is not the servants, your Majesty,' Ghias Beg said carefully. He paused. How did a father plead his Emperor to return to his daughter?

'It must be the servants,' Jahangir said firmly. 'If I am not at her apartments, they do not perhaps listen to her orders.'

'That can be easily remedied, your Majesty.'

'Yes.' Jahangir turned to one of the maids dawdling in the corridor. 'Send a message to Nur Jahan Begam that I will visit her this evening.'

'Thank you, your Majesty.' Ghias bowed and backed out of the corridor. It had been so easy to ask this favour without even asking for it. He had fretted all night about his daughter. She had been unhappy when he had seen her. She had pretended otherwise, but she had cried, and Mehrunnisa cried so little, unlike other women, whose tears were at a rush to come for demands and wants and fears. Or if she did, Ghias never saw that sorrow. Not when she had had the miscarriages, not when Ali Quli had died... although that last, it had been a freedom of sorts. And so, in the morning, after a night spent thinking these things, Ghias had decided he would speak to the Emperor.

When he left, Jahangir went down the marble steps into one of the courtyards. The slaves, eunuchs and concubines lounging under the shade of the mango trees rose to melt away. He waited until they had all gone and then sat down at the edge of a pond. The carp in the pond came to nibble at his shadow, greedy and waiting to be fed. He waved a hand over the water and watched as they skittered in the direction of his hand, mouths open and gulping.

Here was a chance to see Mehrunnisa again. Again and at last. In this last week, he had not known how to go back to her. Every morning he woke to an empty bed by his side, an emptiness around him. And his days were then filled with state duties, visits to Empress Jagat Gosini's apartments at night to take part in interminable entertainments and cups of wine. His head ached from wanting to be with Mehrunnisa. Jahangir had his eunuchs tell him every detail of her days, he knew she went to the jharoka balcony on the two mornings he had not gone, that she spent the rest of the day in the shooting ranges. He listened to all of this with a calm face, but inside a hunger rioted.

Jahangir removed his imperial turban and laid it on the stone edge of the pool. The afternoon sun stood guard over him, reflecting off the slabs of marble in the courtyard. He would have to wait till the evening to see Mehrunnisa. Why had he said evening, why not right now? Surely, twenty minutes would have been enough for her to prepare herself.

Once, Mahabat, Sharif, and even Jagat Gosini had tried to keep him from Mehrunnisa, to keep him from seeing her, from marrying her, citing her family's disloyalty to the throne, her husband's perfidy, saying that for sure she would harbour resentment against him. All these reminders had returned in the past week, borne on a breeze of slyness. Mahabat's and Sharif's voices had taken on a strength that had waned after Mehrunnisa's first jharoka, and Jagat Gosini had solicitously showed him the imperial *farmans* she had signed with the royal seal. But they had not been able to see that their Emperor was grieving. It was Mahabat's and Sharif's behaviour that was unsettling. What was it they feared? A rise in status in her family? Mehrunnisa's voice at the jharoka? But why?

He sat there for a long time, his head uncovered, his hair soaking up the heat of the sun. After his evening prayers and the final audience at court, Jahangir bathed and dressed in a hurry, shouting orders at his servants. He went to Mehrunnisa's apartments and she was there, waiting for him, serious. She had done nothing to apologize for. As Emperor, he could not apologize either. There was no fault in either of them.

He carried with him an embroidered bag of velvet as a gift. Earlier in the afternoon, he had sent for this most precious piece of metal in the empire. Jahangir put the bag in her hand and enclosed her fingers over it.

'What is it?' she asked.

He said nothing at first, a curious light of excitement in his eyes. Then, 'What you have wanted, Mehrunnisa.'

'I have you.'

Again he was quiet, watching her. 'Without it you do not have me completely.'

Could it be... no, but this was so soon, so sudden... Mehrunnisa glanced down at the bag in her hand. Whatever was inside was heavy, tiny but heavy. Through the cloth she felt its smooth and round edge. She laid the bag against her chest, and the coolness of the metal seeped through the weave.

'Thank you,' she said, numb of all other feeling, without any other words to speak of her enormous gratitude. With this piece of metal, she *owned* the empire. Possessed power over every corner of its lands, all of its people, why, even the earth on which it rested and the sky above it.

Jahangir stayed the night in Mehrunnisa's apartments. They slept wrapped around each other, frightened by what had happened this last week. A fight... a non-fight... a misunderstanding. How easy it was for this to happen, how easy to inflate a small incident out of all proportion, to bring a wedge between them.

Every night a sword was brought to the Emperor's sleeping chamber, a different one each night, the scabbard encrusted with rubies and pearls, or pearls and emeralds. Jahangir slept with it by his side—this was a ritual his father had begun, that a Timurid Emperor never closed his eyes without protection, no matter how heavily guarded he was on the outside. And so this night, the sword found its way to Mehrunnisa's chambers and lay within Jahangir's reach by the bed.

When the eunuchs returned from this errand, they talked in the zenana. Lamps that routinely waited to be extinguished only after news of Jahangir's whereabouts were now put out, and the women went to bed knowing that somehow, with some sorcery, the newest Empress had once again managed to beguile the Emperor.

And so Mehrunnisa's star rose again.

Abul Hasan leaned against the wall, arms folded across his chest, watching his sister's profile outlined against the window. The sun lit up circles around her, escaping through the pattern of the filigree work of the wooden shutters. She was reading an embellished scroll held up to the light. Abul waited for her to speak, as patiently as he could.

'What is it?' he asked finally, with a note of fretfulness in his voice.

Mehrunnisa looked up, her face aglow. 'A royal farman.'

'What has the Emperor given you this time?' He bent to pull it from her hands and frowned. 'An order for a mansab to one of the courtiers. Why do you have it? What does it have to do with you?'

'Everything, my dear Abul.' Mehrunnisa patted the divan. 'Sit down.'

He sat and then saw the little green Malacca velvet sack, embroidered with pearls. Even as she read, Mehrunnisa had her hand on the bag, her fingers rippling over the pearls. 'What is that?'

Mehrunnisa smiled. 'So many questions, Abul. You ask too many questions. Tell me, what does it feel like to be allowed to enter the hallowed walls of the imperial zenana?'

A week earlier, she had sent instructions to the guards to allow Abul in. Every mole on his face, every hair on his head, every bend of his limbs was described in detail. As Abul stood outside the gates, the Kashmiri guards and the Ahadis examined him minutely, and then sent a message to Hoshiyar Khan inside the zenana. Hoshiyar came and conducted his own thorough examination. The eunuch studied him carefully, asked a series of questions about his uncles and grandfather—where they lived at different times of their lives, which women they had married, who had given birth to those women. A thick shawl was brought to cover Abul's head and the upper part of his body, and then Hoshiyar led Abul in this half-darkness, with only the vision of his own feet to guide him, through sandstone courtyards, gardens with lawns glittering with morning dew, and marble floors so sleek he slip-slid his way over them. A woman passed by once, silently, but her curiosity was vastly evident. She hesitated near him, the bottom edge of her silk ghagara's skirts swishing to a halt. He saw the pleats settle into folds, saw the sun pick out the hundreds of ruby buttons nestled in the gold embroidery. She stood very close, and even in the sweating heat of the shawl, Abul could smell the jasmines in her hair, and something else, some undefinable, unreachable perfume. Hoshiyar had his fingers tight around Abul's elbow, but his touch made Abul stop, and for this woman. Who was she, that she might command the direction of Hoshiyar's steps? A few long moments passed. The woman and Hoshiyar Khan did not speak with words, and if otherwise, Abul had no idea of what they said. He thought she was looking at him as one did in the camel markets, scrutinizing the shape of the camel's hump, the health of its legs, the grace of its stride. Abul did not dare to lift his shawl and look at her. He might be the brother of Nur Jahan Begam, but his head was still not worth too much.

This was an enormous amount of fuss, Abul thought, and just to see his sister. He could remember her birth well, although he had been only four that winter evening in the desert outside Qandahar. He could remember his fear, fed by hunger and fatigue, as the storm howled about them, as his mother's whimpers broke through the canvas of the tent into his ears. This was how Mehrunnisa had come into the world. In the beginning, he hated her for this, for being so demanding, for crying all the time, for creating worry for them all.

Of when Bapa gave her away and brought her back, Abul had no memory, for it happened in the span of a few hours. Only later, at Agra and Lahore, as they followed Emperor Akbar's court where he went, did he begin to notice her, to teach her *gilli-danda*, or laugh at her attempts to climb a tree, her ghagara tucked dhoti-like between her legs. They had grown apart from each other, of course, as a boy and a girl brought up in the same house do, stretching their love and liking for one another over years and miles.

'You have changed, Mehrunnisa,' Abul said softly. Even as he spoke, his hand reached to her side to the embroidered bag.

She slapped it away. 'Why? Does this'—she waved around the cool room—'and this'—she touched the turban on her head decorated with a long heron feather, and only those in favour with the Emperor were allowed to wear it—'make me different?'

'No,' he said. Now he leaned forward and tipped a gold vase of yellow roses on the rosewood table beside him. The vase's neck moved through the air as though it were bowing to royalty, and as Mehrunnisa lunged for it, Abul moved his left hand quickly towards the bag in her lap. 'These are outward signs. Tributes from Emperor Jahangir. And good to have. But something else...'

Mehrunnisa had fallen across the carpet, holding the vase in her arms, the flowers thrust into her face, but when she moved, the bag went with her, still in her hand. Abul took the heavy vase from her and ceremoniously put it back on the table. She laughed, turned on her back, and put the bag on her stomach. Its drawstring was looped around her wrist. 'Do you want to see what is in it?'

'Please.'

'All you had to do was ask, Abul.' She threw it at him, and he caught it eagerly and with surprise. It was heavier than he expected, and whatever was in it banged sharply against his palm.

Abul opened the bag, and a small, heavy, silver disc fell into his palm. He turned it over. Nine circles were carved on the front, and within each, etched in Persian, were the names of the house of Timur. The first read, 'Amir Timur, Lord of the auspicious Conjunction, Lord possessor of the four Corners of the world' and so on until 'Akbar Padshah, the Emperor most mighty', and finally the ninth circle in the centre of the disc, 'Nuruddin Muhammad Jahangir Padshah Ghazi, Light of Religion and Conqueror of the World'.

Abul's hand shook. The metal was cool to his touch, and the carved writing was black, filled with the grit of ink. As his fingers moved, little flakes of dried ink came away on his skin. He put the disc to his cheek and then ran his tongue over its chilly smoothness. 'The royal seal.' Abul's voice was hushed and reverent.

'Do not eat it. It's the only one I possess,' Mehrunnisa said from the carpet where she still lay, her hands light on her stomach. When Abul looked up at her, there were many expressions on his face, awe and wonder, of course, but also gratitude. He had heard of the seal—there was not one man of consequence in the empire who had not, and who had not wanted its imprint upon a farman or an edict addressed to him, which would be kept for years, from generation to generation.

'How?... Why?... Where did you get this from, Mehrunnisa?'

She turned to her side and raised herself on one arm. 'Is it too soon? I did not ask... but I wanted it. And the Emperor wanted to give it to me. Should I have waited longer, Abul?'

Abul wiped the seal on the front of his qaba, and then he again rubbed it on his face, breathing in its metallic smell, wanting to absorb it into his skin. With it, mountains could be moved, cities devastated, rivers run off course. It would buy almost anything in the land, including the head of almost *every* noble. Such was its power. And now Mehrunnisa had possession of the seal. But how? It was said to reside with Empress Jagat Gosini, how did Mehrunnisa get it? He looked at her with suspicion.

'Don't be an idiot, Abul. I did not steal it.' Mehrunnisa sat up. 'Give it to me.'

'A few more minutes, Mehrunnisa.' Abul moved away from her hand and folded his arms, the seal resting in his armpit, solid and comforting.

'You can see it, hold it, even taste it'—this last Mehrunnisa said with a laugh—'whenever you want. I do not intend to lose it to another woman in the zenana. It will be here when you come to visit me.'

Abul put the royal seal in the palm of her hand and watched Mehrunnisa. She wet a lump of ink with some water from the vase, making a thick paste in the jade inkwell cup. The seal was dipped into the ink, drained on the side of the cup, and then pressed onto the farman. She laid a weight on each of the four corners of the farman for the ink to dry.

Abul stared at the glistening black imprint. 'Are you the Padshah Begam, Mehrunnisa?'

She did not look at him. 'That is just a title, Abul.'

Now his attention was finally diverted from the seal. He had heard the undertone of roughness in her voice. 'Wait for a while then. Good things will come to you, Mehrunnisa. But they must come in little bits, too much and you will be bludgeoned with them. You will not know what to do. And the seal, you hold this, is it not enough for now?'

'For now,' she said. 'For now it will do very nicely.'

'Tell me how.'

'You heard about the hunt?' He nodded and she continued. 'When the Emperor came to my apartments later, the week after the hunt, he gave me the royal seal.'

Abul moved closer to his sister. 'What did you say?'

'Nothing at first.' She bent her mouth to blow on the farman. 'Well, nothing in the end either. I thought about it, whether I should have the seal now... or later. Whether I should wait until I had formed... connections in the zenana, when the women, the eunuchs, the slaves and concubines all knew who I was.'

'They will now, Mehrunnisa,' Abul said softly. 'No one will be able to ignore you now.'

As Mehrunnisa talked, Abul thought again of how much—and how quickly—she had changed. She spoke of the other farmans she had signed, of her ships. It awed Abul when she said this, *her ships*. Last month, she had sent Hoshiyar to Surat on the western edge of the empire, to the shipyards there to oversee the building of three ships. The money came from her jagirs, land that Jahangir had given her. And the Emperor had given Mehrunnisa the choicest districts in the empire, where the earth was lush and fertile, where wheat grew with a mere sprinkling of seeds and a clouding of the sky. She owned cities—the shops and bazaars, the houses, the fields around them, the people in them, everything. Sikandara, on the Yamuna River south of Agra, was a giant customs house, and duties were collected on goods from all over the eastern wedge of the empire. And all this money came to Mehrunnisa.

Abul was envious; it was hard not to be so of so much good fortune. But there was also a part of him, a larger part, which was glad for Mehrunnisa. She shared her wealth with all of them. Because of her he had a new title, Asaf Khan. Their father had a larger mansab, more responsibility, and more visibility in the empire. Maji was Matron of the Harem. He knew that he only had to ask for something and she would give it to him. The years apart, when they had grown into adulthood as separate people, could not take away their childhood closeness.

He wondered if Mehrunnisa could do anything about his daughter. Arjumand was nineteen now, and of all Abul's children, she gave him the most delight. Five years ago, because of Bapa's standing at court, Arjumand had become betrothed to Prince Khurram. But in these five years, so many things had happened to move the dirt from under their feet and throw it upon their family, to sully their name. The engagement had been forgotten. Abul had watched his daughter grow silent, the laughter inside her vanished as though swept away. She was still cheerful when he wanted her to be, still brought his chai to him when he returned home, still stood by his side asking how his day had been, but it was all done with a noticeable effort. Arjumand was a woman now and needed to be married. She had formed hopes when she saw Prince Khurram, perhaps even fallen in love with him, as a girl should when she first sees the man she is to marry.

Abul wanted to ask Mehrunnisa if the marriage could now take place. But he could not bring himself to ask. At least, not yet.

So he said instead, 'I should leave now, Mehrunnisa. I was given two hours to visit you.'

She patted his arm. 'Go then. And come back again soon.'

He unbent his knees and rose from the divan. Abul stood looking down at his sister, hesitation in every movement. His hand went to the little red cloth bag tucked into his cummerbund.

'What is it?' Mehrunnisa asked, a sudden wariness in her eyes.

'Nothing...' Abul turned to go, and then turned back. He took the bag out of his cummerbund and held it where she could see.

'What is in the bag, Abul?'

In response, he undid the drawstrings of the bag and let its contents spill into his palm. The brown-black kidney-shaped seeds glowed against his skin like a hive of bees.

Mehrunnisa beckoned with her head, and Abul came up to his sister. She touched the seeds with her finger. 'Datura,' she said. Then very quietly, 'Are you asking for allegiance, Abul?'

His mouth dry, Abul said, 'Yes.'

'Why? Have I not done enough?'

'Yes. But will you swear for me now, Mehrunnisa? Upon the seeds?'

Once, a long time ago, when they were both children, they had played this dangerous game, swearing loyalty to each other after some stupid incident that neither could talk of. What it was, Mehrunnisa could no longer remember... she rummaged through her memory now. Abul had visited the public houses? Or they had together? Something like that. Something neither Bapa nor Maji could hear about. Abul had offered her the white crushed powder from a single datura seed, and they had both eaten it. Bitter to the tongue and oily, for hours afterward they had swayed in almost-delirium, constantly drinking water, eyes shut against the painful light of the world. Mehrunnisa's stomach had cramped, and that was when Abul had called for Maji. Their mother had given her a paste of tamarind and willow charcoal, and Mehrunnisa had vomited the contents of her stomach onto the stone floors of the central courtyard. And then only had the pain in her belly ceased, then only could she open her eyes to the light without cringing. Neither spoke of what they had eaten, though; they had promised not to.

'We could die, you know,' Mehrunnisa said. Now she knew that she had perhaps almost died from that taste of datura, that without knowing how much they should eat, she had overdosed on the powder.

'I know,' Abul replied. But he did not move to put the seeds away in the bag. 'This is how we promise, Mehrunnisa. Are you now afraid?'

A little smile came upon her face. 'No, I am afraid of very little, Abul. But we are much older now, and should know better.'

Abul opened another cloth shoulder bag that he had brought with him, and took from it a marble mortar and pestle. He placed one seed into the mortar and ground it to a powder. Then, dusting the residue from the end of the pestle, he placed it between them.

'We have a bond nothing and no one will touch,' he said. The same words he had spoken the first time, Mehrunnisa thought; Abul did not forget much. He wet his right index finger with his tongue and dipped it into the powder. Then he put his finger into his mouth.

Mehrunnisa watched him, waited until his finger came out of his mouth clean. Her heart hammering inside her chest, she said, 'We have a bond nothing and no one will touch.'

With a finger that trembled suddenly, Mehrunnisa sponged up the gritty white powder and brought it to her mouth. The stinking, fetid smell of the datura plant assaulted her nostrils, but she did not waver. The powder dissolved on the tip of her tongue, still as bitter as she remembered it, with the undertaste of oil. When she lingered thus, Abul grasped her hand and pulled it out of her mouth to check whether she had eaten the datura.

'Now what, Abul?' she said.

He reached into his bag and brought out a jar filled with the paste of tamarind and charcoal. 'Eat this, right away.' He fed her the paste and then scooped some into his mouth. A few minutes later, retches rose inside both of them, and they ran for the gold flower vase, tipped out the roses and the water outside the windows, and, one after another, with their heads bent towards the opening, emptied the contents of their stomachs into the vase.

Mehrunnisa leaned weakly against the wall, heaves still shaking her body.

'Are you all right, Nisa?' Abul rubbed her face and wiped away the sweat on her forehead. 'Shall I call for a hakim?'

She started to laugh then, without control, her arms around her brother. 'How stupid we are, Abul. We could have died, you know.'

'Thank you,' he said. Then he pulled away from her and looked into her smiling blue eyes. 'Now I know, Nisa.'

Fifteen minutes later, their retching had stopped, but they could not help laughing. It was not, thank Allah, the mad laughter under the influence of the datura, but the mirth of defiance, of having seen death in the face and turned away from it.

The farman had dried; Mehrunnisa rolled and tied it up. Then she snapped her fingers, the door to her apartments opened silently, and Hoshiyar materialized in the doorway. He took the farman from Mehrunnisa and, without a change in expression, took the vase she handed him.

'Clean that, Hoshiyar.'

'Yes, your Majesty.' He held it away from his nose and stood waiting for Abul.

Mehrunnisa took her brother's hand and kissed it. As he stepped out, she said, 'I have not seen Arjumand in a few months. Will you ask her to come for a visit soon?'

A lot of people watched Mehrunnisa's swift ascendancy with interest, both within and without the walls of the imperial zenana. For the harem's inmates, it was a source of wonder. Most of the women had not even seen her, so vast were the women's quarters, but they heard of her from the slaves and eunuchs. The women all steadily, one by one, fell into camps. There were those who approved of Mehrunnisa for whatever reason—she would benefit them, or they did not like Empress Jagat Gosini, or more probably because these women, whether they were other wives or concubines, mothers of Jahangir's sons or not, did not have either the ambition or the tenacity to aspire for supremacy. So they were happy enough to let Mehrunnisa have it, as long as their lives went on with the same ease and comfort.

There were those, of course, who watched her with a growing dread and dislike. For Empress Jagat Gosini, the hurt was immediate, and it was accurately placed. Having been at the very top, she was losing the most when Mehrunnisa wandered near that position. So some of the other women in the imperial zenana gathered around Jagat Gosini, and were thus, by their very association, against Mehrunnisa.

And then there was the Dowager Empress, Ruqayya Sultan Begam. Still bitterly enraged at Jagat Gosini for slashing her income—from luxurious to merely lavish—Ruqayya was ecstatic about Mehrunnisa's growing power. If she could not rule the zenana anymore, at least she would through Mehrunnisa. Or so she thought.

They met again over the next few months, either late at night or in the afternoon when the heat had driven most of the harem into their cool rooms for a nap. Ruqayya taught Mehrunnisa the value of diversifying her assets—some of her money should be in land, jagirs and such, some in the cities of great trade value, and some in the sea, ships that plied the Arabian Sea routes from India to Mecca and Medina.

As she sat in Ruqayya's apartments, Mehrunnisa watched as a great many eunuchs and slaves came and went, bending to the

Dowager Empress's ear with whispers. Ruqayya would say then, 'Did you know Mirza Kamran's daughter, the one who is to be married in two weeks, has lost her dowry necklace? It cost fifty thousand rupees, and poof, now it's gone. Their tailor's son, the one who made eyes at her, who always lingered over her when taking measurements, has started constructing a new house though.'

Mehrunnisa would be bemused at this piece of information. *Who* was Mirza Kamran? Ah, one of the courtiers of the first tier in the Diwan-i-am. What other significance did he have? None that Mehrunnisa could think of, and yet, here was this intrigue that had somehow found its way to Ruqayya's ears, and in all probability, Mirza Kamran still thought his tailor's son was at the house only to stitch clothes for his family.

Ruqayya's hand would flash, quick as a silverfish, into the bag by her side, and money would glitter in the informant's palm—a gold mohur, a silver rupee, sometimes a bracelet or a bangle, depending on the weight of what she had heard. Ruqayya was normally stingy, normally bewailing her now-straitened circumstances , but *this* was what money was for, Mehrunnisa, she would say. Not for ships or jagirs, gardens or sarais, but for knowledge. The most powerful weapon in any arsenal.

Outside the zenana walls also, among the courtiers of the empire, the English merchants in Agra, and the Jesuit priests, Mehrunnisa was much talked of. Here too there was marvel and disbelief. How could a mere woman have so much authority? That did not stop these men—who would not credit her with intelligence or influence—from thronging her jharoka appearances, deeply curious.

Much closer to home, in the *mardana*, the men's quarters of the imperial palaces, Prince Khurram paid attention to Mehrunnisa too.

Khurram's interest in Mehrunnisa was not merely incidental.

There were four contenders for the throne, four sons of Emperor Jahangir: Khusrau, Parviz, Khurram and Shahryar. All four had equal rights to the empire. With as many wives as their father had, many sons had been born. But survival was another matter. A son could be, and was, lost to something as flimsy as a fever. The year Shahryar was born, there was another son, Jahandar, but he did not live past a few months.

The four princes were each of them born to different women, the first three to imperial wives, and Shahryar to an imperial concubine who had been fortunate enough to please Jahangir for just one night. There was no explicit law of primogeniture in the Mughal empire, either; as they reached manhood, as they waited for the end of Jahangir's reign, all the princes would jostle for the crown. This had happened when Jahangir had come to the throne, and it had happened with their grandfather, Emperor Akbar, as it had with their great-grandfather, Emperor Humayun.

Now though, in the year 1611, the four sons had each a different history.

Khusrau was born of the ill-fated Man Bai, Jahangir's first wife. He was the first son, the first heir to the throne, and his birth had been much awaited. And in his early years, he showed great promise. He was a fine young man, handsome to look at, gentle with his servants, a boy who spoke well, in whose person rested the future of the empire. Also, the prince had powerful connections.

Khusrau's uncle, his mother's brother, was Raja Man Singh, a Rajput warrior who had been much respected by Akbar, so much so that the Emperor had given him charge of the most important campaign in Mewar and the governorship of Bengal. When Khusrau was seventeen, his marriage was arranged with the daughter of another influential noble at court, Mirza Aziz Koka. With two such men as his advisors, Khusrau could do little wrong. But in the end, it was their voices that misled him. When Jahangir was yet a prince, Raja Man Singh and Mirza Koka encouraged Khusrau to rebel and try to gain the throne for himself. But the two nobles underestimated not only their authority in the empire but also Jahangir's influence over the court and Emperor Akbar.

It was at this time that Khusrau's mother, Man Bai, died of an overdose of opium. She had watched bewildered as her son fought with his father, as her pleadings made no impression on him. In the end, weakened by this struggle, she killed herself. And so Khusrau, at eighteen, knew that he was responsible for the death of his mother.

Jahangir became Emperor of Mughal India and crushed his son's two supporters. Mirza Koka was stripped of his titles and lands, and Raja Man Singh was eventually relieved of his governorship of Bengal. Khusrau was merely imprisoned. But Khusrau had rebelled again... and again, fleeing his confinement, trying to muster an army to fight his father, even, at one point, attempting to assassinate Jahangir. The Emperor would not allow his son to be put to death, so Khusrau was blinded instead. Later, physicians were summoned to restore his sight, and they did so, but only partially in one eye.

Here was Khusrau then, at twenty-four, half-blind and deranged, roaming the gardens of his palace, still plotting the overthrow of his father, but weak in supporters. He had a son, Prince Bulaqi, a potential contender for the empire, but then Khusrau's other brothers were in line before him.

Prince Parviz was born of Sahib Jamal, Jahangir's third wife. Jahangir married her in the same year he married Jagat Gosini. Parviz had early on succumbed to the scourge that afflicted so many members of the imperial family—drink. Of the four royal princes, he was the only one away from court, preferring to stay in the Deccan under the guardianship of the Khan-i-khanan Abdur Rahim, ostensibly directing the interminable campaign in the south. If

Parviz wanted the throne, he had not enough strength to either ask for it or demand it. It was easier for him to rise every day to the soft touch of the women of his zenana, much easier to drown his nights in wine.

Prince Shahryar had been born of a royal concubine the year Jahangir ascended the throne. He was only six years old, still a child, still untried. Shahryar played with his nurses, went swimming in the Yamuna River, and ate what he pleased, and all these made him contented. What more could a child want?

And so came Khurram, Jahangir's third son, born of Jagat Gosini, brought up by Ruqayya. His name was given by his grandfather, Emperor Akbar, for that was what his birth was. 'Joyous'. Khurram was, almost universally, beloved of everyone. Unlike his older brother Khusrau, Khurram had the simple advantage of pleasing his grandfather and not displeasing his father. The prince also knew that all this beneficence was just by chance. Had he been offered riches like Khusrau, or wine like Parviz, or just simple-minded nurses like Shahryar, he, too, would have been languishing like them. Somewhere, the fates had been kind to him.

Khurram had been with Ruqayya in the zenana until he had reached manhood and was taken out of the women's palaces and brought up in the men's quarters of the fort. He was well aware of the intricacies of harem life, of how the women fought, slyly and with diplomacy befitting the greatest monarch, for even a toehold in their world. He had watched Ruqayya bend other wills to hers, and seen how she had been instrumental in influencing his grandfather.

The prince knew that Mehrunnisa's voice was growing stronger in his father's zenana, far surpassing even Jagat Gosini's. He was twenty years old, his father only forty-two. If the crown were to shift heads today, it would come to Khurram. But in ten, or maybe even twenty years, when his father actually died, loyalties could migrate like sands in a dust storm, obliterating all traces of one-time affiliations. And at that time, if Mehrunnisa's rise to power now were any indication, she would be the person who decided where the crown would be vested.

So this prince, the best of the four sons of Emperor Jahangir, aware of his own importance, and aware too that this importance was only fleeting if he did not work to keep it, decided to go in search of Mehrunnisa.

In another part of the harem palaces, Empress Jagat Gosini pondered on her upcoming meeting with Mahabat Khan. She had not stopped fighting yet, but then, she did not know yet of her son's impending betrayal.

Chapter Five

The Conqueror of the World was the slave of a woman—
his consort, Nur Mahal, or Mehrunnisa, as she was
afterwards styled. Her father... and her brother... had a
large share in the administration of affairs; while her
niece... was the wife of Sultan Khurram... All these
personages were at this time in close alliance...

—WILLIAM FOSTER, ED.,
The Embassy of Sir Thomas Roe to India

BY 1570, EMPEROR AKBAR HAD FINISHED CONSTRUCTING THE LAL QILA,
the Red Fort, on the banks of the languid Yamuna at Agra. A year
later, he would begin construction of an entire city at Sikri, calling
it Fatehpur Sikri after the conquest of Gujrat. Fatehpur Sikri sat on
the banks of a large freshwater lake, sixteen miles from Agra, near
no other source of water. It was built as homage to a Sufi saint to
whom Emperor Akbar had gone in pilgrimage, praying for an heir
to his empire. The saint promised him three sons. Ten months
later, Jahangir was born at Sikri. Akbar had two more sons. But it
was Emperor Jahangir who ascended the throne.

Fifteen years after Akbar's court moved from Agra to Fatehpur
Sikri, the city was abandoned as the Emperor went to Lahore to
take command of the campaign against the king of Uzbekistan. He
never came back, and neither did the current imperial court. So by

1611, the city lay in the searing heat of the Indo-Gangetic plains, its red sandstone buildings dulled to a blush, its courtyards empty of human voices, its gardens wilted under the fierce sun, dust cloaking its many windows. The paths were filled in, no longer deeply rutted by horses, elephants, camels and bullock carts.

It was here, as the sun, hued in orange and tangerine, dipped into the even lines of the earth, that one lone figure rode through the deserted bazaar street toward the *Diwan-i-khas*, the Hall of Private Audience of Fatehpur Sikri. Lining the grimy path, the trees grew stunted, their branches reaching flat into the sky, their leaves shrivelled. Mahabat Khan could see glimpses of the lake as he rode, his horse kicking up dry brown dust clouds. Its waters were blue, silver-streaked in the twilight, but the plains had already come to claim its edges, muddying the lake. In a few years, it would dry up, evaporated into oblivion by the sun. And Fatehpur Sikri, that monument to a great emperor's whimsy, would be left standing at the brink of nothing.

Once this had been a thriving city, the seat of the imperial court. Once, the many palaces had echoed with the laughter of the harem ladies, incense from sandalwood sticks had swirled between the pillars, marble floors had been piled with Persian rugs, oil lamps had lit shadowed niches, and illicit lovers had met in the dark shade of the tamarind trees. The sixteen-mile road between Agra and Fatehpur Sikri had been one long bazaar street with sarais for weary travellers, shops and houses. Here Emperor Jahangir and Mahabat had been children together, growing up in the imperial zenana under the watchful eyes of the many women. They had hunted together, played together, sat at their books with the same mulla. Theirs had been a strong friendship forged through boyhood fights and reconciliations, acts of bravery and mischief. Later, Mahabat, Sharif and Koka had convinced Jahangir to rebel against Emperor Akbar, telling him that the one sure way to control the empire was to have possession of the royal treasury at Agra. Jahangir had listened, as he had always listened to them, desperately hungry for the empire that would be his anyway at Akbar's death. Through all those trials, they had stood by him, with him, knowing there was no turning back. One misstep and Emperor Akbar would have their heads adorned on stakes on the ramparts of Agra Fort.

The sandstone minarets of the Diwan-i-khas came into view, and Mahabat led his horse to the front courtyard, looking around as he did so. Fatehpur Sikri was a ghost city, some said even inhabited by ghosts, drifting around its courtyards and palaces, murmuring snatches of songs of days gone by. But Mahabat was here to meet no ghost. He felt excitement sing through him, as though this were a rendezvous of the heart—some other noble's wife or daughter, where half the lust would come from its being publicly denied. He jumped down from the horse and tossed his reins to the ground.

He ran across the courtyard, his boots flapping lightly on the stones, up the steps to the entrance. He paused for a moment, letting his eyes adjust to the cool gloom. A lamp flickered in a corner niche. Mahabat looked up at the exquisitely carved marble pillar in the centre of the room, which held up the balcony in which Akbar used to sit while giving audience to a few select nobles. Even in decay, the Diwan-i-khas glowed with Akbar's vision.

'Mirza Mahabat Khan.'

The words were spoken softly from one end of the room, echoing through its silent walls. Mahabat turned to the sound. She was wearing white. A white muslin veil covering her face, a white ghagara sweeping through the dust of the floor, silver bangles that slid down her arm in a tinkle. In the murky light, she looked like a ghost. She moved noiselessly through the doorway and into the room. Mahabat put his right hand to his forehead and bent in front of her, bowing from his waist in a konish.

'Your Majesty.'

'Thank you for coming to Fatehpur Sikri,' Empress Jagat Gosini said.

'Thank *you*, your Majesty. I remember well that I asked for the meeting.'

'As I had once before, all those years ago, Mahabat.'

'Yes.' Mahabat tried to look at her face, to read her expression, but the veil was too thick. 'Why Fatehpur Sikri, your Majesty?' he asked. 'Wouldn't it have been easier to meet at Agra in one of the imperial gardens?'

She moved, her hands fluttering under the veil. 'No place at Agra is safe anymore. Mehrunnisa's spies are everywhere. It would seem even everything *I* do is reported to her. I chose Fatehpur Sikri because it is so far away. I asked the Emperor for permission to pay my respects at the Shaikh's tomb.'

Jagat Gosini moved to the centre of the room and sat down against the main pillar. Mahabat watched her, then went to the other end to lean against a wall. The Empress was truly royal, he thought. Only a queen would sit in the dust and dirt of many years and not care that it would soil her clothes.

Outside, his horse snickered, and Mahabat swung sharply to the sound, listening. He tiptoed to the doorway again and looked out. Nothing. The courtyard was washed with the liquid blue of twilight, hard to see in, but there was nothing.

'Something has to be done, Mahabat.'

'Were you followed here, your Majesty?' he asked in a low voice.

'No, Mahabat.'

'And your servants, where are they?'

'At the Shaikh's tomb, in prayer. Sit down, Mirza Khan.'

Mahabat came back into the Diwan-i-khas and slid down the wall to his haunches, his hands resting loosely on his knees. His ears strained for sounds from outside. True, he had ridden in on another horse, not his own, but it stood there in the courtyard, groomed and fed, too well cared for to be looked after only by spirits. Anyone passing by...

'Do not worry. Who would come here? My servants can be trusted, Mahabat. No one else has a reason to be at Fatehpur Sikri today.'

He finally turned his attention to her. 'What is it the new Empress has?' he asked. 'Is she beautiful?' At this there was an inward smile. He had seen the portrait, he knew of Mehrunnisa's beauty; or rather the painter's brush had caught something that was sure to be flattering to both Jahangir and Mehrunnisa. But the painting was long returned to the imperial atelier. He could only remember now that he had thought Mehrunnisa to be exquisite.

'She is considered to be so, Mahabat. She is old, you know, and time takes with it all charm.'

Mahabat nodded. One woman would not praise another, especially when they both had the same to offer the Emperor. He bent his head in acknowledgement and in apology. 'She sits at the jharoka, your Majesty.'

Again he said the wrong thing, and Mahabat could sense a stiffness in the Empress. Her voice was cold, cutting. 'She rejected one of your applicants the first day.'

Mahabat waved a hand. 'That was a small matter. The man was a cousin, or so he asserted. Lately, many have come to be cousins, with relationships distant and diffused. I allow it—it is one of the doubtful privileges of my position. It was not that she denied my cousin but that she denied me, your Majesty. The Emperor has never said no to me before. And he did that day at her behest.'

'And this was what I warned you of all those years ago when I said she would be deadly for us. Not just to me in my position as Padshah Begam but to you in court.'

'I still do not understand it,' Mahabat said. 'Her husband caused the death of Qutubuddin Koka, whom the Emperor loved as a brother. Such bonds are not lightly broken. Yet, he seems to have forgotten Koka's death.'

'We tried to remind him, you and I,' the Empress said. 'But it did not work, did it? For you did not do your part well enough, Mahabat.'

It was a slight, but he let it pass. 'Who could have known? There were so many things wrong with her family; they were disgraced, they could not have possibly gained favour with his Majesty. Nothing but this marriage could have changed their circumstances. There were serious obstacles to love. If it is love.'

A silence stretched between them as the Empress looked down at her hands, twisting an end of her veil in spirals between fingers that had suddenly become rigid. Again, he had displeased her. But why? She could not possibly be offended by his question, Mahabat thought. They both knew that love was a word to be used in poetry, in verses of lauding, and had little place in royal affairs.

'Perhaps you have never fallen in love?'

Mahabat smiled. 'I love my wives, your Majesty. And the slave girls and other women.'

Jagat Gosini leaned forward. 'And they? Do they love you, Mirza Khan?'

'Of course.' This he said with finality. 'They have no one else, your Majesty.'

The Empress laughed, and Mahabat flinched. It was an unpleasant sound, reminding him that just as he had met with the wives of other nobles, perhaps his own women had met with—were even now meeting with—other men. Even this brief thought of his harem's supposed infidelity enraged him.

So he said, 'I hear the imperial seal reposes with Empress Nur Jahan.'

His voice cut short Jagat Gosini's laughter, and an edgy silence descended.

'Well done, Mahabat,' she said softly. 'It would seem we both have reason to dislike Mehrunnisa. She has to be stopped.'

'I know,' Mahabat replied. 'And she has to be stopped now, or soon. The past is the past, unhelpful to us unless it can be used against her. We tried at every turn to stop the Emperor from marrying her, but it happened nonetheless.'

'You did not try hard enough, Mahabat.' The Empress's voice was caustic.

He did not respond to that. He *had* tried, but without faith in Jagat Gosini's fears, and so without much enthusiasm, for Mahabat had not cared what Mehrunnisa did within the harem's walls. The jharoka... that was an entirely different matter.

'I can do nothing within the harem, your Majesty,' he said.

'Let me handle that, Mahabat. Your place is at court.'

But she had not 'handled' anything. Mahabat had heard of the hunt and Empress Jagat Gosini's success in it, yet, after that, so soon after that, in a few weeks, she had lost the imperial seal. Jagat Gosini had once warned him about Mehrunnisa, and now, finally, Mahabat found himself listening to her. But she had nothing else— Hoshiyar was gone from her side also. So why had he even bothered with this meeting, inviting the danger of being discovered like this, in the deserted Diwan-i-khas of Fatehpur Sikri, so close to a member of the zenana? One word of this in Emperor Jahangir's ear, and, long friendship or not, Mahabat could very well lose his head.

However, there was one thing Jagat Gosini had that Mehrunnisa did not. 'The nobles at court speak often of Prince Khurram's prospects, your Majesty,' he said.

She smiled, and her voice filled with love. 'He is a good child, Mahabat. And one day, when he becomes Emperor, he will need good advisors.'

'And he is yours.'

'Yes, after so many years, my son is finally mine. No matter what Mehrunnisa does now, once Khurram is on the throne, she will have no might.'

'You are the mother of the next Emperor, your Majesty. No one can take that away from you. *She* will never provide a rival.'

Mahabat's horse shifted about on its feet, metal shoes clicking agitatedly against the stones in the courtyard. He jumped up to look out of the window of the Diwan-i-khas, painfully aware that dark as it was in here, it was darker yet outside, and his turban was framed by the dull light of the room. He could not see his horse. And again, he heard nothing, no footsteps, no sound of anything living, human or animal. And then, a shadow moved in the courtyard.

Mahabat yelled out, 'Who is it? Who goes there?'

But the person, the thing, whatever it was, just melted into the dark of one of the arches. Mahabat's horse whinnied, shaking its head.

'What is it?' Jagat Gosini came up to him. He turned to her and looked into her face for the first time, albeit through the veil. She was frightened. It showed in her eyes.

'We must leave now, your Majesty,' he said, flying across the room to blow out the oil lamp. He waited until his eyes grew used to the sudden darkness, then he held out a hand to her. They went out of the Diwan-i-khas, Mahabat holding the Empress behind him to hide her—her clothes were white, and they glowed in the dark. They ran across the courtyard, through the palaces, stumbling and tripping over untended roots of trees and vicious vines until they came to the Jami Masjid, the principal mosque of Fatehpur Sikri.

The Shaikh's tomb was within the mosque. Here there were numerous lamps lit, in the open verandah in front and within the tomb itself, visible through the latticework of marble screens.

'I must go now, your Majesty.' Mahabat bowed to Jagat Gosini and vanished into the night, leaving her well within sight of the tomb.

She leaned against the walls of the main gateway, waiting until her breathing slowed. Mahabat Khan had shown an admirable courage in bringing her back to the tomb and her servants. He had acted with decisiveness. Jagat Gosini wiped her face with the edges of her veil. She was not foolish enough to think that he had done this for fear of her safety, but mostly his own.

She could hear voices now from within the tomb. The night was still warm, but the sweat on her back cooled rapidly and Jagat Gosini shivered. What was it Mahabat had seen outside the window? A man? A ghost? She ran across the yard to the front steps of Shaikh Chisti's tomb and sat down there near an oil lamp, the screen behind, of interlocking circles in marble, throwing its pattern over her. She could hear her servants' chatter, and Shaista Khan's querulous voice raised above the others.

It was time to leave and go back to Agra, or rather to the sarai a mile away—a sixteen-mile journey was not that easily undertaken in a night's span. But Jagat Gosini sat where she was, thinking. Anger was long gone, or she had cast it away with a force of will. It rose at times, though, as now, when she least expected it. The day Hoshiyar Khan had come to take the imperial seal away would forever prey on her thoughts. When he had said why he had come, she had been too stunned to think.

'Where... Where did this request come from?'

'At his Majesty's behest, your Majesty,' Hoshiyar had said.

She had possessed the seal for six years, since 1605, when it was wrenched away from Ruqayya's unwilling hands at Akbar's death and Jahangir's ascension. As the head eunuch of the imperial harem had waited, Jagat Gosini had gone to the teakwood trunk in her apartments and taken out the bag. She had handed it to him, and he had still waited. One by one, the other paraphernalia of the seal had gone to him——the *qalam* wood pen used to sign farmans, the nephrite jade inkwell, the wedge of ink in a gold box, and the gold knife with its ruby and pearl hilt used to chip at the ink. She had kept the heavy silver water vase that she had commissioned for diluting the ink. Hoshiyar knew of its existence, of course, but he had not asked for it, and neither had Mehrunnisa. They had allowed her that small dignity.

As he had left, Hoshiyar had said, 'Her Majesty has asked permission for her brother's visit, your Majesty. In two weeks. He will pass by the courtyard in front of your apartments in the third *pahr* of the day.'

So Empress Jagat Gosini had stopped Hoshiyar and Abul on their way. She had been curious about Mehrunnisa's brother. As she had stood next to him, she had tried to make out his face through the shawl, judged how high he rose from the ground——a mere elbow length above her——inspected the silk of his pyjamas and the embroidery on his qaba. All this had told her nothing and yet had told her something about Abul. He had fidgeted, moved his head this way and that as though trying to see her; he was a man of volatile emotions, short of patience.

She wondered just how much care he had for his sister. His coming to visit her was no indication; any man would visit a sister who had entrapped his Emperor. Jagat Gosini remembered that Abul's daughter was betrothed to Khurram. This was a fact she never forgot, and it was something she had been very careful to guard from both Jahangir and Khurram. If the marriage took place, Abul would be father-in-law to her son, and if his daughter had the same charms as her aunt, she could lose Khurram all over again.

'Your Majesty?' Shaista Khan stood next to the Empress.

She looked up at him. 'It is time to go, Shaista. Call for the horses.'

The servants carried lanterns to provide light on their ride. Guards ran ahead of her entourage, their feet slapping on the earth, as the horses pounded through the darkness, flinging dust into the night air. All the while, her veil plastered to her face, the reins taut in her hands, Jagat Gosini thought.

Khurram would never marry Mehrunnisa's niece, not if she had any say in it. He would not become part of her family. And without someone like Khurram—an heir to base hopes upon—Mehrunnisa had nothing.

As the moon swelled to fullness at the end of February, the festival of Holi was celebrated in the imperial palaces at Agra. The days were increasingly hot, the nights still pleasantly cool. The winter's wheat harvest had been cut, threshed, stored and traded, and now it was time to celebrate.

Holi was a Hindu festival, born of legends of kings and demons, gods and devotees. It was a time for enjoyment, whether its revellers were Hindu or Muslim, or indeed, pledged to any other religion. This liberalism had not always existed. When Emperor Babur conquered India in 1526, some eighty-five years ago, celebrating a Hindu festival was not even considered. He had instead instituted a *jizya*—a tax paid by a head count by those whose minds professed Hinduism. But then Babur had never really considered India home, or her people his. It wasn't until Akbar ruled that the jizya was abolished and Hindus were put on equal footing with the Muslims at court—an extremely political move, for the country itself was largely Hindu, the Rajput warriors at court were Hindu, and many of Akbar's wives were Hindu.

Once that barrier was destroyed, everyone could enjoy every festival. Even the Jesuit priests were allowed to celebrate mass, to convert the people of Hindustan to Roman Catholicism. They were even tolerated when trying to persuade the Emperor himself to their religion. This last would never happen, of course, no Mughal Emperor of India could profess anything but Islam, but the priests still tried.

Holi was celebrated for five days. On the first night, the ladies of the harem went out into the courtyards of the palaces and swept dried leaves and twigs arranged there by the *malis*, with gold-handled brooms. This was what the peasant women did outside the walls of the harem, clearing the ground around their huts of winter's debris. They piled the branches into heaps and set fire to them. All around the city of Agra, bonfires illuminated the cool night sky. The burning of fires signified the end of a long winter, the welcome of new life in spring. Bazaars stayed open late, selling silver-leafed cashew burfis, gold rounds of *jalebis*, saffron-tinted kheers, and other sweets and savouries.

In the palace kitchens, the Mir Bakawal hung over huge vats of bhang—hemp—marinated in water. The next day the cooks would mash the bhang to a white, sticky paste and then boil it with milk, sugar, almonds and sultanas. There would be no taste of the hemp left, only a sweet almond-flavoured milk, drunk in abundance, with one glass powerful enough to turn eight hours into a pleasant, many-coloured haze.

The palaces woke to the first rains of the year. In the streets, children rushed about wetly, screaming with delight, throwing *gulag*—coloured powder—on each other. In the imperial zenana, the morning started with the customary glass of bhang, then the ladies went out into the gardens to play. They smeared each other's faces with pomegranate reds, sunflower yellows, indigo blues, paddy-field greens. Little squirt guns were filled with coloured water. The idea was to sneak up on an unsuspecting victim and douse her with the water. Faces, arms, legs, clothes were all stained in a mélange of dyes. The stains would remain for the next three or four days, resisting baths and washings—they were the proud signs of having played Holi. By afternoon when the rain stopped, most of the jugs of bhang provided by the cooks were empty, and the ladies of the harem floated around dizzily, happy and careless.

Prince Khurram went looking for Mehrunnisa as the sun climbed high above Agra. The initial euphoria of the morning had worn off, and the women lay under the shade of the mango and tamarind trees in the gardens, talking softly, listening to music, and eating their noon meal. He walked through the courtyards holding a fistful of purple gulag, searching through the groups of people. He was accosted at almost every step, coloured water thrown on him from behind, from a verandah, from a balcony. And Khurram good-humouredly fought back, chasing a slave girl, cornering her against a pillar, and rubbing the gulag over her body as she giggled in delight. He was more decorous with the older women, bending so they could powder his face and sipping bhang from the glasses they offered him.

Finally, an hour after he had thus danced his way through the zenana palaces, he saw Mehrunnisa sitting with his father under the shade of a slender-leafed mango tree. Emperor Jahangir was leaning against the tree trunk, and Mehrunnisa sat forward, one elbow resting on his knees. They were not talking. As Khurram watched, his father's hand went to touch Mehrunnisa's back, and she turned to smile at him. They were alone, and this surprised Khurram. He had never seen his father alone—always surrounded by wives, a number of eunuchs and slaves—never with just one wife.

The prince went up to the Emperor and bowed with the taslim three times. Then he bent to kiss his father's cheek, and Jahangir patted him on the shoulder.

'*Al-Salam alekum*, your Majesties,' Khurram said.

'Welcome, Khurram,' Jahangir replied. 'Sit with us for a while.'

'I hesitate to disturb you, Bapa.'

In reply, the Emperor glanced at Mehrunnisa. It was only a slight movement of his head, nothing blatant, but Khurram saw this, and before he could look at Mehrunnisa, his father said, 'We have not seen you in many days, Khurram.'

'Happy Holi, your Majesty.' Prince Khurram rubbed the gulag on Jahangir's face, but respectfully, and he turned to do the same to Mehrunnisa, who had her chin up to him. She was smiling, her blue eyes muzzy with bhang. They were both quite drunk, he realized. Her hair was matted with maroon, and not an inch of her skin showed through a dusting of other colours, the powders even creeping under her fingernails. Mehrunnisa's ghagara was drenched in some undistinguishable shade, and her veil bloomed a green that could only come from indiscriminately mixing colours. Jahangir had suffered a similar fate, his silk kurta not white anymore, the skin on his neck an alarmingly unnatural red.

'Happy Holi, your Highness,' Mehrunnisa said, and she dabbed a finger into Khurram's palm and drew a line of purple across his forehead and down his nose. 'Now that is a definite improvement on your looks, Khurram.'

He shrugged. 'I can only agree with your Majesty. Perhaps it is so.'

Mehrunnisa laughed, a slow, languorous sound. 'When did you become so humble, Khurram? I have never known you to be anything but imperious, anything but arrogant. I know you well, remember.'

He nodded, sat down next to them, and dusted the rest of the gulag from his hands. They did not speak for a while. The afternoon passed lethargically, every minute unhurried but not weighty. Khurram could sense Mehrunnisa turning her head, looking at him for a few minutes, and then turning away. A bee came humming by, and he swiped at it, watching his hand move deliberately through the air. He had drunk more bhang than he thought he had.

'Tell us what you have been doing, Khurram,' Jahangir said.

'The usual things, your Majesty. I apologize for not coming earlier to pay my respects, but I thought you might need some time.'

'And how is your child? Well, I trust,' Jahangir said.

'A delight, your Majesty. I will bring her to visit.'

The Emperor and the prince talked thus and Khurram tried very hard to concentrate on what he was saying, but the heat went to his head. He watched as Mehrunnisa put her hand in Jahangir's and his father absentmindedly kissed her fingers and then kept her han.! to his chest. This open affection between them, taken so much for granted, flustered Khurram. The *touching* did not bother him, he had been brought up in a zenana and had one of his own now. Khurram had seen his father leave for his bedchamber with a hand on a slave girl's hip, and there had been no mistaking that gesture—it spoke of sex and lust. But this... this intimacy not of the flesh but of the mind, which bespoke a comfort Khurram was not familiar with, this disconcerted him. He knew his mother and Jahangir had never had this indefinable quality of ease. Khurram was not envious of Mehrunnisa for his mother but for himself. *He* wanted this intimacy that his father and Mehrunnisa had. And not knowing what it was, or how it could be acquired, but seeing it so evidently, disturbed him. As he conversed with his father, he moved restlessly, dashing bits of grass from the carpet.

Khurram wished he had found Mehrunnisa alone so he could talk to her, to tell her that she had his support in anything she wanted, well, anything within reason.

'Why are you here, Khurram?' Mehrunnisa said suddenly. She had stopped Jahangir in mid-sentence, and more surprising than that, he had let her. Now his father was alert too.

'Your Majesty, I come to bid you welcome into my father's harem.'

He said this without thinking. It was a phrase of politeness, of etiquette, but it was not enough.

'Just that, Khurram?' She said this softly, now leaning back against the Emperor. Khurram did not know how to react to this. She was telling him that the Emperor and she were one, that if he had anything to say to her, it would be best said in Jahangir's presence. But how could he even start what he wanted to say? That he came to make his bid for the throne before his father had any idea of relinquishing it. That he had no design of displacing Jahangir but merely securing his own place for the future. How could an intention such as this not be misconstrued?

'Your Majesty,' Khurram said, thinking for the right words, words that would please and not offend, 'you are new to his Majesty's harem. I offer my compliments at your place here. Would you wish to command anything of me, I will be a willing servant.'

Jahangir laughed. 'Well said, Khurram. Your flattery does us all proud.'

'I do not flatter, your Majesty,' Khurram said in a flurry. 'The word has unpleasant connotations. No, I merely speak of my affection for my new mother.'

Jahangir opened his mouth to reply, but Mehrunnisa put a hand on his arm and he stopped. 'He speaks well, your Majesty,' she said. 'Here is a son we can all be truly proud of. Go now, we must rest. We shall remember this courtesy, Khurram. *I* will remember it.'

Prince Khurram rose from the grass and bowed to them. As he walked away, he was aware that they were still looking at him, but when he turned, Mehrunnisa had rested her head on Jahangir's chest and had her eyes closed. Khurram muttered to himself, cursing the bhang he had drunk, which had made his language too flowery and indistinct. But then again, how to ask without seeming greedy? More to the point, *what* to ask for?

Under the mango tree, Mehrunnisa and Jahangir slept for an hour, still sitting as they had. When Mehrunnisa woke, she knew the Emperor was awake too, although he did not move; the beat of his heart under her ear was less steady, not the regular beat of sleep.

'He comes to be nice, Mehrunnisa,' Jahangir said. 'But he wished to know if you will nurture his dreams.'

'Should I do so, your Majesty?'

'I am not dead yet, Mehrunnisa.'

She looked up and put a hand over the Emperor's mouth. 'You must not even say this. Where would I be if you are gone? What could I do without you?'

He smiled at her. 'I have many years left. But I can remember wanting the throne for a long time. I believed my father greatly unjust in not giving it to me. More importantly, I feared that Murad and Daniyal would lay claim to it, even though I was the eldest born son.'

'Khurram is the most likely to succeed you, your Majesty. The other three... they are nothing compared to him,' Mehrunnisa said.

'True, in Khurram I have my heir.' Jahangir's voice hardened as he spoke. He was still bitter about Khusrau, a son he had once loved dearly, who had betrayed him in rebellion, whom he could not seem to forgive. Khusrau reminded him too much of himself, of when he had rebelled against Akbar and caused him pain, and Jahangir did not want that wash of guilt. Parviz was a drunkard, a weakling, not cut from the cloth of kings. He too reminded Jahangir of himself in many ways—his drinking, for one. Jahangir had eaten opium since he was very young, lost many an hour in cups of wine. Mehrunnisa checked this when she could, when he allowed her to, but it still seduced him beyond all reason at times. And at those times, he was too much like Parviz.

'So shall I talk with Prince Khurram, your Majesty?'

Jahangir kissed her on the head. The coloured water had dried in the heat of the day, leaving little flakes of maroon and red scattered over her hair. As long as he lived, Mehrunnisa would get what she wanted—she only had to ask. But when he was no longer here, things would be different. She would just be a Dowager Empress, with no son to lay claims upon, no right to occupy the front of the zenana screen at court. No voice in anything. But through Khurram... if his support for Khurram came through her, she would have some authority. For it would seem to his son that Mehrunnisa had strengthened the affections of his father. And Jahangir wanted Khurram to be Emperor after him—he was the only one of his sons who would cherish this empire and look after its people.

'You must bathe now, Mehrunnisa, else the colours will stick to your skin for days,' Jahangir said. He snapped his fingers, and Hoshiyar Khan came running up from behind one of the pillars in a far verandah. 'Prepare our baths, Hoshiyar.'

'Yes, your Majesty.'

They followed Hoshiyar into the palaces at a more leisurely pace. As they parted to go to their own apartments, Jahangir said, 'Khurram would be the best person to give the throne to, Mehrunnisa. But he is still raw, much a child. He needs to be groomed, he needs advice. I can think of no person better than you for this, my dear.'

Mehrunnisa smiled. 'Thank you, your Majesty.' Then she went away to her apartments on feet still unsteady from the effects of the bhang. In a few hours they would meet again, bathed and fresh, the colours of the gulag still glowing on their skins. Mehrunnisa chose a ghagara and choli that matched the colours of her skin so perfectly that it seemed as though she were clad in a skin of green. More bhang flowed, but Mehrunnisa did not drink any. She was thinking about Khurram.

She knew her limitations, or was being fast made aware of them. Power—to speak at court, to change the dictates of a society that demanded obeisance from a woman, to rule over the zenana and its inmates—was a very fragile thing indeed. It would be hers as long as Jahangir gave it to her. But with Khurram by her side, more was possible. Courtiers and nobles already whispered about the succession—like Khurram, they had a vested interest in it too. Where the crown was involved, speculations would be rife about whose head it would adorn next, no matter if it had rested on the current head only for a few short years.

Among the courtiers were some who looked upon Mehrunnisa with dislike, especially the Rajput soldiers who found their loyalties in Empress Jagat Gosini's household. But they would support Khurram; he was Jagat Gosini's son, so there was a natural inclination to do so. More important, if he were to become the next emperor, they would be fools not to have supported him early on.

If Khurram came to Mehrunnisa's side and she advocated his cause, these nobles would be forced to come to her too. This was logical thinking, with the hard head of a diplomat. There was another reason to play the role of Khurram's advisor. Jagat Gosini would be furious, and Mehrunnisa wanted to keep her unsettled in anger, for the Empress would be more dangerous with a cool mind.

Poor Khurram, Mehrunnisa thought as she listened to the imperial orchestra, the bhang glass untouched by her side. He had no idea just how important he was to her. And he would never know. Let him think that he needed her more, and at this moment, bareheaded with just the title of a prince, he did. She was planning for the future.

But she did not want to do this alone, relying solely upon a prince in whom she had no faith yet. There were others whom she could call to her side. Bapa and Abul. Even if Khurram were to mislead her, these two other men, her father and her brother, could always be trusted. Their blood was hers.

And so a few weeks later, when spring had shed its first freshness and was lingering on the edge of summer, a palanquin stopped in the outer courtyard of Ghias Beg's house on the banks of the Yamuna.

The servants were all aflutter, shouting orders, the men averting their faces from the daughter of the house who had so suddenly, with the imperial turban on her head, a new title to her name, become unreachable. Her Majesty was here. *Quick, get the horses out to the stables; find the guards something to eat; run to tell the master.*

Mehrunnisa ran into the house veiled, charmed by this attention, even from old servants who had scolded and petted her when she was young. She had asked for this meeting. It was easier for her to come to her father's house than to have Abul and Bapa come into the zenana. For them to be in the family home would not cause talk. But Khurram's presence was quite another thing. Abul was already there, the prince was not. They waited for him in the reception hall, talking of the family. Mehrunnisa saw Asmat flit by the open door anxiously. Her mother was not happy about this—covertness made her nervous.

And then Khurram came in. He was shy at first, accepting homage from Ghias and Abul, giving it in his turn to his father's wife. They all waited for Mehrunnisa to speak. It was up to her to tell them why they had been summoned in secrecy. But when Mehrunnisa started to talk, it was about commonplace things.

'William Hawkins has left the court to return to his own

country,' Mehrunnisa said. 'He was fatigued here, the heat too much for him. What thin skins these *firangis* have.'

So they talked of William Hawkins, a merchant who had styled himself as an ambassador from England and had wanted Jahangir to sign on trading privileges for the English. The three men knew that Mehrunnisa and the Emperor had flirted around the treaty, but lightly, and enough to keep the merchant in India. He had amused them, amused all of them with his fluent court-ready Turki, but his manners were coarse. He swore colourfully, he did not perform the taslim in court as many times as he should have, his voice was at times gruff. But on the whole he had been entertaining. When he wanted to leave, Jahangir had offered him an income and a house in Agra for as long as he wanted to live here. He was even given a mansab of four hundred horses and the title of an English Khan. But Hawkins wanted to leave, frustrated and no longer hopeful that Jahangir would sign a treaty. So he was let go, kindly and with many gifts.

'What of the Jesuits, your Majesty?' Khurram said.

'What of them, Khurram?'

The Portuguese Jesuits had been in India for many years now, well before the first Mughal conquest of India. They were here to proselytize, or so they claimed. Their churches' steeples rose in Agra, the money and the land for the building given to them by the Emperor. Their priests had converted three of Jahangir's nephews to Catholicism, gaining a foothold into the royal family, but they would not advance further. And as Catholics, the nephews could not hope to raise their eyes to the crown of the empire. Despite all these outward signs of God, the Portuguese Jesuits manned the Arabian Sea routes, providing protection for the pilgrim ships travelling to Mecca and Medina, charging taxes and levies for that protection.

'The cost of trade is too high,' Khurram said hesitantly. 'But who else is there? Why is it that the empire cannot provide safety for its own ships? Why do we have to rely upon others?'

'The English, perhaps?' Abul said. He had known William Hawkins well during his stay at Agra. And Hawkins had been full of stories of English power at sea—bragging about the defeat of the Spanish Armada twenty-five years ago. But twenty-five years was a long time back. What was it they could do *now*, and in waters foreign to their own, where different winds blew, and the earth took altered shapes?

But they had all heard the stories of yet another Englishman, one who had barely touched the empire's soil, a man called Henry Middleton. He was on his way back to England too, and he carried Hawkins with him. But when Middleton had first arrived, he had been allowed to unload his goods for trade at the dock at Surat and then been unceremoniously driven down the Tapti River into the Arabian Sea. Enraged, Middleton had assaulted—there was no other word for it—Indian vessels he had met in the Gulf of Aden on his way out to England, forcing a heavy ransom or trade in some very unfavourable terms. The ships had come limping back to port at Surat, riding lightly on the water, void of their cargoes but full of tales of bitterness against the English. Among those ships was the *Rahimi*, which could carry, with a full cargo, fifteen hundred passengers. In the royal palaces, the insult to the *Rahimi* was the greatest affront to the empire—Ruqayya owned this magnificent ship and had complained bitterly about her loss of income. Middleton undid all of Hawkins's efforts at diplomacy.

Mehrunnisa said, 'Do not judge this Middleton too harshly. He was provoked, robbed of his own belongings here by Muqarrab Khan.'

'John, Mehrunnisa,' Ghias Beg spoke for the first time. He had watched his daughter quietly all this while, admiring her knowledge.

She turned to him. 'I know, Bapa. Muqarrab has converted to

Catholicism; he calls himself John now. He did what he did to Middleton because of the Portuguese. They do not want the English here.'

'Why?' Ghias asked, and when Abul and Khurram motioned to speak, he held a hand up for their silence.

'If the English are really that adept in the seas, if their navy is really that powerful, we can use them. They could protect our ships instead of the Portuguese, or rather, we can give both the firangis a chance for it—and profit from it. As long as the Portuguese are unchallenged, they grow arrogant,' Mehrunnisa said. Then she shook her head. 'But Middleton's behaviour in the seas, against our ships, it does not bode well for a good relationship. Where is a demonstration of naval strength in that? He harassed defenseless trading vessels.'

'But with reason, as you just said, your Majesty,' Khurram said. 'If nothing else, we know to be uncertain of Muqarrab Khan's loyalties. Let the English come back to India if they wish to. We will welcome them.'

They talked into the night, and the candles burned low into their silver saucers. Most of the talk was about the firangis. They did not touch on the zenana, or Khurram's claims to the throne, or what Ghias Beg and Abul Hasan wanted from this new rule. They all wanted something, even Ghias, who was not merely content that his daughter was powerful; he wanted the riches that power could bring. It was his one weakness, one that Mehrunnisa understood. For now, it was enough that they could talk, in private, in a place where the walls would not speak of their conversations.

Thus the *junta* was born.

And so Mehrunnisa stepped tentatively into history's pages, dipping her foot into the ink that inscribed the names of men and writing her own.

She had, perhaps, acted too hastily in forming this junta, in bequeathing her allegiance to Prince Khurram.

For though no one knew yet, least of all Mehrunnisa, there could be another person who had the same claims as Khurram to the empire. And more, much, much more claim to Mehrunnisa's affections and loyalty.

Chapter Six

Few marriages in polygamous households have been so happy... Arjumand Banu... surrendered her mind and soul to her husband. Yet the marriage had primarily been a political one. It symbolized the alliance of Mehrunnisa, Itimad-ud-daulah and Asaf Khan with the heir apparent.

—BENI PRASAD,
History of Jahangir

COURT WAS IN SESSION IN THE DIWAN-I-AM AT THE AGRA FORT. EVERY DAY, except for Fridays, Emperor Jahangir held court here—here the official business of the empire was conducted, news brought from every corner of its vast lands, and petitions read. It was late in the afternoon, the sun tumbling westward in the sky, waning in its strength. Coming into the Agra Fort from the westward Elephant Gate the nobles and commoners passed by the guards first, their passes checked there, before they stabled their horses in a front courtyard and then walked up the cobbled ramp into the Diwan-i-am. They would find their places in the square marble hall, with floors of marble coated end-to-end with the finest silk carpets Persia could provide, and forty marble pillars holding up a sandstone ceiling covered with a thin leaf of beaten gold. They took off their shoes and sandals before entering the hall, and this was court etiquette.

The Diwan-i-am was open on three sides. On the fourth it abutted the walls of the imperial palaces. Here Emperor Jahangir sat in a high marble throne with a canopy of gold cloth fringed with emeralds and supported by pillars of gold. On either side of the throne, built into the wall, were the zenana balconies, visible from the hall only as fine mesh screens of marble.

Mehrunnisa had come to the harem enclosure before Jahangir, finding her seat up front, near the screen, so close that if she put her fingers through, she could touch the Emperor's back. She leaned to look at the assembled nobles in the Diwan-i-am; they could not see her, of course. Just below Jahangir's throne were the royal slaves, two boys of seven years each, standing on huge wooden elephants so that their fly whisks would reach the air around the Emperor. Near them were the attendants, and Mehrunnisa counted their numbers silently—the keeper of the imperial ensign, which was a gold ball clasped in gilt hands hanging from a chain, the imperial standard, which was a yak's tail, the Emperor's flag imprinted and embroidered with a lion crouching in front of a rising sun, and the other flags.

The top nobles of the empire stood grouped around these men, Mahabat Khan and Muhammad Sharif, the other rajas of the empire—kings in name only, for their kingdoms belonged to the empire—and foreign ambassadors. Ghias Beg and Abul Hasan stood here too, just below Prince Khurram, two inches above Mahabat and Sharif; their places had been ordained the day Mehrunnisa married Jahangir. This was the exalted first tier of the empire, and they were separated from the second tier by a thick, hip-high silver railing. Beyond this railing was the next rank of people, merchants and businessmen, cut off from the commoners of the third tier by a red lacquered wood railing. Behind the commoners were the royal elephants, their mahouts seated atop their necks, awaiting the muster call.

Awnings of gold cloth stretched over the outer yard to provide shelter from the sun for those who were not weighty or important enough to be placed either in the Diwan-i-am itself or even before the imperial beasts. And every day, no matter what the weather, whether it rained or the sun was particularly unforgiving in temper, the court appearance of Emperor Jahangir always drew crowds numbering over a thousand, sometimes two.

The zenana balconies also bustled—every woman who could find a free hour from her siesta or her studies came to the court. Mehrunnisa had always come with Ruqayya, and then they had sat at the back, following the implicit hierarchy of the harem, the heads of other ladies blocking their view, the words from the Diwan-i-am coming splintered to their ears. Empress Jagat Gosini had sat in front, of course. And she did so still.

Mehrunnisa turned to her. Jagat Gosini sat to the Emperor's right, Mehrunnisa to his left, even though she thought that the premier position ought to be hers. The Empress did not turn to Mehrunnisa; her back stiffened though, and Mehrunnisa knew she was aware of her without moving her eyes away from the Diwan-i-am. What was she scheming? Did she know of Khurram's defection?

Mehrunnisa wanted to know the answer to this last question more than any other. For she had taken Prince Khurram away as surely as if she were his wife or his mother. And she was neither. She smiled to herself. Let the Empress meet with Mahabat Khan as much as she wanted, let her talk with him and even hold his hand in supposed flight and fright. If Mehrunnisa were to tell the Emperor of this, everything would be shattered for the two. She had no intention of telling Jahangir, not now anyway. But later... if she needed something from the Empress, or simply to break her.

They had met to talk of her, this much Mehrunnisa knew, for her servants had repeated some of their conversation. Not very much, just as much as they could hear. Hoshiyar had brought her news of this meeting through Shaista Khan, Jagat Gosini's eunuch. Did she know that a devil lived within her own walls? That it was Shaista's step she had heard at Fatehpur Sikri?

The kettledrums announced Jahangir's arrival. They all rose in the zenana balconies, and all of them, the nobles in the courtyard, the war elephants, the women of the harem, bowed in the konish. When they raised their backs, Emperor Jahangir was already seated on the satin divan of the throne. The nobles did not sit. No one was given the privilege of bending his legs in front of the Emperor, and even in standing there was an etiquette. Their arms were clasped in front, the fingers of their right hands cupping the left elbow and the left hand the right elbow, splayed just so. Their necks would bend too, conveying submission even as they stood at attention. And no one spoke.

Of the thousand people present at the Hall of Public Audience, not one voice made itself heard. They could speak only when directly addressed by Jahangir. They could not leave until he had left, for if they did, they would give up their places in the hall— and their heads, by sunset.

This rigidity of rules was what kept Jahangir foremost in the empire. The Emperor *was* the empire. There was no mistaking that.

Emperor Jahangir nodded at the Mir Tozak, the Master of Ceremonies. He bowed and unrolled his scroll. The first order of the court was to confirm that yesterday's orders had been carried out. This done, news was read from around the empire.

'In Lahore, your Majesty, a chick was born with three beaks, two on either side of the main one,' the Mir Tozak said.

Jahangir leaned forward. 'Where is it? Command it brought to court so all may see this unusual thing.'

'It did not live beyond two days, your Majesty. But the keepers are trying to mate the same hen and rooster again, so another such chick may be born.'

'A chick with three beaks,' Jahangir said. 'There has been no such thing before, has there?'

The nobles all shook their heads, although the Emperor had unconsciously turned to his left, talking to Mehrunnisa, as if the entire darbar did not stand before him. Mehrunnisa smiled at Jahangir's wonderment. She had once asked him why it was important for such trivialities to be brought to his notice in the Diwan-i-am—surely, only matters of state ought to be discussed here? Jahangir said that nothing was trivial. In him was vested *every* concern of the empire, small and large. The news from its farthest reaches, local and consequential only to its own district or jagir, had to be read in open court. For it was too easy for the nobles and *amirs* of the empire to be swept away by a sense of their own importance, to belittle what went on elsewhere, to think of Agra alone as being significant. It was easy for Jahangir to do so too, but he was not Emperor merely of Agra but also of every other village and town and settlement in the empire. The news brought notice of these little places. And again Mehrunnisa was reminded of what Ruqayya always said, that in knowledge lay true power.

And so other oddities were read out, commented upon by Jahangir, acknowledged by the court. He gave orders on a few matters and simply talked about others. And then the petitions were read out, who was to be given a larger mansab, who was to be commended for bravery, who stripped of his lands and titles publicly. A few nobles came forward to beg Jahangir's permission to marry their daughters. Alliances had been found and decided upon, but the Emperor had to bless any future union.

In this he turned more often to Mehrunnisa. Once, he even used her name, saying, 'What do you think of this, Nur Jahan Begam?'

She said nothing, and the whole court strained to hear even a whisper. But her silence was enough, and Jahangir said to the supplicant, 'Your daughter is too young, Mirza Chingaz Khan, perhaps you should wait a few more years.'

Chingaz Khan bowed and backed away to his place. He had wanted to ally himself with one of the court's grandees, whose mansab was greater than his was, and who had the friendship of Mahabat Khan. For this reason, Mehrunnisa did not allow the marriage. The fewer people who had an opportunity to be grateful to Mahabat, the better. This petition, like all others, had been brought to her the night before in the imperial zenana, and she had read through them and talked with Ruqayya and Hoshiyar about why they were being requested and what the advantages would be. Mehrunnisa had no sheet of paper listing her final decisions. She committed these to her memory, not wanting any physical evidence of her careful deliberation and motives to remain.

At the end of the darbar, the royal elephants were mustered first. Jahangir asked the name of each elephant, where it was born, how much sugarcane it ate each day. Then came the horses, and then the camels.

Mehrunnisa did not watch the muster; instead the two Jesuit priests at court caught her attention. Fathers Xavier and Pinheiro, they called themselves. Unlike the nobles, no daggers or swords adorned their persons. They were a curiosity at court, or had been when they had first arrived, clad in long black robes even in this heat, their heads and faces shaved clean of hair, with round black caps on their heads. They stood out like stones among pearls in this assembly of silks and brocades, rubies and emeralds.

The priests came forward to ask for a higher monthly allowance. They brought only a pair of gloves with them as a present for Jahangir, in kid leather, unadorned with either embroidery or jewels.

Mehrunnisa watched Jahangir's neck turn red as he listened to the two men. He held his anger in with a force of will. They had not performed either the konish or the taslim—their religion did not allow them to do so, they claimed. And the request, such as it was, was made in an insolent tone. That they would approach the throne today, both Mehrunnisa and Jahangir knew, and that their wishes would be acceded to, this also had been decided upon. The whole court knew of Middleton's trashing of the Indian ships in the Arabian Sea, and there was no other protector left but the Portuguese, who accompanied the ships now and guarded them from pirates. So Emperor Jahangir raised their salaries, the money coming from the imperial treasury, and gave them greater freedom to convert his subjects, but not with coercion. He despised having to do this, but his hand had been forced.

When the darbar ended, Mehrunnisa rose to leave, after Emperor Jahangir had gone back into the palaces. And all at once, a thick wave of fatigue blindsided her, and she fell back on the divan. She lay there trembling, her hands shaking. Mehrunnisa tried to wave off offers of help from the slaves and the other ladies. The room went to dark and then a bright white, making it hard for her to see.

Suddenly, Mehrunnisa realized that it had been ten days since her monthly blood should have come. This tiredness was familiar; she had felt it numerous times before Ladli. She had been so engrossed in matters of the mind that she had not listened to her body. She had not thought that there might be a child.

Even as she adjusted to the possibility of a child, she wanted a son. She had Ladli, now there should be a boy child. It had not been important before Ladli, but now, with the empire in her hands, this child should be male. Fear came to crawl up her spine as she saw Jagat Gosini scrutinizing her. Nothing would touch this child, no one's evil eye or malevolent hand. If this were true.

But if this were true... what of the favour she had shown Khurram?

Ladli ran to hide behind a pillar, pulling the skirts of her ghagara in and tucking them between her legs. Then she peered around it, carefully. Arjumand had stopped farther down the verandah. Her back was to Ladli, and she was looking down, seemingly at nothing. Still breathing hard from all the running as she had tried to keep up with Arjumand, Ladli withdrew and waited. Arju seemed to do this a lot nowadays—this standing still, her eyes glazed with thought.

Sweat ran in tiny rivers down the sides of Ladli's face and pooled thickly at the nape of the neck, where her hair was plaited down her back. She wiped her face, bending to use the ghagara's silk, leaving a damp spot on the front. Then she looked out again. Arjumand had gone, the arch where she had stood was empty, and the afternoon light slanted on the verandah floor unblemished by her shadow. Ladli slipped from behind the pillar and ran into someone with a soft thud. She fell to the ground and lay there, looking up at Hoshiyar Khan.

'What are you doing?' the eunuch asked. 'Why aren't you in your apartments?'

'Nothing,' Ladli said, still on the floor.

Hoshiyar bent, and with his right hand, he hauled her up by the waist of her ghagara. When she was upright, he dusted her fastidiously.

'Go back to your rooms. Now.'

He had his hand on her shoulder, and Ladli wriggled out from his clasp.

'It's too hot, I cannot sleep. I will not go out of the zenana palaces, I promise, Hoshiyar. Let me be. Please?' This last she said as woefully as she could, making her eyes round and large, letting a sweet smile come to her face.

'You cannot roam alone in the harem, Ladli. You know this. Where are your servants?' He looked around, but there was nobody. The sun had driven everyone into the coolness of their apartments. The corridor was deserted. 'I will have their heads. What will your Mama say if she knew you were unescorted like this?'

Ladli dug her hands into Hoshiyar's cummerbund and hung from it with her knees off the ground. 'I just want to go to the gardens and play in the shade of the banyan trees, Hoshiyar. Please. Please. Please. Let me go. I will come back before the afternoon chai, no one will know. Please.'

The eunuch pulled her away from him and held her at a distance. Again, she smiled at him. 'All right,' he said, but reluctantly. When he left her, he would go in search of Ladli's servants, yell at them, and tell them to go look after her. They were probably asleep right now, lolling around in the shade, unmindful of their duties to the royal daughter.

Ladli watched him walk away and went on slowly herself, although she wanted to run. Arju could have gone anywhere in the time it had taken for her to negotiate this bit of freedom from Hoshiyar. And why was he outside in the afternoon, in any case? Hoshiyar was Mama's eunuch; his only job was to look after Mama, yet he found time to be everywhere Ladli was. He even came upon her during her studies with the mulla, especially when she felt like teasing the old man by making up a nonsensical song, or by writing all her essays backward, until he sat there literally scratching his head in distress. And at this time—Allah only knew how Hoshiyar knew—he would put his head into the study room and say, 'Behave, Ladli.'

Implied was the *or else I will tell your Mama*.

Ladli looked back. Hoshiyar was gone. She picked up the skirts of her ghagara and ran down the steps into the gardens, flitting like a bee in the sunshine from one bush to another. Where was Arju?

Finally, exhausted by the heat, she sat down in the shade of the banyan and put her arms around herself. She missed her mother. Ever since Mehrunnisa married the Emperor, she was no longer as free as she had been. She was almost always tired, also. Once, Ladli's every word was listened to with gravity. Now her mother hardly paid any attention to her chatter, always engrossed in reading some farman, or listening to what Hoshiyar had to say instead. The Emperor seemed to have more time for Ladli. He let her climb into his lap at night while he was reading, but she was not allowed to speak. Once she had even fallen asleep thus, and when she woke, Jahangir's pearl necklace had dug small, round holes into her cheek. He always smelt nice though, a whiff of tobacco and wine and sandalwood. And he was kind to her; he still gave her presents, even though Mama was now married to him and he did not anymore have to please her through Ladli.

But where *was* Arjumand? One afternoon a week Arjumand was given permission to come into the zenana to visit. Ladli always waited eagerly for these visits from her cousin, for Arju brought news from outside, news of what her mother was doing, or her brothers and sisters. But lately, Arjumand either didn't come at all, or she arrived very late, until only a few minutes were left for visiting.

Ladli was grateful Arjumand even came; none of her other cousins did. And Arjumand was nineteen years old, quite old to Ladli. But she was so pretty, so graceful, sewed so well, and when they played at cooking together, she made the most delicious make-believe pulav. Much better than Ladli's efforts, for she always forgot the bay leaf or the ghee-roasted sultanas. And Arju was quiet. Hoshiyar had once said that she should follow Arjumand's example, be calm, sit in one place for longer than a minute. But Arjumand was almost too quiet. She had a sadness about her, she always listened when they heard voices outside her apartments, and if it were a man's voice, she would grow all aflutter. And when they saw who it was, Arjumand would become quiet again.

Ladli decided that Arjumand was sad because she always got lost when she was in the zenana. That was the reason she usually gave to explain her lateness. So today, Ladli went to the gates to meet her. Arjumand came in without seeing her young cousin, and her steps took her towards the gardens. Ladli followed her, suddenly very suspicious. Arjumand had a lover. That was the only explanation for all this furtiveness.

'There you are, Ladli baba.'

Ladli looked up as a slave girl came across the lawn to the banyan. She wrinkled her nose, and the girl smiled. She bent down to pinch Ladli's cheeks, quite painfully, and Ladli twisted her face away.

'Such a darling child. Do not make faces, dear child. Come inside and sleep now.'

'I don't want to.'

'How beautifully you say this! Come,' she said as she caught Ladli's plait and pulled her by it.

Ladli struggled. Ever since Mama married the Emperor, she had suddenly become everyone's darling child. They hugged her a lot, gave her kisses full of wetness, pinched her cheeks, and cracked their knuckles about her ears, ostensibly to take away the evil eye. When Mama and she had lived in the zenana with Dowager Empress Ruqayya, no one had even known Ladli existed. Now everyone knew and wanted to tell her just how precious she was, hoping that she would talk to Mama about them.

'Come,' the slave girl said again, her face puffed with sleep, her ears still echoing with the scolding Hoshiyar had given her.

Ladli drew her foot back and kicked the slave girl on the shin, hard, until her own toes hurt. As the girl howled and let go of

Ladli's hair, she ran away, first slipping through the banyan's roots and then out into the sunshine.

And it was then she saw Arjumand, behind a jasmine bush, or rather almost inside it, leaning over the top with her feet off the ground, her stomach resting on its branches.

'What are you doing?'

Arjumand whipped around as fast as she could, a look of guilt crimsoning her skin from the neck upwards. 'Ssshhh... keep quiet, Ladli.' She extricated herself from the bush, pulling at her ghagara and veil, and leaving little shreds of green silk on the branches.

'You have torn your dress, Arju,' Ladli said.

'Keep quiet!' Arjumand almost yelled. She pounced on Ladli and wrestled her to the ground, one hand clamped over Ladli's mouth. Bending close to her cousin, Arjumand said, 'When I take my hand off, you must NOT talk. Is this clear?' Ladli nodded, eyes huge with fright. 'I know you like to talk, and a lot, but not a word from you, Ladli.'

'Let me go, Arju,' she said, her voice muffled under Arjumand's hand. Her cousin seemed to have forgotten that she still lay there; Arjumand's eyes had shifted to whatever was beyond the bush.

'Sorry.' Arjumand took her hand off.

Ladli rose from the grass. Tears came rising behind her eyelids. How could Arju do this? Quiet Arju, who had always been so gentle with her, never even raised her voice before. Ladli sat on the grass, uncaring that her ghagara was getting more soiled and stained with green, and she cried. Her face became red; she sniffed and waited for Arjumand to notice.

Arjumand did look at her, though distantly, and said, 'Keep quiet, Ladli.' Then she turned again and held out her arms. 'Come here, I am sorry. I truly am. Come, darling child.'

Still sniffling, Ladli allowed Arjumand to pull her into her lap. She sat there, letting her tears soak through the silk of Arjumand's choli. She was the only one, apart from Mama and the Emperor, who could call her darling child. She could also hug Ladli as much as she wanted. She smelled nice, of perspiration and the sun, of jasmines. Arjumand kissed Ladli on the head. 'I said I was sorry.'

'All right, but don't do this again.'

They sat thus for a while, Arjumand rocking her seven-year-old cousin in her arms, until Ladli said, 'What are you looking at, Arju?'

The rocking stopped, and the irritation came back to Arjumand's voice. 'None of your business. Go back to your rooms. Why are you here, anyway?'

Ladli jumped out of her lap and stood over her, hands on hips. 'You were supposed to come and see me, why didn't you? What are you doing here?'

'Don't—,' Arjumand said, but Ladli had already gone into the jasmine bush. It was in bloom, and the flowers, white and tiny, punched the air with their fragrance. She moved a few branches carefully, which promptly slid out tentacles to poke her skin, drawing blood in some places, in others leaving scratches of white. The view was one of the zenana lotus pools. The lotus flowers bloomed the colour of pearls, white with a pink blush on them. They stood erect on slim stalks above their thick round and green pads. There was a bench at the far edge of the square pool, and Prince Khurram sat there, head uncovered in the sun, throwing stones into the water. As Ladli watched, a slave girl came up behind the prince and touched his neck. He turned, and, laughing, pulled her over the bench and into his lap.

Arjumand moved to stand by Ladli.

'It's Khurram,' Ladli said, quite unnecessarily. 'What are they doing? Cannot she feed herself?' Khurram had taken a cherry from a silver bowl by his side and put it between his teeth. He then offered it to the slave, who leaned forward to take the cherry from the prince with her mouth. Juice ran down her chin, and the prince caught it with his finger. 'Look, Arju,' Ladli said.

But Arjumand was done with looking. As long as Khurram had been on the bench alone, she had filled herself with the sight of him. She sat down on the grass and pulled Ladli away from the bush. 'Sit and stay still, Ladli.'

Ladli sat, watching her cousin. 'Go to him, Arju.'

'And what am I to say? Your Highness, I am the woman you are betrothed to, the one you have forgotten.' Arjumand said this slowly, with an ache in her chest. But the betrothal was five years ago, there was no reason for Khurram to remember this. *She* remembered, for she had seen him at the ceremony—to him she was just another veiled figure, a political alliance. What was holding up the marriage? Their family was back in the Emperor's good graces; her aunt had married him now. It was not as if Arjumand could go to her father and ask him—what would she ask him? They would all laugh at her impatience.

And how did one go to one's elders and say, So how are the arrangements for my marriage progressing? How did one even talk of such things? One never did. One day, Bapa had come to her and said she was to be betrothed to Prince Khurram. Arjumand had bent her head in agreement. So one day, she would be married to him. That also happened without thought. But this... this waiting... this uncertainty, no one had prepared her for this.

All of Arjumand's friends were already married; they had two or three children, and here she was, at nineteen, betrothed to a man who did not know of her existence, and if he did not marry her, no one else would. Besides, Arjumand thought, she did not *want* to marry anyone else. She loved the prince.

Arjumand and Ladli sat in the shade of the jasmine for a while. Every now and then they would hear a giggle, or a shout of laughter, or murmurings from behind them. At each sound,

Arjumand's head plunged lower and lower. She swiped at her eyes, and Ladli looked at her intently to see if she was crying. No, just a bit of dust, Arjumand said.

'What an idiot Khurram is, Arju,' Ladli said suddenly. 'Who would not want to marry you? He only has to look at you once.'

Arjumand smiled a little. 'Thank you.'

Ladli nodded. Arju was the beauty of their family. She moved as though floating in air, she was so gentle with her words, when she laughed it made Ladli want to laugh too, just to join in with what she did. And Khurram sat there with a coarse slave girl, who could not even speak without her mouth tripping over her thick village accent. What was the attraction in that?

'I will tell Mama,' Ladli said. 'She will make Khurram marry you.'

'No...,' Arjumand said automatically. Then she turned pleading eyes to her younger cousin. 'Do you think you could talk with your mother? She can do this; she has the Emperor's attention. I mean... it is not much to ask, is it, Ladli? Khurram is betrothed to me, after all.'

'Mama can do anything, Arju.'

'Yes, she is... somehow... so powerful. So like a man,' Arjumand said. 'I wish I had her courage at times.' Her face drooped. If only she could speak of what she wanted, it was not enough to just want.

Ladli sprang up and darted around the jasmine bush. Her bare feet made no sound on the sandstone slabs surrounding the pool, and it was not until she stood at Khurram's elbow that he looked up. The slave girl had her face hidden in his shoulder, her back, now bare, to Ladli.

'What do you want, Ladli?' Khurram asked. 'Go to the Empress and don't disturb me here.'

'Oh, your Highness, I beg forgiveness for disturbing you, but my cousin has sprained her ankle and needs help,' Ladli squealed mendaciously, wringing her hands in mock despair.

'Get one of the eunuchs to help her.' Khurram turned to the slave girl.

'But, your Highness,' Ladli pulled at his cummerbund, 'please, everyone is away, she is in great pain.'

'All right.' Khurram got up in exasperation, pushing the girl off his lap. His mood was spoilt in any case. The slave would just have to wait for his favours.

'Call for help,' he said to the slave girl, then he turned to Ladli. 'Where is this cousin of yours?'

Ladli marched back to the bush, leading a reluctant Khurram by the hand. Meanwhile, Arjumand had been listening to the conversation with horror. The brat. She would whip her as soon as she had a chance. Now she had to feign an injured ankle.

Khurram and Ladli came around the bushes. Arjumand sat there, her head bowed and her face blooming with blushes.

'There she is!' Ladli announced triumphantly.

Khurram knelt down next to Arjumand. 'Have you hurt your ankle?'

'Er… yes, your Highness.' Arjumand flashed an angry look at Ladli, who promptly winked back at her.

'Which foot is it?'

Arjumand reluctantly pointed to her right leg. Khurram moved her skirts slightly, noticing the little slivers of thread where the silk was torn, and lifted her foot. Such a perfect foot, the prince thought, such slender ankles offset by gold anklets and henna. He ran his fingers over the skin, but he could detect no swelling. Khurram looked up at her face to see if she was as beautiful. Her eyes were not lifted to his. He saw a clean scoop of chin, skin radiant and flushed from the heat, long lashes lying against her cheeks.

'Does it hurt very much?' Khurram's voice was low; his

caressing hand sent thrills through Arjumand.

She nodded dumbly, mesmerized by him. When she finally looked at him, he was smiling. Ladli stood aside, watching them both. They seemed to have forgotten that she was there, but Khurram would not easily forget her cousin now.

The prince lifted Arjumand and carried her back to the palace. Because he told her to, she put an arm around his shoulder, stunned by his nearness, by his aroma, by the sound of his heart so near hers. She could not speak, and did not want this moment to end. Khurram asked her name, and Ladli helpfully told him who she was.

Hoshiyar Khan came running out of Mehrunnisa's apartments and gathered Arjumand in his arms. He looked at her ankle—like Khurram, he could see no swelling—but, unlike Khurram, he was suspicious. The eunuch glared at Ladli, and she grinned back at him.

'Take good care of her, Hoshiyar,' Khurram said.

'I will, your Highness. I will take her directly to the Empress,' Hoshiyar said, swinging around to carry Arjumand away. Ladli followed them both, skipping, and turned to wave at the prince. 'Thank you, Khurram.'

He looked at her bemused, but all thoughts were with this creature he had held in his arms. Mehrunnisa was beautiful, but another such as her in the same family? They had been blessed; there was no doubt of that. How had she escaped his notice thus far? And how could he get her?

Prince Khurram turned away, pondering this, and then he turned back and ran up the steps that led to Mehrunnisa's apartments. Once he thought of something, he wanted it to happen immediately.

Khurram entered the darkened room. It was cool inside; heavy curtains had been drawn across the windows to keep out the afternoon heat. He stood at the door for a moment, letting his eyes adjust to the darkness, until he saw Mehrunnisa. She lay on a divan, a hand propping up her head.

'What is it, Khurram?'

'Your Majesty,' Khurram spoke rapidly. 'I have met a most wonderful woman. I want to marry her.'

'What's stopping you?' Mehrunnisa raised an eyebrow. 'Why come to me? You should go to the Emperor.'

'Your Majesty, she is your niece.'

'Oh?' Mehrunnisa mentally ran over all her nieces. Which one was Khurram talking about?

'Arjumand Banu.'

The Empress threw back her head and laughed richly. 'You want to marry Arjumand?' She grinned at the bewildered look on Khurram's face.

'Yes, your Majesty, please... don't tell me she is already betrothed,' Khurram said in despair.

'She is already betrothed, Khurram.'

'Oh.' The prince bowed his head. How could he have not thought that she would already be taken? Such beauty and grace. Such a lovely woman.

Mehrunnisa watched him curiously. 'You have no idea who she is, do you?'

'I just met her today, your Majesty.' Khurram raised his eyes. 'Is the engagement of a long standing? Is the man of a good family? Is he worthy of her?'

'Yes to all the three questions. You really do not remember, do you?'

'Remember what, your Majesty?'

Mehrunnisa was silent. She had been aware of the pact made between the Emperor and Abul, that each would give his child in marriage—this Abul had taken great pains to remind her of before her own marriage to the Emperor. But in the last year Mehrunnisa had done nothing about this matter. Her own affairs had kept her busy—getting the seal, courting Khurram to her side, giving importance to Bapa and Abul and their mother, to say nothing of spending time with Jahangir. But there was also the hope that *they* might have a child too. And if they did, and if it were a son... his needs would have to be met, his future wants looked after. How would bringing a culmination to this other tentative alliance affect her child?

'She is betrothed to you, Khurram,' Mehrunnisa said finally. It had to be said, and it was better she said it, for Khurram would find out anyway.

'To me?'

'Yes, your Highness.' Mehrunnisa smiled. 'The engagement ceremony was performed at my father's house five years ago.'

Now he did remember the betrothal. But his mother had told him then not to expect much out of it, and Jagat Gosini had also said that the girl had the face of a pig and limbs as heavy as iron. Khurram had tried to look at her during the ceremony, through two layers of curtains, one that parted the men of the family from the women and the other the veil that covered her head. And then he had forgotten about it. He had been fifteen that year, shy and embarrassed at all the attention from everyone. A wife was an inevitability; he knew this as a prince. And not just one wife, but as many as his father thought necessary—for the good of the empire. For the heirs they would bear, for the alliances they would bring to the royal family. Marriage was for the good of the empire. Besides, with the description Jagat Gosini had given him, Arjumand had passed from his mind.

'She is so lovely,' he said with wonder. And she was. Could his mother have been mistaken? Shown another girl at the betrothal instead of this one? Or perhaps Arjumand had changed over the years? 'I had no idea, your Majesty.'

Mehrunnisa watched Khurram carefully. 'She is lovely, yes. She will make you a good wife.'

He looked at her with awe, his eyes shining with pleasure. Suddenly he was very young and hopeful, in the first flushes of love. Khurram knelt by Mehrunnisa and kissed her hand fervently. 'Can I hope for the marriage to be arranged very soon, your Majesty? I shall be ever grateful if you would talk with my father about this.'

She patted his hand. 'It will be so, Khurram. I shall talk with his Majesty tonight. And soon, very soon you shall be a part of our family.'

The prince literally floated out of the room in happiness. When he had gone, Mehrunnisa lay back on the divan and closed her eyes. Any fear she had felt, any sort of discomfort at the idea of Khurram and Arjumand's marriage evaporated. Instead of driving them apart, it would only bring them together. They would all be tied now in bonds of marriage and blood. Through Arjumand—if Khurram's devotion to her already was any indication—she would have Khurram's support. This much Mehrunnisa knew, that Arjumand's loyalties lay with her aunt and with her father.

As for the child... she touched her stomach lightly. There was still no sign of her monthly blood, but she did not know this for sure, for there had been other times when she had not been regular. The fatigue was there though, forcing her to rest in the afternoons, to sleep even for a few hours when the sun was at its peak in the sky.

The wedding ceremony was performed at Ghias Beg's house. For days before, presents flowed from the imperial palace to the bride's house. The groom had to send her the wedding dress, for she would leave her father's house so completely upon her marriage that even the clothes she wore would mark her as now belonging to her husband. A henna party took place in Mehrunnisa's apartments, where the women sang songs and painted thin pipes of henna paste on their hands and feet. Even Khurram came for this, allowing his hands to be painted in the same colours that decorated his wife's.

The presents were lavish—pearls, rubies, emeralds, and diamonds wrapped in black velvet; silk and satin embroidered ghagaras and cholis; casks of wine and liquor; sweets on huge silver platters. The imperial treasury doled out vast sums of money for the cooks and cleaners, the musicians and other entertainers, and the *shamiana* awnings that would cover the courtyard.

The entire empire rejoiced at Prince Khurram's wedding. News had already gone to every town and village of the beauty of his new wife, more importantly of her relationship to the Empress, and her father and grandfather's position at court. What could be more natural than this alliance?

Emperor Jahangir was happy too, because he saw how contented Mehrunnisa was. This marriage had focused attention on Mehrunnisa, for everyone involved was pleased—Ghias that yet another woman from his family was getting married into the imperial family, Abul that his daughter would no longer be sad, Khurram because he was in love with Arjumand. This match had nothing but advantages.

Any doubts Mehrunnisa might have had were now vanished. She had other things to occupy her, for she was now certain she was with child. She told Emperor Jahangir the night before the wedding. Almost at once he began thinking of a name for the boy—for it was to be a boy, of course—which mulla he would study with, and whether he would look most like Mehrunnisa or him. In another month, they would have to announce this to the empire; for now, it was their secret to know and keep and cherish.

So Mehrunnisa joined in prayers the next morning along with

the qazi who was officiating at the ceremony. She thought no one could possibly be as happy as she was then, and how could she grudge even a fraction of this to her niece?

But Mehrunnisa did not know then, would never know, that by giving her blessings to this marriage she had set into progress a chain of events that would eventually erase her name from history's pages.

Or that Arjumand would become the *only* Mughal woman posterity would easily recognize. Docile, seemingly tractable and untroublesome Arjumand would eclipse even Mehrunnisa, cast her in a shadow... because of the monument Khurram would build in Arjumand's memory—the Taj Mahal.

Chapter Seven

Her abilities were uncommon; for she rendered herself absolute, in a government in which women are thought incapable of bearing any part... Noor Jehan stood forth in public; she broke through all restraint and custom, and acquired power by her own address, more than by the weakness of Jehangire.

—ALEXANDER DOW,
The History of Hindostan

THOMAS BEST STOOD ON THE DECK OF THE *RED DRAGON*, FEET FIRMLY rooted, hands on hips. The ship pitched in a wave and he moved easily with her, crouching low on his knees with the practise of many years, until the swell passed. Best raised one hand to his eyes and squinted at the burning Portuguese pinnace, *Ozeander*, silhouetted against the dark night sky like a candle. A slow smile spread over his face. Best saw her men throw lifeboats overboard and then jump out into the dark waters. They fell in quiet splashes, and across the expanse of the sea. Best could hear their curses and shouts. It was tempting to send his crew after those men, but he knew that too much time would go to waste. Even standing here admiring the death of the *Ozeander* was wasteful, but Best could not resist it.

'Captain, we should retreat before the Portuguese send reinforcements.'

Best turned to his first helmsman, a short, swarthy young sailor, seventeen winters old, whose skin had been burned almost black from the sun at sea.

'Yes, weigh anchor and move into open sea. We will wait out there.' Best turned back to the burning ship. A loud boom signalled that the fire had reached another barrel of gunpowder. Fresh tongues of fire wrapped around the *Ozeander*'s keel, and she listed to one side.

The message was passed on to the rest of the fleet, and they quietly weighed anchor. A slight wind blowing from the east helped billow the sails, and the ships moved out into the Gulf of Cambay.

Thomas Best had arrived at the mouth of the Tapti a few months ago. As he had sailed up the river to Surat, he had not known of Sir Henry Middleton's reception in Gujrat or the consequences of his ill treatment of the Indian ships in the Gulf of Aden, or even that Middleton had harassed them. Best had already left England, and there was no hope of hearing from fleets of the East India Company before they arrived back home—in the open seas, England's few friends were rarely met, while enemies were more and more often to be encountered.

Best had immediately sent out word for Jadu, the Indian broker used by both Hawkins and Middleton. Jadu had come, bowing and scraping to the English merchant, with a letter from Middleton. In it, Middleton had outlined his disgrace at the hands of Muqarrab Khan, the governor of Gujrat, and his subsequent decision to return to England. As for the rest, the stories from the Indian ships, these Jadu had provided him. Best had been perplexed. Should he return to England without trying to get a trading agreement? Was India to be given up as a lost cause?

He had decided to take a trip into Surat to survey the situation for himself. Armed with a circle of guards, one hand on the dagger in his belt, Best had walked through the streets of the busy town.

Paths had cleared for him in the crowds, and not just because he had towered over the men in the streets. Merchants and local traders had called out greetings to him and bowed, as though in fear. They had seemed to know who he was, know also of the mighty *Red Dragon*, which had been anchored fourteen miles away in open sea, off a sandbar in the bay; Best had travelled inland to Surat on the Tapti River in just a little boat. In a few days, he'd realized that Middleton, in his short and unfruitful stay at Surat, had terrorized the natives. Where diplomacy had not succeeded, aggression had. Best had quickly gone to work, accosting Muqarrab Khan and persuading him, with the help of ample bribes from his cargo, to sign a formal treaty allowing English trade with Gujrat.

It was a weak agreement, flowery with phrases that said little and meant even less, but it was *something*. For the first time the East India Company had legitimacy in India. What Hawkins and Middleton had failed at—and the fortunate Hawkins had been the Emperor's favourite companion at one time—Best had achieved.

Best smiled grimly. The consequence of that trading agreement had been an attack by the *Ozeander*. He had been warned of this, of course. By Hawkins and Middleton, and even by Jadu, who had not thought to mention the Portuguese until Best's gold coins were safely tucked into his cummerbund. The treaty in his shirt pocket, Best and his men had fled down the Tapti, back to the *Red Dragon* and the rest of the fleet. A day after they had been on board, the pinnace *Ozeander* had come up the gulf from the south, hoping to send Best, the *Red Dragon*, and the scroll of paper he possessed, to rot in the deep waters off the bar.

Best turned to look back towards land. The *Ozeander* was sinking slowly, still aflame. Of her men, Best could see nothing; like the rats from the ship, they too were doubtless headed to the shore.

A Happy Christmas to all, Best thought wryly as the burning boat lit up the dark eastern sky like a Christmas tree. He should have been home in England now, with the Yule log burning in the fireplace, a mug of apple cider by his side, snowflakes settling gently outside the casement windows. Instead he was here, in this infidel land, fighting off an old European enemy.

Even here, so far out from the sight of land, it was deadly hot, even at night. The air was damp with moisture, the wine he had drunk at the Armenian wine houses in Surat came pouring out of his pores, and the sun burned his skin in blotches and bleached his hair. But the discomfort was nothing, would be nothing when he returned to England with the treaty—surely the Company's directors would award him with a rich purse?

If he returned to England with the treaty. Best was not stupid. He knew that the Portuguese Viceroy at Goa would immediately send reinforcements up north to try and drive the English away. That was why he had moved his fleet into open sea—it gave him more room for maneuvering, and, God forbid, if they lost, they could flee without being captured.

Sure enough, the next day, the watch at the bird's nest high atop the *Red Dragon* yelled out a warning. Five Portuguese warships, armed and weighted down with cannons and guns, came into sight. The battle lasted two days, and both sides suffered heavy losses. But the Portuguese were bested, and they sent frantic messages back to Goa. A few days later, another fleet came to the aid of the floundering Portuguese ships, and the English fleet successfully defeated them too. The Portuguese limped away, their ships damaged and smoking from fires they put out with difficulty.

Best, knowing that they would need time to recuperate, guided his fleet back to the bar off Surat. There he set foot on land again for the first time in three weeks, and he gave those of his men for whom fatigue was the only injury from the skirmish, leave to indulge themselves as they pleased in Surat. He stayed back, overseeing repairs on the fleet's ships and the wounds of his men.

Each day since Prince Khurram's wedding, soothsayers and seers had come to Empress Jagat Gosini's palace. The lines grew outside the zenana walls: ash-covered mystics, with iron spikes pierced through their cheeks; old, toothless hags who claimed to read the head by just touching it; and priests who cast her horoscope over and over again, drawing out the houses and mapping the configuration of the stars at the moment Jagat Gosini was born.

Shaista brought these men and women who promised wonders, and the Empress allowed him. She had not moved out of the palace for days, not since she had forced herself to go for Khurram's marriage ceremony. With each ritual, Khurram had been absorbed more into Ghias Beg's house and his family, and Jagat Gosini had watched her son slip away from her as surely as though he had been pulled from her arms again. The pain was the same as when Khurram had been taken away first by Ruqayya, only perhaps more intense. As soon as Empress Jagat Gosini had heard the talk of Khurram's betrothal to Arjumand being consummated at last, she had sent for her son.

Khurram at first had not responded to her summons, and then he had come, but so reluctantly that it was as though he was willing his legs to walk into her apartments. His face had been shuttered from his mother. He kept turning away from her as she had spoken, his answers to her questions had been mumbled. But he had been resolute. Jagat Gosini had tried to tell him that the alliance would not be to his advantage—true, Arjumand's aunt had some small ascendancy over the Emperor right now, but that would not last, and what value would this marriage have then?

The Empress had talked to her son through the night, but he would not bend. He would marry Arjumand. Finally, when her heart had been heavy with ache and her eyes had smarted from crying and a lack of sleep, Khurram had risen to leave. He stood at the door and asked, 'Have you seen Arjumand, your Majesty?'

Jagat Gosini's spirit rose. 'She is not fit for you, Khurram.'

'I see.' Khurram then left, and the Empress hoped again. But only briefly. The marriage had taken place, she had attended the ceremony as she had had to, and Khurram never came again to visit her.

Shaista Khan coughed at Jagat Gosini's elbow. She leaned towards him. Another seer was at the door, your Majesty. He begged an audience. The Empress leaned away and pulled her veil over her head. Let this seer come too, let him promise her good fortune as the others had, now she had only promises left, nothing more substantial than that.

The man came in and bowed. He carried a wooden cage with iron bars and a pack of cards. Jagat Gosini took a deep breath and then wished she had not. He had not bathed in quite a few days and was redolent of that very human unwashed smell. Sweat and dirt matted his long hair. His face was black from the sun and his teeth a rotting red from too much paan. For a man who had so much distaste for his body that he did not look after it, or take care to wash it at the Yamuna's ghats every morning, his eyes were bright and lively, shining with a strange intelligence.

The man spread out his cards on the carpet and let the parrot out of the cage. It waddled over—fly it could not with shorn wings—picked out a card, and turned it over. Sketched on the card in garish colours was a woman. An apsara, he said, a handmaiden to Indra, King of the Gods. She would bring beauty to her Majesty's life.

And so it went on for the next few minutes. One card after another lifted and turned over, a message read from it. After a while Jagat Gosini did not listen anymore. She wished the day were over so she could retire to her bedchamber to sleep.

'Courage, your Majesty.'

Her head whipped up. Had he really said that? But no, he was cooing to his parrot as though it were a lover. 'Come, my darling, pick another card.'

'Is everything lost to you already, your Majesty?'

Now the seer looked at her and smiled. It was Mahabat Khan. Empress Jagat Gosini sat up.

'What are you doing here?'

'I have news, your Majesty.' Mahabat shuffled the cards again with his grimy hands. He fanned them out. 'Empress Nur Jahan is with child.'

Jagat Gosini stared at him. 'You must be mistaken, Mahabat. I have heard no such thing.'

'True, nonetheless, your Majesty. And please, do not address me so.'

'How long?'

Mahabat took out little chips of almonds from a dirty bag tucked into his cummerbund and held them out to the parrot. It came over to peck in his palm. 'I do not know, your Majesty. But just recently. It is early yet.'

Empress Jagat Gosini leaned back into her divan. Mehrunnisa was pregnant. She would have a child, a son surely, and the Emperor would love her even more. Why did this have to happen? What of Khurram?

'Children,' Mahabat said, still looking at his parrot, 'have a way of returning where they belong, your Majesty. Prince Khurram is young, easily flattered by the attention given to him. This child will change things. He will realize it.'

And for the first time in days, the lethargy lifted, and Jagat Gosini's mind exploded with thoughts. True, Khurram would return to her. But Mehrunnisa's child was a threat to all of them, mostly to Khurram. Was she the only one who saw this?

'Mahabat, she must not have this child.' The words came out even as they were formed in her, and once she said them she could not take them back. Jagat Gosini looked around, but they were alone, and Shaista had gone to get the seer a glass of water to wet his lips.

'Much better that she does not, your Majesty. A woman is always most vulnerable at this time, when her body and her mind are given over to the task of making a child. If anything were to happen to her... who would be blamed? Especially if this is done discreetly.'

They heard footsteps, and Mahabat hastily pointed the parrot to the cards again. Shaista came in, and following him were three more soothsayers. The minister scooped up the cards and shooed the parrot into the cage in a hurry. In another minute, he had left, bowing to the ground and backing out without lifting his head. The soothsayers' gazes stuck to him until he had gone, and then they asked questions. Who was he? Which village did he come from? What was his reading? Jagat Gosini fended off the queries and banished them, with strict orders to Shaista not to bring in any more men.

Jagat Gosini sent word out asking if the news of Mehrunnisa's pregnancy was true, and when she knew it was so, she distributed the news, slyly, into the various other zenana quarters. Fear came to live with a lot of women, and where fear came, anger followed. And with the temper came the cunning, the planning, the deceit. Many women had been known to carry a child inside them... and then, one day, to lose that child even before they saw its face.

'Runners have come from Surat, your Majesty.'

'What news?' Mehrunnisa asked eagerly, reaching for the mailbag.

She unrolled the letter and read it in silence. The English had successfully repulsed and then defeated the Portuguese thrice in the last few months. It was unheard of; the Portuguese had reigned supreme over the waters of the Arabian Sea for over a century, and now this captain, Thomas Best, had defeated them. Was this letter an exaggeration? Mehrunnisa smoothed out the paper on her knee. It was signed by Muqarrab Khan himself, the governor of Gujrat. He would not lie, surely. Muqarrab was now a Christian, influenced by the Portuguese into their religion and their needs, which they had told him were one, for they alone knew how to please this new God Muqarrab had agreed to serve.

'Where is the Emperor?'

'In his *Ibadat Khana*, your Majesty. The Jesuit fathers are in conference with him,' Hoshiyar replied.

'Send a message requesting an audience immediately.' Mehrunnisa put the letter back into the bag and rose to go to her husband. The Ibadat Khana was the House of Worship built within the palace complex of the Agra Fort. The first Ibadat Khana—and the idea for it—belonged to Emperor Akbar in Fatehpur Sikri. It was not a temple but an octagonal hall, the ceiling slotted with glass to allow light, and everything within it an unblemished white marble—the pillars, the floor, even the sun coming into the hall. And here Akbar had invited the religious elite of the various religions of India to sit in his presence and argue the merits of their own faiths. There were Jain and Buddhist monks, the Jesuit fathers brought from Goa, Hindu priests, every Muslim sect in the land, and the Zoroastrians.

A balcony ran around the top of the Ibadat Khana, fenced off by a marble screen reaching to the ceiling. Here the women of the zenana came to listen to the philosophies in the hall below. They were always silent, knew that the men in the hall thought the finer points of most religions to be their exclusive purview and a woman's job was merely to follow the dictates of her husband's or her father's or even her son's creed. Questions were not admitted—

indeed, the men below did not even know there were women listening, or if they did, they allowed it by ignoring it.

Mehrunnisa climbed the steps to the balcony and pressed her face against the screen. It was night, the room was but dimly lit with small torches in sconces on the walls. The men argued—some loud and forceful, some more timid but still so persistent that they repeated their sentences over and over again until they had been heard. The Jesuit fathers, Pinheiro and Xavier, were there too.

They had suddenly grown small, Mehrunnisa thought. They had tried, for many years, to convince first Akbar and then Jahangir of the finer points of Christianity. But for both the emperors, there were too many flaws. Monogamy could not be accepted. How could a monarch marry only one wife? An empire ran on politics, and if God dictated a king's behaviour, He did so through the king, and then, the king was only obeying God in accepting more than one wife. This, quite apart from the fact that the empire benefited from the numerous unions. There were other perplexities. What was a virgin birth? How could that even exist?

Mehrunnisa and Jahangir had talked of the arguments from the various religious leaders. Even Hinduism was incomprehensible. Widows could not marry again, the soul was reincarnated, and most terrible, the practice of Sati, where a woman killed herself in her husband's funeral pyre. But there were Hindu queens in the zenana; they had their beliefs and knew better than to argue with Jahangir about them. It was enough—actually, more than generous—that he allowed them their faith within the walls of his harem.

Mehrunnisa watched as Father Pinheiro bent to Father Xavier. They talked under cover of the noise in the room. Had they heard about Best? If they had heard of the new Englishman in India, it was unlikely they would know of the defeat of their fleet in the Arabian Sea. Hoshiyar came into the Ibadat Khana now, and the Emperor rose from his divan in the centre of the room.

'I must retire from this discussion,' Jahangir said as the leaders dropped into silence and bowed to their Emperor. 'But please do continue if you wish.'

They only waited until Jahangir left before commencing again. But to fill the Emperor's absence, fifteen Ahadis, the personal bodyguards of the Emperor, filed into the room, daggers in their cummerbunds, spears in their hands, their faces unyielding. Here in the Ibadat Khana, if the Emperor were not present to stop it, blood would flow in the name of God—so excitable were the men. The Ahadis were there to maintain order; any man who threatened another, no matter who he was, how exalted his position, would be first thrown into prison, and then let out only to be banished from the Ibadat Khana. Raised voices were allowed, but hands could not be raised.

'Mehrunnisa.' Emperor Jahangir came up behind her. 'Have you come to listen?'

'Your Majesty, I have received communication from Surat.' Mehrunnisa showed him the letter. 'The English ships have defeated the Portuguese at sea, not once but thrice.'

He read it carefully. 'So it is true. Muqarrab Khan writes to say that the empire should come to the aid of the Portuguese.' Jahangir shook his head. 'This cannot be.'

'Do you think they know?'

They both leaned their foreheads against the screen and looked down. Father Xavier glanced up, but he could see nothing, so they did not move away.

'The Portuguese are too arrogant, Mehrunnisa, too sparse with their gifts now. They are my guests at Agra and have been accorded all the respect due to a guest. But they misuse this,' the Emperor said. He spoke softly, but even had he yelled, he would not have been heard in the noise that rose from the floor of the Ibadat Khana. He held up the letter again. 'Muqarrab has given this Best a treaty to trade with Gujrat. Should we extend the territory?'

'So much favour, your Majesty? And so soon?' Mehrunnisa asked.

Jahangir laughed. 'Let him think so at least. The treaty will not bind us to anything definite; we can follow Muqarrab's admirable example and say quite a lot and still say nothing.'

'Yes,' Mehrunnisa said, 'and an English ambassador should be commanded to court, your Majesty. Not one,' she inclined her head towards the hall, 'who makes pretensions for being a man of God and deals in mortal things, but who is a noble, who can claim a high birth, and is more worthy of your notice. This may be a beginning...'

'We shall see if it is. At least we do not *need* either the Portuguese or the English in the Arabian Sea. We want them, but do not need them yet.' Jahangir put an arm around his wife's shoulder and pulled her close. 'I do remember about your ships, my dear. Have they come home from their first journey?'

She shook her head. 'I have heard nothing.'

'They will, and soon.' He pulled away to look at her face. Mehrunnisa was not wearing her veil; there was no one to see her but Jahangir and Hoshiyar. The Emperor cupped his hands around her chin and kissed her gently, on her mouth, on her nose, and her closed eyelids. Then he enfolded her like this, with her head bent into his chest, with just her forehead touching his heart, and his arms about her neck. 'How are you feeling, beloved?'

He spoke still more softly now; Hoshiyar, at the door to the balcony, would not hear them, and the shouts from the hall below resounded through the screen.

'Tired,' Mehrunnisa said. She smiled into the embroidered cloth of his *nadiri* coat. 'Tired when I am reminded of it.'

'Does Hoshiyar know?'

She shook her head.

'Why?'

'I'm not sure why. Perhaps...' Her voice faltered. 'It is the others I lost at this time. Perhaps it is that this child is, will be, so precious to history. I fear at times, mostly for his safety.'

Jahangir pulled her more completely into his arms. Now her face was flat against the silk-covered buttons of his nadiri. Mehrunnisa was tired, too tired to even stand on her feet, so she climbed onto Jahangir's feet, balancing on the incline, as he held her even tighter. 'You must never fear, Mehrunnisa. As long as I am here to look after you, everything I have, my army, my treasury, is for you to use. As for the child, you must tell Hoshiyar at least. But he must have guessed, surely?'

She smiled, blissfully wanting sleep. If Hoshiyar had guessed, he was being very discreet. He set down trays of cashews and sultanas by her side if she was hungry, but he had not yet brought the mixture of ghee, sugar and almonds that was to fatten a woman at this time and, in doing so, fatten the child in her womb. As Jahangir and Mehrunnisa left the Ibadat Khana for the welcome quiet of the outside night, she slipped her hand into the Emperor's. They walked back to her apartments.

An imperial farman was drawn up and sealed by Mehrunnisa in Jahangir's name. It allowed the English very vague trading privileges in the empire, as obscure in language as Muqarrab Khan's own treaty had been. Mehrunnisa used Muqarrab's document as a model for her own and added a new command—a representative of King James was to be introduced in the Mughal court.

Thomas Best was nonetheless thrilled. It was the first imperial acknowledgement of English presence in India, four years after William Hawkins had set foot on Indian soil. He quickly wound up his business and set sail for England.

But this was the next morning's achievement. Mehrunnisa did not think that night, either in her waking hours or in her dreams, of Thomas Best, of Khurram and Arjumand, or of Abul or her Bapa. Her time was given over to the child. What would he be like? Would he look like Ladli? And this was entirely possible, because Ladli had very little of her father in her. And what would Ladli think of this new brother? It was too early; there was no outward sight of the child, nor a quickening inside her. The symptoms, such as they were, came as a sudden fatigue that turned her arms and legs into liquid, or a hunger that seemed to eat up the skin of her stomach, or the bile that rose to her throat at the sight of *every* food—even water had its distinctive and disgusting taste—or that she could smell every aroma around her. Even Jahangir's perfumes, ones he wore and then chose not to wear for Mehrunnisa's sake, were irritating at times. If she could not smell the sandalwood of his bath, she could smell the soap used to wash the Emperor's clothes, and the sun that had dried it, and turned away from both equally.

There was no doubt in her mind that there was going to be a child. Mehrunnisa did not want to tell anyone yet because she was afraid of the evil eye and the sharp tongue of jealousy. And there would be rage in the zenana. She knew of other attempts to make a woman miscarry, attempts that had succeeded. A push down the stairs, a potion in the wine cups, a chant to invite misfortune. She would protect her child from all of those. Jahangir would not think such deceit possible in the women of his harem. But Mehrunnisa knew that she had angered too many women here, taken away privileges they once considered their own, and not just Jagat Gosini, but others too.

But no matter, she thought. She would protect this child. Let them try to take him away from her.

A few nights later, when the moon died into nothingness, Mehrunnisa opened her eyes. Her heart beat rapidly, and sweat spread thickly between her breasts. Something had woken her, what was it? A sound? Was someone in the apartments? No, it had been a dream, a strange and frightening dream where she was being chased by a faceless person. She stumbled and went down, hands came to touch her...

She rose from the mattress and went outside into the gardens. The eunuchs on guard were all asleep, leaning against the pillars in the verandah. *This* was like a dream, that they would be so careless as to close their eyes while guarding the Emperor. Mehrunnisa did not wake them but went down the steps into the lawn. The night was dark as ink. A breeze whispered through the leaves of the tamarind tree, and a form, white and ghostly, flitted from one bush to another. She stood in the centre of the lawn, not afraid of the spirits, not knowing whether she was awake or asleep still and all this was just an extension of her subconscious.

Hoshiyar came up to her and touched her on the shoulder. Mehrunnisa turned. What was he doing here? Hoshiyar's duties kept him by her side only during the day. Never before had he come at night.

'I cannot sleep, Hoshiyar.'

'Perhaps a walk around the gardens, your Majesty.'

She was glad to have his arm to lean on as they walked over the wet grass, the skirts of her ghagara gathering dampness. When they moved onto the bare earth around the grass, the ground was smooth, beaten into the consistency of soft cloth. At one point, the cotton of her ghagara caught on the branches of a shrub, and Hoshiyar carefully extricated it, but a little tear was left. Soon she was tired and said so. They made their way back to the verandah, not the one she had come from, but another one. This one was paved with flat stones of marble. As Mehrunnisa climbed the steps to the verandah, she noticed that the marble glowed even in this dark night, gleaming as though newly polished.

She put her foot on the top stair and it gave way. Hoshiyar had come up behind her. 'What is it, your Majesty?' he asked.

Mehrunnisa cried out as her body lifted into the air. Her hands scrambled for Hoshiyar's qaba. She caught the front lapel, and the buttons came ripping into her fingers. She slid down the length of the verandah, Hoshiyar following her, for she had knocked him off his feet. The stones were cold under her back, and too, too smooth. Mehrunnisa finally collided into the pillar on the farther end, her right ankle twisting under her thigh, her knee smashing into stone, the jolt travelling through her stomach to her chest. She heard Hoshiyar crash also, somewhere close to her.

Even through the pain she could smell something odd, something different. The aromas of the garden at night, the sun-fired essence of the brick pathways, the cool scent of marble... but also something else. Something from the kitchens, from the cosmetics case, from the bath for lustrous hair. It was the acrid tang of sesame oil.

How strange, Mehrunnisa thought as her body started to shut down in response to the pain to give her the relief of unconsciousness. As she drifted away, another ache came, huge and overwhelming. Her lips moved. 'My child.'

Chapter Eight

He complained much about his mode of government,
telling him that it was indecorous to let a woman govern
the empire.

——WILLIAM IRVINE, TRANS.,
Storia do Mogor by Niccolao Manucci

'SHALL I ORDER YOU ANOTHER SHERBET, FRIEND? WITH FRESH ICE?'

Mahabat Khan looked up from his goblet at the sound of the Amir-ul-umra's voice. 'Yes, please.'

Muhammad Sharif signalled to the attendants. A pretty slave girl came forward to do his bidding.

Mahabat Khan moodily swirled the khus sherbet in his goblet, tracing patterns on the frosted silver with his finger. He dipped his hand into the goblet, pulled out a shard of ice, and sucked on it, letting the cool water run down his throat. It tasted of the mountains in the north, the Himalayas, abode of King Himavat. Whose daughter—and so the Hindus would have it—was the wife of Lord Shiva.

But here there were no mountains, no mounds of earth to guard from the sun. The Indo-Gangetic plains stretched vastly, arid and open. The night air was still, pregnant with expectation of yet another monsoon. Heat lay cloaked over the city of Agra, stifling every breath, dulling the senses. Mahabat wiped his perspiring brow and looked up at the starlit sky. A few more days, he thought, for the monsoon rains to come to the plains. The rains would fall in a deluge, soaking the thirsty, dry, cracked earth, giving life to the countryside. Fields would be green again, flowers would bloom, and people would be happy, their moods lifted. The monsoons sustained them all. If they were late, the rice crop, which depended on the rainfall, would be harvested late, which would mean bad-quality rice, or worse still, a failed harvest.

The two friends were seated in an outside verandah at Sharif's house overlooking the garden. Coloured paper lanterns hung on chenar trees cast a soft glow. In deference to the heat, the stone floor was covered only with reed mats. Every half hour, a servant sprinkled perfumed rose water on the mats, and for a few minutes coolness rose around them, until the heat sucked it away.

Three dancing girls swayed in front of Sharif and Mahabat. They seemed miserable as they languidly moved their arms about, sweat pouring down their lithe bodies. They moved out of step with the music, like puppets on indifferent strings, jerking about without grace or rhythm.

'That's enough. Go to the kitchens and get something cool to drink. I don't want you to die of a heat stroke,' Sharif said. It was tiring even to *look* at them.

'Send the slaves away too,' Mahabat said.

Sharif indicated with his head. All the slaves left the courtyard.

'What is bothering you?' Sharif asked. 'You have been restive ever since you came to dinner. Is it the heat?'

Mahabat lay back on the divan. His voice was peevish. 'The heat will dissipate with the monsoons. But my problem seemingly has no solution.'

'Oh?' Sharif raised an eyebrow. 'A woman? A married woman?'

'Yes,' Mahabat Khan said morosely, then, seeing the smile on his friend's face, he added hastily, 'no, no. It is not a romantic attachment. I am talking of another woman, one who has successfully made my life hell. My standing with the Emperor has been lost because of her.'

Sharif became grim. 'Be careful, friend. What you are saying is treason.' He looked around cautiously. 'If someone was to hear...'

'Who will hear?' Mahabat demanded. 'Aren't you safe even in your own house?'

'Yes...,' Sharif said slowly. 'But she has great resources, she knows everything.'

'Sahib, a message from his Majesty.'

Both men whirled around. An attendant was standing behind them with a letter in his hand.

'Don't sneak up like that,' Sharif said angrily, reaching for the letter. He glanced at Mahabat, and the same thought crossed both their minds. Had the man overheard their conversation?

Sharif read the letter. 'Mahabat, it is for you,' he said. 'The Emperor commands your presence in the zenana next week.'

'Tell the Emperor I shall be there,' Mahabat said to the attendant.

When he left, the two ministers fell silent. Much had changed since Mehrunnisa had married Jahangir. She now completely ruled the Emperor and, in consequence, the empire. It was too much. For six years they had been the two most important men in the Empire, second only to Jahangir, and then, in one day, they were relegated to minions. Jahangir no longer came to them for advice, he did not consult them on matters of state; all affairs passed through Mehrunnisa's hands. Now a new treaty was finding its way to the English captain's hands, signed by the Emperor himself. They had had no knowledge of it until the runner had dashed out of Agra with the farman rolled into a silver baton.

'I went to see Empress Jagat Gosini again, Sharif,' Mahabat said.

The Grand Vizier of the Mughal Empire did not look at his friend as he spoke. 'You are a fool, Mahabat. A fool twice over. I know you went into the zenana this time, into her very apartments and sat before her. Do you think there is no danger of your being found out? And what purpose have these futile meetings served?'

Mahabat turned to Sharif with surprise. So much fury, and so many words! Sharif rarely talked, preferring to let his glance, the language of his body, do the talking instead. In all the years Mahabat had known him, in all the years of their friendship, the voice had belonged to Mahabat. What he said, Sharif did. If Sharif protested at all, it was but a bland protest. 'You call me a fool, Sharif?' Mahabat said quietly. He drew his dagger out of its sheath and laid it on the divan between them.

Sharif laughed, quite unpleasantly. His own dagger came out of its home, bigger, squarer, the blade thicker, the ends double-edged and so honed that when he flipped it on the divan next to Mahabat's, it cut an opening in the velvet covering. 'If you had listened to what I said, you would have seen yourself for the fool you are, Mahabat.'

They held each other's gaze for a few moments, Mahabat itching to lay hold of his dagger, but he knew that Sharif's hand was swifter, his movements faster. Friendship or not, Mahabat could find his hand nailed to the divan with the tip of Sharif's dagger between the bones. Still, he wanted to fight. The heat made him unreasonable, made them both unreasonable, else why would Sharif snap at him thus?

'You are right,' Mahabat's voice was subdued. 'I wanted to go into the zenana, into the Empress's apartments... it was a momentary thrill. I went to console Jagat Gosini on Khurram's marriage. But Sharif,' he waited until the minister had sheathed his dagger until moving his hand to his own, 'Empress Nur Jahan is pregnant.'

'Why did you go then, knowing this? Mahabat, have you no children?'

'You know I do, my friend.'

'And what were your women during those months? And what were they for months afterward with a mewling baby to look after?'

Mahabat smiled. He did this so rarely that his face fell into unused lines, and when at rest, which was almost always, no wrinkles came to mar his smooth brown skin. 'Hoydens and witches. They did not want to be touched; I could not talk to them, and if they talked it was to whine and groan and fuss about the heat, or that they could smell too keenly, or that they were hungry when food lay aplenty in front of them. I had to banish them from me, to return only when their good humour returned, and only when they could pay more heed to me than the child.'

'Really?' Sharif lay back on the divan and raised his head just enough to sip at the khus from his goblet. 'The way you worry about the new Empress's pregnancy, I thought your women had all been angels.'

'What?...' Mahabat said, and then he stopped. This time the smile was genuine, one of pure delight. 'The Emperor would never put up with this. He dislikes it when his women complain, and once they are sent away, they never return.'

'His Majesty does have a large number to choose from, Mahabat, unlike you and I,' Sharif said.

'So let her be, you say. Why didn't I think of this before?'

'Because you want to act on every change, Mahabat, without pausing to reflect if it should simply take its course. Without wondering whether that change will be to our advantage,' Sharif said gruffly.

Mahabat put an appeasing hand on his friend's arm. 'I apologize for pulling the knife. We are both irritable today.'

'And what did you say to Empress Jagat Gosini?'

'I told her of the pregnancy.' Mahabat's voice fell. 'I told her, no, I suggested that there might be ways to end it. The other women will be jealous, and envy lends courage to even the weakest enemy. Something will happen—'

'You are an idiot, Mahabat,' Sharif said abruptly. He sat up and pulled the cloth of his white kurta from his back, where it lay stuck with sweat. 'Now, something will happen. The women will try. The Emperor will be dragged into their quarrels, and do you think he will have much time for us then? Why bring his attention unnecessarily to his new Empress?'

'Enough with calling me a fool and idiot, Sharif,' Mahabat said, raising his voice. 'What if she does have the child? And it is a boy? He will be the next heir, and she will have far more power than she does now.'

'Think, Mahabat.' Sharif put his face close to his friend's. 'Think for a moment of what you are saying. Even if the child is a boy, he has at least fifteen years to grow up to manhood, before that he is only the promise of an heir. And who is going to protect the child in the interim? The Emperor's other sons are much older, do you think Prince Khurram will allow his claims to the crown to be so easily dissolved?'

'I should have said nothing,' Mahabat said quietly.

They sat in silence for a while more, Mahabat now ashamed of his actions. What Sharif said was true, let Mehrunnisa have the child, and she would find herself more and more occupied with it, leaving her little time to meddle in court affairs. The other day, in the Diwan-i-khas, Jahangir had made a shocking statement. He had said, 'Before I married her, I never knew what marriage really meant, and I have conferred the duties of government on her.' All the nobles had hushed after that. What was there to say? To give a mere woman so much power, even though she was an Empress, was offensive.

'You were right, Sharif, about my meeting with Jagat Gosini.

I should have gone to the Emperor himself,' Mahabat said, thinking out loud. 'Yes,' he nodded to himself, 'the Emperor is the one to approach.'

'Don't,' Sharif said as he laid a warning hand on his arm. 'The Emperor is blind when it comes to Empress Nur Jahan. Say nothing against her.'

'Someone has to make him see reason.' Mahabat jumped up and started pacing around, hands clasped behind his back. 'You know what the Emperor said in front of the nobles. You know how they laughed at this obsession. I must tell him of this. He must realize how much he has become an object of ridicule at court.' Mahabat stopped in front of Sharif and flung his arms out. 'See where we are now, Sharif. You are the Amir-ul-umra of the empire, the Grand Vizier. And what decisions do you make? Have you had any say in court appointments lately? All you do is decide budgets for the zenana—that too approved by the new Empress. Are these the duties of a Prime Minister? If the Emperor is now ludicrous, we are even more so, bested by a woman.'

Sharif looked at Mahabat. He was so restless that he could not even stand still, shifting his weight from one foot to another. Mahabat had always been thus, never content until he was *doing* something. Never content, and this was ironical, until he was at worry about something or the other, wondering how to fix things, unable to even take the word patience into his mouth. And so here he was barging ahead into another indiscretion.

'Sit down and give me the courtesy of listening to me,' Sharif said. Mahabat shook his head vigorously, so Sharif continued, 'Do not talk with the Emperor about Empress Nur Jahan. When have we ever been able to sway him once his mind was made up? Wait awhile, let matters follow their own paths, let us see what happens.'

In reply, Mahabat paced the courtyard again, his bare feet not making a sound on the red sandstone slabs. Sharif watched his friend whip himself into fatigue for several minutes until at last Mahabat said, 'All right. I will wait.'

'Let us go to bed,' Sharif said. 'It is late.'

An attendant came into the verandah, and this time, they both saw him. He had another message. It was addressed to Mahabat in a woman's hand, but not Empress Jagat Gosini's. He read it out loud to Sharif, without reading it first by himself. Mehrunnisa was seriously ill; she had slipped and fallen in the zenana at night. The royal hakims were not optimistic about the survival of either the child or the new Empress.

The next few days passed slowly. Little was done at the morning and afternoon jharokas, less at the court in the Diwan-i-am. The first two days, for the first time since he had sat on the throne, Emperor Jahangir did not come to the jharokas. It was awkward and frightening for the nobles and commoners who came to the morning audiences. The Emperor was always there—whether he was unwell or not, whether he had slept or not, he would be at the balcony, unshaven, irritable, or just plain sick with such a fever that it marked his forehead with a pale, unhealthy glow. They were so used to seeing Jahangir and Mehrunnisa by now that they waited for the two hours of the audience and then went home, and during the time they waited, they stood as though in the presence of royalty, and not one word was spoken as usual.

It was as though a blight had come over Agra. News travelled through the bazaars in the city of Mehrunnisa's death, and then of a miraculous revival. Potions and poultices were discussed. *Surely if she took a little bit of turmeric and ginger in buffalo's milk it would bring down the fever. Or her Majesty's stomach would be settled with some* ajwain *water, the seeds roasted on a dry pan and then boiled with water and jaggery to take away its bitterness.* For every ailment possible, a cure was brought forward from remedies handed down from one generation to the next, and from travellers and merchants from countries around the world. No one really knew what had happened. The imperial palaces and courtyards were usually like a reed fishing basket, pouring water when raised— there were so many people going in and out of the fort that news was always plentiful.

But since Mehrunnisa's fall, the palaces had shut down. No music was played, hence musicians sat idle outside the walls, no business was conducted, so the zenana stewards waited for their mistress's summons, no runners were allowed in. Every detail of Mehrunnisa's illness was pure conjecture. The night she had fallen, the royal hakims had been summoned—so far they had not come out of the zenana palaces.

In Mehrunnisa's apartments, the hush that seemed to weigh down the empire was at its quietest. It was mid-afternoon, and drapes of a thick blue velvet had been drawn over the windows. The cloth did not quite meet in the centre, and an arrow of sun slanted its way into the room.

When Mehrunnisa's eyes opened, the light was what she first saw. It came through in a straight line and then inched its way up the divan. She put her hand into it and watched the diamond rings on her fingers glitter. She was lying on her stomach, her face turned towards the windows. At some point, yesterday, the day before, she had woken from this interminable sleep to tell Hoshiyar to always let some light in.

The Emperor was next to her, by her feet. He was sitting cross-legged on the floor, a book on his lap, his eyes on the pages, but his lips were moving. Jahangir was praying. She watched him for some time, turning her head slightly on the pillow to look down at him, a deep and immense love flooding over her. How could she ever repay this devotion? For devotion it had been. Every day and night when she had woken, Jahangir had been there by her side. In the beginning, for the first few days, the pain overwhelmed every other sensation. If the hakims came to ponder over her, she neither saw nor heard them. Hoshiyar, and sometimes Jahangir, forced khichri and water into her mouth, and she ate and drank because they said so. Not because she wanted to. Ladli was brought to see her too, and she ordered that her daughter was to be kept away until she was better. Mehrunnisa had no time for Ladli right now and did not know how to wipe away the fright in her daughter's eyes. Every thought, every wish was given over to the child inside her.

She put her hand under her, to her belly. But even as she lay there, she knew the dampness between her legs was unnatural. For the first few days there had been some bleeding, it was inevitable, the hakims had said. But even now... tears came sliding down her cheeks, soaking into the silk of the pillow cover. Even now it had not stopped. Her stomach cramped, her insides felt raw, the life inside her had been beaten out like clothes on a stone on the banks of the Yamuna. Why, Allah? Why did this have to happen? *Why did this have to happen again?*

'Mehrunnisa.' Emperor Jahangir put down his book and slid up to her. He knelt by her side and put his face into the curve of her neck. Then he wiped away the tears that came as fast as he could extinguish them. 'It is all right. Shhh...'

Jahangir did not know what else to do, what to say to her. The hakims had told him that the only way for her to let go of the sorrow was to let it escape. That she must cry, that the pain would eventually wane. But it had been days and this had not happened. And when Mehrunnisa cried, as she did almost each time she woke, it broke everything in him. He was helpless. He watched her, he murmured words of comfort, or what he thought were words of comfort, he held her to his heart. And she cried on. Jahangir put his face to hers again and felt the jut of her cheekbones in his skin.

She had no will for anything anymore, she looked at him, dim and uncomprehending, as though he were a stranger.

He climbed up on the divan next to Mehrunnisa and put a leg over her. This time, she turned to him, grasped the collar of his nadiri coat, and in a few minutes her sobs weakened and then ceased until he could just hear her breathing. Jahangir smoothed her hair from her forehead; it lay in dank strands, thick with sweat, and dulled from not having been washed.

'Your Majesty...,' she said, and looked up at him with a question.

The Emperor shook his head. 'No. There has been too much bleeding.' He was terrified that she would give in to the sorrow again, that it would take her from him, that this wretched illness would be her death. But he would not lie to her; she did not expect it from him, so he would not lie.

But she did not cry again. 'I see... how did I slip?'

This was the question Jahangir most dreaded. But again, he would not lie. 'The verandah floor had been oiled, Mehrunnisa, with sesame oil.'

'Ah... someone did it then.' For the first time in days, anger reared itself. Mehrunnisa could not stop the trembling that beset her. How did they dare this? Who had dared this? It had been hard enough for her to keep a child inside her—Ladli was a gift from Allah, a miracle after so many other miscarriages. Someone had *oiled* the floors, that was why they had gleamed on a night with no moon, that was why she had been left with the smell of sesame seeds just before escaping into unconsciousness.

'Who?' she asked, a fire in her eyes.

Jahangir shook his head. 'But it will not happen again, Mehrunnisa. I promise you this.'

She pulled away from the Emperor and tried to sit up, but her limbs were too heavy, too unused from lying down all these days, and she fell back.

'Rest, my dear,' Jahangir said. 'I am here to watch over you. Will you eat something?'

'Yes.' Mehrunnisa did not feel like eating, but she did feel like living. She would hunt down the people who had done this to her, have them buried in the ground in the summer sun so that the heat could broil their brains in their heads, so they would die knowing that Empress Nur Jahan was not to be trifled with.

When the food came, she ate obediently, sitting up to lean against Jahangir as Hoshiyar fed her with his hands. Then the Emperor ordered her to sleep again, and she slept, because she needed it to gain strength, not because she feared being awake.

Mehrunnisa slept through the rest of the day and the night, and Jahangir stayed by her, leaving only for his own night's meal. Hoshiyar came and went from the room, no one else was allowed in. The Emperor watched his wife by the light of the evening oil lamps. Her breathing was even, she did not move in sleep unless it was to shift her head to a more comfortable position. She slept as she should, from fatigue and not from illness.

When the muezzins from the mosques around Agra called the faithful to the last prayer of the day, Jahangir laid out his prayer rug facing west towards Mecca. *Allah-u-Allah-u-Akbar*. There was peace in their liquid voices during this last prayer, when the sun was setting, the skies painted with gold and orange, fires for the evening meal filling the streets of Agra with the scent of woodsmoke.

When he finished, he stayed kneeling on the rug, his hands resting on his thighs. For the last few days, he had stormed about the zenana palaces in a rage. Every single woman in the harem was questioned, where she had been that night, who she had talked with, who her visitors were for the past month, who had sesame oil as part of her toilette kit. There were many of the latter, of course, but Hoshiyar had asked each of them for samples of the oil, and they had been compared with the one on the floor. Jahangir had been disbelieving at first. Who would have dared to try and harm his wife? Who had done this? Why had no one seen this happen? Someone had actually taken a bucket of oil and mopped the floor with it—this was the only way it could have been done.

Jahangir had not slept in many nights. And he made sure every single person in the harem—wives, concubines, slaves, eunuchs and guards—did not have a second of rest either. He slashed all their incomes in half, so they would feel pain. Not the pain Mehrunnisa felt, but still. He tripled *her* income—gave her more jagirs and districts as she lay on the divan, ordered three more ships to be built in her name in the dry docks at Surat. Jahangir did all of this openly, advertising his favour for Mehrunnisa.

He rose from the prayer rug and rolled it up. Then he went to sit by the window, looking out at the wedge of the moon in the sky. Where had it been the night Mehrunnisa had most needed it? Where had he been? Asleep in his apartments, thinking her asleep near him too. He had failed in his duty to look after her. He had promised her this, and he had failed. But it would not happen again. He bent his head. *Thank you, Allah. Thank you for bringing her back to me.*

The Emperor went to lie down by Mehrunnisa, and in sleep she turned to him. His eyes closed, his heart was light for the first time in days. There was to be no child. The hakims had said there would be no more children.

But he had Mehrunnisa. And that was enough.

'Where is her Majesty?'

'She has gone to visit her mother,' the guard replied.

Mahabat Khan felt a glow of exultation. Surely, this was a good omen. With Mehrunnisa out of the palace, he could more confidently present his case to the Emperor.

'You can go in now,' the guard said, opening the doors to Jahangir's apartments.

Mahabat entered and performed the konish. When he straightened, he noted with surprise that Jahangir looked healthier than he had seen him before. This was his first private audience with the Emperor in months. Once, Sharif and he had had free leave to come and go from Jahangir's apartments as they had wanted. They had not needed permission to visit. Mahabat stood where he was, watching his Emperor. Jahangir had not looked up from his book yet.

The Emperor's face had a hearty glow, not the sickly red of too much opium; his eyes shone bright from under bushy eyebrows, for once not unfocussed by liquor. Mahabat hesitated, already unsure of himself. If Mehrunnisa was capable of regulating Jahangir's intake of wine and opium, she was indeed capable of performing miracles. What chance did he have against such an adversary?

'*Al-Salam alekum*, your Majesty.'

'*Walekum-al-Salam*,' Jahangir replied, and then he raised his eyes. A smile lit his face. 'Mahabat, I am pleased you are here.'

'Your Majesty commanded my presence?'

'Yes,' Jahangir said. 'Come in, dear friend, and sit down. We have much to talk about.'

Mahabat quickened his steps. The Emperor spoke to him with such affection, as he had before. And to be asked to sit in his presence was a great honour indeed. This meant a long talk. He bowed again and sat down on the edge of the divan.

'How have you been, Mahabat?' Jahangir asked.

'Well, your Majesty,' Mahabat replied. 'And you are looking well too, with Allah's grace. It has been hard to tell this from the jharoka or the Diwan-i-am audiences, and I am grateful for these summons.'

Jahangir bent his head. 'I have much to thank Allah for. These are joyful days, Mahabat. Her Majesty has recovered.'

'Your Majesty, the empire rejoices with you,' Mahabat said

cautiously. He spoke with courtly etiquette, but inside Mahabat a little spurt of fear reared its head. What would he say? Was it better not to say anything, as Sharif had suggested? Guilt came to nag him at the thought of Sharif, for the Amir-ul-umra did not know that Mahabat planned to disregard his advice yet again.

'I have been neglectful of my duties, Mahabat,' Jahangir said, 'which was why I commanded you here. Have you heard the latest news of the affairs in the Deccan?'

'I have, your Majesty. Ambar Malik has successfully repulsed all efforts to recapture Ahmadnagar,' Mahabat Khan replied.

Ambar Malik had been an Abyssinian slave in the service of Chingaz Khan, the conqueror of Berar, south of the border of the Mughal Empire. He had risen in the ranks and proved himself to be a soldier of astonishing capability and bravery. Ever since Jahangir ascended the throne, he had made surprise attacks on the Mughal army guarding the southern border of the empire.

The threats were inevitable. With the empire as vast as it was, a change of the crown from one head to another seemed to provoke every enemy king into action. They sent messages of congratulations, of course, writing with one hand while the other rested on a sword. They searched for a weakness in the new regime, a wavering on the part of the new Emperor, anything that would expand *their* borders. And so it had been a year after Jahangir's coronation on the north-western frontier of the empire. The Shah of Persia had called Jahangir 'brother' and written him a cloyingly sweet letter while his governors had raised their war standards on the boundary. So Jahangir had sent a mighty Mughal army on a 'visit' to the border town of Kabul, merely, he had suggested to his brother the Shah, to recuperate and be put through their training.

With Ambar Malik in the south, however, no such diplomatic tactics worked. He did not just threaten; he actually came roaring into battle, forcing a retaliation.

Two years ago, Ahmadnagar had fallen to Ambar Malik. The Khan-i-khanan, Abdur Rahim, who was commander-in-chief of the imperial army, had been sent to the Deccan to look after matters there. But Abdur Rahim had surrendered Ahmadnagar to Ambar Malik. Then, the Khan Azam had boasted that he would recapture the lost territory in two years, if only he was given command of the imperial forces. Jahangir had agreed and had sent the Khan Azam Salabat Khan to the Deccan to replace Abdur Rahim.

'The Khan Azam has bragged of his skill in commanding a victorious army. I see no signs of victory against that wretch Malik,' Jahangir said.

'That is true, your Majesty. Malik is a formidable enemy. His resources are not large, but there are rumours that the kings of Bijapur and Golconda are supporting him with provisions and an army.'

'Yes, but the imperial army has to defeat Malik once and for all. His very existence is a scourge to us. The reason I have summoned you here is to command the Khan-i-khanan to return to the Deccan and relieve the Khan Azam of his duties. Send Abdur Rahim on his way immediately. Let him regain what he lost if he wishes any patronage from the court again.'

'As you wish, your Majesty,' Mahabat said happily. This was a sign of favour. Jahangir could just as easily have sent a message to Abdur Rahim himself, but he had chosen to convey it through Mahabat. He leaned on Mahabat yet again, came to him for support. As it once had been. As it should be again. Sharif would be glad too. He would also show the Emperor that he had his well-being, and that of the entire royal family, always at heart. So Mahabat said, 'It is also advisable to have someone in the Deccan to oversee Prince Parviz. Your Majesty must have heard of his behaviour.'

'Yes, yes.' Jahangir waved a hand irritably. 'My son is a

drunkard. I know that. But the Khan-i-khanan has not proved himself to be an able guardian. Should we send someone else to look after Parviz, Mahabat?

The minister shook with pleasure. He had been right! He would tell Sharif of this, and Sharif would have nothing to say in return. Another request from the Emperor. 'Perhaps you should strongly reprimand Abdur Rahim to look after the prince, your Majesty. A word of caution from you will make him more diligent in his duties.'

'I don't want to see Abdur Rahim. Tell him he has to try and wean Parviz from wine.' Jahangir nodded dismissal and picked up his book.

Mahabat Khan bowed low and slowly backed out of the room. At the door he hesitated. 'Your Majesty...'

Jahangir looked up from his book.

'It is a rather delicate matter. If I may presume...'

'Of course, come back here, Mahabat.'

Heartened by Jahangir's tone, Mahabat walked slowly towards the Emperor.

'Your Majesty, I speak for most of the nobles in the court. Please, do not take my words amiss. I speak from a deep loyalty and love for you. You are my Emperor, my king and my lord. My concerns and cares are for your health and well-being—'

'Yes?'

'It is regarding Empress Nur Jahan.' Jahangir's face shut down, and he closed his book with great deliberation. Mahabat hurried on, 'It is unseemly to leave the entire supervision of an empire so large in the hands of a woman. The whole court is shocked that so wise an Emperor as your Majesty should leave affairs of administration under the supervision of an Empress.' He stopped and waited, but there was no response. So Mahabat said, 'We are all very unhappy about her Majesty's recent illness. Please do convey our condolences to her for her womanly troubles. But as unfortunate as the recent past has been, perhaps had she concerned herself with only zenana matters, it might have been avoided.'

Mahabat had no more to say, at least for now. He waited, his eyes on the ground, for Jahangir to speak.

'Your concern for me, for my zenana, is admirable, Mahabat,' Jahangir said. Mahabat listened to his voice, leaning forward to catch an inflection of distaste or even sarcasm. But no, the Emperor was actually commending him. And now words came flooding from his tongue. Had Sharif been there, he would have forcibly dragged Mahabat out of Jahangir's presence, but Sharif was not there, and even the echo of his warnings had long died from Mahabat's ears.

'Your Majesty,' Mahabat raised his voice confidently. 'Your rule has been wise and just. You have shown yourself more than capable of carrying on the responsibility left to you by your gracious father. How can you now give up that responsibility? Is it to be said that the great Emperor Jahangir was ruled by a mere woman? I beg your pardon if I have insulted her Majesty. But the facts speak for themselves, we all wish to be under your able guidance so the empire may flourish once more.'

Mahabat Khan stopped and looked at Jahangir. He had dug past the Emperor's imperial facade to his most vulnerable points. There were two things Jahangir wished for most. One, following in the wake of his father, Jahangir wished to feel himself worthy of the throne. Now Mahabat was giving Jahangir the assurance that not only was he as capable as Akbar but he might in certain points supersede his father if only he divested himself of Mehrunnisa's influence.

Second, Jahangir had a need to be known as a kind and just Emperor, not only while he lived but also to posterity. He wished for the citizens of India to laud him as a great king, many years after his death. There again, how would posterity view him? As a man ruled by his wife?

'Mahabat,' Jahangir said quietly, 'do you wish to be given command of the army in the Deccan?'

'No, your Majesty,' Mahabat said, surprised. 'But... of course... if your Majesty wished for it, I would obey immediately. But, if I may presume to say so, I have no such wish.'

'I see. You may go now, Mahabat. I thank you for your advice, you can be certain that it will be well considered.'

Mahabat Khan bowed and backed away to the doorway, and once there, he bowed again before letting himself out. He had been right in talking with the Emperor. Everything, especially Jahangir's offer of the Deccan command, had indicated this. He almost ran with happiness to Muhammad Sharif's house on the banks of the Yamuna. Along the way he did not forget to send a message to the Khan-i-khanan, Abdur Rahim, to return to the Deccan campaign at his Majesty's orders.

But Mahabat had talked to his Emperor as no man should have talked with his sovereign. In his frustration, he had crossed an invisible line—one that separated the king from the common man.

Mahabat Khan seemed to have suddenly grown less fond of his neck.

Chapter Nine

...during the rest of the reign of Jehangire, she bore the chief sway in all the affairs of the empire.

—ALEXANDER DOW,
The History of Hindostan

ONCE AN ACCUSATION HAS BEEN MADE, HOWEVER DAMNING IT MAY BE, doubt begins to blot the hearer's mind. And so it was with Emperor Jahangir. At first he was deeply furious with Mahabat. When the minister left, he picked up his book to read again, but the words made no sense, the language did not engage him, and a red haze swam in front of him. Jahangir almost called out to Hoshiyar twice, to command Mahabat's body relieved of the burden of his head by sundown, and then stopped himself. What purpose would it serve?

He did not sleep that night, the bed beside him empty of Mehrunnisa's presence, and he turned and tossed and thought. How did Mahabat have the audacity to come to him with such a proposal? They were childhood friends, yes, but only in infancy had Mahabat, Koka and Sharif been allowed to forget that Jahangir was royalty and they mere commoners. Their friendship had very loose ties indeed. Blood did not bind them, and neither did marriage or any other bond. This the three men had never let out of their sight, and if they had had the temerity to do so, even by suggestion, Jahangir had reminded them who he was. He was their Emperor.

In him was vested their well-being, their fortunes, their titles, their very lives. They could not question him. It was as simple as that.

When the earth swung around, with a few hours left to greet the sun, Emperor Jahangir was still awake. Clouds had filled the skies outside his windows. These were monsoon clouds, purple, angry, pregnant with moisture. By morning the rains would come. Already it was cooler. Jahangir rose to go to the window. He leaned over the balcony into the night air, breathing deeply to settle his thoughts. Was it true, what Mahabat said? That the nobles snickered openly at his obsession for Mehrunnisa? That they called his love for her by this abominable name? Had they lost respect for him?

Jahangir was crushed all of a sudden. For many nights he stayed awake watching over Mehrunnisa as she lay in her bed, not even wanting to live. During the days he attended his audiences and court business, but without any heart. These were duties, they had to be done, what he wanted was to be with his wife. Now he remembered that a few nobles at court had lounged indolently in front of him, leaning against a pillar, clasping their arms below their elbows in huge breaches of etiquette; at the time, he had noticed but had not paid heed to it. Etiquette had not seemed important when his very life was in danger of being overthrown.

And again he thought of Mahabat's coming to speak to him, *daring* to speak to him. How could that have happened unless, for some reason, for the very reason Mahabat had spoken of, Jahangir had lost the reverence of his people?

He fretted thus until Mehrunnisa returned back to the palaces the next day. At court, the Emperor was more solemn—no more lounging was allowed, infractions against his person or his court were reprimanded, order brought to its knees again. The murmurings ceased, silence regained its hold at court, and the only voice heard was Emperor Jahangir's.

That night, the chief writer of the harem was reading out her journal to the royal couple. The writer was employed specially to keep a day-to-day journal of zenana happenings. Everything of significance was recorded in that book: names and relationships of visitors to the harem women; purchases made by the ladies; their requests for money; and even the length of their private conversations with eunuchs. It was a highly efficient spy system. The ladies were watched every day, and nothing they did went unnoticed by the spies interspersed throughout the zenana. It was hard to tell who was a spy. It could be a maid faithful for twenty years, a new eunuch appointed for the purpose, a mali in the garden brought in to water the flowerpots... it could be anyone.

Mehrunnisa played listlessly with the rubies on a silver plate next to her, dropping the stones through her fingers. Jahangir watched her thoughtfully. She had seemed pleased at the gift but had not listened when he had given her suggestions about how the jewels should be set. In her turban? That was fine. A new necklace? That was fine too. A set of six sherbet goblets in jade? Fine again.

She paid no notice to him anymore, weighed down with her sorrow. It came and went as it pleased, with no warning, one moment she would laugh and he would join in so happily, at another she would be silent, barely lifting her head.

Now she did not listen to the writer, where once she would be sitting on the edge of her divan, nodding as the writer spoke.

'Mehrunnisa,' Jahangir said gently, 'would you like the writer to leave now?'

'As you wish, your Majesty.'

'Would you like to listen to some music?' he asked.

'No.'

Irritated by this response, Jahangir put his hand under her chin and raised her eyes to his. 'Well, I would like to listen. Hoshiyar, command the orchestra to play.'

'Do not, Hoshiyar,' Mehrunnisa said. 'The music will tire me.'

'Everything tires you now, my dear. The music will only relax you.' The Emperor's voice held an edge to it.

She shook her head, and Hoshiyar stood between them, hesitant, not quite knowing what to do. 'If only I could believe you were solicitous of my health, your Majesty.' She said this softly, leaning towards him.

'What?' Jahangir flared up. He had tried to tell himself that this swerving of her moods would end, that in a few days she would settle down. It was for her he had done this, courted the insolence of his nobles and his empire, why was she so ungrateful? How could she even think that he did nothing for her?

'I hear Mahabat Khan came to visit, your Majesty. I also heard he was most concerned for you, and unconcerned for me, and that you did nothing about it.'

'Mehrunnisa.' He opened his arms, but she moved away. 'Please, my love, come here and listen.'

Tears came to her eyes and she shook her head. He watched them fall down her face, and an ache began to grow inside him. She was still so lovely to look at, so graceful as she sat there, her ghagara spangled with tiny emeralds that glittered in the lamplight. Her wrists were slung with the gold bangles he had given her, but her eyelashes were wet with crying. He had given her everything material, anything that his empire could command was at her service, but she would not be appeased. How could give her the child she so wanted?

'You have Ladli, Mehrunnisa.'

She raised angry eyes at him. 'She is a girl, only the child I carried would have been worthwhile. You know this, your Majesty. What use am I now?' Her words were bitter, hurtful.

Suddenly he was furious. Jahangir turned away from her and signalled to Hoshiyar. The eunuch nodded his head, and the music began to play from the orchestra balcony above them. Slave girls brought in wine and poured out a gobletful for the Emperor. Why was he even doing this? Why cajole a stubborn wife out of her obstinacy? If she wanted to mourn, let her.

He drank steadily and in silence. Mehrunnisa stopped crying. She had waited for the ache in her heart to settle, to go away somewhere, to be banished. But it would not. She was angry too, and in this anger, she asked, 'You have said nothing about Mahabat Khan, your Majesty.'

'What do you want me to say, Mehrunnisa? He asked for an audience, for a chance to speak of what was in his mind. I allowed it. I would allow it again; Mahabat Khan is a trusted minister, he is a friend of old, he has nothing but my best interests at heart.' He drained his wine and held out the goblet for more.

Hoshiyar Khan coughed in the background. 'Your Majesty,' he addressed the Emperor. 'Prince Shahryar requests an audience.'

Jahangir waved a languid hand. The door to the hall opened, and a boy came into the room, or rather, his nurse, wife of one of the nobles at court, dragged him in. Shahryar was nine, born the same year as Ladli. All of Shahryar's brief life had been spent under the supervision of nurses, one after another, almost one every year. Just as he became attached to a woman, developed an affection and learned to sleep through the night without any fears, the guard would change around him. This was on Empress Jagat Gosini's orders. She knew that Khurram could have little threat from Shahryar, but she wanted to make sure that even that smallest danger was removed from her son's life. There had been a precedent for a nursemaid gaining power in her charge's name—Emperor Akbar had had one such wet nurse who had ruled the empire for a few years before he had dismissed her. So Jagat Gosini kept Shahryar unsettled at all times. Even this young, the prince knew he could trust no one, that his nurses were playmates for a short time and that they would be whisked away.

Prince Shahryar was a beautiful child, Mehrunnisa thought. His hair was still curly and long like a girl's, his eyes were a bright black, but behind this outer face, she did not think much existed. The prince was like well-kneaded dough, easily shaping himself into whatever plans the people around him suggested. He had no mind of his own. When his nurse whispered in his ear, Shahryar came forward to perform the taslim, and he did this awkwardly, without any grace.

'*Al-Salam alekum*, your Majesty,' Shahryar said. He looked around the room.

It was a large, rectangular hall with a high-domed ceiling. A balcony ran all around on top, supported by an arched hallway below. The corridor on one side was lined with another set of open arches leading to the gardens. The prince wriggled his toes in the deep pile of the red carpets on the marble floor. In one corner, a silk-covered divan reposed, strewn with jewelled cushions and velvet bolsters. Mehrunnisa and Jahangir were surrounded by attendants, eunuchs, slave girls and servants. In front of them, gold and silver trays bore flasks of wine, paan and sweets and delicacies from the imperial kitchens.

Shahryar looked greedily at the sweets. He did not see such richness in his apartments. Every nurse had her own rules, and this current one did not think that sweets were good for his health. He tried to be respectful and stand with his head bowed in front of his father and stepmother, but his gaze kept moving to the tray. The gulab jamuns looked so plump and soft, surely they would ooze sugar syrup when he bit into them. The *son papdi*, dressed with pistachios, was flaky, made with a light hand—this would melt upon contact with his tongue. And the burfis, in all different colours, made of wheat and chickpea flour and coconut, gold and purple and green and white... all scattered with cashews, sultanas and raisins roasted in ghee. He hung over the tray without realizing, his mouth open.

'Would you like some sweets, Shahryar?' Mehrunnisa asked, unable to bear the sight of the boy salivating over the plate.

He stepped back hurriedly, tripped on the edge of a carpet, and went down. His nurse picked him up. Shahryar bowed and said, 'Whatever you wish, your Majesty.'

'Oh, take him away. Take him away now,' Mehrunnisa said. Did the child not even know what he wanted? She pushed the plate of sweets at the prince. 'Here, take this and go.'

Shahryar's face became red. His nurse caught him at his collar and started to pull him backward from the room. Mehrunnisa rose from her divan and went up to him. She patted him on the head and he recoiled from her hand, not used to gestures of affection. 'Go, Shahryar,' she said more gently. 'Come and visit us at another time, now is not good.'

'I apologize, your Majesty,' the prince said, beginning to cry.

'You have nothing to be penitent for, Shahryar. Go now.'

Shahryar left the room sniffling, and Mehrunnisa returned to the divan, ashamed of herself. The Emperor had not moved at all through Shahryar's visit, or if he had, it was only to drink. How many cups had he had already? Five? Six? Perhaps more, but today, Mehrunnisa had no strength to argue with him, no will to stop his goblet from rising to his lips. She sat trembling at her place, her mind rioting with thoughts. What was this uneasiness? She had never felt it before, not even when she had had the previous miscarriages. But somehow, the promise of this child and that he would be a son, and that she would teach him how to rule the empire—this had come upon her in the two short months she had carried the child with such a force of feeling that it still stayed. Even now, when there was no child.

Mehrunnisa doubted herself too now. The hakims said, in no

uncertain terms, that there would never be another child. They explained their reasons for this, but she scarcely heard them, concentrating instead on those words, *no more children*. Why was this happening to her? Why was her body so traitorous? And what did the Emperor think of this? Ever since Mahabat's visit, something had changed. Hoshiyar had told her of the meeting, and of what had been said during it. At another time, when she was less vulnerable, less fearful, Mehrunnisa would have been in a rage with Mahabat, but now...

Mehrunnisa had returned to the zenana as fast as she could after hearing of Mahabat's visit from Hoshiyar, even though she was to have stayed at her father's house a few more days. But it was important that she be by Jahangir's side, and yet, each time he spoke, each time she opened her own mouth, nothing but bitterness seemed to come out. She was irritated even with the mild, donkey-like Shahryar, who was so harmless. When she looked at Shahryar, she thought of the child she should have had. *He* should have lived; if this boy could, why not her own son?

Mehrunnisa rubbed her face and leaned sideways against a silk-covered bolster. What stupidity it was to think over and over again about the child, what he could have been, what she would have done with him. The reality was that he was not here, would never be here. Where was her resolve? Where was her strength? If she lost this, she would lose Jahangir.

She cried again, and this time, she noticed, the Emperor did not reach out to her. He sat by her side, so close, and yet they had nothing to say to each other, no words of comfort to offer. The deep trust between them seemed to have been slowly rinsed away by something neither of them could control.

Mehrunnisa heard Jahangir ask for yet another glass of wine, and suddenly, after all these days of mourning and feeling angry and sorry for herself and generally living on the periphery of life, something snapped in her brain. She sat up and put a hand on Jahangir's arm.

'This will be your last cup today, your Majesty.'

He shook his head. 'Remember that it is not your place to tell me what to do, Mehrunnisa. I am your Emperor. *You* must listen to me. If I wish to drink, I will do so.' Jahangir drank the wine fast, until he was choking, and then held out his cup for more. It was filled, and defiantly he raised it again to his mouth.

Mehrunnisa grabbed the cup from him, spilling wine on the front of the Emperor's embroidered qaba, and threw it against a pillar. The cup, made of white jade studded with rubies, shattered into tiny pieces, the wine leaving a stain on the marble of the pillar.

He wrenched at her shoulder until she faced him, and then his hand swung in an arc through the air and came into contact with her cheek. The slap rumbled through the room and brought on its heels a huge silence. The musicians in the balcony above stopped playing, the slaves and eunuchs froze where they stood. No one knew what to do. And neither did Mehrunnisa, for a few seconds. Then her arm went back, her fingers in a fist, moving from below to connect with Jahangir's chin.

Within minutes, they were rolling around on the floor, yelling and screaming. They spit at each other, tried to claw each other's eyes out, and punched one another. Mehrunnisa's veil came off her head and her hair came undone. Jahangir ineffectually tried to ward off her blows with his hands. Shame had already come to leave its mark on him. He knew he should not have hit a woman, he had been taught not to do so, and even deep in his cups, he had never done this before. But this time... something had turned in his brain, had taken over his thinking. He stopped fighting, gave up, tried to shout at Mehrunnisa that they should halt, but she was too enraged and he could not stop her.

The attendants watched amazed as the couple rolled over

again; this time Jahangir lay on the ground and Mehrunnisa sat astride him. She slapped Jahangir four times with an open palm.

The servants dithered in the background, shifting from foot to foot. No one had ever before hit the Emperor, either in his childhood or his youth. And here he was, meekly taking a beating from his wife. Should they go and break up the fight? The event was unprecedented; no other Mughal Emperor had fought with his wife so disgracefully before. What were they to do?

Just then, the room resounded with yells from the orchestra balcony, followed by a series of deep, skin-thumping thuds.

In the hall below, Mehrunnisa looked up in surprise. Who was dying? She jumped off Jahangir and gave him her hand. They ran up the stairs to the orchestra balcony. When they got there, one of the sitar players was lying on the floor, shouting out nonsense, 'Save me. O Lord, save me!' He wriggled on the floor, beat himself on his chest, and screamed out each time he did so. Then he saw them and stopped, rising to perform the taslim. 'Your Majesties, I hope the fight is over.'

The Emperor and Mehrunnisa stood panting at the top of the stairs. Now they were both ashamed. The orchestra had very effectively broken up their quarrel by creating a diversion.

'Hoshiyar, scatter gold over these men, they have done well,' Jahangir said. He turned to Mehrunnisa. 'Shall we leave to take care of our persons, my dear?'

Mehrunnisa nodded and followed Jahangir down the stairs and back into the reception hall. Her hair had escaped from its plait and her scalp burned near her nape where the Emperor had yanked it. She could feel an ache on her right cheekbone, and her eye was already swelling shut. They both had wine spilled on them and were now redolent of it. Mehrunnisa's anger had abated somewhat. Even her pain had gone, she thought, in the fighting her pain had gone.

Jahangir was limping, and she asked, 'Did you twist your ankle, your Majesty?'

He turned to her. 'It is best you go to your apartments, Mehrunnisa. I will take care of myself, and you must get Hoshiyar to look after you.' When she opened her mouth, he cut her short. 'We should not have forgotten who we are. Fighting like animals, with no sense of decorum... what are people in the empire going to say about this? Come to me, Mehrunnisa, only when you wish to ask pardon, and no sooner than that. I will wait for your apologies. But only for so long.'

She stood mute, stunned, disbelieving that Jahangir would talk to her like this in front of all the servants. She walked away slowly and went to Ladli's room. Her daughter slept slanted across the divan, the silk sheet thrown off, her pyjamas riding up to her knees. Mehrunnisa climbed onto the divan and put her head next to Ladli's. The child's hand came up to touch her hair.

'Mama?' she said wanderingly, half-asleep.

'Yes, beta.' She gathered her into her arms, and Ladli sighed. She did not ask why her mother came to her like this at night after so many nights away. Mehrunnisa was tired, so shattered by everything that had happened lately.

One evening, as Mehrunnisa had lain recovering on her divan after losing the child, Hoshiyar had brought Ladli to see her. Ladli had stood at the door to her apartments, eyes luminous with fright, tears trembling just behind, until Mehrunnisa had called to her. Then, she had run in to cling to her mother, so tightly that Mehrunnisa could not breathe until the embrace ended.

'I am sorry, Mama,' Ladli had said. 'You really wanted this child, did you not?'

'Yes,' Mehrunnisa had said, 'Yes, beta. I wanted him very much.'

With her face still buried in her mother's neck, Ladli had said,

'And would you... have loved him more, Mama?'

'No,' Mehrunnisa had said automatically, only half-listening, starting to weep again.

Her daughter had swabbed gently at Mehrunnisa's face with her little hands and said, 'Better to have a girl, Mama. A boy... he would have to fight for many things when he is older. Boys always fight, don't they?'

Mehrunnisa remembered now how she had turned from Ladli and called to Hoshiyar to take her away. And those words she had paid so little heed to—*and would you have loved him more, Mama*—came to crush her. She had thought Ladli not important, what kind of a mother was she? What kind of a person was she? No matter what happened now, she would always have Ladli. She started to cry, and in sleep Ladli patted her, reacting instinctively. Mehrunnisa closed her eyes after a long time, terrified and lonely. She was comforted by Ladli, but she also wanted the comfort of Jahangir's presence.

What was happening to them?

The eunuchs and slaves stayed in the reception hall only long enough to sweep up the shards of the wine cup and straighten out the divan and the carpets. They blew out the oil lamps and left the room in darkness. Then they ran through the palaces of the zenana, waking the women to tell them of what had happened. The story fled from ear to avidly listening ear, brought laughter and glee to faces. With each telling it took on horrific proportions, Mehrunnisa had slapped the Emperor, she had punched him in the stomach, he had hit her back—true, of course, but the tale became cheerfully embellished. They had said bitter things to each other. Jahangir never wanted to see her again. She was expelled from the harem, sent to live with her father and mother. The horse hooves heard in the street outside was the carriage carrying her away.

The rumours found their way to Prince Khurram's apartments also, where he lay in bed with Arjumand. They were to have their first child in two months, and unlike Mehrunnisa, her niece had no trouble keeping the baby inside her. Her stomach was hugely rounded, and she had all the satisfying symptoms of a healthy pregnancy—the bloated face, the heavy feet, the loss of hunger as the child grew within to compress her stomach.

Arjumand woke to the voice of the eunuch who bent to fill Khurram's ear about the fight before padding out of the room. She was turned away from her husband, her back to his, but she was listening nonetheless. Khurram put his arm around her and rubbed her stomach lightly.

'Did you hear?' he asked softly.

'Yes,' she replied. 'I have been awake.'

'This is disgraceful,' Khurram said. 'If you fought with me like this, I could not bear it, Arjumand.'

She turned around, but laboriously, rising first to sit, then to turn, and then to lie down facing her husband. She touched his face in the dark with her fingers. 'We are different, your Highness. You must know that I would never disrespect you like my aunt does the Emperor. My aunt does not do her duty; she is in the zenana to bear children, now they say there will be no more. I would never do this to you. I know my place.'

'Yes, and this is what I love about you, my darling. Mehrunnisa emasculates my father, makes him less of a man by insisting that she play his role.' Khurram gathered her closer, as close as her distended stomach would allow him.

Arjumand did what Khurram wanted her to do, what she had been taught a woman should. It was her duty to follow her husband's commands, to be what he wanted her to be. It had surprised her at first that her submission was such a novelty for him. Then she realized that all the women around Khurram before her—Ruqayya, his mother, and Mehrunnisa—were used to demanding things that strained the binds of convention. He had thought this behaviour natural, until Arjumand had taught him otherwise. She put Khurram on a pedestal, deferred to him, touched his feet every morning for his blessings on her day. Arjumand would never trample over her husband, this she had decided many years ago, for she saw what this did to a woman's reputation. No one thought of Ruqayya or Jagat Gosini or Mehrunnisa as feminine, they were strident, troublesome... almost man-like. This, Arjumand decided, she would *never* be.

'Khurram,' she said. 'I do not like that you spend so much time in conversation with my aunt. Forgive me for saying this, but you must rely upon my father and my grandfather. They are men of experience and wisdom, they will definitely know how best to advise, much better than the Empress. Do you not think so?'

'Of course,' he said. 'But the Empress is in distress right now, Arjumand. The fight with my father cannot be very pleasant. What will happen to them? I wonder if this news is true, that she has been sent away. I cannot believe his Majesty will allow her to go, he was so anxious when she was unwell.'

'Do not talk of her, Khurram.' A terseness came to Arjumand's voice.

'But she is your aunt, Arjumand. Don't you care for her?'

'Of course,' she said hastily. 'I do worry about her too. But this predicament is of her own making. Had she respected the Emperor as she should have, this would not have happened. If she insists upon making trouble for herself, we can do nothing about it. Remember, my lord, that if she had the child, and if it had been a boy, she would not have been so pleasant to you.'

Khurram laughed. 'Arjumand, you worry too much. No one can take away my right to the throne after my father.'

'It is not just your right anymore, Khurram. Think of the son

I am carrying, your first son, the child who will be Emperor after you. I do not feel that the Empress would have taken either you or our son into consideration if she had one of her own.'

He was silent, thinking about what she said. Arjumand's breathing evened as she fell asleep. But for Khurram, rest did not come that night. It was all very well for them to form a junta, all very well to have Mehrunnisa at the head of it... until now. His own father had been held up to derision because of her. How long would it be before that extended to him? And the crown was uncertain, as much as he tried to convince himself otherwise—if the nobles at court thought him easily led by a woman, they would not support him. At least his father had the advantage of already holding the title of Emperor. Arjumand was right—she was an unnatural woman.

So Khurram allowed himself to be led by yet another woman, but the hand was soft, the tug gentle, and he did not realize it was happening. Arjumand was outraged that Mehrunnisa would have so much power and authority despite being childless for the Emperor. Only the mother of the future heir could, and should, have any domination in the empire. So she told Khurram this, and neither of them remembered that had it not been for Mehrunnisa, that at one word from her, their own marriage—that gave birth to such ideas and the future sons for the empire—would not have taken place.

During the next two weeks, just as there had been a hush during Mehrunnisa's illness, mouths now flapped energetically. Jahangir did not visit his wife, and the Empress made no move towards an apology. It gave the gossips something to talk about, and it gave them hope that there would be a shift of power in the harem and more excitement in their lives.

It was the end of the reign of the Empress.

Chapter Ten

But the queen, after the custom of petted women, showed herself more angry and offended than before... In the end, through a third person, she gave Jahangir to understand that the only way of being pardoned for the affront was to throw hinges at her feet.

— WILLIAM IRVINE, TRANS.,
Storia do Mogor by Niccolao Manucci

'ALL IS WELL AND IT IS TIME TO RISE!' THE NIGHT WATCHMAN SANG OUT. He tapped his stick on the hard dirt ground of the street outside the palace, one tap for each hour of the morning.

In her sleep, Mehrunnisa heard those taps, and with her eyes still closed, she counted them. It was the second pahr of the day. She heard Hoshiyar come into the room, and she opened her eyes as he approached the bed.

'How does it look today, Hoshiyar?'

He touched the skin on her forehead, between her brows, and she felt his callused thumb rub over a ridge. 'The colours are muted, your Majesty, but the scar will remain.'

'Bring me a mirror.'

When Hoshiyar held the mirror in front of her, Mehrunnisa sat up to peer into it. Outside, the sky was scrubbed with the pale greys of dawn, and only a little light came into her apartments. Her wounds had all healed, except for the gash on her forehead, where one of Jahangir's rings had cut into the skin. This had bled for a day after, and then the skin had knitted itself tight, and when she spoke she could feel it strain on her face. It was not a big cut, less than the end of her little finger, and now, in healing, it puckered up, shaped like a spear.

The other discolourations were gone. The Emperor's hand had left its imprint on her cheek, near her hairline, four neat lines of fingers. She had bumped her head as they had rolled around and that had swollen over her eyebrow, shutting one eye. Mehrunnisa wailed at the sight of her face the next morning, she had lost everything now. How could she even go before Jahangir with this face?

But Hoshiyar had worked miracles. He made her drink goat's milk with saffron each morning, and he applied a thick paste of lime and chickpea flour on the skin. He also brought strange-looking, strange-smelling poultices that made her gag, but she submitted to them, sitting for hours as they dried to cake on her face.

Now only the scar remained. And as Hoshiyar said, it would stay.

'Is it time to dress?'

'The nobles will be gathering at the jharoka in half an hour, your Majesty.' He brought her a copper vessel with water, and when she put her chin forward, he washed her face. Two slave girls came in silently and bowed.

Mehrunnisa brushed her teeth and stood as they dressed her. This was an effort each morning; even waking up was an effort. She had returned to the jharoka audiences a few days after the fight. In the beginning, the crowds were thin, the nobles arrogant, their voices louder than usual, their bows much shallower. But she did not let them cow her. She kept her tone firm, no flattery pleased her, no disrespect made her lose her temper. But each day she came back physically exhausted. And each morning she forced herself to go again.

As she walked down the corridor of her apartments, she looked across the courtyard at Jahangir's palace. He would be awake too, and getting ready for his jharoka appearance. They had long settled into this routine where each of them gave audience in different parts of the fort, where they had different petitioners. Would she see him today? If she did, would he look at her? She stumbled, on nothing really but her thoughts, and Hoshiyar caught her elbow.

'Courage, your Majesty,' he said in her ear.

Mehrunnisa nodded. Courage she *would* have, after so many weeks of weakness. The child was gone, so what of that? She had Ladli. She had her pride. She was still Empress Nur Jahan. But... if only the Emperor would return, a voice inside her spoke. It was lonely and frightening to live like this. In the beginning she had still been angry, although most of that anger had been frittered away in the fight. She did not want to apologize, to be the first to bow her head, to acknowledge wrong. Everyone insisted on this, and her back grew rigid with each insisting. Bapa sent messages, Abul ridiculed her, and Ruqayya grew strident, thinking all her advantages lost. There had been other times, Mehrunnisa remembered these well, when again the weight of all opinions had tried to pin her down. But she had resisted, as she resisted right after the fight.

The desolation crept in at night. Hoshiyar was there, Ladli came to share her bed sometimes, but it was Jahangir she wanted. The performance at the jharoka, the impertinence, was repeated every single day. Slaves backed out of the room only till the doorway before turning. Someone had moved the royal seal from her desk to under her desk, as though saying it would not long be hers.

If she were to go to the Emperor and beg his pardon, there would be nothing left for her in the zenana, this much Mehrunnisa knew. Her name, her title, her possessing the royal seal—all these would mean little now. But she also knew she had done wrong, that Jahangir had been more than indulgent with her. She knew that she was stupid to stay away, and anxious that some other woman was right now capturing his affections. How would she bear this? After all these years of wanting to be Jahangir's wife, how could she live with this? But then, how to go back and apologize without losing face? The Emperor had shown no indication that he would welcome an apology either...

But that morning at the jharoka, Jahangir did show Mehrunnisa his favour. When she entered the balcony, she saw the Ahadis, the Emperor's personal bodyguards, lined up on either side of the courtyard. The captain of the team announced her, the rest of the men watched the nobles as they bowed. She was announced three times, even though she stood in front of the men, until the captain was satisfied that the taslim had been performed as it ought to be, as it ought to be in front of Emperor Jahangir himself.

When it was over, Mehrunnisa ran back through the corridors of the palaces, her veil streaming behind her, and rushed into Jahangir's chambers. He had returned earlier and was now in bed again for his two-hour nap before the day's duties began.

She knelt before him and kissed his hands. 'I am sorry, your Majesty. Please forgive me.'

He touched the scar on her forehead. 'Will that go?'

'Hoshiyar says no. But I am now'—Mehrunnisa laughed and put her arms around him—'marked by you, your Majesty.'

'You do not mind?' he asked.

'Not if you don't.'

'I have been miserable without you, my love. Come to me as you will, with scars and warts and even grimaces, no perhaps not grimaces, but come to me as you will, and never go away.' Jahangir made space for Mehrunnisa on the divan.

They lay together, hip to hip, shoulder to shoulder, with

Mehrunnisa safe against Jahangir's chest. The monsoon rains had begun, and outside the windows, it fell heavy and steady. Coolness swept into the room, and the curtains—of a light silk the colour of pond water—crested inward and ebbed.

'Mehrunnisa,' the Emperor murmured.

She made a sound, lulled into lethargy by the rain.

'Do what you will with Mahabat.'

'Can I?' she asked, her voice drowsy.

They slept then, as they had since they were married, their breathing hushed and comfortable, secure that no one was ever going to break them apart. But before their eyes closed, Mehrunnisa asked a favour.

When the rains broke late that afternoon over the Anguri Bagh within the Agra Fort, a few clouds still abided in the skies, dense with wetness. The lawns were damp, and the leaves of the tamarind and the *champa* glistened. Water in the square ponds lay rippleless, mists rising from the surface. The Anguri Bagh, the garden of grapes, was so named not because grapevines stretched around but because the bottom courtyard was laid with a honeycomb of brick plots filled with damask roses, mimicking a cluster of grapes.

The roses were in full flower this summer, dead wood pruned carefully and lovingly, earlier in the year, by the royal malis. Each plot held just one plant of the Ispahan, the pink damask rose brought from the hillsides of Isfahan in Persia. The plots overflowed with the thick, green, shiny leaves and stems, crammed with the pink flowers turning their lovely faces to the sun.

The women came out of the harem palaces in crowds. They sat on the stone steps that led into the courtyard, watched as their children swung from the lower branches of a tamarind, running away in glee as the leaves shed water. In the soft light of the monsoon sun, the Ispahan roses gleamed with drops of rain—

diamonds scattered on pink satin. The zenana women leaned into one another, wondering why they had been summoned here. Whispers rose and hung in the washed afternoon air, passing from mouth to ear, mingling with the shrieks of children's laughter. One word was oft repeated. *Mehrunnisa.* Something to do with Mehrunnisa... but what? Was she going to be publicly humiliated?

The women fell quiet as eunuchs came into the Anguri Bagh, bearing large gold and silver platters heaped with pink rose petals. *What was this? An offering for a prayer?* A eunuch swept the marble pathway that cut across the centre of the courtyard of brick plots, his broom moving in noiseless swishes. *What was this for?* Then, two eunuchs knelt on the eastern edge of the path and laid down the petals, each petal turned up. As they worked, another slave followed them, dripping a single drop of rose water into the centre of every petal's cupped and upturned face. The work was painstakingly detailed—the petals were inspected for bruises and marks, used or discarded accordingly, and laid exactly half an inch from each other until the path was no longer the white of unblemished marble but a pink, perfumed, glittering carpet cutting a swathe through the living Ispahans on either side.

An hour passed, and then two, and the afternoon wore on. The women waited, sensing something was about to happen, something huge and significant. When the heat of the afternoon surged, the rose petals let loose their fiery aroma into the air, cloying and filling.

The women did not see Mehrunnisa until she was among them. She stood at the top of the steps on the eastern edge of the fort, the Yamuna flowing behind her, the dusty plains in the background, and waited for them to look at her. Then, slowly, and with great deliberation, she went down the steps to the edge of the pathway. When her foot first touched the rose petals, voices rose within the women's minds and hearts—*careful, watch where you put your feet. These are the Ispahans.* But not one word was spoken aloud.

Mehrunnisa wore white—a widow's colour—her ghagara made of chiffon was peasant-plain. Her choli was white too, but this was thickly studded with diamonds, and her face glowed in the reflected light from the stones. The women watched, mouths watering, eyes greedily catching the brilliancy of the diamonds. Mehrunnisa wore no veil, nothing else to cover her but her hair, which went down in a smooth sheet of soot black to her waist. As she walked, the skirts of her ghagara swirled over the rose petals, destroying their careful arrangement on the marble slabs. Mehrunnisa went up to the centre of the pathway and stood waiting in the sunshine. The diamonds on her twinkled with every breath, capturing the light from the sun.

Emperor Jahangir entered from the other end, the western end of the courtyard. He did not notice, and did not acknowledge, the bows of the women of his zenana, nor did he reply to the salutations. He too walked down the steps to the yard below, weaving his way through the crowds, and went down the pathway to meet Mehrunnisa.

The women leaned forward in their seats. This was so obviously staged, so patently a drama of some kind, a ritual, but what was it? They watched as Jahangir moved closer to Mehrunnisa, his shadow moving gracefully ahead of him. He stopped, perhaps just a carpet-length from her, and his shadow stopped with him. They stood looking at each other, and ears strained to hear words. But no, there was no sound. Only... the Emperor started to move forward again, and every woman shouted out the same phrase in her mind. *Move away, Mehrunnisa. Move away. Step aside.* But she did not move. She did not look down either as Jahangir's shadow—just his head and chest—draped over the bottom half of Mehrunnisa's ghagara.

A deep sigh drifted through the courtyard as every eye there gazed upon the dark grey shadow across Mehrunnisa's feet. So sacred was the Emperor's person that even his shadow could not fall upon anyone near him. If it did, it meant he had fallen at their feet, bowed before them—it was unthinkable.

Mehrunnisa stepped away and went to her husband. As they stood there, now side by side, letting the zenana see them together, she said, 'Thank you, your Majesty. You have restored my name to me.'

He clasped her hand and they went back to their apartments, scattering the rose petals as they walked. 'Let them all know, Mehrunnisa, that there is no one quite as important to me as you are. It shall always be thus.'

The women of the imperial harem left the Anguri Bagh, overwhelmed by what they had seen and filled with yearning. Each had wanted to walk upon the rose-strewn pathway, each wanted to feel the soft bruise of the petals under her feet, to stand in the bright sunlight and have Jahangir's shadow cast its darkness upon her. To be the most brilliant rose among the royal damasks. To be literally *feasted* thus, so sumptuously, with roses. This was a banquet like none other. The flowers were used, of course, to adorn marriage beds, or sling about necks in garlands or nestle in hair. But this—to so negligently strew them on the floor, and in such large quantities so as to divest a whole garden, and simply for treading upon with feet—this was unprecedented.

For the next few weeks, the women talked of nothing else. Those who had watched the reunion gossiped about it, exaggerating almost everything. The choli Mehrunnisa wore, it had a thousand diamonds sewn into the fabric, each exactly like its neighbour. Her feet did not burn when the Emperor's shadow fell upon it because she was a sorceress. How else could she have cajoled the Emperor into denuding the rose garden for a few seconds of pleasure?

Prince Khurram heard of the event; he was not there, and until it happened, did not actually believe his father would debase himself thus. But he did hesitate when news was brought to him. Arjumand and he were in his apartments that afternoon, and he was reading to her as she poked a needle into some silk, but her fingers were fat with the pregnancy, and the needle slipped more often than not.

'The entire garden of Ispahans,' Arjumand said softly, imagining the scene in her head. 'Would you do this for me, Khurram?'

'Of course,' he replied, but his mind was not with her.

'Would you?' She nudged his chin toward her.

He rubbed her back with one hand, the book still in the other. 'Yes, my dear. I would. I will make a garden for you, a forest, anything you want.'

'His Majesty adores my aunt, Khurram,' Arjumand said, a little wistful now. And so Khurram loved her too... did he not? But such lavishness for her aunt, who was an old woman, a beautiful woman, true... envy pricked inside her, tiny at first and then, suddenly raging. 'How can his Majesty allow her to demean him so, and in public?'

But Khurram had turned away from his wife and was looking out the windows. Arjumand talked on for the next half hour—she would never do this to Khurram, never demand an apology like this, she was always considerate of his reputation. Behind all her protestations lay jealousy. Like the other women of the zenana, Arjumand wanted this feast of roses for herself, wanted it to bear *her* name, not Mehrunnisa's.

Khurram heard little of her tirade. He was thinking, and he did not confide his thoughts in Arjumand. Instead, Khurram went to pay his long overdue respects to Mehrunnisa. Khurram was not stupid, ambitious he was, but not so filled with pride that he could not see that Mehrunnisa had come back to reign over the zenana and over the court. He did not see the feast of roses as an opulent mark of favour from a man to his beloved; he saw it for what it actually was—his father had bestowed power unto Mehrunnisa, now and for always. And she too was now stronger somehow. After the events of the past few months, a second skin had formed over her, thin as an eggshell, resilient as iron.

In an inner sanctum of the fort at Agra, within the walls of the imperial zenana, lay the Khel Aangan. It was a courtyard of sixty-four unblemished black and white marble squares, hand-polished to a seamless shine. The roof yawned to the sky above. On breathless summer days, as the sun drenched the palaces, the black squares swallowed the light; the white reflected it pearl-like in a mosaic of deep pools and still, white water. The squares measured ten feet on each side. On one side of the courtyard, raised from the ground, was a marble balcony strewn with divans and pearl-studded cushions.

As the sun set over Agra, lingering in the western sky for a brief equatorial moment before being scooped into the earth, torches flared to life in sconces set high on pillars that surrounded the courtyard.

Hoshiyar led Mahabat Khan into the balcony and let go of his hand.

'You may open your eyes now.'

Mahabat opened his eyes slowly, his heart thumping. He first looked at Hoshiyar, unwilling to let his gaze stray, aware that he was within the imperial zenana, where few men unrelated to the royal family were invited. Mahabat had been in the periphery of the harem before, of course, in reception halls where he had met the Emperor, and gardens where he met Jagat Gosini. But he had never been this far inside.

The eunuch nodded. 'You may look around, Mirza Khan. It is safe.'

'Thank you for bringing me here.'

Hoshiyar let a small smile crease his mouth. 'Her Majesty commanded your presence. She does you a great honour, Mirza Khan, by allowing you within the walls of the harem. It is an even greater honour that you were given permission to come this far with only your eyes closed, not covered with a sheet like the physicians. She has trusted you.'

'I know,' Mahabat said, acerbity in his voice. Hoshiyar was reminding him, none too subtly, of his meetings with Empress Jagat Gosini in the zenana gardens all those years ago. Then, Hoshiyar Khan had been Jagat Gosini's eunuch, with the Emperor's ear and the Empress's faith. Now, he served another mistress. Just how much had he told her about Mahabat's meetings with Empress Jagat Gosini? Mahabat waved his hand. 'You may go now.'

Hoshiyar bowed. 'I most certainly will, Mirza Khan. The Empress must be informed of your arrival.'

When he left, Mahabat looked around him. It was dark by now, the sky a soft velvet studded with glimmering stars, but it was the courtyard below that drew his attention. The light from the torches and oil lamps glowed gold in the warm air. Mahabat leaned over the balcony, his blood alive with excitement, assaulted by the perfume of incense. His hands trembled as they rested on the marble balustrade of the balcony. No other man he knew had seen this famous Khel Aangan, the courtyard of play. Legend had it that Emperor Akbar had had the workmen sent into exile once they had finished work on this part of the imperial zenana, so they could not talk of it, in seriousness or in jest. And no one would build another quite like it.

And now he, Mahabat Khan, was here. When the summons had come to him the night before, Mahabat had stared at the curved writing for a long time, disbelieving what his eyes read. *In the Khel Aangan,* she said, *will you honour me with your presence, Mirza Mahabat Khan. His Majesty wishes to reward you for many years of devotion, so you are to be invited to the zenana as my guest. I have heard much of your prowess in Shatranj; perhaps when you visit you will agree to play a game with me?*

Mahabat had touched the paper, disregarding the eunuch who waited for a reply. It had been well written, lyrical, almost poetic. And though it had been polite, what he had held in his hands had been an imperial summons, one he could not refuse. When the eunuch had departed with his answer, Mahabat had swallowed a deep draught of his wine. Setting the goblet down, he tried to think of a precedent. It was not entirely uncommon for Mughal Emperors to invite strange men to the zenana, but only when they were vassal kings or other high dignitaries. It was a sign of favour, usually done in the hope that the honour would make the guest more amenable to signing a treaty or offering his support to the empire. In just one other case had the man thus honoured been a commoner. Emperor Jahangir had ordered the ladies of his harem to go unveiled in front of Ghias Beg. But Mirza Beg was Mehrunnisa's father, and grandfather of Prince Khurram's wife. His blood lay in the imperial harem; he had strong ties to it. Mahabat could claim no such kinship. Now these summons. No title, no amount of wealth, no grants of land could match this.

It had been a month since his talk with Emperor Jahangir, Mahabat thought as his legs weakened under him. He sat down on a velvet-covered divan, his hands suddenly cold. This summons was a result of that talk, of that he had no doubt. But why? He must have displeased Mehrunnisa when he had gone to the Emperor with his complaint. Yet here he was being rewarded.

An elephant trumpeted softly, and Mahabat rose from his seat to look down into the courtyard again, his mind imprinted with the picture in front of him, his brain storing every exquisite detail.

The floor stretched gleaming in front of him, shining dully in the lamplight. The board was set with live pieces for chess, and

Mahabat's eyes greedily skimmed over the pieces. The rukhs on either end and on each side were calf elephants sporting tiny howdahs, a mahout standing next to each elephant, hands on their charges' necks. These were the Emperor's special elephants, born in the imperial stables, their bloodlines impeccable, dating to Emperor Humayun's time. They were trained especially for this game; in a few years they would be too large to fit into the courtyard, or to stand comfortably on the squares of the board.

The knights were foals, drenched in imperial livery, bridles, bits, saddles embellished with real gold and silver. Next to the knights were the commanders of the Emperor's army— *mansabdars*—holders of mansabs of ten thousand infantry and cavalry. Mahabat looked at their strange vestments with surprise. The eunuchs masquerading as commanders were dressed in long, thick cotton robes, much like the Jesuit fathers at the church at Agra.

In the very centre, behind the row of eight foot soldiers, were the Shah and his Grand Vizier. The pieces were all dressed in white satin and black velvet, contrasting white and black pearls sewn into their clothes and the elephants' head coverings. Mahabat shut his eyes and opened them again. No, it was not a dream. He was here, in the Khel Aangan, the board set for Shatranj, the pieces like jewels glimmering in the lamplight. He had only heard of the Emperor's collection of pieces before, now he had seen them for himself. Mahabat felt a sudden chill cast over his bones. One thing was certain. Although it was a privilege to have been invited to play a game of Shatranj with the Emperor's favourite, he would not allow her to win, etiquette be damned.

'Mirza Mahabat Khan.'

Mahabat turned around, his hand automatically plunging to the ground, his head bowed in the konish. When he straightened, he allowed his gaze to fall on her almost diffidently. No story he had heard about her beauty, no portrait he had seen of her—not even the one he had stolen from the Emperor's atelier—did justice to the woman before him. She was taller than he had expected, coming almost to his shoulder. She was clad in a deep sunset red, her choli fitting over her breasts, the sleeves long and caressing her wrists. Her ghagara was strewn with ocean-blue aquamarines, catching the light in the courtyard with every movement. She was wearing a veil of a thin red muslin, but her face was visible behind it. Mahabat reacted to her instinctively as a man would to a beautiful woman, straightening out his qaba, running a hand over the slick dome of his well-oiled head.

Mehrunnisa smiled, her teeth flashing suddenly, and Mahabat caught his breath again. This was why Emperor Jahangir was so enamoured of her, why she seemed to obsess his every thought, why she had so much power over him.

'Thank you for responding to my request, Mirza Mahabat Khan,' the Empress said, her voice soft, the tones dulcet and charming.

Mahabat bowed. 'I could not have refused, your Majesty.'

She gestured toward the divans. 'Please sit down.'

Mahabat hesitated. 'Your Majesty, it would not be right to sit in your presence.'

Mehrunnisa laughed as she sat down gracefully on a divan, tucking her feet under the glittering fan of her ghagara. 'Come now, Mirza Khan, we are all friends here. I always allow my friends to sit in my presence. Besides, we will be here a long time playing Shatranj. Sit down, Mirza Khan.'

Mahabat sank uneasily onto the feather-stuffed divan, his back straight. 'Will his Majesty be joining us?'

Mehrunnisa shook her head. 'His Majesty is unwell tonight. It is nothing serious, just a headache. I hope my company will suffice, Mirza Khan.'

'Your Majesty, this is a great honour for me. Words cannot express—'

'I know,' the Empress said, cutting off his sentence midway, 'it is indeed a great honour. And one you must remember.' She clapped her hands. At her signal, the pieces in the courtyard below them bowed to the imperial balcony, the elephants lumbering to one shaky knee at their mahouts' command. 'Are they not enchanting? I personally designed their costumes.'

Mahabat nodded. 'Your Majesty, this is all delightful. The pieces, their livery—but I do not understand the clothing of the mansabdars.'

As she moved, a waft of civet and musk swirled over Mahabat. 'If you will grant me one request, Mirza Khan. I thought we should play by the rules of the Portuguese. And perhaps then we will better understand why they give us so much trouble. I hear you know their game? The mansabdars have been replaced by bishops.'

She said 'beeshops', much as Mahabat himself would have said the word, and he found himself leaning toward the Empress. He drew back hastily. 'I do know their game, your Majesty. They allow castling and the Grand Vizier to move unlimited steps in any direction.'

Mehrunnisa looked long at Mahabat. 'The Grand Vizier is called the queen on their board. *She* is the one given so much influence. A most wise policy, you must agree. No mere Vizier can be given such power.'

The confusion about the summons crystallized into clarity in Mahabat's mind. If she wished to give the queen such power, so be it. He would play by her rules and defeat her. This game of Shatranj, he saw, was to be symbolic of their individual authorities over the empire, and Mahabat would show her just how influential he could be. When he spoke his tone was polite. 'I beg to differ, your Majesty. The Grand Vizier is the Shah's most important ally.

He protects the Shah. And doubtless has been with and known the Shah all his life. Such relationships are difficult to dissolve.'

Mehrunnisa laughed. Mahabat watched, fascinated, as she drew her veil from her face. Her skin was so exquisite, like a pearl, he wanted to touch it. Her eyes blazed at him. 'Mirza Khan, you are a worthy adversary. But I do not agree with you. Relationships, even long ones since childhood, are easy to invalidate. You see, a wife must be everything to a man, not his friends. To a Shah, a queen is everything.'

Mahabat was still recovering from his first sight of her face, and her words slid over him unheeded. The veil lay in a pile of red cloud around her shoulders. Now he saw the lines around her mouth and eyes. She was not young, not fresh of face, yet the experience of years had brought loveliness to her eyes. All of a sudden he remembered her first husband, Ali Quli, a man he had intensely disliked. He had been a mere Persian soldier fled to India, whom Emperor Akbar had honoured with this woman's hand. What a waste, Mahabat thought, still speechless. He stared at her until Hoshiyar Khan coughed.

'Shall we play now, Mirza Khan?'

Mahabat looked down at his hands. He had not really heard her words, but now they came to him again. *The queen is everything.* He shook his head. Mahabat had seen and been with many beautiful women, yet the Empress was truly stunning. When he looked up, she had pulled her veil over her face again.

The Empress held two exquisitely carved Shatranj Shahs in her hand, one in ivory decorated with rubies, the other in ebony studded with diamonds. She closed her palms over them and put her hands behind her back. 'You choose, Mirza Khan.'

'Your Majesty...'

'I insist, you are my guest. You must choose.'

Mahabat pointed to her right hand. She brought it forward and unclasped her fingers. The ivory king lay against her palm.

She laughed softly. 'You have the advantage, Mirza Khan. Make sure you use it well.'

'I most certainly will, your Majesty.' Mahabat kept his gaze away from her, determined not to be distracted by her presence.

Mehrunnisa turned to the courtyard again. The pieces all stood still, watching the imperial balcony without seeming to do so. Then she inclined her head to Mahabat. 'Call out your moves, Hoshiyar will relay them to the board.'

Mahabat leaned over the short rail of the balcony and let his eyes sweep over the board. The white pieces stood to his right, the black to his left. He searched through his memory for tales of Mehrunnisa's prowess in Shatranj, but he could find none. Rumour had it she was now an excellent shot at hunting expeditions, that she wrote poetry and songs, but there had been no stories of her chess-playing ability. If she wanted to play by Portuguese rules, they would. He cast his mind over the games he had played with the Jesuit Fathers.

'Pawn to Shah four.'

Hoshiyar Khan stepped to the edge of the balcony and called out Mahabat's move. In response, the foot soldier, a eunuch in front of the Shah, moved forward two spaces. He did not look up at the imperial balcony or acknowledge the command. Very well trained, Mahabat thought. But it was early yet.

The Empress made a similar move, until their two Shah's pawns were facing each other.

'Knight to Shah's bishop three,' Mahabat said.

Mehrunnisa leaned over the balcony, placing her arms on the ledge. 'Knight to queen's bishop three.'

Mahabat moved quickly, placing his Shah's bishop four paces ahead of his queen's bishop. The Empress matched his move.

'Tell me, Mirza Khan, what do you think of this ambassador who is to come from England?'

'Sir Thomas Roe?' asked Mahabat, using a castling move. He watched as the rukh's mahout knocked on the elephant's head and it neatly sidestepped two squares, the Shah whipping around the elephant. His Shah was now protected by the rukh and three foot soldiers.

The Empress said, not looking at the board but at Mahabat, 'Knight to Shah's bishop three.' Then, she said again, 'Yes, this Sir Thomas Roe. He brings with him a letter from King James, proclaiming he is a representative of the throne.'

Mahabat turned to her. 'Your Majesty, he is said to be a legitimate delegate of the king of England—'

'I know that,' Mehrunnisa cut into his speech, 'but the English want a royal farman from his Majesty to trade with the empire. Why would a king be involved in trade issues? The Emperor never is. Why would this English king? You are taking too long, Mirza Khan. Your move.'

Mahabat turned to the courtyard again, his words tripping out, his mind now on other matters. 'I beg pardon, your Majesty. You have moved so fast in retaliation, I have not had the time to think.'

The Empress titled her head with a smile. 'As it must be. Now, make your move, Mirza Khan, and tell me more about this ambassador and the land he comes from. Where is it?'

Mahabat called out his move, commanding his rukh to move one away from his Shah. Now it covered his Shah's pawn from capture. Then he responded to the Empress's questions. 'A small island in Europe, your Majesty. The ambassador does not speak either Persian or Arabic, but he will, to learn the etiquette of the court, the manner in which to address his Majesty. If only you could meet him too. But alas, it is forbidden for the ladies of the imperial zenana to be seen by strange men.'

Mehrunnisa castled, mirroring Mahabat's earlier move. Her eyes were bright with amusement when she spoke. 'Alas indeed,

Mirza Khan. Which is why it is so important for his Majesty and me to have excellent ministers as yourself in our employ.'

Mahabat felt a wave of anger wash over him. She talked as though he was some minion, some minor minister, not Mahabat Khan, one of the Emperor's most trusted and loyal servants. And yet who was she? A woman picked out of the dust and elevated to this exalted status of Empress.

'Your Majesty is too kind,' he murmured, calling out his move. His queen's bishop pawn moved forward one pace. So far they had played automatically. Mahabat had led with his advantage as the opening player, and she had matched his moves or mirrored them.

Mehrunnisa moved her queen diagonally forward, Mahabat saw it but also saw his Shah secure in its stronghold. He moved his queen's pawn two squares.

In response the Empress commanded her pawn to execute Mahabat's pawn. Still unconcerned, he watched the black-velvet-clad foot soldier draw his sword and make a motion of slicing off the white soldier's head. The white soldier fell to the ground, then slithered away to the side, where, for the first time, he raised his head and looked straight at Mahabat.

'I am suspicious of this ambassador, Mirza Khan,' Mehrunnisa said, her voice soft and lifting. Mahabat listened, entranced. She spoke of state matters, yet her tone was one belonging to a bedchamber. 'The English have made many promises, mostly to protect our ships in the Arabian Sea from marauders and the Portuguese. All to naught. Is *this* ambassador to be trusted?'

'I think so, your Majesty,' Mahabat said, moving his pawn to threaten the Empress's knight. She moved it out of danger to Shah's knight five. Mahabat bade his queen's bishop pawn to capture the Empress's pawn, and he watched the same drama unfold. Yet it seemed half-hearted, the Empress's black pawn almost seeming to fight with his pawn before striding off the board. When the soldier reached the edge of the courtyard, he bowed to the Empress and she nodded to him. 'The English ambassador may not be trustworthy, but they have proved their might over the Portuguese at sea. It may be worthwhile to keep them pacified for some time. Until his Majesty decides what to do. Your Majesty is very kind in wanting to be informed of these matters, but there are many ministers at court willing and able to serve the Emperor, with their lives if necessary.'

Mehrunnisa laughed. 'True. But ministers have only their lives to give. The queen, why, she can provide this Sir Thomas Roe with a treaty for trade in Gujrat. More beneficial to the empire, don't you think?' She commanded her queen's knight to trample over Mahabat's just-victorious pawn.

Mahabat stared at her, anger flaring again from deep inside him. In the last four years, since her marriage to the Emperor, Mehrunnisa had cheated him time and again of honours and privileges. She had petitioned Jahangir to act contrary to Mahabat's wishes, making a fool of him in court. How did she now dare talk to him this way? Any awe he might have felt at being in the imperial zenana had vanished. He had been invited here to be humiliated, belittled by this woman who thought she led the Emperor and the empire by the nose. He looked at the far end of the courtyard where the captured pieces stood. Two of his pawns, one of the Empress's. On the board, her queen's knight, which had so recently swooped upon his pawn, now stood defended only by her queen's bishop. Which she would surely not dare to sacrifice also. A stupid move, Mahabat thought grimly. A move worthy of a woman whose only charms were her face and her body.

'Knight to queen four,' he called out, his voice harsh in the silent courtyard. His knight moved to swallow the Empress's knight.

When the pieces had settled down and the board stood still, except for the occasional twitching of a foal's or an elephant's tail, Mehrunnisa turned to Mahabat. 'Very good, Mirza Khan. Very good indeed. You know,' she said, changing the topic rapidly, 'I do not trust Shah Abbas of Persia.'

'Why, your Majesty?' he asked, a little smile on his face. If she wanted some time to think, he would grant it to her.

'Qandahar is being constantly threatened by him. He wishes to annex it to his lands. It is an important stronghold in the defense of the empire. If we were to lose Qandahar, it would be easy to menace the rest of the empire.'

Now she had Mahabat's complete attention. *Was* there a problem with Shah Abbas? He remembered danger from the Shah to Qandahar early in the Emperor's rule. But that threat had been successfully repulsed, and Shah Abbas had conveniently blamed the fighting on the governors of his border provinces.

'I have not heard of any disturbances in the north-western frontier of the empire, your Majesty.'

'Doubtless you have not, Mirza Khan,' Mehrunnisa said. 'I was merely wondering about the possibility. We cannot afford to lose any of the cities, especially not Qandahar.'

'Your move, your Majesty,' Mahabat said. 'If I may be allowed to say so, you are taking too long.'

Mehrunnisa nodded. 'But...' She leaned over the board again, looking hard at the pieces. Then she said, 'Queen to king's rukh five.'

Mahabat looked down at the board, tiny beads of sweat dotting his forehead. The air in the courtyard suddenly seemed close. The sun had set, but the heat of the day lingered. Someone snickered; it was Mahabat's Shah. All his pieces seemed to be smiling. The Empress's queen was too close to his Shah, with nothing to protect the Shah but the three pawns. He moved his king's knight back in a panic.

'As I was saying,' the Empress said softly, 'I have a special fondness for Qandahar; it is where I was born.'

Mahabat forgot to be polite. 'But your Majesty has never visited Qandahar since birth, it seems like an odd fondness,' he sniped, irritation colouring his voice. He was scrambling on the board and he knew it. Somehow, with all her sweet talk, this woman had him running. First the English ambassador, now the Shah of Persia. What was this, a lesson in diplomacy? Taught to one who played the game better than she ever could?

'True,' Mehrunnisa replied, seeming not to note the disrespect in Mahabat's tone. She killed Mahabat's king's bishop pawn, and now her queen stood near his Shah. 'But I have a great fondness for Kabul also. My father was treasurer there for four years.' She sat back on her divan, every muscle relaxed. 'Check, Mirza Khan.'

Mahabat wiped his face with the sleeve of his qaba. Where had he gone wrong? Now he saw clearly that she had offered her queen's knight as a sacrifice, and like a fool he had taken it. He moved his Shah to the rukh's place, his voice trembling as he called out the move.

'The Emperor and I are much concerned with the rumours about the governor of Kabul, Mirza Mahabat Khan. The Emperor has sent him a missive commanding his presence at court to answer to those rumours. But Kabul cannot be left without a strong leader, one who will protect the Emperor's interests and possibly fend off any threat on the border.'

'I will search for such a man, your Majesty,' Mahabat said, desperately, as the Empress's queen moved towards his Shah. He was trapped. He took the queen with his knight. But there was no way out for his Shah.

Mahabat turned to Mehrunnisa, his eyes haunted. By tomorrow, news of his defeat would be all over Agra, in a few weeks the empire would know. Mirza Mahabat Khan had been beaten by the

Empress, a mere woman. She was smiling under her veil as her king's knight moved forward to Shah's bishop seven. Mahabat's Shah was now smothered by his own three pawns and his bishop.

'But there is no need for you to trouble yourself,' she said. 'I have already done so. I suggested to his Majesty that you would he the perfect choice.' She paused. 'Checkmate, Mirza Mahabat Khan.'

Her voice was soft, but he did not mistake the menace in it. He was to be sent away from court as governor of Kabul. She had outmanoeuvred him, not just in Shatranj but also at court. Mahabat's head bowed in a brief, grudging admiration. Sharif had been right all along when he had warned him of Jahangir's affection for this woman. He remembered the Emperor asking him if he wanted to go to the Deccan to oversee the campaign there—Jahangir had been warning him to keep his thoughts to himself, but Mahabat had not heeded that hint. Now he was headed to Kabul, so far away from Agra, across the entire breadth of the empire. It was death without dying.

He took a deep breath and exhaled it slowly. 'I thank you for your confidence in me, your Majesty. The appointment to Kabul is a great honour indeed.'

A wary look came to her eyes. 'Is it? I wonder. You must leave soon, Mirza Khan, within the week.'

Mahabat rose and bowed to the Empress. 'It shall be as you command. Perhaps his Majesty will require my services at court again sometime in the future.'

She waved her hand at him as though he were a servant. 'Perhaps, but it will be unlikely.'

As he left, Mehrunnisa dipped her hand into the embroidered bag by her side and threw a handful of mohurs into the courtyard. They spun golden through the air before scattering on the ground. The Shatranj pieces scrambled for the mohurs. 'Well done,' she called out. 'You will be better rewarded tomorrow.'

The eunuchs bowed and filed out of the courtyard. She watched as the servants doused the torches on the pillars, leaving only two oil lamps burning by her divan. One obstacle had been surmounted. Kabul was far enough away from the court that Mahabat would be powerless to influence the Emperor against her, but not so far that her spies could not keep her informed of his movements.

So Mahabat left on his long journey, carrying with him a deep and abiding loathing for Mehrunnisa. In the coming months and years, he would have much time to ponder what he had done wrong, whether he could have done better. One conviction would never change.

If Mahabat ever got a chance to destroy Mehrunnisa, he would not hesitate. And they did not know then that this opportunity *would* come one day.

Chapter Eleven

*I never saw so settled a Countenance... but mingled with
extreme Pride and Contempt of all. If I can judge any
thing, hee [Khurram] hath left his hart among his fathers
women, with whom hee hath liberty of conversation.
Normahall... visited him... She gave him a Cloake all
embrodered with Pearle, diamondes and rubyes; and carried
away, if I err not, his attention to all other business.*

—WILLIAM FOSTER. ED.,
The Embassy of Sir Thomas Roe to India

'ZAHARA BAGH IS BEAUTIFUL, YOUR MAJESTY.'

Mehrunnisa and Jahangir were walking close to each other,
ahead of the rest of their entourage. Her arm was around the
Emperor's waist, his rested on her shoulder. 'It is named for
Emperor Babur's daughter.' Jahangir looked around. 'It was laid
out by my great-grandfather. When he first came to India, he was
unhappy. The heat was terrific, it sapped his strength, and there
was nothing to provide respite from the sun. Since he could not
return to Kabul, he brought his favourite garden here.'

The royal party moved slowly through the garden, shaded by
mango trees. The fruits were near ripening, weighing down the
branches with patches of brilliant, succulent yellow. When they
passed under the trees, a swarm of green parrots rose squawking
from their perches and flew away.

In the centre, at the meeting point of the four water channels, was a *baradari*, a pavilion built of red sandstone. It was a large, open building, with pillared, cusped arches supporting a domed roof. Despite the heat of the summer, roses, marigolds and carnations bloomed around the edges of the grass, lovingly watered by hand.

The central theme of all Mughal gardens was water; at placid repose, flowing, tumbling in a waterfall, seen, heard, or felt in a misty spray. Zahara Bagh was divided into four quadrants by the water channels that crossed from east to west and north to south, meeting in the middle. Hence, the gardens were called *charbagh* or, literally, four gardens. The channels were used not only to irrigate the plants and trees alongside but also to provide cool relief from the summer heat in the plains. Where Emperor Babur had just been a nomadic chieftain before the conquest of India, now there was an empire to rule, with a wealth of natural resources from the earth, jewels of unimaginable lustre, and bountiful soil that gave birth to golden wheat and rice. But water had been hard to find, and before the monsoon rains, the tufan winds—terrible, parching gales that scorched moisture from the very skin—thundered through the country. So when he had built gardens that brought to his mind images of paradise, water had abounded.

Jahangir and Mehrunnisa had just returned from a hunting trip. For Mehrunnisa the mortification of that early hunt with Jagat Gosini had long faded away. Today, with her face dusty, gunpowder peppering her skin, the smell of it and sweat still lingering on her, she was happy. She had shot four tigers from the howdah, and these with only six bullets. Mehrunnisa touched the twelve gold bangles on her wrist. Tiny, perfectly cut emeralds, the colour of the ocean at rest, caught the light of the sun. This was her reward from Jahangir for her prowess in the hunting field. And so her jewellery boxes were filled with tokens of his affection.

'It is peaceful here,' she said. This was Mehrunnisa's first visit to Zahara Bagh, and the quiet of the garden was soothing after the cacophony of the hunt.

'I thought we should stay here tonight. The moon will be full.' Jahangir looked up at the bright sky.

'How do you like it here, Khurram?' Mehrunnisa turned to the prince, who was walking beside them in full hunting gear. He had shed only his musket.

'Very much, your Majesty.'

Khurram's gaze, though, was on the bangles Mehrunnisa wore. He watched the green of the emeralds turn dark and light as her hand moved. Mehrunnisa smiled and held her hand out to him so that he could touch the stones. He did this reverently, fascinated. Prince Khurram had excelled at the hunt too, but it was for him as easy as breathing. His eye was sharp, his aim unwavering, he could even catch a gazelle in full flight.

They reached the baradari. A gentle breeze drifted through the open pavilion, with an underlying edge of coolness picked up from the shade of the mango. The floor was covered with reed mats and strewn with velvet bolsters. Mehrunnisa, Jahangir and Khurram settled down and waited for lunch.

The Mir Bakawal headed a line of attendants. The imperial kitchens had been moved to the grounds behind the gardens, downwind from the baradari, so that no smoke from the fires or smells from the cooking would sully the air in the pavilion. The Master of the Kitchen now brought in a large, red, satin tablecloth, which he ceremoniously spread on the ground in front of the Emperor. Twenty slaves filed in, each carrying gold and silver dishes. They set them down, and an attendant placed a large stack of porcelain plates next to the food. The head server then knelt. As he lifted ornate lids off the dishes, the aroma of delicately spiced curries and rices filled the baradari. There were dishes of lamb marinated in yogurt, garlic and coriander, and baked in an oven, fish from the Yamuna grilled with pepper and salt, partridge and pigeon meat from the hunt, still simmering in rich brown gravies of onion and ginger, and five types of rice, tinted with saffron and liberally tossed with cashews, walnuts and raisins.

As the server heaped plates with food, the attendants brought in gold goblets studded with rubies and diamonds into which they poured chilled khus sherbet. Jahangir indicated his choice by pointing, and his plate was prepared for him. The attendants waited in silence as the royal party ate. They did not speak during the meal. Food was best enjoyed without the distraction of conversation. They ate with their hands, using only the right hand, picking at their food delicately so that it rode only up to their knuckles. A food-smeared palm was bad etiquette.

Mehrunnisa chewed on a mouthful of rice with a gravy-smothered piece of chicken. What was in it? Ginger—its fresh scent exploded on her tongue—some cumin seeds, and something else... something tart. Ah, the powder of dried mangoes. She nodded at the Mir Bakawal, who was standing with his arms folded, watching them with anxiety. The food was excellent as usual, the gravies weightless and well cooked, the fish flaky, each piece soaked in garlic and lime. The Master of the Kitchen bowed his head at the compliment, which was given to him at *every* meal. But at this one, Mehrunnisa thought, it was doubly important. It must have been difficult for him to move the entire kitchen from the fort to the gardens, hard to cook in the open air, where even water had to be brought. She had suggested to Jahangir that they return to the zenana for their food, and he had laughed at her concern. There were men enough to take every dish, plate and ladle to Zahara Bagh. Enough slaves to bring every teaspoonful of water, teaspoonful by teaspoonful, for the cooking. But won't it be a discomfort for the kitchens? Mehrunnisa asked, still not used to the casual way in which even the most elaborate events took place. What else have they to do? the Emperor replied. This is their job, their work, their life itself. So Mehrunnisa complimented the Mir Bakawal—he would talk of this to the cooks who waited behind the garden walls in silence, straining to hear if they liked the food.

She ate and contemplated Khurram. It was barely a year since Arjumand had her first child, now she was pregnant with the second already. Khurram and her niece had a boy, whom Jahangir had named Dara Shikoh. This one would be a boy too, Mehrunnisa thought, from the easy way Arjumand carried him inside her. An ache began to grow at this idea, but Mehrunnisa stifled it. This kind of thinking had debilitated her, taken from her the will to live even; it would not do. She had Ladli. And so she had reminded herself, at first almost every few minutes, and then day after day, and then, it was only at times like these that the thought sneaked in at all. She had Ladli.

Something had changed between them with Dara's birth. Khurram did not come as frequently as he once had for their meetings; often, it was only Bapa, Abul and Mehrunnisa who met, with Abul offering apologies for his son-in-law's absence. For this hunt too, Khurram had not wanted to come, but Mehrunnisa had sent him a letter and insisted, albeit gently, that the Emperor would be glad to see him.

Khurram did not glance up from his food to catch her eye. When he did eventually, the meal was over, and attendants were bringing warm water for them to wash their hands.

An hour later, Jahangir laid his head down comfortably on a pillow as the musicians outside the baradari played soothing music. He was asleep in a few minutes.

Mehrunnisa made a sign to Khurram. He got up and followed her outside. They cut across the lush, green lawn and reached a square water reservoir filled with goldfish and white lilies. A willow curved over gracefully, sheltering them from the sun.

Mehrunnisa sat down at the edge of the pond and took off her jewelled sandals. She put her feet into the cool water and watched as the goldfish curiously nibbled at her feet. Khurram sat next to her in silence, waiting for her to speak.

'How is Arjumand? I hope the confinement is progressing well.'

'Yes.' A flush of happiness spread over the prince's face. 'She is doing well. The soothsayers say it will be another son. It does not matter much to me, but Arjumand is content.'

'You love Arjumand very much.'

'More than life itself, your Majesty,' the prince replied fervently. Then he stopped and said, 'This sounds too grand, too much like what I should say to you, her aunt, rather than what should be. But it is the simple truth.'

'It is good to love your wife, Khurram,' Mehrunnisa hesitated, 'but remember, as a royal prince it is your duty to marry often and to show impartiality to all your wives. You have another wife, one before Arjumand. I hear you visit her less often.'

'This from you, your Majesty?' Khurram asked. His smile was wry. 'I beg your pardon, but I have known you since I was a child and so feel I can safely say this. Empress Jagat Gosini complains of the Emperor's neglect of her, others do too.'

Mehrunnisa laughed, and the sound tumbled around the silent gardens. The eunuchs in the baradari leaned their heads out to look at them, but they could not hear the conversation. She touched Khurram's arm. 'That was well said. But matters are different with the Emperor, Khurram. He has too much else to do, the court, the people, the empire, all these have his attention. When he returns to the zenana, he comes to me. I do not need to remind you of this.'

'I apologize, your Majesty.'

She nodded and fell silent. She had not expected to be

questioned thus by Khurram. On the other hand, that mocking, light tone had been absent from their dealings for a long while, and she welcomed its return. Yet... behind those words lurked insolence. Even if he had not meant it to be so. But had he meant it? Khurram too had taken off his sandals, and they sat shoulder to shoulder on the stone edge of the pool. 'I shall never marry again,' he said. 'No political marriages, no more marriages of convenience, I have all I could want in Arjumand.'

'It is very well to love Arjumand,' Mehrunnisa said quietly; 'but think of all the alliances you can make for the good of the empire, alliances which will link us with other kings. You cannot put love before duty.'

Khurram frowned. 'Why must it be a royal prince's duty to follow these orders? Why cannot I make my own choice?'

'You complain of a lack of freedom, Khurram?' she asked. 'You want choice? Will you then give up your royal birth and your right to the throne for these?'

He whipped around to her. 'I can have them and still be free. My father did, he chose you, your Majesty.'

At his words, the anger that had simmered somewhere inside Mehrunnisa flared to life. He was reminding her of her lowly birth, of the fact that her father was a Persian refugee, and that she had brought no political connections to the marriage. His *wife* was that Persian refugee's granddaughter.

'Arjumand has my blood in her. Did you forget that so soon?' The prince began to talk, but Mehrunnisa shushed him. 'I know your first wife is descended from Shah Ismail of Persia, but I do not see that her ancestry makes you any more fond of her. Just as the Emperor is fond of me, the woman he chose after having married nineteen others for the empire, you too find yourself by Arjumand's side. Are you now disrespecting your wife?'

He moved away, his face flushed. Khurram apologized, over

and over again, mumbling and incoherent. He had not meant to be disrespectful, surely your Majesty could not think so. He had much to be grateful for, and it all came from her family. Mehrunnisa let him talk, did not interrupt him and waited until her own rage had calmed a little. He *had* wanted to be spiteful, and in the process had overlooked the fact that anything he said to her would reflect upon him too. They were now tied in marriage. Let him be unsettled, she thought. It would make what she had to say much easier. He must never again forget who she was, or what she could do for him.

'Then you will agree with me, Khurram, that some inconveniences have to be borne to enjoy greater conveniences.'

'Yes, of course, your Majesty. But what do you have in mind?' he asked. 'Has another alliance been offered?'

'Yes,' she said finally. 'I wish, your father and I wish, for you to marry again.'

'Who is it?'

No more protests, Mehrunnisa thought; he was more curious to know who it was than he was on insisting on his undying love for Arjumand. 'Someone you know well. And someone who will make you a good wife—Ladli.'

'Ladli!' Khurram repeated. 'But she is a mere child.'

'She is eleven years old, Khurram. I am not suggesting a marriage yet, merely a betrothal. We can wait while she grows up.'

'How can I marry Arjumand's cousin?'

'A precedent has been set before, need I remind you of this? Dowager Empress Ruqayya was Emperor Akbar's first cousin, another of his wives was their common cousin. Why now an exalted sense of morality?'

Khurram stared at her. Who was she to tell him of the responsibilities of an Emperor? She spoke as though his becoming an Emperor depended upon her good graces. He was the natural heir to the throne; his two older brothers, Khusrau and Parviz, were wastrels, and Shahryar was still a child. Why, even Emperor Akbar had indicated that he was the best loved of all his grandchildren. What right did this woman have to dictate his responsibilities or belittle his moralities?

'I shall think about it,' he mumbled.

'Think well, Khurram,' Mehrunnisa said, getting up and slipping her wet feet into her sandals. 'Remember who you are.' She stopped and said in a gentler voice, 'I do not mean to command you into this decision. But what can be so wrong about it? Ladli is a charming child—and I say this not just as her mother—she will become a charming woman, one much like Arjumand.' She laughed. 'Now I sound like the mother of a bride, lauding my daughter's advantages. But think that this will not disadvantage you either.'

The Empress and the prince walked back to the baradari in silence. Khurram did not venture into conversation again, his brow furrowed in thought. Mehrunnisa let him be. The idea she had suggested would take time to settle in his mind. It was a little thing to ask. He was her niece's husband, why not her daughter's? Soon he would see why this was important.

But she remained uneasy. They were still strong, surely, the junta. The same loyalties existed. Surely.

Chapter Twelve

The shippe, which arrived at the barre of Suratt the 13th of September, 1613... was taken by the Portungales armado of friggots, notwithstandinge theire passe which they had of the Portungales.

—WILLIAM FOSTER, ED.,
Early Travels in India, 1583–1619

THE *RAHIMI* RODE ON THE WATER, HER MASSIVE SAILS DISTENDED WITH breeze. She was on her way back to Surat from Jiddah, the Red Sea port near Mecca.

'Land ahoy!' the *panjari* seated in the bird's nest atop the main mast yelled out.

The deck was immediately crowded with passengers and sailors, all eager for the first glimpse of land after almost four months at sea. They were finally home. They pressed eagerly into the railings, chattering with one another, faces lit with smiles, eyes searching for the land the panjari had seen. The gulls had come to the *Rahimi* two days ago, bringing promise of home as they had squawked and swooped around the ship. But such promises were not easily believed, for birds had flown over the ship before and vanished into the vast and empty sky, and no land had been sighted.

Most of the passengers aboard the *Rahimi* were pilgrims on their way back from the Haj in Mecca. They had been away for a long time—in some cases, two or three years. They mingled easily on the ship's polished decks with the crew, men and women together, waiting. At first there was nothing, the lines of the horizon were flat and unmarred. And then there was a blue-black smudge, like a fingerprint. Finally, it *was* land. It was India. Shouts and yells resounded over the water. The gulls got their reward as pieces of bread were thrown into the air.

In a few hours, just as the sun was setting, the *Rahimi* furled her sails and glided smoothly to anchor off the bar at the mouth of the river Tapti. The next morning at sunrise, boats would row out to the *Rahimi* and carry its passengers and crew fourteen miles inland along the river to Surat.

With the sun dipping behind her in the Arabian Sea, the *Rahimi* was a magnificent sight. The ship could displace up to fifteen hundred tons of water at full cargo, her main mast rose forty-five yards to the sky, her sails were so huge that they were identifiable from many miles away, and she could carry fifteen hundred passengers. On this voyage, the *Rahimi* had aboard seven hundred pilgrims from Mecca and a full complement of crew. The cargo holds below deck were stocked with silks, spices and other goods for trade. She was the largest ship that plied the Arabian Sea routes, and her bulk and enormity did not make her less stately or elegant. Her sails were handwoven in thick canvas, and shot through with one-inch strips of gold embroidery—on a bright day, she seemed on fire. Her fittings were of the shiniest brass, and her wooden decks were swabbed daily.

All these were on Dowager Empress Ruqayya's orders. The *Rahimi* belonged to Ruqayya.

As night fell, the passengers retired to their cabins, delighted to be back and awaiting their first step on their homeland the next day. The captain and crew rested after a long, arduous voyage. As the ship slept, five Portuguese frigates silently moved into position around the *Rahimi*.

When morning came and the sun rose behind the hills in the east, the lone lookout woke guiltily. He had fallen into sleep aided by wine; the captain himself had brought him a cup. But the night had been calm, there had been no trouble. He rose from the deck, rubbed his aching back, and yawned. A frigate loomed in front of his eyes. For a moment this did not register, and then he turned and ran.

'Captain!' he shouted, racing toward the captain's cabin, 'we are surrounded by the Portuguese.'

His cries woke the whole ship, and within minutes the deck thronged with passengers and crew, who came pounding up from their cabins. They stood gazing with awe at the mighty battleships. As they watched, a lifeboat was lowered from the side of a frigate and a small party of Portuguese rowed over to the *Rahimi*.

'Let down a ladder,' the Portuguese captain yelled.

'What is the problem? We have paid for our *cartaz* and have not violated any conditions on it,' the captain said. Upon hearing the word, the pilgrims on the *Rahimi* shuddered, but they said little, watchful of the frigates surrounding them. The cartaz was the pass all ships departing the Indian coast had to carry. It was a passport for the ship, detailing ports of call, routes to be taken in the Arabian Sea, and even items for trade by name and quantity. The top page of this hated cartaz was stamped with the picture of Mary and Jesus—hated because it was abhorrent for the Muslim pilgrims headed to Mecca to travel under the auspice of a God they could not call their own.

'Let me see your cartaz.'

The Portuguese pass was brought out and lowered by a rope. The Portuguese captain perfunctorily examined it. Then he demanded a ladder again; it was let down, and they came aboard. 'The *Rahimi* is being appropriated by us. You have violated the rules.'

'What rules?' the *Rahimi*'s captain yelled. 'You cannot do this; the *Rahimi* belongs to her Majesty, Dowager Empress Ruqayya Sultan Begam.'

'We do not know yet,' the Portuguese captain said. 'Your cargo will be examined and we will check for violations. The crew is under arrest, give yourselves up peacefully and you will not be hurt.' He turned to his first officer. 'Get a crew over here to guide the *Rahimi* to Goa.'

The man nodded and went off to signal his frigate.

'The Emperor will hear of this.' The captain of the *Rahimi* turned to his first officer and said, 'Send a message to his Majesty in Agra.'

'No one is to leave.'

A murmur started in the crowd. The men began to press in around the Portuguese officer, some started to shout, and some of the women cried. The *Rahimi*'s captain pushed them back. 'Let the passengers go. They have waited too long to come home.'

'They can wait a little longer. My orders are to escort the *Rahimi* to Goa intact, with all the crew, passengers and cargo.'

In an hour, the entire crew had been rounded up and sent to the Portuguese frigate. A new crew came aboard. The passengers were ordered to their cabins and they did what they were told, fear taking hold of them. They had been so close to home, they could see the land, and now... now what would happen? As the sun rose in the sky, the *Rahimi* weighed anchor and set sail south to Goa, the seat of the Portuguese Viceroy in India.

Mehrunnisa pushed her notebook toward Siddhicandra. 'What do you think?'

He read carefully, marking out specific passages. 'Your Majesty, the essay is very good, but you have made some elementary mistakes. Like here...' Siddhicandra pointed out with his quill.

She sighed. 'Sanskrit is more difficult than I thought, so many grammatical hurdles.'

Siddhicandra smiled. 'It is just a matter of time and patience, your Majesty.'

The twenty-four-year-old monk had a youthful face, his skin unfettered by lines. And nature had been kind to him, shaping the muscles on his back, shoulders and abdomen as with a sharp knife. His cheekbones and chin were strongly cut, his head was shaved and no bumps marred his skull. The monk wore saffron clothing, loose cloth draped upon his body, his feet were bare, he rarely walked in sandals, and he usually bore a thin muslin mask across his nose and mouth so even in breathing he would not endanger insects that might otherwise find their way into his lungs.

Siddhicandra was a Jain monk. Jainism, a religion founded by Mahavira, had found its roots many centuries before the advent of Christianity or Islam. In India, it was followed mostly by the *baniyas*, the merchant class in Gujrat. The main precept of Jainism was kindness to all creatures, big and small, which meant no meat, and, in cases like Siddhicandra's, even an unwillingness to step on, or breathe in, life the eye could not discern.

But it was the monk's demeanour that enchanted Mehrunnisa. Siddhicandra moved as though at rest, his limbs fluid. She had never seen him angry or even upset. He was very young, almost too young for such self-control. She had invited him into the zenana to teach her Sanskrit, logic and poetry, in all of which he had an excellent understanding.

For all his calmness, Siddhicandra was a man not connected with the royal family, and so could not come into the harem and sit with the women. Mehrunnisa had followed those rules, though only in spirit. She had a scaffolding erected outside the balcony of her apartments, and once a week, Siddhicandra was lifted on a swing-like contraption to come level with her balcony, and thus she studied with him. He was but three feet away from her, but hanging in mid-air—not exactly *within* the walls of the imperial zenana.

They worked in silence, and while Mehrunnisa struggled with learning the conjugation of verbs, Siddhicandra read a book he had brought with him. She had asked for him as a teacher because he brought peace with him when he came. Sanskrit she would probably never master, although she did try. But what she wanted most was to know how he could let the world fight and destroy itself around him and yet not be affected by it. He had *no* wants, none at all. He did not even seem to need anything.

'Tell me, how does it feel to be surrounded by men who enjoy all earthly pleasures and not enjoy them yourself?' Mehrunnisa asked.

Siddhicandra put down his book. 'Your Majesty, it takes a strong mind. For years, I have cultivated my mind to obey the rules of my religion. My mind is detached from its outward shell'— Siddhicandra gestured toward his body—'and is thus not attracted either by the pleasures of my body or those of others.'

'Have you never indulged yourself? Even a little?'

'No, your Majesty, it has not been necessary. I have never felt the need.'

As he spoke, Emperor Jahangir came into the apartments. The monk immediately bowed his head.

'Your Majesty, I have been chiding Siddhicandra for his unreasonable celibacy,' Mehrunnisa said. 'And that too in one so young and beautiful of form...'

'Then I shall join you in persuading Siddhicandra to give up his quest for chastity.' He turned to the young man. 'Why do you persist? Don't you see all around you the luxury and sensuality of a good life?'

'Besides, austerity is only for those who have been sated by sensual pleasures,' Mehrunnisa added. 'What is the difference between Jainism and Hinduism? The asceticism that Hindus have to undergo comes only in the fourth phase of their lives; they live first as the child, then the student, then the husband and householder, and finally, when they are old, they renounce the world for God. But the Hindus have already, in their youth, experienced pleasure and give it up only at an old age. How can you renounce worldly pleasures without experiencing them? How can you know if one path is better than the other if you have travelled but in one direction?'

'Your Majesty,' Siddhicandra responded, 'what you say is true. But reflect for one moment upon the world we live in. Would you frankly acknowledge that the old today are as disciplined as they were a few generations ago? It is the youthful who have more control of their minds and bodies and who have the strength to give up physical gratification.'

Mehrunnisa fell silent. What was he saying? That she was too old to gain any sort of peace? This power she had now, that Jahangir had given her, was exhilarating. But it came with an unsettled mind. She worried all the time—there was always something or the other to give her pause. Now it was Khurram. She had not heard from him, had not seen him, either at the darbars or in her apartments. Was he hiding from her? Why had he not responded to what she had suggested?

She would never be able to duplicate Siddhicandra's sheer uninterest in anything but his God. Even here, in the zenana, looking through the doors at the thickly piled Persian carpets, the silk-covered divans, he was not tempted to lay his body upon them to rest. Where did this will power come from? He was barely two years older than Prince Khurram, but in everything else, he could not be more different. She listened as Jahangir and the monk sparred with each other in argument. They talked often like this;

for the Emperor it was unimaginable that the body must not be listened to, that its needs be ignored. How else would heirs to the empire be born? Without want, there would be no getting anything. Ambition needed to exist. And Siddhicandra insisted upon his love for his God as fulfilling his needs.

The Emperor turned to Mehrunnisa during a lull. 'Convince him that he needs to take a wife, my dear. How can he not have what we have?' He put his hand on her shoulder, and Mehrunnisa leaned against Jahangir.

'What is it?' he asked, moving her face until he looked into her eyes. 'What bothers you?'

They forgot that the Jain monk sat in front of them on the scaffolding, that he still watched them and listened to what they were saying.

'I asked Khurram if he would be willing to marry Ladli,' Mehrunnisa said. 'Not now, of course, but soon.'

'And there is a problem here?'

'I do not know,' Mehrunnisa said slowly. 'He has said nothing.'

She then told him about the whole of their meeting at Zahara Bagh. Of what they had said to each other. Jahangir asked if she wanted him to interfere, and Mehrunnisa thought about it and then shook her head. She was Ladli's mother and should manage this herself. Besides, she could not go to the Emperor for help each time she wanted something.

They talked thus for a while, still not aware of Siddhicandra. Finally, he asked for permission to leave. Siddhicandra beat against the ropes two times, and the workers below began to haul down the swing. As he left, he said to Mehrunnisa, 'Your Majesty, no man can be moved against his will. If the prince hesitates, it is not because he is influenced by a wife or a father-in-law. It is his own determination that dictates his decision.'

'As you resist your Emperor's command to take a wife,' Mehrunnisa said, leaning over the parapet.

'Yes, your Majesty.' Siddhicandra raised his hand in salute as the swing took him down to the ground.

The Emperor and Mehrunnisa watched him go. 'Do you think he is right, your Majesty?' Mehrunnisa asked. 'Is Khurram not to be influenced?'

Jahangir shook his head. 'Khurram has not Siddhicandra's austerity, nor his strength of character. None of my sons have this. Perhaps I am at fault for having been too indulgent, but,' he grimaced, remembering how once he had been misled too, 'I cannot make too strong a claim to a lack of weakness myself. Do what you will with Khurram, Mehrunnisa. Nothing would please me more than to be able to call Ladli a daughter-in-law. And I have three other sons.'

She laughed for the first time, the worry lifting from her. Of course. None of the other three had Khurram's charm, but charm could be cultivated, could it not?

Hoshiyar came to stand behind them and they turned to him.

'Your Majesties, the Dowager Empress Ruqayya Sultan Begam seeks an audience.'

Mehrunnisa leaned over to kiss the Emperor's cheek. 'I should go to her, your Majesty.'

'Both of you, your Majesties. She wishes to see both of you,' Hoshiyar said.

Ruqayya met them at the door to her apartments. The curtains had been opened, and summer filled the room with light and air. There was no darkness anywhere, no sense of the sloth and ease the Dowager Empress liked around her. Ever since Emperor Akbar's death, Ruqayya had been thus—lying on her divan with the hukkah smoking gently in her hand, the essence of opium in the water pipe swirling about, waiting for news, waiting for knowledge. Her quickness had gone, and she had let herself grow more fat and more grey in the head. So this was a change indeed, Mehrunnisa thought, as the Emperor and she bowed to Ruqayya.

'Come in, come in,' Ruqayya said. 'Do not dawdle outside.'

She settled them on divans and subsided opposite them. When her little Chinese dog came up to nip at her fingers, she slapped it irritably and shouted to her eunuch to take it away.

'You commanded us, your Majesty?' Jahangir said. He was always this polite, insisting that all the women his father had married required this respect; they were all, in a sense, in the place of his mother. Ruqayya especially had been Akbar's favourite, and that favour Jahangir gave her too. Besides, she had looked after Mehrunnisa in those years when she was a widow, she had made their marriage possible, and for that he would always be grateful. He did not always listen to her, as he had not when he was a prince, but that was entirely another matter. He gave her the courtesy of seeming to listen.

The Dowager Empress frowned. 'I have heard news from Surat. The *Rahimi* has been captured.'

'By whom?' Mehrunnisa sat up on her divan.

'The Portuguese Viceroy at Goa. She has been taken there as she was, with her crew, the cargo, even the passengers.' Suddenly Ruqayya seemed old and tired. Defeated. Once news such as this would have sent her into a flying temper, flinging curios and shouting curses at anyone who would care to listen. But the capture of the *Rahimi* seemed to have broken her.

'Why?...' Jahangir said, and then he stopped. He turned to Mehrunnisa, and she was watching him. They both knew why. It was the imperial farman to trade that the Englishman Thomas Best had carried with him to England. Unable to defeat the English, the Portuguese had turned on Indian ships.

'I will not see my beloved ship again,' Ruqayya's voice rose to a wail.

Mehrunnisa smiled and then quickly hid that smile. Ruqayya had *seen* the *Rahimi* only once in fifteen years. It was not easy, living as they did at court at Agra or Lahore, to travel to the westernmost reach of the empire merely to visit a ship. It was easier to own the ship and send it to sea from this far. What Ruqayya was bemoaning was the rich cargo in the *Rahimi*'s hold.

'Do not smile, Mehrunnisa,' Ruqayya said sharply. 'How would you feel if this were one of your own ships?'

'I apologize, your Majesty,' Mehrunnisa said. 'But did the *Rahimi* infringe any of the conditions on the cartaz?'

'Of course not,' Ruqayya snapped. 'I have a very honest captain, and he has strict orders not to do any such thing. The *Rahimi*'s cartaz was up to date, and all the customs duties had been paid.' She looked at Jahangir. 'What are you going to do about this? Will you let them get away with something so unlawful? if the Portuguese have the temerity to reach within the zenana itself, how long will it take for them to grab for the throne?'

And so she scolded them for a while longer and they listened. Ruqayya was not always reasonable in her arguments, but she was afraid. The *Rahimi* had contained most of her wealth—she had disregarded the advice she had given Mehrunnisa about diversifying her investments and had put most of her money into this journey to Mecca.

Jahangir and Mehrunnisa left her apartments after an hour and went back to their own. On the way, they talked. No word had come from the Portuguese Viceroy about the *Rahimi*'s capture, why it had been done, when the ship would be released, and what conditions had to be met before that happened. Ruqayya was right about one thing. There was no possibility that the Viceroy did not know who owned the *Rahimi*. The biggest insult was that it was taken from the bar at Surat, on the very shore of the empire. It was an act of war. The Portuguese had been indulged too long, given the right to ply their religion and their might at sea. But they had forgotten that it was a benign hand that allowed this. They might have been in India longer, but the Emperor still owned every breath of their bodies. They had forgotten this.

A farman was sent immediately ordering the release of the *Rahimi*. The Portuguese Viceroy returned a polite but impudent answer. The *Rahimi* would not be released until certain conditions had been met; English privileges were to be revoked; and the Emperor had to surrender the English in India to the Portuguese Viceroy.

Mehrunnisa was enraged by the demands. Letters flew back and forth between Agra and Goa, neither side willing to concede defeat. The tone of the letters, on both ends, was diplomatic at first, and then threatening. The Empress did not want to insist too much or too harshly, for Ruqayya had set her mind on getting her ship back. The empire could not go to war with the Portuguese, at least not yet. And because Mehrunnisa did not insist, the Portuguese Viceroy sent her a bundle of passes, to distribute as she wished. He knew she owned ships too, and he was enticing her with these passes in which the terms were so liberal, the payment so light, that Mehrunnisa's ships would be travelling as though for free in the Arabian Sea. The frigates would still defend her ships from pirates and marauders, she could trade at whatever port she wanted, customs duties were banished and not even to be thought of. Mehrunnisa knew this to be a bribe, but it was so tempting to use this new cartaz that she hesitated returning them.

And as much as greed overcame her, the simple fact was that the Portuguese still provided protection, such as it was, to the Indian ships. The English had promised to guard them instead, but this would only be done upon drawing up a formal treaty between England and India, for trade all over the empire. For the treaty to be drawn up, the new and first official ambassador, Sir Thomas

Roe, had to come to the courts. Roe was on his way, the Englishmen said. The problem was that it was not enough that Roe was on his way. He had to be here to sign a treaty to provide security for the Indian ships. The promise of Roe was not enough.

So Mehrunnisa accepted the 'gift' from the Viceroy but still insisted upon the return of the *Rahimi*. He still resisted, and as the months passed, the standoff continued.

While the Emperor and the Portuguese were debating on the matter of the *Rahimi*, Rajput chieftains in Mewar revolted against the imperial army.

Mewar lay within the Mughal Empire, a thorn lodged in its heart. For years, ever since Emperor Akbar's rule, the Rajputs of Mewar had defied invasion. They had lost land, of course, as the edges of the kingdom had been eroded away and added to the empire's boundaries, and now Rana Amar Singh, ruler of Mewar, had been pushed into hiding in the Aravalli range of Rajasthan. Here he reigned, his back against the rock of the mountains, one hand forever on his sword. When Amar Singh's father was dying, he saw his son's turban tumble off his head, and he took it as an omen that Mewar would soon be lost to the Mughals. But that prophecy was yet to be fulfilled. It had been twenty years since Rana Pratap Singh's death, and Amar Singh still ruled over the hillside he could now call his kingdom. Below him, in the flat land of the plains, was the brilliant blue of Pichola Lake, the half-built palace of his ancestors, the lush green of the fields fed by the lake's waters.

Rana Amar Singh had grown old in his mountain fortress. He was tired of living thus, sleeping—if he slept at all—under an open sky, battling the sudden monsoon rains that left his men and his army sodden, trying to rear his children on the hills, where every bush hid a legion of cobras and vipers. They had never known the luxury of a roof over their heads that was not made of loosely knitted jute, or the comfort of a bed that did not have a boulder to support it.

Even Amar Singh's memories of the palace that lay below him were faint at best. The conflict with Akbar had started while he was still a child, and the most he could remember was his father's stubbornness and determination that Mewar would never call itself part of the Mughal Empire. That no matter how vast the empire stretched, how many other kingdoms it encompassed, how many other Rajput kings swore fealty to the Mughal Emperor and gave their daughters into the imperial harem, this Rajput warrior would be a warrior until death. And that meant Pratap Singh's head would not bow to Emperor Akbar, and so Amar Singh's could not to Emperor Jahangir. Father had fought father, and so son fought son.

For years, the Rana's men had come down from the Aravalli when night had provided them cover to pillage a caravan of hapless merchants, to set off mines against the ramparts of the fort on the Pichola, which now housed the Mughal army, or to fill the ponds with poison. This was the only way they could battle.

But this time, the Rana had come down from the mountains to stay. The Mughal army in the plains had grown weary of the fight. Soldiers had fled, leaving in large numbers each day; not even the promises of promotions or higher pay would have made them stay. The Rana had come, they had fought him, and the crafty Amar Singh had then retreated to his mountain home. Nothing had been achieved. It had been in a situation like this, with half the army gone, the other half indifferent, that Amar Singh had come down for one last foray—and taken over his ancestor's palace on the banks of the Pichola.

When the news of this latest rebellion reached the royal court at Agra, Emperor Jahangir forgot, briefly, the problem with the Portuguese. And when he talked with Mehrunnisa, she forgot her hostility against Khurram. Mewar should not have mattered so much. But the Mewar problem had uneasy roots for Jahangir.

Akbar had sent Jahangir there when he was a prince, but Jahangir had not had the patience to stay and see the campaign through. Instead, he had decided to storm the treasury at Agra; the bitter years of estrangement from Akbar had followed, and Mewar had been overlooked. When Jahangir came to the throne, he tried to subdue Amar Singh again, but just as he had rebelled against his father, Khusrau chose the moment of the second Mewar campaign to rebel against Jahangir. And again, Mewar was forgotten, as Jahangir went racing after Khusrau to Lahore. So that pocket of land remained independent within the empire—and not placidly independent either.

'I can no longer go to the battlefield, Mehrunnisa,' Jahangir said. 'Who shall I send to lead the army? Amar Singh will surrender himself, or his life, this much I am determined about. This has gone on for too long.'

They talked of the possible candidates. Parviz was in the Deccan, supposedly overseeing the campaign there. Besides, Parviz could not be given command of the Mewar invasion—he had already had that when Khusrau had rebelled, and he had proved useless. There was no question of Khusrau even being considered— a blind prince to be put in command of an imperial army? He could not even climb his own horse unassisted, let alone chase the wily Amar Singh up and down the gullies of the Aravalli. Shahryar... he was still a child. And that left only Khurram.

Mehrunnisa suggested his name, and Jahangir agreed. Prince Khurram had not been tried on the battlefield yet, but he was a royal prince and had some notion of how to command an army, or if he did not, he would learn.

So Khurram left for Mewar.

He was sent away with many gifts of elephants, horses and silks. Khurram did not take Arjumand with him, because she was pregnant yet again, with their third child. Mehrunnisa did not talk with Khurram about Ladli, and he said nothing to her either. But she wanted him to think, and deprived of Arjumand's nearness, he might begin to think that Ladli would make a good wife also. Mehrunnisa had paid heed to Siddhicandra's warning that a man's decision was made at his own will, but she did not believe in it too much. If anything, Arjumand was too much like her, and had—this Mehrunnisa admitted to herself just once—as much of a hold on Khurram as she had on Jahangir.

She remembered Jahangir's words too, that he had three other sons. Yet, when a problem of such magnitude as Mewar presented itself, who did they turn to? Why then even consider those other three sons as possible husbands for Ladli? No, it must be Khurram. How it would come about, Mehrunnisa did not know.

The court had been at Agra for many years now, mostly because it had not been necessary to move. But now Jahangir decided to shift to Ajmer, north of Mewar, to be near Prince Khurram's campaign. The entire city of Agra emptied. Houses were shut up, and furniture drenched in neem oil to keep away white ants and termites. The bazaars closed down as the traders went with the court.

Now all eyes turned towards Mewar. If Khurram successfully routed Rana Amar Singh, the empire would be rid of this forty-nine-year scourge. But more importantly, given his suddenly tenuous relationship with Mehrunnisa, he needed support from other quarters.

Chapter Thirteen

Each encampment requires for its carriage 100 elephants,
500 camels, 400 carts, and 100 bearers. Besides, there are
employed a thousand Farrashes… 500 pioneers, 100 water-
carriers, 50 carpenters, tent-makers and torch-bearers, 30
workers in leather, and 150 sweepers… On account of the
crowding… it would take a soldier days to find his tent…

—H. BLOCHMANN AND H.S. JARRETT, TRANS.,
Ain-i-Akbari

IT WAS NO UNUSUAL THING FOR THE MUGHAL EMPERORS TO PACK THEIR
belongings and move away from one place to another, spending
months and perhaps years on the road. In their hearts, the Emperors
were wanderers. Emperor Babur had been a nomad chieftain, much
like his ancestors, Timur the Lame and Gengiz Khan. It was not
until the last four years of his life that his household had taken root
in India, where he finally laid out gardens and started to build a
fort. His son Humayun had much less time. He was driven out of
India by the Afghan kings Babur had displaced, and *his* son Akbar
had grown up thus, living in a tent, not knowing in the morning
where he would lay his head at night.

So when Akbar came to the throne he started to build.
Foundations were laid, entire cities were born—at Agra, at Fatehpur
Sikri, at Delhi and Lahore, and at Kabul and Kashmir. Akbar was
leaving his mark on India's map. *This* was what his empire would

stand for, these magnificent creations of sandstone and marble, this rerouting of rivers to form vistas from terraces, this moving of the earth from one spot to another. This was the glory of the Mughal kings.

But somewhere in Akbar's blood too lurked that gypsy gene. He set down roots in all these major cities of India, and moved from one to another as he wished. Summers were spent in the lush coolness of Kabul and Kashmir, winters were sometimes at Lahore and sometimes at Agra, and Fatehpur Sikri, of course, was abandoned early on. This travelling became so established a routine that for the first few years of his reign, Jahangir followed it, deviating only when Khusrau's rebellion took him to Lahore earlier in the year than expected.

The Mughal Emperor was, in many senses, the empire itself. Where he sat, the throne stood, his voice alone directed the lives of the hundred and thirty million people within the empire. So when Emperor Jahangir decided to go to Ajmer, the soul of the empire moved with him.

When Jahangir's great-grandfather was a mere chieftain in Kabul, his camp packed up in a few short hours, and everything—the tents, the cooking vessels, the water jars, the women, the children, the horses and camels and goats for milk—was transferred to another site in a day or two's travel.

Things were no longer that simple. When Emperor Jahangir travelled, the court and the harem travelled with him. The imperial army came along too. The royal tents were elaborate now, no longer made of canvas but of silk and wood and embroidery in gold zari, standing at two or even three storeys high.

A few days before Jahangir and Mehrunnisa set out towards Ajmer with their retinue, the *Paish-khana*, or advance camp, left Agra, travelling the route to be taken by the Emperor. There was no question of Jahangir waiting while the tents were pitched, so there were two identical sets of tents made. One, the Paish-khana, travelled before the Emperor, found a suitable spot, and set up the camp, awaiting the arrival of the entourage. After a stay of a few days, the royal party would move on to the next site and would find all in readiness of their arrival.

The caravan was so massive, consisting of camels, horses, elephants, goats and cows along with the numerous humans, that it travelled only eight miles a day. Whole villages came out to watch. Children would wake early in the morning to line up along the road, sitting on rocks with a jute parasol over their heads, an earthenware jar of cool water beside them, rice and *ber* fruit pickle wrapped in banyan leaves to keep hunger at bay. This was how they entertained themselves for the eight hours it took for the entire procession, from head to tail, to pass where they sat.

The Mir Manzil, or Quarter-Master of the court, was in charge during journeys. It was his responsibility to scout the area and find a flat piece of ground suitable for encampment. Once found, the land was marked out into a rectangle and the ground levelled painstakingly. Then, large platforms of earth were raised to pitch the tents. The entire rectangle was enclosed by a *gulabar*, or the grand enclosure. Huge wooden frames, eight feet in height, covered by red calico cloth printed with reproductions of vases of flowers, were erected all around, forming an enclosed area. For purposes of security, while the Emperor was in residence, the imperial army surrounded three sides, and the fourth contained the offices and workshops of the court.

In the main courtyard of the encampment, a large pole, forty yards high, was set up, supported upright by sixteen ropes pegged to the ground. On top of this pole was a large lantern. This was the *Akhash-diya*, or the light in the sky. It was visible from miles around at night and helped guide soldiers and hunting parties to the imperial campsite. It burned all through the day and night, and ladders were used to climb to the top to feed the fire.

On the eastern side, a two-storey pavilion made of canvas and wood was erected, which formed the Diwan-i-khas. This was the place for jharoka during travel, and Jahangir went there daily for his morning prayers. A smaller tent, the *ghusl-khana*, or private audience room, was erected inside the enclosure where the Emperor and Empress gave audience in the evenings. Beyond the ghusl-khana were the royal tents, enclosed by a set of screens lined with Maslipatnam chintz and painted with colourful flowers.

Behind the Emperor's tents were the zenana quarters. Mehrunnisa, as the Padshah Begam, occupied the most important spot. Spiralling outward from her tent were the dwellings of the other ladies of the harem, each distanced according to her status and title. The floors of the tents were spread with thick reed and cotton mats and then covered with Persian carpets and divans. Each tent also had ornate wooden doors. Finally, on one side of the royal encampment, the merchants and traders accompanying the Emperor set up their shops and bazaars.

The camp was enormous; each set of tents required for its transport a hundred elephants, five hundred camels, four hundred carts, one hundred mules and a hundred bearers. The elephants carried the heaviest equipment, large tents and poles. The smaller tents and luggage were borne by camels, and mules and carts transported kitchen utensils. The bearers carried the lighter and more valuable items; porcelain and gold plates used at the Emperor's meals and the delicate curtains and rugs that adorned the royal tents.

The imperial harem travelled in howdahs strapped onto the backs of elephants. Each howdah was made of gold, silver or wood, decorated with precious stones and screened with silks and satins. The ladies also travelled by palanquin, a long bamboo bed covered by satin or brocade, carried by bearers.

Prince Khurram arrived in Mewar at the head of an army of twelve thousand infantry and cavalry. Along the way, as they rode hard from Agra, he consulted with his commanders, listened to their advice, and did what he thought was important. Even before he had left Agra, he had ordered an army of five thousand men to fly across the empire to Mewar. Most of these men were not soldiers; they were scouts and spies. Trained in the imperial army for this purpose, the men had chameleon-like, movable, and forgettable faces. They spoke almost every language in the empire—their gurus had been brought in especially to teach them the intonations and inflections and mannerisms of each dialect. The spies had no wives or children, no families who could lay claim upon them. The army was their life, the Emperor their only master.

By the time Khurram arrived near Mewar, the spies had done their jobs well. Many now lived in the surrounding villages and towns, mingled with the local people, heard their stories, and learned about Rana Amar Singh's exploits. It was almost impossible to invade the land around the Pichola lake. The Rana had set up outposts in a fifteen-mile radius around the lake, and mines had been dug into the hard, flat ground. The imperial army's abandoned cannons, now in Amar Singh's possession, would be used to ignite the mines. The earth was so flat here that even at night Prince Khurram's army would announce its arrival long before they were within fighting distance.

The prince again listened to counsel from his commanders. He was enraged at how effectively the Rana had fettered his hands. Mewar had been ignored for too long, much longer than a simple conquest of the palace at Pichola Lake—it would have taken Amar Singh's men months to lay the mines. The plans had been in place for a long time, first the mines were set, then the existing imperial army was driven off, leaving behind their cannons and muskets, firepower without which the gunpowder under the earth would be harmless.

Mirza Aziz Koka, Prince Khusrau's father-in-law, had been left here, in command of the army that had so shamefully lost Mewar. When Khurram arrived, Koka tried to tell him what to do, what plan of action to follow, how to lay out the campaign. They fought bitterly with each other, and Khurram wrote to Jahangir asking that Koka be removed from the scene of the battle. The message came to the Emperor while he was still on his way to Ajmer, and Jahangir agreed, ordering Koka to meet up with the travelling court and explain his side of the story.

Then Khurram and his men set about methodically ravaging the countryside around Mewar. Villages that had supported Amar Singh, either this time or in the past, were destroyed. Prince Khurram gave the people fair warning to leave; he did not order the villagers harmed. Mango and guava orchards were burned down, and only blackened stumps stood where once lush greenery had provided shelter for the parrots and fruit to fill empty stomachs. Villagers who had not heeded Khurram's commands were driven from their homes. Imperial elephants demolished their brick-and-mud houses. Wells were filled in, or poison was added to the water. The wheat and rice fields were burned. The army smashed old Hindu temples that had stood for centuries. For days, smoke smouldered in the air, darkening the skies, until the winds came to blow it away.

From his newly acquired fortress on the banks of the Pichola, Amar Singh watched this destruction. He heard the cries of the villagers and their curses against him. Was this destruction, this absolute annihilation, this loss of their property, their lands, their cows and oxen and goats, their very livelihood, worth the Rana's pride? Were they not Rajputs too, just like him? Hordes of villagers migrated from around Mewar to find new homes elsewhere. They could not come back for a few more years at least. It would take time before their water was pure, before their fields could hold life, before the pain would be erased from their memories.

Rana Amar Singh listened to everything—and still held out.

So Prince Khurram devised a new plan. He set up outposts all round Mewar and surrounded the land encircling the Pichola. Nothing was allowed in. No butter, no milk, no wheat or rice, no water, *nothing*.

Weak with hunger, Rana Amar Singh was drawn out of his stronghold for a brief fight, and during that battle he lost fifteen of his elephants, among them one he had grown up on, played with in his childhood, a friend more dear to him than most humans. He heard that the elephants were sent to Emperor Jahangir and that they were now part of the imperial stables at Ajmer.

Rana Amar Singh held a conference in his palace. His commanders all came for the meeting, their faces ravaged by the harsh sun, their bodies thinned to starvation, their voices all but burned out from the months of battle. Peace was the only alternative to death. For if peace did not come, death almost certainly would.

Now it was time to surrender.

All through the day and towards the end of it, dust had been whipped up in huge clouds, blotting the sun, bringing a premature darkness, until Khurram had run to huddle within his tent. When the wind had died, a cloak of earth—so thick had it been that it could no longer have been called dust—lay over the tents, the horses and camels, the men who had not gone for cover. And then the clouds had gathered in the skies. Lightning had flashed, thunder had boomed, and the rains had come in torrents, pelting down in a fury, washing away the dust of the morning from the tents until they had been wetly green again.

It had rained for two hours now, and Khurram could hear the water gushing through the gullies dug outside. The months at Mewar had almost all been like this. The weather was extremely unpredictable: when it rained it threatened to drown everything;

when the winds blew they killed every breath with the dust they carried; when the sun shone, skins were parched; bodies forever longed for water. Nothing was moderate here, nothing merely pleasant. And in this inhospitable climate, Khurram had waged war against the Rana. But now, he thought, it was finally over. He had been victorious.

The rain was held at bay by the waxed canvas of his tent, but within, moisture collected and hung as the gathered nobles talked and laughed. Wine was passed around and the voices grew louder and harsher. Sweat poured down faces. The talk turned to nonsense, to stories of imagined valour. Some of the commanders staggered to their feet and postured as they showed how the Rana had been routed, how his elephants had been captured, how he himself had been tamed. After all this time, they could finally celebrate. Mewar was now part of the Mughal Empire, the Rana was no longer a threat, the years of fighting were over. And they had been responsible for this. Jahangir would reward them richly, jagirs would be given out, titles bestowed, wealth amassed, and the Emperor's favour would fall upon them. They drank some more, their speech began to slur, everything was funny.

Khurram turned away from his men and sank deeper into the cushions of his divan. He felt over the front of his qaba, and his fingers traced the square, folded sheet of paper resting in an inner pocket. Then he picked up his goblet and drank from it. Lime juice with jaggery to sweeten it. Khurram did not drink liquor; he never had. He touched the letter again, wishing the commanders would leave so that he could read what Arjumand had written to him.

How many months had it been since he had seen her? Eight? Nine? Time blurred here, for each month had been the same. No change of seasons, nothing to engage his attention. Without Arjumand, there was nothing for him. Khurram had been ordered to command the army against Amar Singh, and he had obeyed. Not just from filial loyalty or a sense of duty as a royal prince, but because Arjumand had said that he must go. They had decided that he would not accept Ladli as a wife, and this would definitely upset Mehrunnisa, but a victory in Mewar would counter that with the Emperor. So Khurram had fought the Rana, not for the empire he wanted to inherit, not because it would bring him glory, not even because he wanted to please his father, but because he wanted to please his wife. Every action he had taken, every foray he had planned, every move his commanders and his men had made had been with Arjumand in mind. The sooner he vanquished the Rana, the sooner he could be with Arjumand.

He looked around at his men as they grew louder and more brash. One tipped over from his divan, and in doing so, upset a goblet of wine. It soaked into the carpet, and a red stain blossomed in the silk pile. The smell of fermented grape came to gag the prince. Khurram wanted to ask them to leave, but this was their celebration too. Tomorrow, Amar Singh was to come to the camp for the official surrender. And then, in a few days, weeks at most, Khurram could go to Ajmer, where Arjumand was with the Emperor and Mehrunnisa. He hugged his arms around himself at those words. Tomorrow, a few days, weeks... after all these months, finally he could speak of returning to Arjumand in smaller measures of time.

Ray Rayan, major-domo of Khurram's household, noticed the prince's restlessness and broke up the celebrations.

'His Highness is tired.' Ray Rayan pointed to the flap of the tent. The excited nobles stopped talking and turned drunkenly to Khurram.

The prince lifted his shoulders gracefully. 'What he says is true.'

When the last noble had left or been dragged out, and the flap of the tent was pulled down, Khurram eagerly reached inside his qaba. He put the paper to his face, smelled the light hint of rose water in which Arjumand had dipped the edges, rubbed it against his cheek. She had touched this letter, she had been thinking of him when she had written it, she must know that he would think of *that* as he read it. Their third child had been born a few months ago at Ajmer, another boy, and the Emperor had given him the name of Aurangzeb.

Khurram unrolled the letter and let his eyes run greedily over the graceful, flowing handwriting. 'All is well with the grace of Allah.' Here was that first line of assurance; before Arjumand began her letters, she always put this line on the top. It was something she had learned from her grandfather; Ghias Beg had taught her to tell the reader, upon first perusal, that the letter bore no bad news. And leaving out that line would be warning of what was to come. She wrote:

> My dearest lord,
> I miss you. There must be ways, surely, of saying this more poetically, with more emotion and distress, with more feeling. But for me, these three words are enough. You are not here by my side, your absence is felt every day and every moment, without you there is no life in me. When is this to end? Why must I be confined thus to the bearing of children, and not be with you? Why can I not bear those children where you are?
> I apologize for these words and this language, but I am anxious for your safety. If I cannot see you, or be near you, how can I look after you?

Khurram clutched the letter to his chest and rocked back and forth on his divan. It was not enough to have just the letter from Arjumand; he wanted her in his arms. He was the one who should look after Arjumand, so he had promised when he had married her.

And why this separation indeed? Because Mehrunnisa had suggested it, she had said that Arjumand was pregnant, that she could not possibly travel with the army, that she would slow them down, that the child, possibly a future emperor, could not be born on the roadside without the royal physicians in attendance. That Khurram would endanger his wife's life if he insisted upon taking her with him. It was this last argument that had given Khurram pause. And though Arjumand had wept and thrown a tantrum, he had withstood her demands. She could not come with him in her condition. But now, after all these months apart, all these months when Khurram felt as though his body was here in Mewar but everything else, his thoughts, his heart, his every breath was where Arjumand was, Mehrunnisa's reasons no longer seemed valid.

The Empress had wished to separate them, to bring a break in their relationship, to cause them this grief. What would have been so bad if Arjumand had travelled with Khurram and lived in his camp? He would have brought the royal hakims with him to be at her service when she needed it. As for the child, Arjumand had already been safely delivered of two other sons, with seemingly no distress at all. And even if Aurangzeb was going to be emperor after him—this Khurram did not think very possible, because there were those two other sons, Dara Shikoh and Shah Shuja, whose claims were a mite stronger because they had come into the world earlier—Emperor Akbar had been born in a tent while Humayun was fleeing India.

Khurram held up the letter and started to read again.

My aunt has received five passes from the Portuguese Viceroy at Goa. I went to ask her for one, just one cartaz for your ship that is to leave Surat soon for Jiddah, but she refused. She had given them all out already, she said, but I know at least three rest in the pockets of her ships' captains. She is a vicious woman. I know you will never marry Ladli, but is there any necessity to plague us so just because of one refusal?

I upset myself with these thoughts, but one remains always constant. That you must return, my lord, safely and with victory adorning your forehead. The Emperor will see that he has a son he can be proud of; for my part, no woman was ever so fortunate in the man she loves. May Allah be with you.

The prince kissed the letter, folded it up, and put it into a silver box that he kept with him always. In the box were Arjumand's other letters. He suddenly realized how silent it was—the rain had stopped as abruptly as it had started. He could still hear water flowing through the camp sewers, but his men were now moving around outside. Khurram put his head through the flap of his tent. The humidity of the night had come to take the place of the rain. Mosquitoes buzzed furiously, fireflies came out to twinkle in the darkness, and in the centre of his camp, some of the soldiers had set up logs of neem wood in a fire pit. It was too hot for a fire, but the acrid, smoldering smoke of the neem would keep the mosquitoes away in the night, and for the first time in many months they could even light a fire for this without worrying that Amar Singh would ambush them.

Khurram withdrew and went to his desk. He pulled out a sheet of paper and sharpened his quill with his knife. He would write to Arjumand immediately. Then he pushed the paper away. No, he would be with her soon, before the letter found its way to her hands. He dipped the quill in the ink cup and sketched the outlines of his ship in Surat. Khurram had started dabbling in overseas trade only recently, mostly because Mehrunnisa found so much in it to interest her. The money was excellent, so Ruqayya had always told him, and Khurram had seen her throw bags of mohurs at servants who brought her something she really wanted. Why, the Portuguese had captured Ruqayya's ship, so there must be some value in this kind of trading. Besides, Khurram needed the money, he had only the income from his jagirs and his mansabs, and he wanted more so that he could buy Arjumand as many jewels as she wanted, and as many jewels as he pleased. He was poor, he thought, compared to Mehrunnisa. The Emperor had the most income, as was only befitting, but *he* should have been next in the empire, instead of being third, behind Mehrunnisa.

If Mehrunnisa would not give him a cartaz, he would write to the Portuguese Viceroy himself. The Viceroy would be a good ally and would not refuse a royal prince, especially one who had the most chance of becoming the next emperor. He took out a fresh sheet of paper and began to write.

Khurram was just finishing the letter when Ray Rayan lifted the flap of the tent. 'Your Highness, would you like to come out? The men wish to see you.'

'Yes.' Khurram put his seal on the letter, folded it and handed it to his eunuch. 'See that it gets to Goa as soon as possible.'

He went outside to the circle around the fire. The soldiers cheered when they saw him.

'Hail to the conqueror!' they shouted, waving their arms and clapping their hands.

He stood there smiling, exulting in this praise. All the commanders were older than he was, but he had planned every detail of the siege. And these men had followed his orders, trusted in his judgement. He let them hoot and yell, and then he held up a hand. The soldiers quieted down, wine bottles were raised to their mouths, and they waited for Khurram to speak.

'We have succeeded,' Khurram said. 'It has taken us a long time, but now it is all over. The credit lies with all of you, brave soldiers and able commanders. The Emperor will be pleased with your service to him and the empire. Tomorrow, the Rana comes to the camp to surrender.' At this, the soldiers began to snigger and boo, but Khurram stopped them. A few weeks ago, his father had written to him. Even then it had been evident that the war against Mewar was over. *Treat the Rana with dignity and honour,* Jahangir's letter had said. *He is a king; he comes to us still a king. Regard him as one king would another, Khurram.*

So, standing there in the hot light of the neem fire, Khurram told his men of the Emperor's wishes. They fell quiet, looked at each other with shame, and bowed their heads. Khurram clapped his hands when he saw their sombre faces. It was enough that he could tell them of this—he knew he would be obeyed.

The prince signalled to the musicians behind his soldiers. Music started to play, and the nautch girls came out from behind the tents. They swayed in front of the soldiers, the light searing through their thin muslin skirts and veils, illuminating a slender thigh here, the shape of a barely covered breast there. The soldiers drank some more, flung silver rupees into the air, lurched drunkenly after the women, who giggled and escaped their hands. They would eventually succumb, of course, but the longer they held out, the more money they would make.

Khurram turned to go back to his tent. Someone touched his arm, and he turned back. The girl was young, perhaps no more than sixteen. She had a warm, earthy beauty. Heavy breasts, well-curved hips, a tight waist. Her skin was clear and golden in the light from the fire. She smiled at him, her eyes full of a rich promise.

She put out a hand. And Khurram, suddenly hungry for the taste of a woman's skin, took it and led her to his tent.

Rana Amar Singh came into Khurram's camp to the sound of trumpets. The imperial army stood along the path the Rana was to take, and when he walked among them, the men bowed. They had fought him for very long, and though Amar Singh was subdued, even cornered, he was still a king. Their commander had said so, and if Khurram was going to treat the Rana with respect, they could do no less.

Amar Singh was now in his sixties, his hair and thick moustache were white, in startling contrast to the brown of his face, where the sun of Mewar had painted its colours. Amar Singh had come into the camp almost tentatively, not quite sure of his reception. He was in full armour, and his boots and mail clanked as he walked. His back was straight though; even had he been boorishly received, Amar Singh would not have let his pride fall as his kingdom had.

Khurram stood outside his tent and watched the Rana. Amar Singh went down on his knees and touched Khurram's boots. The prince immediately bent and raised the old man to his feet.

'There is no need to ask for forgiveness, all is forgiven,' Khurram said. 'You have shown your fealty to the Mughal Empire by coming here today. The Emperor shall protect you at all times, and it is your duty to respond to his call when he needs you.'

'I will do so, your Highness.' Rana Amar Singh lifted his head and looked at Khurram. He gestured to the soldiers behind him. 'Please accept these offerings.'

The soldiers came forward and set down a huge ruby. It was enormous, about the size of a polo ball, and it glowed like the heart of a fire. So the rumours about the existence of this ruby were true, Khurram thought. It was said that the ruby had belonged to the Rana's family for many generations, and his gift of the stone proved his loyalty and complete surrender. He had to restrain himself from grabbing the ruby and running his fingers over its many-faceted face. What a lovely jewel it would make, set in a turban, the light catching its pomegranate redness. But Khurram would have to give the ruby to his father, and it would most probably end up in Mehrunnisa's hands. He looked at the black velvet cushion he held with wistfulness, thinking, at least for now, this stone was his. The

Rana's soldiers also brought in bales of silks and jewelled daggers. Seven elephants and nine horses were led into the enclosure. Each animal was clad in cloth of gold and silver with gem-studded reins and bridles.

'I am ashamed of the meagre offerings,' Amar Singh said. 'But as your Highness probably knows, they are the only things left to me.'

'This is more than generous,' Khurram smiled. 'We have captured all the other animals in your private stables. The Emperor is pleased with your surrender. A royal farman will be sent to you bearing the imperial seal. The farman will provide you with protection and will name you as a vassal to the empire. As proof of the Emperor's intentions, please accept these gifts from me.'

Khurram turned and signalled to Ray Rayan. The eunuch brought forward a robe of honour and a jewelled sword that the prince gifted to the Rana. Attendants led an Arabian mare into the enclosure with a jewelled saddle and an elephant strapped with a silver howdah.

The Rana bowed his head. 'Thank you, your Highness. Your kindness is much appreciated.'

'One more thing,' Khurram said. 'You are still a king, Amar Singh. You will retain your title and your lands. Mewar is given to you as a jagir, yours to rule while you live.'

The Rana spent a few days at camp, where he was feted and his every need tended to. After he left, his eldest son Karan came to pay his respects to Khurram, according to custom. The heir apparent never accompanied his father to pay his respects to an Emperor or a prince; he always came later. Karan would go with Khurram to Ajmer and pledge allegiance to Jahangir on behalf of Amar Singh. Khurram accepted this, and did not insist upon Amar Singh's accompanying him himself. This much dignity the old Rana was allowed. And so the empire and Jahangir told Amar Singh that he had fought a worthy fight, that he was a mighty king too.

Soon after Karan's arrival, the royal party broke camp and began their journey back to the court at Ajmer.

Prince Khurram returned to the imperial court victorious in a siege his father had once fought as a prince. With this triumph, many things changed. Khurram found a confidence he had not had before. He could lead an army, so he could wear a crown. He would find a way to tell Mehrunnisa that a marriage with Ladli was impossible.

court would celebrate, and she had to be prepared for the festivities.

Mehrunnisa sighed. There was so much to think about, and here she was, wondering about her toilette. What was to be done with the Portuguese? Ever since the capture of the *Rahimi*, they had taken possession of at least a hundred more Indian ships. If they could dare to seize the Dowager Empress's ship, how long before they took one of hers? Mehrunnisa had ordered the Portuguese to return the *Rahimi*—there was no question about the ship not being restored to Ruqayya—but her language had been honeyed, her tongue imprisoned by the passes the Portuguese Viceroy had sent for her ships.

And Khurram would come home a hero, feted and pampered, still as much a worry as the Portuguese Viceroy. She rose from the divan and walked around the room. She needed to make a decision, needed not to feel helpless against these men. Mehrunnisa stopped and dug her toes into the pile of the carpets. She willed anger to flood through her, to take over her thoughts and drown out everything else. If the Portuguese wanted war, they would get war.

A few minutes later the Empress whipped around to Hoshiyar, her mouth set in a tight line. 'Send an order to Muqarrab Khan. He is to lay siege on the Portuguese city of Daman.'

'Your Majesty, why Muqarrab? He will do all he can to help the Portuguese. You must know that he has been converted to their religion. He is on their side.'

'He cannot openly defy imperial orders. If he does, it will mean death. This order will test his loyalty to the empire. Muqarrab will get no more indulgences from the court. Yes,' Mehrunnisa nodded, 'it will have to be Muqarrab Khan. As governor of Gujrat, he is closest to Daman. The Portuguese will not be granted any more privileges. They have enjoyed the magnanimity of the Emperor for too long and have misused their power. Daman must be captured.'

Chapter Fourteen

The Prince entered the Towne, and all the great men in
wondrous triumph. The King received him as if he had no
other, contrary to all our expectation.

—WILLIAM FOSTER, ED.,
The Embassy of Sir Thomas Roe to India

MEHRUNNISA GLANCED AT THE LETTER IN HER HAND THOUGHTFULLY. NEWS
had come from Surat. The Portuguese had burned four Indian ships
at the Gulf of Cambay in direct disobedience to imperial orders.

Hoshiyar Khan coughed. 'What is the reply, your Majesty?'

'Do you know what is in this letter?'

'I have an idea,' Hoshiyar said. 'I talked to the runner who
brought the letter.'

Mehrunnisa nodded. Hoshiyar had probably not just talked to
the runner but as the letter had found its way to her on the silver
salver, it had also probably unrolled itself. The seal was broken, but
she said nothing about this. Finally, after all these years, she had
come to trust Hoshiyar. What she knew, he knew. He would never
betray her.

She spread her fingers on the satin cover of the divan. The
tendrils of jasmine vine, drawn on with henna paste, were now
feeble orange. Tonight, no, tomorrow, soon anyhow, she would
have the maids repaint the henna. Khurram was coming home from
Mewar, bringing the captured Prince Karan Singh with him. The

Hoshiyar bowed and turned to go, but Mehrunnisa's voice stopped him. 'Also prepare a farman to Agra. The Jesuit church in Agra shall be shut and the salaries paid to the priests stopped. Send the priest Jerome Xavier to Muqarrab Khan, he is to keep Xavier in custody until further orders come from me. All the Portuguese in India are to be arrested and their belongings seized.'

When Hoshiyar left, Mehrunnisa wrote to the captains of her ships; they would find the letters waiting for them when her ships returned to Surat. The passes from the Viceroy were to be sent to Goa with thanks from her Majesty. She had no more use for them.

The imperial farmans were prepared and sent to the zenana, where Mehrunnisa read them with care before affixing the seal of the Emperor. Then she picked up a smaller green jade seal in the shape of a rose with six petals, dipped it in ink, and firmly affixed it on the farmans. The seal read, 'By the light of the sun of the Emperor Jahangir; the bezel of the seal of Nur Jahan has become resplendent like the Moon.'

She used her personal seal rarely, but in this case, she wanted the Viceroy to know that this was on *her* orders. That she would play no more games of diplomacy with him, that if he wanted to keep his head in India, it should be bowed towards her.

Next to Jahangir's name, Mehrunnisa wrote with an unwavering hand, 'Nur Jahan, the Queen Begam.'

The streets of Ajmer were decked with flowers and banners. Torches flared from sconces in doorways, pillars were wrapped in marigold garlands, and the stone-flagged paths had been washed clean. Fire and colour welcomed Khurram. The streets were thronged fifteen deep, men and women pushing against each other and the imperial soldiers who kept them from the path. The balconies of the houses overhanging the lanes were filled with women and children, leaning over the parapets to look at the head of their triumphant prince, hoping for an upward glance.

Khurram rode into the city in style. He sat upright on his black Arabian mare, his person glittering with jewels and brocade. Gone were the dull mud colours of the campaign, the heavy weight of the armour he had worn daily for months, the unwashed hair, and the sweat-rimmed collars. Khurram was well rested; he had slept on the road to Ajmer on divans sent for his comfort by Mehrunnisa, and the cooks from the imperial kitchens had come to meet him halfway so that delicacies their Majesties ate would fill his own mouth. Unlike the mad dash from Agra to Mewar, when speed had been necessary, this trip had been more leisurely. The imperial favour shown to Khurram was not only for Khurram himself but also to awe Prince Karan, the mountain prince, and to show him the grandeur of the empire.

And here, Khurram thought, as he nudged his horse into a slower trot, was another example of magnificence. Karan rode behind him astride another horse, not as splendidly clothed as Khurram's but one befitting a prince nonetheless. Khurram glanced at Karan and then looked up at the balconies. The women clapped, their expressions pretty with delight, and threw down jasmine flowers that floated star-like in the afternoon air around Khurram. He lifted his face to the gently falling flowers which settled like snow over his hands and his horse. The crowds cheered wildly, and he bowed to them from the saddle, over and over again.

When he reached the royal palaces, he saw his mother and various ladies of the harem gathered there to welcome him. He jumped off his horse and ran to Jagat Gosini. The Empress embraced her son.

'Welcome back, beta,' she said. 'You have made us all proud.'

'Thank you, your Majesty. Where is my father?'

'He awaits you in the Diwan-i-am.'

Khurram hurried to the Emperor. The drums of the prince

sounded in the hall, and he entered after the last note had died down. While all the courtiers bowed to him, he went down on his knees in front of Jahangir and kissed the ground. Jahangir rose from his seat and came down to Khurram.

'You have brought much happiness to all of us, Baba Khurram,' Jahangir said. He raised his voice to the assembled courtiers. 'I declare that from this day, the prince shall be known as Shah Jahan.'

Khurram knelt again, clutched his father's hand, and kissed it reverently. Jahangir had said nothing about a new title in his letters; Khurram had expected to be feted, a mighty prince returning victorious from war, but this... to be called Shah Jahan, King of the World. He grew dizzy with happiness. The title of Shah was one none but a reigning king had held since the time of his ancestor Timur the Lame. And he was just a prince. He started to cry, his heart full at such honour, and Jahangir raised him to his feet and wiped his tears away.

'Come, you must not cry,' the Emperor said, half-laughing, half-crying himself. 'You are a warrior, Khurram. You have done what I was not able to.'

They stood together in the midst of the court, Khurram with his head on Jahangir's shoulder until attendants came up behind them, bearing in their arms the nadiri, a coat of honour Jahangir had designed for himself and ordered that no one else in the empire could wear unless it was bestowed upon him by the Emperor. Jahangir lovingly wrapped the nadiri around his son and stuck a jewelled dagger in his cummerbund. He then ordered that a special chair be brought into court for Khurram. The chair was set just below the Emperor's throne. It was a great privilege, for never before had anyone, royal or otherwise, sat in the Emperor's presence at court.

Mehrunnisa watched the display of affection from the zenana

balcony. She had not gone out to meet Khurram when he had arrived because Jagat Gosini had wanted to be there instead. Hoshiyar, already leaning to her ear, told her that their conversation had been short—an embrace, a few words, that was all. Arjumand sat next to her, her face pressed against the screen, alit with smiles. They both saw Khurram glance up at the balcony, but he could see little of them; the marble latticeworked screen hid them from view. Arjumand put her fingers through and waggled them, and Khurram raised his hand from his lap in response.

'He has made us all proud, Arju,' Mehrunnisa said.

Arjumand turned to her aunt, her face suddenly hard and unyielding. '*I* am proud of my husband, your Majesty.'

It was as if she had reached out and slapped Mehrunnisa. The women in the zenana balcony grew quiet.

'Why the disrespect, Arjumand?' Mehrunnisa said softly. 'I am as proud of Khurram as you are. He is like a son to me. You must know this.'

Arjumand looked away and did not reply. Mehrunnisa let her be, and said something of no consequence to Hoshiyar, something meant to be humorous, and the ladies laughed dutifully. All of this escaped Ladli, who, like Arjumand, had her face glued to the screen. When she turned into the balcony, her eyes sparkled with laughter.

'He is so handsome, Arju,' she said, and went to sit next to her cousin. 'You are very lucky. If only I could be so lucky too. Mama,' she turned to Mehrunnisa, 'you must find me a husband like Khurram.'

And again there was that silence until Arjumand said to her aunt, 'Yes, your Majesty, find Ladli someone *like* Khurram. Just *like* him. That will be best for everyone.'

Mehrunnisa sat without moving, anger coming into her unbidden this time. She could not trust herself to speak. Ladli had begun to chatter again, leaning against her mother. She smoothed her daughter's hair out of her eyes, and Ladli smiled briefly at her mother. Mehrunnisa's hand trembled, and she moved it into her lap. Just *like* him, Arjumand had had the gall to say. When had the mouse-like Arjumand acquired such courage? Had the bearing of three heirs suddenly placed iron in her blood? Who did she think she was? Khurram *would* marry Ladli, there was going to be no argument about that. And Arjumand was the last person who could have a say in this matter. Were she and Khurram stupid enough to think that the Emperor's affections for his son were stronger than his love for Mehrunnisa?

Sweat dampened her armpits and Mehrunnisa shivered. She was startled as Ladli came forward to kiss her cheek, put her arms around her neck, and say, 'Mama, the darbar is over. I am going with Arju to welcome Khurram. You must come too. He's a hero!'

Ladli ran away, one edge of her ghagara tucked into her waist to keep her from tripping—she had not yet learned how to fly in the voluminous skirts with the ease of a woman. But Ladli was growing up. She was fifteen, the age when Arjumand herself was betrothed to Khurram, the age at which *she* could just as easily be betrothed to Khurram.

One chance, Mehrunnisa thought. She would ask Khurram again, and he would get only one chance to respond. His star may be on the rise now, but hers was firmly lodged in the skies and would not fade until Jahangir died. If Khurram said no again... there was no way she would allow the crown to adorn his head.

After the last spin, when the slave's hand left his arm and she melted away with a whisper of skirts on the marble floor, Khurram stood quiet, swaying on his feet. His eyes were shut under the blindfold, the cloth of which covered his ears too, but he could still hear if he strained to do so. The prince stumbled and someone giggled to his right, and then the sound was snuffed out. Khurram breathed evenly through his nose and mouth, waiting for the weakness to leave his legs, waiting for his centre of balance to return.

It was some weeks after his court appearance, and Khurram was playing *ankh michauli*—blindman's bluff—with the ladies of his harem. This was one of his rewards from Arjumand. Tonight, she was fatigued, lethargic from symptoms that presaged another pregnancy. Arjumand was fertile like volcanic earth, Khurram thought; he merely had to *look* at her and a child would grow within. And when she tired from carrying the child—if indeed it was a child inside her—she let him take one of the harem women to his bed. But only every now and then.

Night had long settled over the courtyard in Khurram's apartments, and a bright moon rose to cover the marble slabs with a coating of pale lilac. The verandah arches were in deep darkness, and no lamps had been lit. This was on the prince's orders; if he was going to be blindfolded, the women should have no light to escape from him. Before the cool cloth was tied over his eyes, Khurram stood in the shadowed yard, looking long and hard at the slaves and concubines around him. They were all clad in white, glimmering silks, brilliant zari embroidered into their bodices and ghagaras, wrists bare of bangles, diamonds glittering in their ears. They wore no anklets and their feet were bare, so they could flit about him without noise. The blindfold covered his eyes, and then someone twirled him around in circles and let him go until he no longer knew which direction he faced or who was in front of him.

A hand, soft as rose petals, touched his right shoulder and went down his back. Khurram whipped around, arms outstretched, but she had disappeared. He took a few tentative steps and brushed against a slender hip. Khurram touched the woman, let his hand linger over the curve of her waist, ran a finger under the tie of her ghagara's skirts. She was wearing brocade, he could tell by the feel of it, its pattern was raised into the surface of the cloth in grey satin thread. She stayed perfectly still as his hands moved over her. Nalini... of the luscious mouth, of the daring eyes, of the body that threshed wildly beneath him. But tonight, Khurram was in the mood for something gentle, someone who gave rather than took.

He moved on in complete darkness, led only by his sense of touch and smell. As he had stood waiting for the blindfold, he had memorized almost every woman's dress, and simply by its texture—whether silk, or satin, or velvet, or brocade, or cotton—for that would tell him who they were and whether he wanted them.

They came to caress him often, but in silence, and he followed where he heard their feet lead. Khurram played this game with the same ferocity and intensity with which he had fought the war in Mewar. With every stroke, his heartbeat raced. And yet there wasn't one woman he wanted to leave with to his bedchamber. Until he came to the woman who stood against one of the pillars of the verandah.

When Khurram first clasped her wrist and pulled the palm of her hand to his mouth, she let him. Her skin was smooth, perfumed with an aroma that filled his nostrils. What was it, Khurram thought. Musk? No, something more forceful, with an underlying hint of camphor and incense from censers... *luban*... frankincense. Intrigued by this unusual choice of scent—the other women were bathed in flower scents—Khurram ran his tongue over her palm. He heard the woman take in a breath, and then gently, she tugged her hand away. For a moment, a fleeting moment, she touched his face, cupped her fingers around his chin, and then she turned to flee. Khurram ran behind her, listening hard for the sound of her feet on the cool marble stones. He bumped into a pillar, other hands came to hinder his progress, but he still pursued the woman with the delicious aroma.

When he caught up with her, he framed her against another pillar, his hands on either side of her waist. Khurram would not let her go now. If anyone could sate this hunger of his, it would be this woman. He touched her. Felt the smooth skin between her bodice and the top of her ghagara. Felt the cloth—it was *malmal*, the softest cotton woven in the imperial ateliers. Her shoulders were bare, and he ran his hand down from there to the edge of her velvet bodice. He put his face into the scoop of her neck, listened to the crazy beat of her heart, filled himself with the touch of her skin, the sound of her body, the smell of jasmines in her hair.

Then, the prince raised his head and caught hold of the woman's hand. He fumbled for the white rose that was fastened in a buttonhole of his white kurta and gave it to her. 'This one,' he said aloud. 'She is to be the one for tonight.'

At the sound of his voice, the game was over. Eunuchs filed in carrying torches. They lit the oil lamps and filled the courtyard with light. Khurram, still holding on to the woman, used his other hand to pull off his blindfold.

Shock jolted through him. Ladli stood there. A slender, barely clad Ladli, her eyes grey and unreadable, the white rose in her hands. Khurram stepped back, still stunned. What was Ladli doing here, among the women of his harem? Why was she here? He moved away but could not take his gaze off her. He looked at what he had so recently touched, that slim waist, that neck, that thick swathe of ink-dark hair tied at her nape.

'Of course you cannot have Ladli, Khurram,' a frigid, distant voice said at his shoulder.

Khurram turned to see Arjumand by his side. She said no more, but she too was looking at her cousin, her eyes like stones. He nodded at once, and when Arjumand pointed to one of the other women, Khurram almost ran to grab her hand and drag her from the courtyard. The others went away too, one by one, until only Ladli was left standing against the pillar.

She was trembling, with jitters that seemed not to stop. She raised the rose to her mouth and held it there. Then she slid down to sit on the floor, knees pulled into her chest.

'Of course,' she said out loud to the empty courtyard.

As the weeks passed, Mehrunnisa waited for an opportunity to talk with Khurram. She had learned the value of patience, the value of waiting for the right moment to speak. Khurram and she met, of course, at various places and for various reasons. She called a meeting of their junta; it was awkward and uncomfortable, but they met nonetheless. Mehrunnisa told the three men what she had done about the Portuguese problem. Khurram stubbornly insisted that she could have been more diplomatic—why lay siege on Daman? The empire had always been tolerant of the Portuguese, and after all, they were just reacting to the favour being shown to the English merchants.

'What do you think, Abul?' Mehrunnisa snapped at her brother.

'Do not fight,' Ghias said from his divan. 'You are not children anymore. Listen to what his Highness has to say, Mehrunnisa.'

Khurram did have more to say, of course. 'Your Majesty,' his tone bordered on the edge of insolence, 'the English have only thus far promised us protection. Where is this protection? And where is this great ambassador who is yet to set foot on Indian soil? Why provoke the Portuguese before we know for sure that the English are on our side?'

'They burned four ships, Khurram. If that is not an invitation for retaliation, what else is?' Mehrunnisa leaned forward and put her face a few inches from Khurram's. 'Are we to sit by idly while the Portuguese do what they want? Should there be no response from the court and the Emperor to this affront?'

He looked away. 'I did not know about the ships, your Majesty.'

Abul and Ghias both said, 'Mehrunnisa is right.'

'Yes,' Khurram mumbled, redness creeping up his neck. 'Perhaps so.'

There was no *perhaps* about it, Mehrunnisa thought. They argued next about why she had not consulted with them before taking this step. Because she had consulted with the Emperor. That kept them quiet until the meeting broke up. Ghias stayed back. He was worried about all this fighting. Mehrunnisa should watch her tongue. But she did not listen to her father. Once she had. When she was younger, before she was an empress, even when she was just newly an empress. But too many years had passed. In the beginning of her reign, the three men had been necessary for reasons other than the kinship that bound them. Now, it was no longer so.

Besides, Ghias had grown old. He was too tolerant, and he could not know what lay at stake for her. As his life ended, hers would begin. She had to plan for the future where Jahangir no longer existed. This the Emperor himself told her. Jahangir knew too that he was nine years older than Mehrunnisa, that he would likely not live as long as her, that she would probably outlast him for many years. If he was not here to look after her, he wanted to know, before he died, that she would be well looked after. Hence, he encouraged the courting of Khurram for Ladli—that child was the only connection Mehrunnisa would have to the royal family once Jahangir passed away.

To Mehrunnisa and Jahangir, these conversations late at night were not morbid. They were simply facts of life. Every time the Emperor built a sarai for tired travellers, a mosque, commissioned even the building of a church, or added a palace to the fort at Agra or Lahore, he was aware of his mortality. He would go, but hundreds and hundreds of years later, these pieces of stone would speak of his life.

During the time that Mehrunnisa waited to speak with Khurram, her temper rose and ebbed almost every day. Empress Jagat Gosini was feted along with her son, an irony that made Mehrunnisa deeply angry. Ruqayya was his mother, *she* was the one who had brought him up, lavished her love upon him. But Ruqayya was at Agra, still despondent about the *Rahimi*, and refused to travel with them to Ajmer. So Jagat Gosini preened about with the pride of a rain-foretelling peacock, her feathers fanned, dancing in Mehrunnisa's face.

The irritations were numerous. One evening, at the entertainment, Jahangir leaned over Jagat Gosini, caught Mehrunnisa's chin, and kissed her on the mouth. It was a slow kiss, a kiss of love.

She put her arms around his neck and said, 'Your breath smells sweet, your Majesty.'

Jagat Gosini sat between them. She had turned her face away but could not help watching as they hung over her lap.

Jahangir turned to her. 'What do you think, Jagat?'

'My lord, only a woman who has had an opportunity to smell another man's mouth could tell you that your breath smells sweet. I have had no such experience and can only say that it always smells sweet,' Jagat Gosini said.

Mehrunnisa was suddenly ashamed, and then angry with herself for being ashamed. The Empress was reminding her, none too gently, that she had been married before and had had the opportunity to taste another man's mouth. Jahangir laughed, but he had no jealousy.

And so time passed. The furore over Khurram's victory died down as court duties began to occupy both Jahangir's and Mehrunnisa's time. It was Khurram's twenty-sixth birthday in a few days. Mehrunnisa planned the festivities, intending that when

Khurram was flush with pride at the favour shown to him, she would again ask him to take Ladli as a wife.

'Your Highness, please step into the scales,' the Mir Tozak said.

Khurram glanced at his father. Jahangir nodded.

Khurram bowed to the Emperor and went towards the golden scales in the middle of the Diwan-i-am. The scales hung by gold chains from a large wooden beam plated with gold and embedded with rubies. The criss-crossed legs of the scales were similarly decorated with a beaten gold plate, which had been hammered into the teak underneath with gold nails.

Khurram put a hand on an attendant's shoulder to steady himself and climbed into the large golden disc. He glanced up at the screened zenana balcony as he sat down cross-legged and attendants brought bags of gold and silver to weigh down the other end of the scales. Khurram clutched the gold chain of his scale, felt the smoothness of the metal in his hands, and wanted to grab it to his chest. It was all solid gold, with a smidgen of copper to give it its burnished sheen. Above him, the rubies and pearls on the centre beam glowed and blurred before his eyes. What happiness this was.

Emperor Akbar had begun the tradition of weighing himself—on his solar and lunar birthdays—against silks, gold, silver, copper, quicksilver, butter, grains, and anything else he deemed to be a luxury. The items were then distributed to the poor. It was Akbar's way of blessing his empire.

Today, the court was packed with onlookers. The passes for this weighing ceremony had been much sought. Bribes had filled the pockets and deepened the smiles of the imperial eunuchs, slaves and guards.

The weighing began. First, thick silk bags of gold mohurs were loaded on one plate of the scales, and on the opposite scale Khurram was lifted in the air until the scales were level with each other. Khurram was light, and the number of bags of gold, few. The months at Mewar without the comforts of a proper kitchen had eaten the flesh from his body.

'You are too thin, Khurram,' Jahangir said from his throne. 'And thus do you deprive the needy of their gold.'

Everyone laughed. Khurram smiled too. He bowed from his scale to his father.

'If your Majesty permits, I will eat more and become more prosperous.'

The weighing went on for an hour. Khurram was weighed against silver, copper, gold, fruits, mustard oil, vegetables and butter. The precious metals had been provided by the ladies of the harem, foremost among them the Dowager Empress Ruqayya, who was gratefully acknowledging Jahangir's support in the affair of the *Rahimi*. Mehrunnisa had donated some gold too, and as each bag was put onto the scales, the Mir Tozak announced its origins. So Mehrunnisa's name was taken often in the silent court, and the nobles glanced at each other. The junta was as strong as ever.

Mehrunnisa watched from behind the zenana screen as Khurram tried to get up after the weighing. He rose a couple of times, fell, and then a couple of courtiers grabbed him under his armpits and hauled him up. He swayed unsteadily as he performed the taslim to the Emperor again, his gaze blank. Mehrunnisa smiled. The prince was drunk. In the zenana earlier, when Khurram had come to pay his respects, Jahangir had offered him some wine and the prince had accepted. Of all the royal princes, Khurram had been the only one who had abstained from drink. But since the Mewar victory, Khurram drank wine as though it were sherbet. Earlier this morning he had consumed three cups in twenty minutes and walked out with firm feet and a mocking glance. *See, your Majesty, it does nothing to me.*

This was the time to talk to Khurram, Mehrunnisa decided.

When the darbar finished its business, she called for the prince in open court, her voice silencing the talk of the courtiers.

The Emperor inclined his head to listen and turned to Khurram, who was still swaying on his feet. 'Khurram, have you heard Nur Jahan Begam's command? '

'Yes, your Majesty.' The prince bowed, but ended up lurching into a courtier.

In the zenana balcony, Arjumand started to speak; Mehrunnisa held her hand up across her niece's face. 'You have not been given permission to address me, Arjumand. Go back to your apartments. I will send Khurram there when I am finished.'

Arjumand opened her mouth again, but Hoshiyar came to lift her from her seat and usher her out.

Khurram had to be led to Mehrunnisa's apartments, half-carried by Hoshiyar and another eunuch. He stood at the doorway, shaking his head to clear it of the wine. But the alcohol was in his blood, not in his head. Khurram staggered forward, almost fell, and then righted himself. He pitched into the room and flung himself onto a divan.

Mehrunnisa waited until he turned to her. His gaze was insolent, intractable.

'What do you want, your Majesty? Was there any necessity to speak in court, in front of all the nobles? Am I a puppet to be pulled here and there at your will?'

'Watch your tongue, Khurram,' Mehrunnisa snapped. She had meant to be calm, to convince him of what she wanted, but Khurram's impudent speech sent all heed of caution flying from her mind.

'What do you want?' Khurram said sullenly, suddenly finding his hands very interesting. He held one, and then the other, in front of him, turned them this way and that, stroked the hair on his knuckles.

Mehrunnisa hesitated. Her words of diplomacy had gone. If Khurram wanted to ask a direct question, she would ask one too. 'When will you marry Ladli?'

The prince pulled a bolster from behind him and draped himself over it, lying on his stomach, his arms over the thick roll of cotton. Khurram knew what he wanted to say, what he was supposed to say, but for a little moment he shut his eyes and willed the memory of that night to come into his wine-fogged brain. He could still smell her skin; he could not pass an incense censer without remembering Ladli's skin. His fingers throbbed with the yearning to touch her, to see that want returned in her eyes as when he had slipped off his blindfold. Yet... this was a lust, not a passion. So Arjumand told him. So he *knew*. Surely, he was right in what he was going to say. Mehrunnisa could not become his mother-in-law. Surely, he was right... he inclined his head to Mehrunnisa.

'When did the question turn from "Will you marry Ladli?" to "*When* will I marry Ladli?" *Why* should I marry Ladli?'

'Khurram,' Mehrunnisa said sharply, 'do I have to tell you the advantages of this union? The Emperor wishes for it, and that should be enough.'

'His Majesty does not wish for it quite as much as you do, your Majesty. And what advantages could there possibly be in this match? What lands and jagirs will I gain? What precious stones will adorn the cushions of my divan? What connections will I have with powerful nobles in the empire—connections I do not already enjoy?' Khurram let his head flop onto the bolster.

Mehrunnisa flew from her place and stood over the prince. Her hand itched, moved restlessly about, wanted to make contact with Khurram's brazen face. The wine had not made Khurram more pliable; it had made him more bold. He was using this as an excuse to be disrespectful to her. She turned away and paced the carpets as she always did when she was upset. *This* was the man she wanted for Ladli? This was the man she had built up, given consequence? Though Arjumand was not in the room with them, her presence was there. In Khurram's pretended wine-induced insolence, in his language.

'If you are being honoured at all now, Khurram, it is because of me. Without me, you would be nothing. Oh, you might still have pretensions to the throne because the Emperor's blood is mixed with yours, but there would be nothing else. Remember that, and keep your mouth shut if you want to keep your place in the empire. You will marry Ladli, because I order you to. And if you do not, I will make sure the Emperor takes away his favour.'

Khurram turned to lie on his back. 'You overestimate your influence over the Emperor, your Majesty. What wife could be as important as a son?'

She flinched, speaking in a voice low and filled with abhorrence. She had no need to shout anymore. 'And you are a weak man, Khurram. A man with no spine, no substance. You deny me this one request because of Arjumand, but you do not see how this will eventually change your life.'

Hoshiyar had been watching and listening to their conversation, leaning against the wall near the door, his arms folded across his chest. Mehrunnisa turned to him and he hauled Khurram from the divan, put his arm over his shoulder, and dragged him out of the room.

When Hoshiyar returned to his mistress, he found her seated on the carpet, her back straight.

'I offered his Highness some more wine, your Majesty,' Hoshiyar said, bending to Mehrunnisa's ear. 'I told him it would take away the distress. He was very happy at the suggestion.' The eunuch took four gold mohurs from his cummerbund and laid them in front of Mehrunnisa. 'Very pleased indeed.'

More wine. After twenty-six years of not drinking, so much wine in one day. The words they had exchanged would never be taken back now. Bitter words, words of hatred. Khurram had become something beyond her control, or he thought so anyway. She would not ask him again, not after what had happened today, not after she had already asked twice and been refused. Khurram was a fool. He said that a wife was not as important as a son was. Did he really think that? Loving Arjumand as much as he did, how was he so blind to the love between his father and Mehrunnisa? Did he not realize that this was his father's only real marriage? Ever since they had been married, Emperor Jahangir had had only *one* wife.

But he had three other sons.

Chapter Fifteen

> *...I found a change in my health, and by degrees was
> seized with fever and headache. For fear that some injury
> might occur to the country and the servants of God, I kept
> this secret... A few days passed in this manner, and I only
> imparted this to Nur-Jahan Begam than whom I did not
> think anyone was fonder of me...*
>
> —A. ROGERS, TRANS., AND H. BEVERIDGE, ED.,
> *The Tuzuk-i-Jahangiri*

NIGHT HOVERED OVER GOA AND THE ARABIAN SEA, THE SKIES AWASH IN
gold and tangerine. Here, on the very western edge of the empire,
the sun lasted longer, as though unwilling to leave. Long after dark,
a line of silver would glimmer over the flat horizon, like an unseen
city aglow in the distance. The moon had risen a few hours ago,
and as the sun died, it gained in colour. The streets were painted
in silver, the steeples of the Jesuit churches plunged into the sky,
their brass crosses laying shadows across the churchyards. The
Portuguese Viceroy's mansion stood tall and mammoth, made of
open-faced brick, with arched verandahs, turreted roofs and gabled
windows. Goa's harbour could be seen from the balcony of the
mansion, which lay over the open portico in front.

During the day the sands were white as salt, their colours
seemingly rinsed out by the waters edging the vast and impossibly
blue ocean. Palm trees shivered in the humid breeze, and palm

thatch umbrellas adorned the beaches. Time came to a halt in Goa; each day was like the next, beautiful, restful, the shade inviting a siesta to the lulling sound of waves scrambling up the beach and then wistfully draining down.

On this night, the harbour was crowded with a hundred and twenty ships. The ships swayed in the harbour, big and small, arranged like toys on the water, their hulls so close as to touch. The only sound across the waters to the Viceroy's mansion was the creaking and groaning as the wind shoved one ship towards another, and they met uneasily and bobbed away. The sails were furled, gleaming white in the moonlight. The ships were for the most part small, displacing just a few hundred tons, but today they rode even lighter on the water of the harbour. Their holds were empty, their brass fittings removed, their crews on the beach, watching. The *Rahimi* lay in the centre of the other ships. She too was forlorn, dejected—she was not made for this waiting, but to boldly sail across oceans and make war with storms and pirates.

The Viceroy sat alone on his vast and square balcony. A servant bent to his ear.

'We are ready, sire.'

The servant handed him a torch. The Viceroy rose to stand at the edge of the balcony and lifted his torch in the air. From the beach, another spurt of light answered his orders. A few minutes later, the Viceroy watched as a catapult was wheeled to the water's edge, and a round, oil-soaked ball of cotton and wood chips was set on fire. The ball of fire went spinning through the air and landed on a ship in the far right corner of the harbour. For a few long seconds, nothing happened. And then the ship flamed to life as the fire ignited a barrel of gunpowder on the deck. She leaped into the sky and slammed down on her neighbour.

The catapult went to work again. And again. And again. one by one, all the ships in the harbour caught fire. Burning wood splintered into the night sky and fell in a shower of stars. The *Rahimi* was the last to burn. Her deck was littered with embers of wood, but she held out, resisted this invasion until the very last moment. And then she too was aflame. The fire, orange and red, licked along her mast and sails, covered her deck with greedy fingers, ambushed her holds and cabins.

The light from the burning harbour raced across the beach and over palm trees to illuminate the mansion and the man standing on the balcony, a fluted glass of wine in his hand. He watched all through the night as the ships burned slowly, until only their blackened skeletons were left. When morning came, thick clouds of smoke rested over Goa. A few ships still burned, but most had sunk into the now filthy grey waters of the Arabian Sea.

When the Viceroy eventually turned from his night's entertainment to crawl into bed, he felt a faint chill of fear, as though his demise had been announced. But this was nonsense, he told himself. Emperor Jahangir dared to capture Daman, a Portuguese protectorate. The Indian ships were burned in retaliation. Long before the Mughals called India theirs, the Portuguese were here. They had as much claim as, no, more claim than, the Mughal kings. He slept then.

But news of the arson was already on its way to Ajmer, where Mehrunnisa and Jahangir would hear of it. The Viceroy had miscalculated the court's apathy towards trade, misjudged the weight of Mehrunnisa's anger—had forgotten that the Mughal kings were in India to stay and the Portuguese were merely their guests.

Jahangir opened his eyes and groaned. His head ached as though an iron vise gripped it and twisted it slowly. He swallowed, and his tongue felt like cotton, flapping against the roof of his mouth. He could feel heat radiating off his face. The Emperor lifted himself with an effort on one elbow. 'Is someone there?'

Three eunuchs immediately came running and performed the taslim. 'Your Majesty is awake?'

Jahangir sank back into his bed. 'Where is the Empress?'

'She is in her apartments, your Majesty.'

'Send for her,' Jahangir said, his voice barely audible. It was an effort to talk. Every word pounded in his head and echoed in his ears. 'And bring me some khichri.'

The eunuchs looked at each other. The Emperor must be unwell. Khichri was a mixture of rice and lentils boiled together with salt and pepper. It was known as poor man's food, since it was cheap and easy to make. Jahangir rarely ate khichri, only at times when his stomach gave him trouble.

The Emperor moved, searching for a cool spot on the pillow, but the satin covers were drenched with sweat and lay damp and solid beneath him. Shivers sloughed through his body. His hands trembled. Perhaps opium would calm this restlessness. So he asked for it. The eunuchs hesitated. It was not the time of day for opium, but his Majesty had commanded them. They brought it eventually, a small grape-sized ball of opium mixed with sugar, and put it between his lips.

The drug sang through Jahangir's veins, taking over his debilitated body in a few short minutes. The trembling stopped, and sweat began to pour from his hairline down his face.

'Go!' Jahangir said irritably to the eunuchs who hung over him. 'What are you doing standing around?' And then he slipped into the cool embrace of the opium, the daylight turning into night before his eyes, sleep coming to claim him again.

The eunuchs fled from the Emperor's apartments, two to the kitchens to order the khichri, and one to Mehrunnisa. She had just returned from the jharoka balcony and was holding in her hand a letter from Goa. When the eunuch bowed before her, she looked at him angrily. 'What do you want?'

He told her, and even as he spoke, Mehrunnisa rose from her divan and flew to Jahangir's apartments. What was wrong with her husband? When she had woken that morning, he had muttered something about a headache and gone back to sleep, so Mehrunnisa had gone alone to the jharoka. He had been restive during the night, but she had been tired herself, waking only once to move Jahangir's arm from around her waist, where it had left a long streak of perspiration.

She entered the room and saw the bowl of khichri steaming by the Emperor's bedside. Jahangir lay still on his divan, his eyes closed, his breathing laboured and heavy. He did not move when she laid a hand on his forehead. It burned to her touch, and Mehrunnisa drew back.

'Your Majesty,' she said, close to his ear. He did not wake at her voice. She shook his shoulder.

'Hoshiyar!' Mehrunnisa screamed. The eunuch was behind her. Together they tried again to wake Jahangir, but he had slipped into unconsciousness. Mehrunnisa put her face close to his, and the sweet fumes of opium rose to her nostrils.

'Who gave the Emperor opium?' she yelled, turning on the eunuchs. They cowered against each other, fingers pointing in all directions. 'Get out now. You are fools; he is not well and you give him opium? Get out!'

They ran from the room, tripping over each other. Mehrunnisa ordered cold water and towels. While waiting for it, Hoshiyar and she took off the Emperor's kurta and pyjamas. His skin was now moist and still burning hot. They soaked the towels in cold water and wiped his body over and over again until the fever abated somewhat. Then Mehrunnisa covered him with a cool sheet.

'Wake up, your Majesty,' she said. 'Talk to me.'

But the opium had caught hold of the Emperor and would not release him until it had run through his blood and sweated out of his pores. Hoshiyar suggested calling the hakims.

'It is nothing, Hoshiyar,' Mehrunnisa said as she turned to him, a sudden dread coming to swamp her. 'It is nothing, is it not? Just a fever. It will go down. See,' she took the eunuch's hand and laid it on Jahangir's chest, see how cool his skin is now.'

'Your Majesty, let me do this.'

'No,' Mehrunnisa said. 'If word of this illness got out into the court and the zenana, the empire will be in chaos.'

'The Emperor has been sick before, your Majesty,' Hoshiyar said gently. 'Allow me to summon the hakims, they will be able to tell us what we should do for his Majesty.'

She turned to him, her eyes tearing up. 'What have the hakims done before, Hoshiyar? They have hesitated and consulted each other, and looked ponderous and knowledgeable. Yet, not one of them has given his Majesty advice that was actually usable. They are all afraid that if they misdiagnose the illness and the Emperor dies, the weight of his death will lie over them. What use are they?'

He argued more with her; Mehrunnisa did not listen. She would make Jahangir better. He would not die. He *could* not die.

So she sat by his bedside through the night and waited and watched. The sun came up as it did always, rising, then blazing at the centre of the skies to send shadows scurrying into their owners, and then slipped towards the west. Mehrunnisa knew none of this. She did not move for hours except to wash down the fever. Finally, as night came again, the Emperor opened his eyes. She fed him with some fresh khichri and some water, but he vomited it all over himself, too weak to even rise from his bed and lean over the side.

Then he slept, but Mehrunnisa did not. Jahangir's fever came and went. She heard the sounds of the night watchman's tapping stick, the song in his voice as the hours turned. Two o'clock. Three o'clock. Then four and five. Mehrunnisa did not speak, and would not allow anyone into the Emperor's bedchamber.

She put out a prayer rug and knelt on it facing west towards

Mecca. *Allah, let him be better.* She would not ask for Jahangir's life, *that* no one was going to take from her, she prayed that he would get well. That was all she wanted. The tears came too, all through the night, drenching her face. She was afraid, terribly, terribly afraid. Questions swirled in her head. What if she had been wrong in not calling the hakims? What if Jahangir did... no, she would not take that word even into her thoughts. Mehrunnisa climbed into the bed, over the Emperor, and laid herself on him, her face dug into his shoulder, her toes touching his feet. His skin was no longer hot, but now it was chilly. This was not the smell of his skin, the taste of his neck. He moved then, uncomfortable under her weight, and she slid off to lie next to him, deeply ashamed. He was ill, unwell, and here she was draping herself over him so she could be at ease.

'Mehrunnisa.'

She clutched his arm and raised herself to look into Jahangir's face. He had woken again. 'Your Majesty.'

'You are here.' And then he closed his eyes again.

Mehrunnisa called out for Hoshiyar, but the eunuch had gone to rest. She started to pace, hope filling her at the only sound she could now hear. Jahangir drew in breath after breath into his tired lungs and then let it cleanly out. He still breathed through his mouth, but the pitch was easy. Mehrunnisa leaned against a wall and then slid down to sit. Still listening to the Emperor's breathing, she fell asleep where she sat, her arms resting on her knees, her head upright, one ear awake.

When she woke in an hour, it was to a request. Prince Khurram demanded an audience, your Majesty. Mehrunnisa crawled to the Emperor's bedside and touched his arm. The fever had returned, and his skin was on fire. She ordered more cold water and again cleansed the fever, moving slowly, now without hope. Allah, what was happening here? Why give her this hope and then wrench it away? What was happening? When the eunuch asked again about Khurram, she snapped at him to send the prince away. He was coming to gloat, to see if his father was really dying, to see if the empire was now his.

By this time the next morning, the whole zenana knew, of course. What exactly had happened to the Emperor, no one was sure of, for Nur Jahan Begam would not permit anyone to see him. So rumours started to diffuse through Ajmer. She was poisoning him slowly. The Emperor's asthma had come back and this time he could not even breathe, so a copper tube was put into his nose to help him. He was dying, hovering on the edge of life, kept alive only by the sorceries Mehrunnisa practised in his apartments. She was battling the demons who had come to take the Emperor away. Amid all these wild stories one theme was constant: What would happen to them?

If Jahangir died, and so soon, without naming an heir, without settling his affairs, what would happen to them?

Prince Khurram was thinking this very thought as he walked back from the Emperor's apartments. If Mehrunnisa denied his entrance, matters must be very serious indeed. Would his father die? He sent eunuchs and slaves all through the day to Mehrunnisa, demanding, begging, pleading for some information. She returned his every request unanswered.

As he waited, Khurram sent some men to Khusrau's apartments and others to see where Shahryar was. Parviz was in the Deccan, quite probably in a drunken haze right now, unaware that their father was dying. Khusrau was walking in the gardens, alone, and Shahryar was practising at the firing range.

That evening, Khurram called some of the nobles at court to his reception hall at Ajmer. They talked for a few hours before he asked them for their support should the crown suddenly find itself without a head underneath it. His words brought the silence of shock. Surely, the Emperor was not going to die? No, he assured them. Not now, but if... The prince did not forget the Portuguese Viceroy in Goa either. A hundred and twenty Indian ships had been burned in the harbour, but not one had been Khurram's. He wrote to the Viceroy again, requesting passes and protection for his ships, and in return, he promised his patronage when he became emperor.

The fever raged for the next twenty days, fed by Jahangir's debilitated body and the large quantities of wine and opium he still consumed. Mehrunnisa did not want to stop the wine or the opium suddenly, fearing the withdrawal would kill him. After that first day of a death-like stillness, Jahangir often lapsed into a state of delirium, shouting nonsense and flinging his arms and legs about until he had to be forcibly restrained. He did not recognize Mehrunnisa, and she clutched his feet in tears and sobbed through the hours of darkness as the palaces slept uneasily around her.

On the twentieth day, little rashes bloomed under the Emperor's skin and littered his entire body. The smallpox, Mehrunnisa thought in horror. Could it be this? He would never recover, no one ever did. Now, for the first time, she summoned the physicians.

They came in like frightened animals, tails between their legs. They hovered over Emperor Jahangir with silk handkerchiefs over their mouths and noses. Mehrunnisa watched them in disgust. These were the men appointed to drive away ailment from human bodies? What of the oaths they had taken? They were afraid of being exposed to the smallpox; she herself had spent twenty days with Jahangir, barely leaving even to bathe or eat. As the flesh had worn away from Jahangir's stout frame, it had fled from Mehrunnisa's smaller one too, until her arms were like twigs, her waist non-existent, her choli hanging loose on her shoulders. But her will had not gone. Through all these days, when hope had visited and fled, her resolve had remained strong. The Emperor would live. The Emperor *must* live.

The hakims, old and bearded, with mournful faces, bent over

Jahangir's still body, checked his pulse. Hakim Abdullah turned to Mehrunnisa, accusation in his eyes. 'We should have been summoned earlier, your Majesty.'

'Is it the smallpox?' she demanded, waving aside his gaze. 'What does the Emperor have? Can you cure this?'

Abdullah shook his head, and for a brief moment, Mehrunnisa's heart stopped. There was no cure. He was going to say that there was no cure. She ran to Jahangir's bedside and beat the men away. They must not touch him anymore. No one but she must touch her husband's body. And in this fog of grief, she heard the hakim's voice. 'Not the smallpox, your Majesty. But the Emperor has suffered for too long, if the fever does not break in a few days—'

'Not the smallpox!' Mehrunnisa caught him by his bony shoulders and shook him. 'Not the smallpox? Are you sure? Absolutely?' His head flopped, and his long, grey beard flew up and down. She pushed him towards the door. 'Go. Go. All of you. Leave here now. And, thank you.'

Then she ran back into the room and knelt by Jahangir's side again. Four hours later, when he opened his eyes, for the first time in the last twenty days she saw reason in them. 'Are you here, Mehrunnisa?' he asked.

'Where else would I be, your Majesty?'

From that day on, the Emperor's condition improved. Slowly, day by day. He ate more, listened to her when she said he must not drink too much wine. Her faith in his wellness was better medicine than anything the hakims could have prescribed. A month after the first bout of fever, Jahangir was well enough to go to the jharoka.

The courtyard below was packed with nobles and commoners. They cried out as he appeared before them. 'Hail to the Emperor! May he live long!' That afternoon, the Emperor had his ears pierced in thanksgiving, and drew two pearls through the holes. It would soon become a new fashion, as all the men of consequence imitated Jahangir's new mode of adornment.

Mehrunnisa went back to her apartments and slept during that day, knowing that her husband was well again, and that now, finally, she could close her eyes without waking to fear.

Emperor Jahangir came to her in the night, while she still slept, slipped into her bed and drew her into his arms. He did not remember much of the past month, just little snatches of consciousness when he had seen Mehrunnisa's face. He had always seen her there, not once had he woken to a room empty of her presence. She looked so tired now, as though she had given her strength to him when the fever attacked.

Then his mind turned to the Portuguese issue, but only briefly, for news had come again. An English captain called Downton had met the Portuguese in the Suwali channel off the coast of Surat, defeated them, and burned their ships. Sometime during his illness, Mehrunnisa had demanded compensation for the burned *Rahimi*, and the Viceroy had sent three hundred thousand rupees to Ruqayya. She had also asked for more passes. But those were not necessary anymore, were they? Jahangir thought. This last defeat by the English, it bode well for the empire. Let this ambassador come, he was said to be only two sailing days away. Let him come, and Mehrunnisa and he would handle this matter together.

Jahangir thought of Khurram too, but angrily. How had Khurram dared to defy Mehrunnisa and say that he would not marry Ladli?

The Emperor kissed Mehrunnisa's forehead gently, and she smiled in her sleep. He had asked her why she had been with him all these days. And she had said that in his well-being came hers. Despite all her power, all the riches she had, all the armies she could command, the courtiers who bowed to her—in the end, it was simple as that.

Chapter Sixteen

Knowe yee therefore that, for the Confidence and Trust
which We have in the Fidelity and Discretion of the said
Sir Thomas Rowe, We have constituted, appoynted,
ordayned and deputed, and hereby do constitute, appoynt,
ordayne and depute the said Sir Thomas Rowe our true
and undoubted Attorney, Procurator, Legate and
Ambassador.

—WILLIAM FOSTER, ED.,
The Embassy of Sir Thomas Roe to India

'WE HAVE ARRIVED, SIRE.'

The *Lion*'s anchor chain clanked and rattled its way into the
waters on the bar off the coast of Surat. Two sailors, their shirts
stripped from their backs, unwound the heavy reel of chain, their
muscles rippling and gleaming with sweat.

Roe peered towards the shadowy coast, his heart banging with
excitement. There was not much to be seen, a few trees on the
coastline, junks and frigates anchored near the mouth of the Tapti,
and one large white tower signifying a native temple.

He turned away and leaned against the deck rails. Was that all
there was to the land of the great Mughal? Where were the
fantastic palaces from the Arabian nights, the bejewelled women,
the crowded bazaars? He had hoped his first view of India would
have been more heartening after all the time spent travelling at sea.

The journey from England had taken seven months, and it had been a long, gruelling trip. For so many days there had been nothing but water—everywhere—capped only by a sometimes calm sky, a sometimes purple thunderous sky. He had learned to walk on the deck of the *Lion* without retching, and he had prayed on his knees for hours when a storm had tossed the ship and he had been consigned to his quarters, wondering if he would go to a watery grave without even being given a chance to swim.

Still, the appointment to the court of the Mughal Emperor could not have come at a better time. Roe's luck had been at an all-time low, both personally and politically. The meagre inheritance that he had been left with had diminished into nothingness. His two friends at court, Prince Henry and Princess Elizabeth, were gone—the prince dead, the princess married to the Elector of Bohemia. Roe had been a member of Parliament for Tamworth when the East India Company had offered him the post of ambassador to India. It had been a blessing.

For their part, the Company could not have chosen a better representative. Roe was in the prime of his life, in his mid-thirties, ready for a suitable change. He was eloquent and had a dignified bearing and a commanding presence, all qualities fit for a diplomat and an ambassador.

Roe turned to look at the other members of the fleet that had accompanied him from England. The *Peppercorn*, the *Expedition*, and the *Dragon* swayed gently in the calm waters off the bar at Surat. The fleet was the finest and best equipped of all that had so far been sent out to India by the East India Company.

He ran a finger around his tight collar in hopes of easing the discomfort. What kind of a heathen land was this, where the very heat sapped strength from limbs? It was barely eight o'clock by his fob watch, and already sweat stewed inside his clothes. The *Lion*'s captain had tersely told him to leave off the adornments, and that though land was sighted, it would be a few days before they would actually step on it. Still, Roe was dressed in what he considered his official ambassador's regalia, his boots spit-shined, his shirt pressed, his cuffs snowy and flowing. Just in case someone had an eyeglass on the *Lion*, they would not sight the ambassador dressed like a common sailor. Now Roe eyed the captain jealously; he was sweating too but seemed more comfortable in his loose white shirt and trousers. Roe sighed. This was not the least of his troubles. He had had a lot of time to think during his journey here, reading and rereading journals of previous merchants to India and the Company's briefings. The Emperor had made it absolutely clear that he would not accept a mere merchant as an ambassador and his equal at court. It was rumoured that William Edwards, chief of factors and present at Ajmer right now, was styling himself as ambassador. Hawkins also called himself thus, and if Middleton or Best had found their way to Jahangir's presence, they too would have given themselves that lofty title. So where did it leave Roe? He came with that highly suspect title of 'ambassador' too.

But Roe had no intention of being thwarted. The official document from King James crackled in his breast pocket as he straightened up from the railing. He was the first official ambassador from England, and he was determined to be accorded all the rights and respect that would be bestowed upon his king, for he came as a representative of the English court. Roe had with him not only a letter authorizing him as a representative of England but also a missive from James to Jahangir and a letter of instructions to Roe, wherein James outlined his duties in the foreign court. None of the other merchants had this, but Roe was deluged with royal favour and would use any or all of it to prove he was better than Hawkins and Edwards.

In thought, Roe leaned over the deck railing and suddenly found the water rushing up to meet him as his feet lifted into the air. A hand grabbed his coat; he felt the cloth strain over his throat as his arms and legs flayed before he was thumped on the wooden boards of the deck.

'Ere, watch yerself, mate,' a huge sailor yelled in Roe's ear as the deck resounded with laughter. Roe rose and dusted himself in as dignified a manner as he could, blood rising to colour his overheated face. It had been like this all through the journey, this familiarity, this unwanted intimacy. Now he had finally arrived in the empire, and his life could follow the strict formality of the court.

Sir Thomas Roe expected too much and too soon. He came laden with signs of official patronage, true, but there was to be no good reception.

The town of Surat in the province of Gujrat lay under the jurisdiction of Prince Khurram, who had now openly allied himself with the Portuguese. Since Khurram supported the Portuguese, they allowed his ships to trade unhindered in the Arabian Sea but threatened retaliation if the English were allowed to establish an embassy at the Mughal court.

News of the defeat of the Portuguese by Downton, which had so delighted both Mehrunnisa and Jahangir a few months ago, reached both Khurram and Roe when his fleet met with the *Merchant's Hope*, one of Downton's ships on her way back to England from India. While Roe was happy at the news, Khurram was not. The prince did not wish to allow the English to formalize a trading agreement at court, but while he was still a prince, there was very little he could do to stop it. There was, however, one way he could exert his influence—by making sure that Roe did not set foot on Indian soil and by forcing the fleet to return to England divested of its rich cargo.

So the next week exercised all of the ambassador's diplomatic skills to the utmost. The ships were searched from mast to hull, and duties were levied according to their cargoes. The crew were also strip-searched for contraband. Roe sent various letters to Muqarrab Khan, governor of the province, insisting upon his rights and demanding that he and his possessions be left unmolested. Roe maintained that in his capacity as ambassador, he alone was exempt from the normal practise of a thorough customs search.

Muqarrab immediately sent back a polite letter indicating that all goods had to be thoroughly searched but that he would make an exception in the case of the personal belongings of the ambassador, provided the customs clerk could seal them at the dock and then inspect them at Roe's residence at Surat. They talked back and forth thus, in flowery and meaningless phrases, until Roe had to give in. Once he did, Muqarrab had no other arguments to keep the ambassador from coming ashore, and so eight days after the *Lion* anchored off the bar at the mouth of the Tapti, Sir Thomas Roe landed on the coast of India.

The four English ships were decked in their best finery. Colourful pennants, flags and ensigns hung from the masts. A hundred English soldiers equipped with muskets had gone over earlier in the morning. They stood in two rows dressed in full military regalia to form the Court of Guard to welcome the ambassador. The cannons aboard the fleet boomed out their salute as Roe disembarked from the boat, along with the four captains of the fleet.

The English soldiers saluted smartly as Roe passed them on his way to a huge open tent. Carpets were laid on the ground in profusion, and under the great silken canopy some thirty Indian nobles were assembled, waiting to welcome the ambassador.

Roe stopped and frowned upon coming to the tent. 'Why are the Indians still seated?' he demanded.

'My lord ambassador, it is the custom in these heathen lands,' one of his men whispered.

'This is ridiculous. I am a representative of King James. Would these men dare to sit in the presence of a great king?' Roe said irritably. 'I will not enter until they stand.'

One of his attendants ran to inform the gathered Indians of Roe's demands. They talked with each other, while Roe stood outside the tent, his face reddening with anger. Finally, one of the men rose, and the rest of the assembly rose along with him.

Somewhat appeased, Roe marched into the tent and went up to the centre. One of the Indians made a sign to the interpreter, who started a long speech in broken English with a heavy accent. Thirty horses with fine saddles were brought forth as a present to Roe, and he was also given slaves for use in his personal household. Roe graciously accepted the gifts, inclined his head, and marched down to the pier on the Tapti, where he was to be escorted to the house that had been found for him in Surat.

Upon arriving there, he found that, contrary to the governor's assurances, his belongings had not been brought to his residence. The ambassador was told that his luggage had been sealed in the customs house until such time that it could be thoroughly searched. So here he was, in an empty house, with no furnishings or even his bedclothes. A jute-strung cot was found for him and put in one of the rooms. He sent for his dinner from one of the Armenian public houses in Surat's main street and washed down the fiery food with huge glasses of water. Just as he was retiring to his room, a messenger came running in.

'My lord ambassador, your cook has been arrested.'

Roe jumped up from his cot, retying the laces on his boots. 'Why? Where is the man?' He had brought an English cook along with him, unsure of how he would take to native food, and with good reason, Roe thought, flinging on his coat, if this night's meal was any indication of what he would have to eat.

'He is in prison, my lord. It would be better for you to free him tonight, for these heathens do not believe in either long prison terms or in trials. The cook will be sentenced to death in the morning.'

Roe groaned. Would his ordeals never end? The cook had been sent beforehand to the house at Surat to prepare for the ambassador's arrival. On his way through the city, the man had chanced upon an Armenian wine house and there had spent the next few hours getting drunk. Towards evening, the cook had suddenly recalled his responsibilities and had been wandering through the bazaar in search of Roe's house when he had met the governor's brother and his men. The cook had immediately put his hand on his sword and yelled, 'Now thou heathen dog!'

The governor's brother had been puzzled, what was this firangi saying to him? So he had asked, '*Kya kahta?*'

The cook, too inebriated to attempt an answer, had drawn his sword out of its scabbard and had ineffectually waved it in the air. Although the governor's brother did not understand English, he had recognized the cook's actions as belligerent. His men had immediately fallen upon the cook and thrown him into prison.

When the messenger arrived at this point in the story, Roe turned around and went home. He sent word to the governor's brother to do with the cook as he pleased, shrugging off any blame in the matter. The cook was clearly in the wrong, he thought, and if he made too much of a fuss, this small incident could very well blow up into an international affair. After a few hours of deliberation, the man was released and came back to his master's residence much chastened, and unhurt, as a courtesy to Roe from the governor's brother.

Roe's trials were only beginning. The language barrier, the heat, the unfamiliar customs, would all prey upon him in the coming days. The English had been here before, true. But none of their accounts prepared Roe for India. He sent for Jadu, the broker who had served other English masters in Surat, and talked with him for long hours. He heard stories about the Emperor, his recent illness that had so nearly driven him to his death, his four sons, all of whom had equal claims on the throne. Jadu told him about these four princes, how they all wanted the throne, and how only Prince Khurram had any authority at all at court, like he did here, in the province of Gujrat where Surat lay. What of the others, Roe asked? Parviz and Shahryar were weaklings, sire, Jadu said. But Prince Khusrau... at one time he had had everything, now it is all gone. Only a miracle would put him on the throne. Though who knew, miracles did occur.

The days passed thus as Sir Thomas Roe, the first official ambassador from England, lived in his empty rooms with his cot and his cook. His furniture rotted in the customs houses, and he conversed often with the very courteous governor Muqarrab Khan. But his hands were so woefully tied, Muqarrab said; he could do little about releasing the ambassador's effects. A few more days of waiting, perhaps? So Roe waited, wondering if Surat was to be his first and last stop in India.

It was doubtful he would even reach Emperor Jahangir's court.

Prince Khusrau peered at the book in his hands. The words on the page swam, flitted, grew bigger and then smaller. He held his right index finger steadily on the paper, and bent his head close. His mouth formed the word. 'Willow.' Then laboriously, his finger moved to the next word, and he strained to read it. The beginnings of an ache started in his forehead and wound its painful fingers around his skull. His vision blurred, and Khusrau wiped his left eye over and over again. Finally, he had one sentence. 'Under the nodding willow the poppy lies in blood.'

The prince put the book down and lay back on his divan. This was the only sentence he would read today, and every day, although Khalifa read to him, he forced this exercise upon himself. He thought about that arduously gained sentence and saw in his mind the tiny new leaves of a springtime willow, shivering in the breeze, a carpet of poppies—blood—beneath it, the perfume of violets in the cornfields. It was from Bahar's poem *The Miracle of Spring*. Khusrau liked this poem because, unlike others he had read, it painted pictures in his head of what he had once seen. Some of the others were epics, stories of fathers and sons and grandsons, all mighty, all engaged in some battle that won them glory.

A little prick of restlessness ignited something deep within him. Khusrau held himself rigid on the divan, but the feeling spread from his fingers to his hands and arms, through his body, until he was shaking. He felt for a cushion, picked it up, and threw it from him. There was a soft thud, and then the tinkling crash of glass breaking. Tears came to his eyes, Khusrau doubled over and began to bawl. Some part of his mind stayed sane, but it was such a weak part, and this was so overwhelming, that Khusrau could only howl, beating his fists upon the divan, ripping through the cover with his nails, flinging himself to the ground. He began whacking his head on the floor, again and again.

Khalifa came running into the room, her veil flying off her hair. She rushed to Khusrau, fastened her arms around his shoulders, and pulled him onto her lap. He still flayed about, still yelled, his shouts echoed in her ears, but Khalifa held him fast.

'Hush, my lord. Hush.' She said little else, just this, until Khusrau quieted. His wet face was buried into her chest, he gripped her ribs with his hands until a burning spread over Khalifa's skin. But she still held on to him and rocked him.

'Why?' Khusrau asked.

'I do not know, my lord,' Khalifa said, then her voice became hard. 'The Emperor does as he pleases. Blinding you has pleased him.'

They sat like that on the Persian carpets, hand-woven in the finest workshops in Agra, their design so intricate that it seemed as though rubbing the delicate white jasmine buds would release their fragrance around them. But Khusrau could see none of this.

Khusrau was born in 1587 to Man Bai, Jahangir's first wife. He was the first son, the cherished and beloved heir to the empire. There were few in the realm who had forgotten Akbar's heartache and their desperation for an heir before Jahangir's birth. So Khusrau was a blessing.

When Khusrau was seventeen he was married to Khalifa, whose father was the Khan Azam, the first lord of the realm, a minister with a long-standing relationship with Akbar, and a man of enormous influence. Khusrau's maternal uncle was also a man with no little authority at court—Raja Man Singh was a brave soldier, an able commander, and his power was moulded through years of experience and service to Akbar.

These two men, father-in-law and uncle to Khusrau, watched the ferocious sparring between Jahangir and his father. So even before Akbar died, they presented Khusrau to the nobles as the next heir to the empire, bypassing his father completely. Old and ailing as Emperor Akbar was, as much as he was resentful towards Jahangir during the last years of his life, he was insistent upon one thing—the crown belonged to Jahangir. Not Khusrau.

The prince lifted his face finally from Khalifa's chest and peered at her face. His hands no longer trembled, that terrible hopelessness that made him act so madly had gone. He could not see much of his wife. A smile? He touched her mouth, and his fingers moved over smooth teeth that glimmered liked pearls through the fog of his vision.

'I give you so much trouble, Khalifa,' he said.

'No, my lord.' She smiled again, and this time he could hear it in her voice. 'Nothing you do gives me pain. I only wish that you were more easy within yourself.'

The prince put his face against Khalifa's. He had given her a rotten life. She should have been an Empress, ruling over the imperial zenana, and their two sons should have worn the proud marks of heirs on their foreheads. Instead, they lived like this, on the fringes of the court. Once, he had been lauded as the next emperor, now he was nothing. Half-blind—with only memories of how the sun streaked gold and yellow at setting or the gleaming coat and magnificent lines of his favourite Arabian horse—half-demented too. It was said that there was a strain of madness in his mother's family. Khusrau believed it, especially when the attacks of desperation came upon him, every single day. Through all this, the only one constant was Khalifa.

The princess pushed Khusrau to lean against the divan, picked up his book, and began to read to him. He heard the wonders of spring and heard how the line he had so tormentingly read came somewhere in the middle of the poem framed thus: *Bright with a myriad jewels the wheat-swept fields are starred. Under the nodding willow the poppy lies in blood—sudden the blow that smote her, drenched her in crimson flood.*

A message came to them then. Raja Man Singh had died in the Deccan fighting alongside the Khan-i-khanan and Parviz. Sixty of his wives had jumped into his funeral pyre and burned themselves to death, becoming Sati. Khusrau had not seen his uncle in the past few years; Jahangir deliberately kept them apart.

The prince started to howl again, hugely, his madness coming upon him once more. His uncle was dead. His father-in-law had been stripped of his titles and sent to live in his jagir to be a landlord. Who would now help him become emperor?

They all said Khurram would be the next emperor. But what of *his* claim? Why not Khusrau instead of Khurram? He yelled and screamed, and Khalifa tried to pacify him. She too was frightened. She had little trust in her father, having had more confidence in

Khusrau's uncle. Now he was gone. They were alone.

But they were not entirely alone. In another part of the palaces, a woman thought of them. She was determined that Khurram would never wear the crown. And her daughter needed to marry a royal prince. Raja Man Singh was dead, the Khan Azam lived in ignominy; Khusrau had lost his two most ardent supporters. But he still had some charm, some standing in the empire. The nobles did not so easily forget his birth, and Mehrunnisa could now give him consequence.

Sir Thomas Roe was miserable.

He held on listlessly to the reins as his horse ambled down the large unpaved road, gutted here and there by the wheels of carts and carriages. A sudden gust of breeze blew dust into his eyes. Roe pulled his scarf close around his face, covering his mouth and nose.

This was the only concession the ambassador had made so far against the heat and dust of India. Despite suggestions from his native servants, he insisted on retaining his English garb, entirely unsuited to the climate. He was dressed in the manner of an English courtier—silk shirt with an embroidered collar, a waistcoat and a long jacket, tight knee breeches and stockings on his legs. His feet were clad in half-length boots reaching to his knees.

Roe moaned as he looked down at his shoes. The black glossy shine from the morning was now dull with dust. His collar had wilted in the heat, lying about his neck like a dying snake, and his maroon coat was a drab brown. It was the month of November, but in the plains, the afternoon sun was blistering. Someone, and Roe searched through his steaming brain for who, had written home that in India there were only two seasons. The hot weather, and the less hot weather. Roe undid the top buttons of his waistcoat and wiped a grimy hand over his forehead.

'When are we going to stop for lunch?' he asked Jadu.

Jadu was a small, wiry man with a huge, ever-present smile. He grinned at Roe, showing yellow teeth stained with tobacco and a large gap in the front where a tooth had been knocked out during a fight.

'Soon, Sahib. Perhaps you would not feel the heat so much if you dressed like me,' Jadu said slyly, gesturing at his own clothes.

Roe stared at him in disgust. How could he dress like a heathen? He was the official ambassador to India and as such had a dignity to maintain, and that did not include dressing like the natives. Roe looked around him. He was accompanied by an odd assortment of soldiers and servants. Roe had hired fifty Pathan soldiers at Surat to guard him during the journey to Ajmer. Jahangir had promised the ambassador protection, but Roe did not trust anyone in India yet, so he had hired his own guards to protect him from bandits and the Portuguese. It was Mehrunnisa—Roe thought it was Jahangir from the official farmans that made their way to him—who had scolded Muqarrab Khan for the ambassador's delay in presenting himself at court. Roe found himself once again in possession of his luggage, and completely intact, the seals from the customs dock still unbroken. Muqarrab Khan had also sent Roe many gifts, among them oxen with bags of skin to carry water during the trip, baskets of fresh fruit and vegetables, and a few chickens for meat. Roe had also accepted a camel from the governor to carry his luggage. It was all very bewildering; after forcing him to stay at Surat, watching his every move, all at once it was Muqarrab's hand that bade him the most enthusiastic farewell. Roe was suspicious. Why? Was he safer at Surat after all? But he could not stay there, of course—he was here to meet Emperor Jahangir.

The party trudged up the road, raising a mountain of dust in their wake. They crested the rise and Burhanpur came into sight. Roe's heart plummeted. What sort of a town was this? Most of the houses were of mud with thatched roofs, or of an indifferent sun-bleached brick. In the centre stood a huge red sandstone castle, which was home now to Prince Parviz, Jahangir's second son. Burhanpur was said to be one of the strongholds of the Mughal Empire—it was from here the Deccan campaigns were mounted. Hills scorched of vegetation rose in the distance, naked and an unpleasant brown. Then Roe looked down into the valley again. The plains were lavish with a serene green, fed by the river Tapti. As far as his eye could see, on either side of the road, the fields were emerald with wheat and barley. Grey partridges ran around in the fields, feeding on the ripening crop.

A breeze came sweeping up from the valley and sent cool fingers of air over Roe's face. He prodded his horse to a trot, heading down the road to Burhanpur. In the city, they found the sarai where he had been promised accommodation. Roe was given four brick-walled rooms with small windows, but the heat was so overwhelming inside that he decided to pitch his tents in a nearby garden.

A few hours later, Roe was relaxing in his tent when Jadu came in. The broker grinned at him. 'Are you feeling better, Sahib?'

'Much better. The heat is terrible.' Roe sighed. 'When should I visit the prince? And what should I take for him?'

'You should see him tomorrow. He has heard of your arrival and is waiting for you. It will be better to observe court etiquette during your visit. Prince Parviz holds court here just as the emperor does in Ajmer. It will be a good practise for you for when you go to see the Emperor.'

'I know how to conduct myself in court,' Roe replied crossly. 'Remember that I come from the court of—'

'The great King James of England,' Jadu completed for him patiently, having heard that refrain many times. 'Yes. Yes. I know that, Sahib. But the rules and customs are different here. It is better if you are familiar with them. You will have to take rich gifts to the prince if you want him to notice you. You see...,' Jadu hesitated, 'your honour depends upon the richness of your gifts. The more expensive they are, the more you are deemed to respect our imperial family.'

'I see.' Roe rubbed his nose thoughtfully. 'I wish to ask Prince Parviz for permission to set up an English factory here. The sword blades made in Burhanpur will serve the English army well.'

'If you please the prince, he will be happy to grant your request.'

The next morning Roe arose early. He went to the fort with his guards but was forced to leave them at the front gate. This he was told politely by the imperial guards—no one was to enter the prince's presence with his own escort; he would be safe enough inside. So the presents Roe brought changed hands, and the royal servants followed behind him.

Roe was led through a confusing maze of corridors to a central courtyard. One hundred armed soldiers lined two sides of the yard; these were the prince's personal bodyguards. A plush red velvet divan sat on a pedestal in the verandah on the far side. A silver cloth canopy fringed with pearls and supported by four silver pillars topped it. The courtyard was crowded with nobles and army commanders. Roe stopped at the entrance to the courtyard, transfixed by the lushness of what he saw. Every scabbard was adorned with glittering rubies and emeralds, almost every turban and coat was of silk or brocade. Jewels gleamed on fingers. There was colour everywhere—bright, vivid, primary colours—all brightened by the morning sun that slanted through the open roof. There were horses and elephants at the back where Roe stood, their tails gently swishing off flies, adorned as the nobles were, in rich trappings. Roe walked solemnly past the line of soldiers, aware that when he was announced, every single eye turned upon him in curiosity. One of the court officials came up to him.

'Sahib, it is court etiquette to go down on your knees and touch your head to the ground in front of the prince,' he whispered.

Roe frowned. 'I cannot do that. As ambassador of King James, I represent him. How can one royal prince pay obeisance to another in such a manner?'

The official tried to convince Roe, shrugged and melted to the back. Roe marched on, until he reached the end of the courtyard. Three stone steps led to the raised verandah where Parviz sat on a throne.

'I bring you greetings from his royal Majesty, King James of England. We come in peace, to foster a friendship with his Majesty, Emperor Jahangir.'

'You are welcome to India,' Parviz replied in a weak voice.

Roe looked at Parviz in amazement. This was a royal prince? His skin was flushed, his eyes bloodshot, his bones sticking out *everywhere*—in thin wrists, a scrawny neck a prominent forehead. His jewelled turban was so huge that it fell over his eyes from time to time. His coat hung grotesquely loose on his emaciated frame.

Roe's gaze turned to the man standing next to the prince. This must be the Khan-i-khanan, Abdur Rahim, who was the prince's official guardian. The Khan-i-khanan was an old man, at least in his fifties. His hair and beard were completely white, startling against his thickly brown skin, but he held himself erect, and keen, intelligent eyes surveyed Roe. Jadu had said that it was Abdur Rahim and not Parviz who ruled Burhanpur; Roe could see why. The Khan-i-khanan was evidently a man of strong character, one well used to controlling people around him, as he did the prince. Parviz leaned towards Abdur Rahim for approval each time he spoke.

'Tell us about your king,' Parviz commanded.

'What would you like to know, your Highness?'

'Everything.'

Roe described court life in England briefly and as well as he could, the person and family of King James. After a few minutes Roe became flustered and his speech faltered. He had been kept standing. Did the prince not have the courtesy to offer him a seat?

'Your Highness,' Roe said to Parviz. 'It is customary in my country that an ambassador is treated equal to the king he represents. I ask permission to ascend the steps and come closer to you so that we may be at the same level.'

Parviz glanced at the Khan-i-khanan. Abdur Rahim's head shifted in a no.

'That is not possible,' he replied brusquely. 'Why, even if the kings of Persia or Turkey came to visit me, they would stand where you are now.'

'But you would rise from your seat and come *down* to meet them, your Highness. Why should it be different with the ambassador of the court of England?' Roe said a little heatedly.

'It is not different. You are accorded all the courtesies that would be given to them.'

'I beg pardon, your Highness. But at least, order a chair for me, so that I may sit down.'

'No one sits in the imperial presence, that is the rule of the court,' Parviz said. As the prince spoke, his eyes alighted on the packing cases behind Roe, presents from England for the prince. His tone softer now, the prince said, 'I give you leave to come closer to the throne as a courtesy. You can stand near the pillar.' He indicated one of the pillars that held up the silver canopy above his head.

Roe had to give in. He could not very well argue with a royal prince. Roe went to the pillar and slid down against it until his knees were bent. If he would not be given permission to sit on a chair, he would sit on his feet.

A small murmur of amusement brushed through the courtyard. The firangi was stubborn. What would he do at the imperial court, where the Empress set the tone of the proceedings?

Parviz continued to talk to Roe. Finally Roe asked his favour. Would his Highness grant permission to set up an English factory at Burhanpur?

'Certainly,' Parviz said. He looked around for his *bakshi*, his paymaster. 'Prepare a farman allowing the ambassador to set up an English factory here. Bring it to me for the seal.' Parviz turned back to Roe. 'I will retire now to my private apartments and send for you in a few minutes. There, you can sit in my presence and we will talk some more about England.'

'As you wish, your Highness.' Roe bowed to Parviz as he left the courtyard.

Two hours passed and Roe sat in the courtyard awaiting Parviz's summons. Servants ran around busy with their work, but when Roe asked them about the prince, they merely shrugged and gave him a smile. Towards noon, someone brought Roe a plate of food. He ate it and waited... and waited. Finally, at sunset Roe saw the Khan-i-khanan striding towards him.

Abdur Rahim bowed. 'Ambassador, the prince sends his regrets. He will not be able to see you today. He is... ah... incapacitated.'

'What happened?' Roe demanded.

Abdur Rahim spread his hands out in an expression of regret. 'The prince found one of your gifts to be... shall we say, highly intoxicating?' Rahim smiled. 'He has been put to bed and can unfortunately meet no one today.'

Among Roe's gifts was a case of English brandy. The dissolute prince had been drinking from the time he had left the court and was now lying in his apartments in a drunken stupor. Disgusted, Roe left for his camp.

That night, tired from waiting in the hot sun and moving to

The Feast of Roses

where the shade fell, Roe fell ill with a fever. He lay in his bed for days, not knowing where he was, delirious from the high temperature. Missives came from Emperor Jahangir commanding his presence at court, but Roe could barely read them, let alone rise from his mattress and mount a horse. When the fever abated slightly, Roe gave orders for the move. He was still weak, his arms and legs turned to water by the fever, but he insisted upon continuing on his journey to the court of the Mughal Emperor at Mandu.

Chapter Seventeen

He hath one beloved wife among foure, that wholly governeth him.

—WILLIAM FOSTER, ED.,
The Embassy of Sir Thomas Roe to India

THE MAN GLANCED AROUND THE TREE, HIS HEART BANGING LOUD IN HIS chest. The sound seemed to reverberate in the still night air. Then he breathed a sigh of relief. The two Kashmiri guards seemed oblivious of his presence. They stood in front of the entrance to the zenana with spears in their hands. If they caught him here... It had been absolute luck that had brought him so far, past the Ahadis and the Rajput guards outside the palace. He wiped his sweating brow with the back of a grimy sleeve. How was he to get inside?

Just then, someone called out to the two women. They turned to the intruder, their spear tips horizontal with the ground, their feet astride.

'Who goes there?' one of them shouted.

'It is I.' A man came into view. The guards relaxed as they recognized a friend.

The man behind the tree listened to their conversation. The guards laughed and chatted with their friend and in a few minutes were persuaded to leave their post to get a cup of chai.

As soon as he saw his chance, the man slipped from behind the tree and ran to the entrance. The door handles were fastened with a massive iron chain and a lock. He looked around. The zenana wall was not very high, and along the wall were niches to hold oil lamps. The man heard voices. The guards were coming back. Within a few seconds, he had scaled the wall, using the niches as footholds. He dropped silently on the other side just as the guards came back to their posts.

Nizam leaned against the wall, his ear to the stones, and listened intently. The guards had noticed nothing. He grinned to himself. He was now within the walls of the exalted zenana, the abode of the royal ladies, where few commoners had set foot before him. The gardens at the entrance stretched in the darkness, bushes and trees shielding the buildings from view.

Nizam frowned with concentration, trying to recall his conversation with the nautch girl. He had visited her a month ago for the first time, and she had gloated of her success in the zenana. She had serviced the Emperor himself, she had said. Probably an idle boast, Nizam thought, for it was well known that the Emperor had over three hundred women at his harem, and would he have left Empress Nur Jahan's bed for even one night? For a common nautch girl? However, that boast allowed the woman to increase her price—a lot of men wanted to sleep with the woman who had slept with the Emperor.

He had gone to her out of curiosity. At first, the woman had been coy, but a few cuffs on her head had straightened that. She had not seen the Empress but had ventured throughout the zenana. In a few days, the prostitute had given Nizam all the information he had wanted, the layout of the zenana, where the guards were positioned, and, more important, where Mehrunnisa's private apartments were.

Nizam stayed where he was until his heart calmed down. If he returned tomorrow after having glimpsed Mehrunnisa's face, he would win his bet. His friends had dared him to go into the zenana to see the veiled Empress. The price was one hundred gold mohurs, a small fortune.

There was a half-moon tonight, just enough light to see but not so much that he would be seen. He was dressed in black anyway, and if any woman looked out of her windows, she would only see the shadows move. Nizam had also blackened his face and hands with coal shavings. He moved away from the wall, his bare feet light on the grass, and came to an open courtyard. At one end a large palace rose to the sky. This was the Empress Jagat Gosini's palace. The corridor along the face of the building was lit with torches, and two eunuchs marched up and down the length of it. Nizam circled the building and came to another garden. Was this it? No, further down, the nautch girl had said.

Finally he came to a small mosque set in an artificial pond. The white marble dome gleamed in the light of the moon. Nizam swiftly circumvented the pond and reached its eastern side. From there he could see Mehrunnisa's palace. It was a huge sandstone building built around a central courtyard. Four minarets rose from the corners, each topped by a circular balcony with a guard in it. The Empress's private apartments were on the eastern side. Nizam had to enter the palace and somehow gain access to the central courtyard, where he could hide himself. He sped along the lit corridor, darting behind the pillars whenever he heard a sound. The main doorway was open, and he slid through it to the courtyard.

Stone steps led down into the garden. A fountain spewed water in a comfortable gurgle in the centre. Nizam found a stone bench to sit on. From there, he could look up to the first floor, where, he had been told, Mehrunnisa slept. Now that he was here, there was no fear in him anymore. He was so close to the Empress. A few more steps and he would be in her bedchamber. He pulled his shawl close around him and huddled in one corner. As the night wore on, Nizam slept.

Mehrunnisa opened her eyes and stared at the ceiling. The door opened softly, and Hoshiyar Khan put his head around it. 'Are you awake, your Majesty?'

'Yes. Come in. What is on the agenda for today?'

Hoshiyar pulled out a piece of paper from the sleeve of his qaba and started reading. Mehrunnisa listened with half an ear as she looked out towards the verandah. The eastern wall of her room merged into the verandah. Stone arches lined the wall, curtained with thin silk. The sky lightened into shades of pink and red as the sun prepared to rise.

'Good.' Mehrunnisa cut Hoshiyar short. 'Call for my toilette. I will listen to the rest while I am dressing.'

'As you wish.' As soon as Hoshiyar left, two pretty slave girls came bustling in. They helped the Empress wash her face and brush her teeth. She was alone this morning; Jahangir had been hunting and had sent word late yesterday that they were delayed and would spend the night at a sarai. So today she would sit at a common jharoka balcony, where both the Emperor's and her supplicants would come. It would be a long and tiring day.

'Shall I prepare your clothes for the jharoka?' a slave girl asked.

'Not yet.'

Mehrunnisa went out into the corridor and walked up to the edge, from where she could look over into the garden. The palace was just stirring. She put an elbow on the parapet and leaned her chin against her hand as she gazed down into the garden. She stood watching the goldfish swimming in the pools of water, the dew on the leaves, breathing in the earthy smells of the early morning. It was a small moment of peace, snatched from a day filled with duties of state and the other thoughts that troubled her. How was she to approach Khusrau for Ladli? What would he say? He would be grateful, of course, because if her favour shone upon him, he would be elevated out of his worthless existence and given prominence once more. But she would do this carefully. Somehow, things had gone wrong with Khurram. The rot had begun inside their junta, within them, long before the nobles at court were aware of it. But Mehrunnisa knew that rumours swirled around the court that Khurram no longer had her support, and that he no longer gave her his endorsement. He had called a conference of sorts during the Emperor's illness. The fool. Had he not learned anything from Khusrau? Hadn't he stopped to think what would happen if Jahangir recovered?

The Emperor and she said nothing to Khurram about this, but they watched him with care. Uppermost in both their minds was the thought that if Khurram was this hasty in wanting the throne while his father lay ill, would he be as scheming now that his father had returned to health? One result of Khurram's actions was that the rift between them was no longer a secret. The nobles and commanders knew, the zenana knew, and so the empire knew. Cracks had begun to appear in the junta's solid front. As yet there were no repercussions. Not even in the junta itself. Bapa said little, he had grown too old to assert his will. Khurram still came to the meetings, but with each one, another invisible brick built up a wall between them through which only polite phrases passed. And Abul... Mehrunnisa always thought long and hard about her brother's loyalties. Abul and she were bound by blood, but Khurram was his son-in-law... it was an uneasy relationship now.

She leaned her head against a pillar.

Nizam awoke with a start as he tumbled off the stone bench. He shook his head to clear his sleep-fogged brain and stared around him. Where was he?

He heard the tinkle of gold bangles and parted the leaves of a jasmine bush. A woman stood in the upper balcony. Nizam's breath choked in his chest. Was this the Empress? From this distance, he saw the slim figure, hands clad in diamond and sapphire rings, and hair that shone like ebony cascading over her shoulders. The lady moved, and her bangles tinkled again. She rubbed her eyes with her palms and then stretched, raising her arms over her head. Nizam gawked, mouth open. Now he could see her eyes, they were the blue of a finely etched turquoise. This had to be the Empress. He had seen her!

Mehrunnisa straightened from the parapet and rubbed her neck. She had slept awkwardly. The bed had been empty beside her, too large and uncomfortable without Jahangir to edge her to one side. So she had slept aslant, cast the pillows off, waking several times with the dampness of sweat in the folds of her elbows and knees. She lifted the heavy mass of her hair from her nape. If she could cut it off, thin it somehow, these summer months would be more bearable. But the Emperor would not listen to even a suggestion about this; he wanted her hair long. She started to turn away; it was time to dress for the jharoka, the nobles would be waiting.

A movement caught her eye. Mehrunnisa gazed intently at the bushes to her left. The leaves rustled again. Who was in the garden early in the morning? She moved away from the parapet, as though she were going, and slid behind the pillar and waited. When she put her head out after a few minutes, she stared in shock as a man came out from behind the bushes. Who was he? Not one of the eunuchs, and no other men were allowed this far into the zenana apartments, not into her apartments anyway. The man knelt by the pool, dipped his hands in the water, and washed his face.

'Your Majesty.'

'Hush,' Mehrunnisa whispered as she put a finger to her lips and beckoned. Hoshiyar came to stand by her.

'Who is that person?' Mehrunnisa pointed to Nizam.

Hoshiyar gazed at him in surprise. 'I don't know, your Majesty.

He is not one of the staff.'

'An intruder?'

Hoshiyar's glance was troubled. 'This is impossible, your Majesty. Who would dare enter the imperial zenana without permission? Does he want to die?'

'Bring me my quiver and bow. Quick!' Mehrunnisa hissed.

Hoshiyar ran into the adjoining chamber and came back with a gold quiver and bow. The arrow shafts were made of silver, and the tips of gold. She put an arrow on the bow and pulled back the string. She nodded to Hoshiyar Khan.

'Hey you!' Hoshiyar yelled.

Nizam looked up. The expression froze on his face when he saw Mehrunnisa, her bow drawn. Before he had time to react, the arrow left the bow and hissed as it cut through the air. It struck him squarely in his chest and went right through his heart.

The garden was soon full of people. Eunuchs, slaves and attendants rushed out upon hearing Hoshiyar's shout and arrived just in time to see Nizam frantically clawing at the arrow sticking out of his breast. As they watched, Nizam toppled over into the pool. The water dyed a deep red, and his body floated in the pool face down.

'Find out who he is and then feed his corpse to the dogs,' Mehrunnisa said curtly. She went back to her bedchamber to dress for the jharoka. By the time she came out, the body had been taken away and eunuchs were carefully draining the bloody water out of the pool. When the Empress returned to her palace after the jharoka, the pool was clear again and the goldfish swam about undisturbed.

The day passed, and whispers grew into a forest of noise in the imperial zenana. Mehrunnisa had forgotten that all she needed to do was stumble just a little. And many hands would flinch from aiding her. Too many feet would willingly stomp on her while she was down.

Chapter Eighteen

Ah! Is it the same Nur Jahan who
behind the curtain of Jahangir
was but the true Ruler of the Time?
Is it the same Lady
that if her delicate forehead creased
the leaves of governance creased too?
[No], this Nur Jahan, now
is not the same.
No more her conceit, cruel charms,
devastating coquetry!
A criminal,
she has no supporter, no advocate;
forlorn, homeless, belonging nowhere!

—ELLISON BANKS FINDLY,
Nur Jahan

MANDU WAS IN THE DISTRICT OF GUJRAT AND HAD THE REPUTATION OF being the most impregnable city in the world. It sat atop a mountain, within a fort. There was no necessity for a moat, since the walls of the mountain fell away steeply from the fort's edge and plunged into a forested ravine whose depth had never been gauged. There were only two gates to the fort—a southern one called the Tarapur Gate, and one on the north, the Delhi Gate. The roads to both entrances climbed sharply from the bottom of the mountain, and in fact, only the Delhi Gate was accessible at all. Horses and camels found the climb strenuous, humans on foot had to claw their way up and rest every half mile to draw dwindling air into their lungs, elephants lumbered up only with the greatest difficulty, their bulk pulling them ever downward with each step. The only way to storm the fort at Mandu was to cut off supplies at the bottom of the north and south roads and wait until the inhabitants starved. Trying to besiege the fort any other way was an invitation to death—Mandu's defenders would simply pick off their tired targets one by one from the fort's ramparts and send their bodies careening down into the patch of green in the ravine.

The fort itself was two hundred years old, built in the middle of the fourteenth century by Dilawar Khan Ghori and added to by his son—all of this long before the Mughals came to India. So far into the sky, the rains rumbled generously into Mandu and filled the sixteen huge water tanks dispersed over the city. The Ghoris, father and son, had built massive palaces, mosques, cobbled streets, bazaars, colleges, schools, tombs and lush gardens. Mandu was a thriving, flourishing little jewel for over a hundred years. Then its fortunes changed as its owners changed. Battles were fought, although Mandu resisted invasion, kings died, treasuries emptied, people fled down the steep slopes to find habitation in the plains. And Mandu slowly died. Its fortunes changed yet again, when Emperor Akbar conquered the city and added it to the empire, but he did not visit here. Jahangir and Mehrunnisa gave orders for the city to be rebuilt again while they were at Ajmer.

They moved from Ajmer to Mandu once the restoration was complete. The city took on life when palace walls and floors were replastered, smoothed and polished, when the ghosts who had lived there for a hundred years were banished, when the trees, bushes and grass were hacked back to obedience, and the water tanks were cleaned and filled with sweet rainwater.

The skies darkened over Mandu the night of Nizam's death. Mehrunnisa and Jahangir slept outside under an inverted dome of confetti-like stars, all pressing close from the heavens.

The next morning, before sunrise, a terrible jangling sounded all through the palace. Jahangir groaned and buried his face into the mattress.

'Who is doing that?' He put a pillow over his head.

The din grew around them, unceasing, until they could ignore it no longer. Mehrunnisa pulled at the pillow. 'You must rise, your Majesty. It is the Chain of Justice that makes this noise.'

The Chain of Justice was a thickly linked gold chain hung with sixty bells. When Jahangir first became emperor, he thought much about his duties and responsibilities to the empire. So he drew up the twelve rules of conduct, the *dasturu-l-amal*, edicts meant to be followed by all his realm's inhabitants. Some were based on practicalities—like the law of escheat, which said that upon a noble's death, his property would not revert back to the crown but fall naturally upon the man's heirs, his sons. Some were moral; the Emperor imposed a wide and sweeping prohibition on consumption of liquor in the empire. Jahangir did not follow this last rule himself and charitably disregarded its ill usage either at court or in the imperial zenana. His only condition was that no courtier should come before him at the Diwan-i-am or the Diwan-i-khas with alcohol on his breath. Thus the guards checked their mouths each day, along with their passes. There was, however, one rule Jahangir imposed on himself, the Chain of Justice. It was strung first on the battlements of the fort at Agra, its other end tied to a wooden stake on the banks of the Yamuna. It was another way for Jahangir to meet with the people of his empire, the commoners who did not have access to his court. Anyone who had a grievance and felt that the qazis had not properly addressed it in the law courts could come and shake the chain, and they would have the Emperor's ear.

The chain accompanied Jahangir when he travelled and was strung up wherever he stayed.

Over the years, without his knowledge, an etiquette grew around the Chain of Justice. Palms had to be crossed with silver rupees before access was allowed to the chain; the guards screened anyone calling for justice, attendants stopped supplicants at spear point and demanded to know what their complaint was and why. The chain remained largely silent. But not this morning. The might of the sixty bells, all pealing at the same time, bounced and echoed off the walls of the fort at Mandu. The whole city woke to that clamour.

Hoshiyar came running into the room. 'Your Majesties, there is a woman outside ringing the bells.'

'Ask her to stop that infernal noise,' Jahangir moaned, clutching his head. 'We will be at the jharoka in a few minutes.'

'Your Majesty, she refuses to stop. She says that she will stop only when you come.'

Jahangir and Mehrunnisa rose hurriedly and flew through the corridors to the jharoka window. The entire zenana—women, eunuchs and slaves—followed them. The din was almost too much to bear and banged in their ears as they climbed the steps to the balcony. The courtyard below was already crowded with nobles and courtiers, who had also hurried out of their beds. Everyone was curious.

Mehrunnisa looked at the woman who had roused them from their sleep. Her greying hair flew about her shoulders, and her veil had slipped off her head. Unmindful of their presence, she yanked at the chain again and again as tears ran down the grooves of deeply wrought wrinkles on her brown face. She was a small woman, and the chain was heavy, but something gave her the strength to pull at the chain and release it, over and over again. One of the attendants said something to her. Then he had to grab her by the shoulders, shake her, and point to the jharoka balcony. She stopped, and the silence that came fell sweetly upon all of them.

The woman turned and ran up to the jharoka window. She threw herself down on her knees and raised her hands.

'Your Majesty, I want justice,' she cried.

'And you shall have it. Tell us the problem,' Jahangir commanded.

'Your Majesty, my son was killed yesterday,' the woman said, wailing. 'He was my only child, the support of my old age. Now he is gone, murdered.'

'Who killed your son? What was your son's crime?'

'There was no crime, your Majesty. Just a childish mistake, and for that his life was taken.'

'Who killed your son?' Jahangir demanded again.

The woman was quiet. She wiped her tears carefully and looked at the veiled figure by Jahangir's side. She lifted a finger and pointed toward Mehrunnisa.

'She did it!' The courtyard echoed with shouts. Mehrunnisa gripped the parapet and leaned over. What was this? What was this woman saying?

'Silence!' Jahangir shouted, holding up his hands. Anger coloured his face. 'Do you know who you are accusing of murder?'

'Yes, I do, your Majesty. Empress Nur Jahan killed my son yesterday,' the woman wailed. 'You have promised me justice. Sentence the murderer to death.'

The nobles in the courtyard started to murmur. In the zenana enclosure behind Mehrunnisa, one woman cried out, 'Justice from his Majesty, the Adil Padshah!'

Mehrunnisa heard the cry. Whose voice was it? Empress Jagat Gosini? Or one of her underlings? She turned to look back, but the other women, and then the men below, picked up the chant. They started to yell. 'Justice. Justice.'

'Mehrunnisa,' Jahangir said, reaching for her hand. 'What am I to do now? How do we silence them? Is she the mother of the intruder in your palace?'

She had to lean forward to hear his words. A small breeze caught the chant and sent it spiralling over the walls of the palace into the city. 'Justice. Justice.' Mehrunnisa started to tremble, for the first time seeing how much she was really abhorred by almost everyone. People jabbed their fists in the air. They all looked only at her, not at the Emperor.

Jahangir held her hand tight. 'What shall I do?' he asked again.

She could not reply, fear coming to blossom inside her. Once, early in their marriage, one of her cousins had killed a child in the streets of Agra. He had been goading his elephant beyond its normal speed, and the child had darted across the elephant's path only to be thrown violently to one side. The child's parents had demanded justice too. And the Emperor had given it to them by his rules. A life for a life. It had not mattered that the perpetrator had been her cousin; he had been ordered trampled to death by elephants. What would Jahangir do now?

He turned from her to the courtyard and held up his hand, and he held it in the air until the noise stopped. 'What crime is your son accused of?' he said harshly to the woman below them.

'Your Majesty,' the woman replied in a small voice, 'he entered the zenana to catch a glimpse of the Empress.'

A touch of disapproval went through the assembled courtiers. They had reacted instinctively to the call from the zenana that justice must be served; what the crime was, they had not known. The men were quiet now. It was forbidden to see the exalted ladies of the zenana, of any zenana for that matter. Almost at once, the tide of opinion swung back in Mehrunnisa's favour. She had been right to kill the commoner; after all, once he had so deceitfully seen her face, he could not possibly expect to live. If she had not done this, Jahangir would have ordered it.

'Do you consider that a childish prank?' Jahangir asked.

'Yes, I do.' The woman lifted defiant eyes to Jahangir's face. Her tears had dried, her back had straightened. 'He meant no harm, your Majesty. He had heard tales of the Empress's beauty and wished to see her.'

'Since you have brought your plea to me, I will render justice thus. The Empress will be arrested immediately and taken into custody. The case will come before the chief justice of the court tomorrow. I agree to abide by the qazi's decision...' Jahangir's voice faltered, '...even if it is death.'

Nizam's mother bent to touch her head to the ground. Two of the zenana Kashmiri guards came to escort Mehrunnisa back to her apartments. She stumbled on her way out, and Jahangir steadied her. 'Go, my dear,' he said. 'I will take care of everything.'

Mehrunnisa returned to her rooms in a daze, Hoshiyar a few steps behind. In the courtyard behind, the nobles began to clap in rhythm, the sound like evenly paced gunshots. One after another. They did not shout or talk again, they just clapped.

The morning hours passed, and news of Mehrunnisa's downfall reached every corner of Mandu. Courtiers hurried home to tell their wives and those unfortunate neighbours who had not answered the bells' summons. Prince Khurram had been in the courtyard, and his hand had been one of the first raised, his voice had shouted the loudest. He wanted Mehrunnisa destroyed; she was of no use to him anymore. And Abul had stood by Khurram, his hand on the prince's shoulder. The voice that had first spoken in the zenana enclosure had been Arjumand's.

A rush of excitement coursed through the harem. This was no mere fight between Mehrunnisa and the Emperor, nothing she could cajole him out of with her wiles and her spells. This was the end. This was surely the end. Tomorrow, the qazi would render judgement the only way it was done in the Mughal Empire. A life for a life. A death for a death. Anything else, any other leeway granted to the Empress, would smack of imperial favour, of injustice, of prejudice. And so little pockets of hatred filled all over the zenana, fuelled by gossip and revulsion. A group of zenana women composed a ballad and had it smuggled out of the imperial harem. By afternoon, the street minstrels set it to music and sang the ballad through the day and into the night.

Mehrunnisa stayed in her apartments, embroidering the hem of a new ghagara. She worked on it steadily, dipping her needle into a bowl of pearls, threading the silk through the hole in the centre of each pearl, and attaching it to the raw green silk of the skirt. She heard the ballad sung in the deep voices of the men in the streets outside. They called her a criminal, they called for her demise.

Hoshiyar watched over her all through the day. She did not eat, he tried to coax her, but she refused, drinking only water. Every now and then, her hand trembled and she put away the ghagara, clasped her hands in her lap, and waited for the trembling to subside. Then she forced herself to begin again. The song played outside her windows incessantly.

Was she a criminal? Had she done wrong in killing a man who had practically put his neck out with his actions? She felt no guilt, no overwhelming sense of wrong. Nizam—that was his name—had come into the imperial zenana knowing well that if he were caught he would die. She had merely executed the death sentence. Why this tremendous outrage? She was disliked... this she knew. Khurram had reason for it, so did Empress Jagat Gosini and the other ladies in the harem. But Abul, her own brother?

Her hand shook, and she cast away the embroidery. Abul's devotion lay with money and titles. Had he forgotten that the very clothes he wore, the title that marked him as one of the grandees of the empire, the house he inhabited, his daughter's marriage to Khurram, all had come through her?

Mehrunnisa picked up instead the thick volume of the *Shahnama*, the Book of Kings, by Firdausi. Her bookmark, a slender gold wire topped with a ruby button, glimmered at the middle of the pages. Pulling out the bookmark, she began to read of the glory of Persia, of the empire in ancient times until the arrival of Alexander, of the great capital of Persepolis, now south of Shiraz. It took Firdausi thirty years to conceive and complete the *Shahnama*, and in the end, his reward from Shah Mahmud was so paltry that Firdausi wrote a harsh criticism of Mahmud. She turned to the end of the volume to this poem—*Satire on Mahmud*. 'Think not, O King! thy sceptre or thy pow'r, One moment can arrest the destin'd hour...'

She fretfully slammed the book shut and put it down. Only a miracle would save her; how that would come about, she had no idea.

If she were to die, what of Ladli? At this thought, Mehrunnisa looked up at Hoshiyar. He stood with his back to the door of her apartments, and his gaze had not left her in many hours.

'Hoshiyar,' she said, throwing away all fear. 'Call for Prince Khusrau.'

Two eunuchs brought Khusrau into Mehrunnisa's room and then bowed their way out. She rose and reached for the prince's hand. He jerked away and stood where he was, his head inclined forward as though it would help him see better.

'Why am I here?'

'Come and sit next to me, Khusrau,' Mehrunnisa said in as placating a tone as she could. She moved in front of him and led the way. Khusrau followed. He stumbled on the edge of the carpet, righted himself, and dragged his feet along the pile, feeling for obstacles. When his right foot hit the divan, he bent down to touch its edges and sat down. He turned to where the light was brightest, towards Mehrunnisa, for she sat in the slanting rays of the westerly sun, the aquamarines on her ears and around her neck gleaming.

Khusrau leaned back from the light a little. He had aged, Mehrunnisa thought. It had been a long time since she had seen him, for Khusrau had been secreted away in the zenana's darkest apartments by the Emperor. His name was not mentioned in Jahangir's presence, for every time Jahangir regarded Khusrau, all his dislike for this once-loved son came flooding back. So the income that went to him from the imperial treasury was deducted automatically, and he was not invited to state functions.

'Why am I here?' Khusrau asked again, a quaver in his voice. He had been commanded to Mehrunnisa's presence and had dared not refuse. In any case, he did not have that option. He bent to peer at Mehrunnisa, and his beard, long to his waist as a sign of his father's disfavour, caught on his cummerbund. He wrestled with it madly, feeling the tug on his chin, until the Empress's hands came to help him disentangle it.

'How is Khalifa?' she said.

'What do you care, your Majesty?'

Mehrunnisa felt a quickening of rage. Were all the princes to talk to her thus, without respect? 'I hear,' she said crisply, 'that your confinement has depressed her spirits. That she is sad.'

'She is my wife, your Majesty,' the prince said. 'Where else would she be but with me?'

'Khalifa insisted upon being imprisoned with you. She will have to endure the discomfort.'

Khusrau hung his head. What the Empress said was true. When Khusrau had originally been incarcerated by his father, his wife had been offered apartments in the zenana, but she had wanted to be with her husband. That meant she had been placed under the same restrictions as Khusrau, for Jahangir had been wary of allowing Khalifa free access to the outside world, by which she could carry messages to and from Khusrau and his supporters.

That last sentence came out sharper than Mehrunnisa expected. In his own way, Khusrau was being as stubborn as Khurram, and he had less reason to be so. But she wanted something from him. 'Have you seen Ladli?'

'Your daughter? *Seen* her?' Khusrau laughed. 'I have *seen* her indeed, your Majesty, with these two good eyes my father has left me. A beautiful girl. Captivating.' He laughed again, and Mehrunnisa stared at him with distaste. He was so bitter, so without charm. What was she thinking?

'You will marry Ladli, Khusrau,' she said, all pretence at diplomacy gone now. She would order this upon him as she had not been able to upon Khurram. Khusrau had not Khurram's advantages, he could not refuse.

In response, Khusrau's shoulders stopped shaking. 'So this is why you wanted me here, your Majesty,' he said quietly. 'To force a marriage upon me. Why?' He paused. 'Did Khurram say no?'

'You are in no position to deny me this, Khusrau. I can give you as much freedom as you want. Marry Ladli and it shall be yours. Khalifa will have full access to the zenana, and your sons will be given consequence. You yourself will be able to demand all the rights given to the royal princes. Say yes, Khusrau.'

A sudden smile of expectation lit Khusrau's face at that word he had not heard in so many years—freedom. But it came at such a price as to make it unworthy. The prince's voice was low and bitter. '*You* are offering me freedom, your Majesty?' He moved his gaze around. 'From here? I hear you cannot step outside yourself. And that when you do step outside tomorrow it will be to greet your death.'

His words brought a wealth of uncertainty into Mehrunnisa. Had she fallen so low, and so suddenly, that even Khusrau, pitiful

Khusrau, dared to strike out at her? What had he heard that she had not? She turned to Hoshiyar beseechingly, her hands spread out. What was she to do now?

The eunuch shook his head. He had tried to tell Mehrunnisa to wait until the next morning before she approached the prince, but she had not listened. He spoke now. 'Your Highness'—Khusrau slanted his ears to the eunuch—'her Majesty will be absolved of all charges tomorrow. It behooves you to listen to her.'

'Hoshiyar Khan, is it?' Khusrau said. 'My father's most faithful eunuch, once Empress Jagat Gosini's right-hand man. How do you like serving this new mistress, Hoshiyar? Your tenure here is going to be short indeed.' Khusrau got up from the divan. 'Take me back to my apartments, Hoshiyar.'

Mehrunnisa nodded and let the prince go. He walked away with as much dignity as he could muster. When he reached the door, she said furiously, 'I will not forget this, Khusrau.'

Khusrau turned. From this far, he could only vaguely gauge her direction. His smile was grotesque. 'Then you will take it to your grave, your Majesty.'

Chapter Nineteen

*The King is so fickle and inconstant, that what hee had
solemnly promised for an English Factory, was... reversed,
and againe promised, and againe suspended, and a third
time both granted and disanulled...*

—J. TALBOYS WHEELER, ED.,
*Early Travels in India, Sixteenth and
Seventeenth Centuries*

'YOU ARE TO ENTER NOW, SAHIB.'

An Armenian slave came up to Sir Thomas Roe as he waited
outside the Diwan-i-am. Another man accompanied the slave, and
the two were dressed alike in white silk trousers and a thin silk
qaba. Jewelled turbans weighed down their heads, and daggers with
pearl-and-ruby-inlaid scabbards were stuck into their white brocade
cummerbunds.

Roe got up slowly. His body still ached from the fevers he had
suffered for the last month. He had lost so much weight that his
waistcoat hung loosely from his shoulders.

Roe had arrived at Mandu ten days ago, but a fever had felled
him almost as soon as he entered the doorway of his house. The
illness had persisted all through the journey from Burhanpur, and
Roe at times had simply let himself topple on his horse's neck and
allowed it to carry him where it would. He had dared not stop on

the way, for the missives from the court were coming at a furious pace.

It did not help that Roe had fallen sick again upon his arrival at Mandu and so could not wait on Jahangir. The Emperor, suspecting that Roe was faking his illness, had sent a slave to Roe with a wild hog he had killed during a hunt as a present. The slave had stood in the outer courtyard of Roe's house and insisted that he be allowed to see the ambassador. So Roe had staggered from his bed, barely able to hold his emaciated weight on his feet, to meet with the slave and thank him for the meat.

'I have requested the Emperor's permission to salute him in the manner of the court of England,' Roe rasped weakly.

The slaves bowed. 'So it shall be, Sahib. The Emperor knows of your wishes.'

'Let us go then.'

They moved ahead of Roe, the two men walking abreast until they reached the huge wooden doors that led to the Diwan-i-am. Roe flicked a speck of dust from the frilled cuff of his right sleeve. He would have dearly liked to be abed still, nursing himself back to health, but the last message from Jahangir had been particularly demanding and uncharitable to excuses of illness. The Emperor had set a date and time for his official introduction, during an evening darbar, specially convened to meet Roe. It just happened to be on the night of Mehrunnisa's incarceration.

The rumours of the morning's happenings had infiltrated into Roe's house too. He had dismissed them, obsessed in the labour of dressing in clothes that seemed to have been sewn for a much fatter and prosperous man. Nothing fit anymore. His stockings flapped about his knees, loose like pyjamas, and he could move his arms in and out of his coat sleeves without twisting himself out of it. He groaned when he saw his image in the mirror. His skin was the white of salt, his cheeks curved inward into his face, his beard drooped, and his auburn hair was a dull brown. How could he go into court, for the very first meeting, looking like this?

And so still worrying, Roe almost bumped into the Armenian slaves in front of him. They had stopped and now faced the closed doors. An invisible signal must have been given, for the doors began to swing open on slick hinges, and Roe heard his name being announced.

Roe stepped into the Diwan-i-am and bowed low from the waist. He straightened and gasped. Diamonds, rubies and emeralds twinkled in profusion off the clothing and persons of the noblemen. Their coats and trousers glimmered with patterns of gold zari. Prince Parviz's court at Burhanpur had awed him, but here he was stunned. He had not thought it possible that this land, so barren and bereft on the outside, with violent winds and a killing heat, could hold such hidden riches.

The light from the oil and wood torches was pure and clean. Even the smoke from them, that wisped out occasionally, was perfumed with civet. The light went everywhere—caressing the bright and dazzling jewels, bringing out a cool white in the Armenian slaves' qabas, deepening the thick reds of the Persian carpets beneath Roe's feet, painting the faces that looked upon him in unblemished shades of wheat and brown. Roe's palms swam with damp, and he rubbed them on his waistcoat. His eyes and his mind were filled with these flitting impressions of grandeur, more grand and fantastic than anything he had been told, anything he could imagine. The nobles were all silent, gazing upon him, their heads twisted towards him but their chests firmly facing the Emperor, for they could not turn their backs upon Jahangir. It must be awkward, Roe thought, to hold one's head like that for a long time. As though in response, a small, almost imperceptible movement bolted through the Diwan-i-am. There were no smiles, no shrugs, nothing as blatant as that. But Roe, his vision heightened to sharpness, saw it, and realized that his mouth was agape. He shut his mouth and moved forward.

Roe was barefoot, like the other courtiers. He had been asked to remove his boots, and this still rankled, but as his feet sank into the thick pile of the carpets, he marvelled at their richness. And this silence, this quietness even of breath... Roe had never been in a courtyard thronging with men and animals and been able to hear the soft *shirr-shirr* as his feet glided over the carpets.

For a moment he was glad for his illness. Having been deprived of all sensations for over a month from his enforced seclusion and having been too sick to care, now it was like a new birth. The air was scented with sandalwood and patchouli. Roe drew the perfumes into his lungs, walked up to the first railing, and bowed again. The two Armenian slaves in front of him bowed to the Emperor and melted noiselessly to the sides. At last Roe could glimpse Jahangir, well down the path of glittering courtiers. Proceeding to the second silver-wrought railing, Roe bowed again, and then he entered the very last enclosure. Here there was little space for him to walk, the nobles crowded on every side. But they moved aside politely to let the ambassador through.

Now Roe was directly below the imperial throne. He bowed, and straightened, and looked upon Emperor Jahangir. The man who sat on the divan was about fifty years old. His hair—what showed of it under the gold brocade imperial turban—and the long sideburns caressing his cheeks were dusted with grey. Jahangir's eyes were calm, a tranquility that seemed to pervade his whole body. He sat cross-legged on the divan, his back straight, his waist not quite as thin as a young man's. Jewels gleamed everywhere. The Emperor wore pearls, rubies, diamonds and emeralds in his ears, on his fingers, around his neck, studded into his cummerbund. Parviz had been a caricature of a prince, betrayed by the deep and dark circles around his shifty eyes, an insubstantial voice, and an unprepossessing presence. His father was all Roe could have wanted in an Emperor. He had been told that one of Jahangir's wives dominated him and the empire. He had expected then a man much like the ineffectual Parviz, but this was a man Roe could respect.

Jahangir made a sign to the official interpreter.

'The Emperor welcomes you to India, Sir Thomas Roe,' the interpreter said. 'He hails his brother across the seas, King James of England.'

'Thank you, your Majesty. I come as the ambassador of King James and bring good wishes. As a token of friendship I bring these gifts and a letter from his Majesty, King James.' Roe handed the letter to the Mir Tozak. It had been painstakingly translated into Persian. 'This is the letter of commission from King James, appointing me official ambassador of England to your court, your Majesty.'

Jahangir looked over the letter of commission curiously. 'How is your health, Ambassador? You were unwell upon your arrival at Mandu.'

'I am much recovered now, your Majesty. Thank you for asking.'

'That is good. If you need any further assistance, the court physicians will attend to you.' The Emperor looked away, and Roe felt his heart pound again. He had done something wrong. What rule of etiquette had he breached? Then he realized what he had forgotten.

'Please accept these gifts on behalf of his Majesty, King James.' Roe gestured behind him and stood aside. His attendants brought forth brass platters bearing mounds of delicate frothy laces, English swords, scarves, belts, cases of fine English brandy, English hats and boots, and pieces of china.

The Emperor surveyed his gifts. 'What else?'

'I have also brought an English carriage for your use, your Majesty.'

Jahangir clapped his hands. His smile was like that of a delighted child. 'A carriage! Where is it?'

'It awaits you outside, your Majesty.'

'Go outside and see the carriage,' Jahangir ordered. Two courtiers immediately backed out of the Diwan-i-am to see the coach.

While they were gone, Jahangir talked with Roe. He asked him who had accompanied him, and Roe brought Thomas Armstrong forward. Armstrong was a musician and carried his virginals with him. What sound did that make, Jahangir asked. If his Majesty would be so pleased, Thomas would play for him. They listened until the nobles ran back to court with news of the coach. Roe strained to make out what they were saying to the Emperor, but he could understand only a few words of the Turki they were speaking. He bent towards his interpreter, who tried to decipher the rush of sentences. The coach had been harnessed to four impeccably white horses from Jahangir's stables. It was curiously wrought, with big wheels that looked rather flimsy. It had doors and windows like a real house. But most impressive of all was the English coachman who had been brought along from England, sweating outside in the heat of the torches in full gold-braided livery.

Jahangir smiled at Roe again and then turned away. His audience was over. He had been warned that he could not expect but a few words of greeting from the Emperor, but Jahangir had been very gracious indeed. Any business would have to come later, in the slow fashion of this empire. The Emperor would meet with Roe many times, and become familiar with him, before talk could turn serious. And then, if the time was right, the stars beneficial, Roe could ask Jahangir for the trade treaty. For today, though, this was enough.

Roe bowed again, trod backwards to the doors, bowing at each railing until he was ushered out. Still dazzled by the lushness of the

Diwan-i-am, Roe rode home slowly. As he reached the front yard, the fever came to swamp through his bones again. He fell from his horse and, delirious, had to be carried inside to collapse on his bed.

When Roe left, Jahangir got into his new coach and rode around the courtyard a few times. He examined the coach minutely. The cushions were covered with red velvet from China, the body was made of a light wood, nailed with brass nails. Jahangir complained about the Chinese velvet to the courtiers present. Why did the king of England have to send him cushions covered with Chinese velvet? He had heard that there was better velvet to be found in Europe. And the hats and scarves and lace—were those the gifts one king would send to another? Where were the jewels and precious stones? Even Rana Amar Singh, a conquered king, had gifted a large ruby, horses and elephants to the empire.

Jahangir walked around his new coach, swung the doors open a few times, checked the wheels, and finally looked at the English coachman. The man bowed as low and deep as he could, his breath stifling in his tight clothes. The Emperor laughed and sent him away to change into something cooler. He gave him a new salary. The coachman could stay in India as long as he wanted, the imperial treasury would fund him.

Of Mehrunnisa, the Emperor said nothing. The nobles all watched him carefully. But he seemed unconcerned about the trial the next morning. Was this the end of Empress Nur Jahan? they wondered to each other at meetings all through the night. Jahangir behaved as though nothing was going to happen that was not usual or routine. He had not been to see his wife, this much the nobles knew, everyone knew. Once, just once during the day, Hoshiyar Khan had been commanded to meet him, then Hoshiyar had left the zenana.

Well before the break of dawn, the streets of Mandu thronged with people. The nobles passed through the crowds, clutching in their hands the cherished passes for the morning jharoka. They went into the courtyard and waited for the next few hours until the sun saw it fit to rise.

Khurram positioned himself at the very back of the courtyard, where he leaned against a wall and waited. The zenana women stood behind the balcony. There were no petitioners in the crowd; the only event that would take place would be the trial. The men stood shoulder to shoulder. They had been standing for quite a few hours now. The imperial orchestra began to play. As the trumpets lifted into the air, the Mir Tozak shouted, 'All hail Emperor Jahangir, the Adil Padshah!'

'All hail!' the courtiers responded.

Jahangir entered the balcony above them. Backs bowed in the taslim.

'Bring in Empress Nur Jahan,' the Emperor said to Hoshiyar Khan. When Mehrunnisa appeared, she stood an arm's length from Jahangir. Her veil was of a thin white muslin spangled with tiny silver buttons. Through it, she surveyed the sea of faces before her. They were all there—Muhammad Sharif, Abul, Khurram and Bapa. Abul was by Khurram's side again, not right under the balcony as he should have been. No matter. She knew where she stood. Alone.

The Amir-ul-umra was at one corner. She wondered if he had let Mahabat Khan know of this yet. If he had dispatched runners to Kabul, they would not have reached by any means, and by the time they did, this would all be over. But so much repugnance from the men... what had she done to deserve such distaste?

'Your Majesty,' she said softly. Jahangir turned to her, but he did not speak. Mehrunnisa wanted to reach out to her husband and touch his hand, know that he would look after her. No message had come to her from the Emperor, no assurance of safety. Did he think her guilty too? Had he condemned her as the others already had?

But her pride did not desert her. If she were to die today, she would die as an Empress would. Inside, she could even smile, the irony of this not escaping her. She wanted to leave her name in the mouths of people hundreds of years from now. If her actions did not secure her fame for posterity, her death—and dying thus— certainly would.

The Mir Tozak's voice boomed in the silent courtyard. 'Bring forth the qazi.'

The judge was an old man; many summer suns had browned his skin and whitened his hair. He was known to render swift judgements and to sleep undisturbed after sentencing death. But last night, there had been no rest. The only punishment he could deliver was death. And what would happen to him in the months that followed, when the Emperor missed the Empress? Who would he turn to blame then?

He dragged himself to the balcony and performed the konish.

'What do you say?' Jahangir asked. There was no presenting of evidence, no recital of crimes, no defence. This was Mughal judgement.

The qazi opened his mouth, but the words would not come. Mehrunnisa waited for the sound of his voice, for that dreadful word of death. She leaned over the balcony's edge.

'Your Majesty.'

At the shout, the courtyard turned to the old woman at the back. She ran through the men and went down on her knees before the Emperor.

'What is it?'

'If I may, your Majesty.' Cunning lit up Nizam's mother's face. Her yellowed teeth flashed in a grovelling smile. 'The Empress's death will do me no good. I have lost my son; he was to look after me. What will I do now?'

Jahangir leaned over the balcony. 'Shall I then suggest a fine instead of the punishment? Empress Nur Jahan will be ordered to pay you two thousand silver rupees as blood money.' He waved his hand at the qazi in dismissal. 'Your services are no longer necessary. As you can all see, the woman herself does not demand the Empress's life.'

There was silence in the courtyard. No voice spoke.

Mehrunnisa drew back. Money instead of her life. Two thousand rupees only. Her outfits cost more. What was happening here?

'Come, my dear. Let us retire to our apartments.' The Emperor put an arm over her shoulders and pulled her away from the balcony.

When they were gone, the nobles began clapping again. It had all been so skillfully orchestrated, like a well-cued play. The qazi with his flapping mouth and his sweaty palms. The old woman who had cursed and demanded Mehrunnisa's blood just the day before. Jahangir's ready acceptance of her terms. Who had told the woman what to do? Hoshiyar Khan. At the Emperor's behest. Dignity was secured on all ends. Nizam's mother would get more money than she could ever spend—two thousand was an enormous fortune. The Emperor would not lose his title of the Just Emperor. And Mehrunnisa would not lose her head.

In his corner, Khurram turned away in disgust. He had heard of Mehrunnisa's offer to Khusrau and had heard that his stupid brother had refused her. But it still bothered him.

What if Khusrau now agreed?

'How was it?' Coryat demanded. 'What did the *great* Mughal say?'

'Hush, Tom. You speak in jest, I know, but others may misunderstand you. We are here to make peace with the empire,'

Roe said, pushing Coryat aside to enter his house.

Coryat laughed and followed him inside. Thomas Coryat had started his career as a court jester and then entered Prince Henry's household as a personal fool. A few years ago, he had travelled all around Europe on foot and was now in India as part of his Eastern travels. When Roe met Coryat in Mandu, he had already walked across Constantinople, Bethlehem, Jerusalem, Damascus, and most of Turkey. He planned to walk from India up to Samarkand in Uzbekistan and there kiss the stone on Timur the Lame's tomb before heading home to Odcombe in Somerset. Coryat was writing of his travels in the Eastern countries, but his memoirs were so large that he had been forced to leave a part of them with the consul at Aleppo before proceeding to India.

At home in England, Roe and Coryat would have found little in common, but here they sought each other's company, aliens in an alien land. Coryat was now living in Roe's house.

'*Pani lao Sahib ke liye,*' Coryat yelled to the native manservant.

'What did you say?' Roe asked.

'I told the heathen to bring you some water to wash your hands.'

Roe shook his head. Coryat was fluent in most of the native languages of India. He even looked like a native. His skin had been burned nut-brown during his travels, and he wore Indian clothes and sandals. He had let his hair grow long to his shoulders and looked like a fakir. Coryat pulled Roe into the courtyard.

'Ahh...' Roe sank into his chair. 'It feels good to actually sit on furniture. I cannot imagine how these natives sit on the ground all the time.'

'It's easy.' Coryat sprang out of his chair and sat on the floor cross-legged.

'Sit on the chair, Tom. No more fooling around,' Roe said. 'Where is the man? I wish to wash the dust off my hands.'

'What happened at court? Did the Emperor receive you well?'

'Very well. He was polite and extended every courtesy to me. I could not have asked for a better reception. In all'—Roe slanted his head to one side in thought—'I would have to say that it went well. I did not expect the Emperor to be so gracious again.'

'Never mind the Emperor.' Coryat waved his hand. He was still sitting on the ground. 'Did you catch a glimpse of her? Did she speak at all?'

'Who?' Roe asked in surprise.

The manservant came in with rose water. Roe rinsed his hands and dusted off his coat. Two chilled goblets of lime sherbet were brought in. Coryat took a long draught of his sherbet and wiped his mouth with the back of his hand. 'Empress Nur Jahan.'

'Isn't she the one who was recently arrested?'

'Yes.' Coryat leaned forward, smiling into his beard. 'It was a sham, Roe. The Emperor is far too enamoured of his wife—she practically runs the empire, makes all the decisions. He is but a pawn, a fool in her hands. If you want your precious treaty, she is the one to approach.'

'Really?' Roe was disbelieving. He had heard these rumours from Jadu and others. But Roe had seen no evidence of this himself. If this Empress was really so powerful, why had she not commanded him to her presence? The veil, yes, he understood a little of how the imperial harem worked. But did the veil also not restrict her movements? How much could a woman speak, and expect to be heard, if her face was not seen?

'Did you bring gifts for her also?'

'I cannot say,' Roe said doubtfully. 'There was some fine lace and women's hats... the Emperor specially requested those hats from England. You think that it was the Empress who commanded them?'

'Undoubtedly. If the Emperor expresses dissatisfaction at your gifts, you can be sure that *she* is the one who does not like them.'

Roe rubbed his chin. Here was something new to think about. Abul Hasan had visited Roe the previous day, just a courtesy visit, he had said. But he had said much more, telling Roe of Jahangir's complaints about the gifts. The Emperor liked the coach very much and used it often, but the other gifts were so mean, so unworthy of a king of England. After Abul left, Roe had written to his Company's directors and told them to send richer presents on the next ship out to India. If Roe remembered rightly, this noble, Abul Hasan, was the Empress's brother. The same woman who so skillfully evaded death. Roe had been sick for a week after his first audience with Emperor Jahangir, and too busy thinking about that audience to pay attention to the ebb and rise of Mehrunnisa's fortunes. He thought back to his recent darbar. There had been a screened balcony to the Emperor's right. It was said that the ladies of the zenana sat behind the screen watching the proceedings at court. But they had not spoken during the darbar.

'Just how powerful is the Empress?' Roe asked.

'Very. Even more than the Emperor, her word is law. If you paid any notice, you would have realized that the Emperor did not resolve a single matter at court today. The nobles petition the Emperor, but all decisions are made by the Empress in the zenana.' Coryat flopped on the ground and looked up at the clear, starred night sky. 'It is beautiful here.'

'Yes...,' Roe said absent-mindedly. A servant came in and coughed to attract attention.

'What is it?'

'Sahib, there is a messenger here from the Emperor.'

'Send him in.' Roe rose from his chair and straightened his coat.

A tall eunuch, slightly tending to fat, came in and bowed. 'Sahib, his Majesty requests that you send him your letter of commission.'

'Who are you?'

'This is Hoshiyar Khan, Roe, the head of the royal harem, and, if I am not mistaken, personal eunuch to her Majesty, Nur Jahan Begam.' Coryat's voice was languid.

Hoshiyar bowed in his direction. 'You are right,' he replied politely and then turned back to Roe. 'About the letter...'

Roe reached into his breast pocket and drew out the official commission. He turned it over in his hands. 'This is the original. I don't have any more copies. If this is lost...'

'Do not worry, Sahib,' Hoshiyar said. 'I shall take good care of the letter. His Majesty... ah... wishes to read the letter again, that is all. It will be returned to you tomorrow.'

'Very well. But please see that it comes back to me tomorrow.' Roe handed the letter to Hoshiyar. The eunuch bowed and left the courtyard. As soon as he had departed, Coryat stretched out on the cool stone floor.

'It has already started, Roe. Watch out for the Empress.'

'What does she have to do with this?'

'Hoshiyar is her head eunuch. He came from her. The Empress is checking up on your credentials, Roe. She wants to make sure that you are who you say you are, an official ambassador. Unfortunately, our former countrymen have also styled themselves as ambassadors, so the Empress is suspicious of you.'

The next morning, as promised, Hoshiyar brought the letter of commission back to Roe. A faint aroma of Attar of Roses came from the sheet of paper, which confirmed Coryat's suspicions. The Empress had carefully studied the letter and inspected the seal of the king of England to ascertain Roe's authenticity.

Sir Thomas Roe came to understand the truth of Coryat's words about Mehrunnisa. If she were placated, the Emperor's hand would sign the treaty. He asked for silk scarves, more hunting hats in felt decorated with gold braids, lace shawls, anything he considered a woman would like. He had once thought the veil would hinder Mehrunnisa, but he was the one hindered. When he could not see her, or even hear her voice, it was hugely frustrating. Here was an unknown antagonist.

And so Roe plodded on, drafting and redrafting the treaty.

Chapter Twenty

But, beeing to depart, he nor his Party thought not themselues secure if Sultan Corsoronne (Khusrau) remayned in the handes of Annarah: that in his absence the King might be reconciled, and by his liberty all the glory and hopes of their faction would vanish...

—WILLIAM FOSTER, ED.,
The Embassy of Sir Thomas Roe to India

IN MARCH, NAUROZ FESTIVITIES BEGAN, AND ROE WAS AT MANDU TO witness the magnificence of the Mughal court. A massive tent was erected in the centre of the darbar. The ambassador saw with some surprise that one wall of the tent was adorned with portraits from England that he had brought over—those of the king and queen, the countesses of Somerset and Salisbury, and the governor of the East India Company, Sir Thomas Smyth. Frances Howard, countess of Somerset, held a place of honour in the middle of one wall, since she was very beautiful. But the countess and her husband, Lord Somerset, were even then awaiting trial in England for the murder of Sir Thomas Overbury. The Emperor did not care, Roe thought, about the vagaries of the countess's fortunes, it was enough that she pleased his eye.

Gift-giving was a large part of the Nauroz festivities, and Sir Thomas Roe dug into his meagre supplies to impress the Emperor.

He gave Jahangir a long, double-linked gold chain with a large emerald carved with the form of Cupid drawing his bow. Jahangir was delighted with his gift. He summoned all the court painters and jewellers and demanded to know if they had ever seen such craftsmanship before. It was the first time Roe had given the Emperor something he had liked so much, so Roe was hopeful. Perhaps he could talk of the treaty soon? The chain and emerald belonged to Roe himself—he had long given up expecting any rich presents from the East India Company.

Roe asked the Emperor, this time not flirting around the topic. Would his Majesty be pleased to sign a treaty? There was no such thing as immediacy, Roe realized. The Emperor issued various farmans and edicts providing protection to the English from the Portuguese and the Indian customs officials in Surat and Ahmadabad, but that was as far as he was willing to go now. Stay a little longer, Sir Thomas Roe, Jahangir said to him again and again. Stay and enjoy our country. We can always discuss business later.

With Mehrunnisa, Roe had a little more luck. She asked Roe for English protection in the Arabian Sea for her ships. In return, her brother took him to court more often. That was all.

The Emperor began to talk of returning to Agra. As preparations for the trip were being made, news came to Mandu that the bubonic plague had struck down Agra. It had first been brought to the western Punjab from central Asia, and during the winter months it had spread fleetly to Delhi, Lahore and Agra. The first sign of the plague was a rat running through the house to dash itself madly against a wall. If it died on the spot, all the inhabitants fled, leaving everything they owned. And only thus could they be spared the sure death that the plague brought. Agra was not safe anymore. Hundreds died every day. There was seemingly no cure for it. Nothing to do but wait it out.

So Jahangir and Mehrunnisa stayed on in Mandu. And Roe stayed with them, his hopes shrivelling.

The sun set into the winter sky over Mandu, painting it in shades of corrugated pinks and reds. On the other side of the empire, the plague raged, sweeping through whole districts. Houses were shuttered, and the stench of rotting flesh, human and animal, hung in the air. No one was allowed into Mandu, for fear that they might be carrying the plague with them.

Rubbish fires burned throughout the city, sending plumes of blue-grey smoke spiralling into the heavens. The walls of the city purpled, and then took on the hues of the night, black and blue and indigo. For a brief instant of twilight, the skies glowed golden. The air was pure and sharp, ethereal, touchable.

Mehrunnisa jabbed her spade into the lush soil, and a jolt of pain shot through her arm. She shook her hand and dug around carefully. A small, smooth-faced stone showed itself. Mehrunnisa pulled it out of the earth and flicked the dirt from the stone. It was curiously shaped, an oval, maroon in colour with white streaking lines around its base. She flung the stone to a pile on one side and continued digging.

'Mama!'

Mehrunnisa lifted her head with a smile. Ladli stood in one of the verandah arches. 'Here I am,' Mehrunnisa said.

Ladli lifted the thick skirts of her ghagara and walked across the lawns to the garden. Mehrunnisa watched her near, a feeling of peace and love filling inside her so deeply she could not breathe for a moment. Where had the years gone? Gone while she was not watching? Ladli was now seventeen, no longer that impetuous child who had demanded her attention while Mehrunnisa worked in the gardens. She drifted over the lush green grass, her feet hardly seeming to touch the earth. Ladli was a woman, with long, thick hair that came down to a tiny waist, a gentle curve of hips, elegant shoulders. It was, Mehrunnisa thought, like looking into a mirror that erased the years. Ladli even had the same skin upon her face, unblemished and lightly tinted with a saffron glow.

'Can I sit with you, Mama?' Ladii asked.

'Yes.' Mehrunnisa smiled up at her daughter. 'But where? There is only mud here, and you do not like getting yourself dirty.'

Ladli shook her head, the colours of the dying sun catching in her grey eyes for a moment. 'I do not mind.' She looked around for a rock, dusted it with her hand, blew on her hand and sat on it, her knees drawn to her chest.

'What is it?' Mehrunnisa asked gently. She shifted her weight on her haunches and sat back, looking at her daughter.

'Nothing,' Ladli said, her head drooping. 'Why do you garden, Mama? Why not let the malis do their job?'

'I always have, remember?' Mehrunnisa pulled a dandelion out of the ground, her fingers closing around the stubborn plant and yanking at it slowly, until a long line of root hung from the bottom. She threw it into a jute basket and dug into the soil with her fingers. The mud was cool to her touch, climbing under her fingernails and into the creases of her palms.

'But you are the Padshah Begam, Mama,' Ladli said. 'Why do you have to do this?'

'I do not *have* to do anything, Ladli. I wish to.' Mehrunnisa looked at Ladli's slight figure again. She had drawn the edges of her veil around her shoulders to keep away the cool evening air. Mehrunnisa did not feel this coolness, all the bending and digging had brought sweat to dampen her armpits and trickle down her neck into the opening of her choli.

'Do you always do what you wish to, Mama?' Ladli's voice was disconsolate. She yanked her plait over her shoulders, undid the last few inches, and then expertly plaited the hair again. And then undid it again. It was a sign of dissatisfaction, Mehrunnisa knew. She herself walked many miles—even within the enclosed space of her apartments—when she was worried. Ladli fretted with her hair.

'Come here,' she said softly. Ladli almost flew from the rock and flung herself into Mehrunnisa's arms. Mehrunnisa sat back on the ground, Ladli half in her lap, her head in the curve of her mother's shoulder.

'Tell me,' she said. 'If you do not tell your mama, who will you tell?'

For a long time Ladli was silent. Her ghagara was now soiled with dirt, but she had not noticed. Another sign that she was troubled. Ladli was always fastidious, always graceful, bringing elegance into everything she did.

Ladli lifted her head and looked into her mother's eyes. The deep blue of Mehrunnisa's had faded somewhat, but her eyes were still brilliant. 'I miss you, Mama,' she said.

Mehrunnisa tightened her arms around her daughter. She rocked her as though she were a child. 'Where have I gone away that you must miss me? I am here, will always be with you. You know this. What is going on, beta?'

In response, Ladli drew back and went to her rock again. From there, she asked, 'Mama, is Khurram going to go to the Deccan?'

Mehrunnisa picked up her spade again and began to dig around the gourd vines, turning the earth up to show its rich and loamy face. 'That has not been decided yet. The Emperor and I have to talk about it.'

News had come from the warfront in the Deccan. Ambar Malik, the Abyssinian slave who had long established himself as a superior military commander, had disregarded the terms of his latest pact with the empire. Malik would never be king, no matter how many kingdoms he conquered, or lands he reigned over, for his ancestry would always keep him a commoner. So he was content with establishing kingdoms, putting puppet heirs on the throne, and ruling from behind and through them. Now he had formed an alliance with the kingdoms of Bijapur and Golconda. The Mughal army lost vast acres of land from the southern fringe of the empire as they eroded away into Malik's capable hands. Parviz was still in Burhanpur, of course, ostensibly commanding the campaign. But neither Mehrunnisa nor Jahangir could fool themselves into thinking that Parviz was any good at being a commander. He was at Burhanpur because he had to be somewhere. If he were not there, he would be here, where the royal court was.

And again, as in Mewar, the problem that presented itself was, who could be sent to the Deccan?

When Jahangir had sent Khurram to Mewar, Mehrunnisa had thought it would be a good opportunity for him to think about her demand that he marry Ladli. Time away from Arjumand would allow him to see the advantages of the match. But now there could be no such alliance. Mehrunnisa was loath to let Khurram go to the Deccan. If he came back covered in glory from there, as he had from Mewar, her task of getting Ladli married would be doubly difficult.

She was silent for a while, thinking of this, and woke from her thoughts to hear Ladli say, 'So do you think he will go, Mama?'

'Yes,' Mehrunnisa said finally. 'The Khan-i-khanan needs the direction of a royal prince. Khurram will go.'

'And will he take Arjumand?'

Mehrunnisa looked up from her work in surprise. 'I do not know. Perhaps.'

'I see.' Ladli put her feet into the earth near the rock and traced figures idly with her toes. 'Mama?' she said.

'What?'

'Can I... is it possible at all... can you ask the Emperor if I can marry Khurram?' This was said in a rush, accompanied by a deep, rosy blush that crept up her neck to her hairline.

Mehrunnisa sat back, stunned into silence. Why had she not seen this would happen? Ladli spent most of her time in Khurram and Arjumand's apartments, playing with their children, or lying about on a divan. The prince was a handsome man, and he could be charming when he chose, this Mehrunnisa knew from experience. He had Ruqayya's quick laughter, her ready wit. He had a humour that was engaging. And Khurram was, finally, the heir to the throne. Although years had passed since they had fought and parted ways, Mehrunnisa had not been able to give that importance to any other prince. Khurram, beloved of his grandfather Emperor Akbar, was beloved of the courtiers too. Why should it be so impossible that Ladli would find herself in love with him? And how could she tell her daughter that Khurram had had the chance to marry her but had said no? And that he had probably said no at the behest of Ladli's favourite cousin, Arjumand?

Ladli was crying now, deeply embarrassed at having asked such a forthright question. Tears came down her cheeks and flowed unhindered down the line of her clean chin. 'I am sorry,' she said in a low voice. 'I know Khurram is too magnificent for me to even look at him. But I thought that if he went away to the Deccan, he would go for a few years... and he may forget me.'

'Come here, beta. Let me explain something to you,' Mehrunnisa said. Her heart tore inside her at Ladli's tears. She knew how shattering love could be when it was not acknowledged, and when it would never be so.

Ladli shook her head. 'You said you can do whatever you want, Mama. Every day I see you do things other women would never think of doing. The Emperor listens to you. Ask him if Khurram can marry me?'

'Ladli...' Mehrunnisa hesitated, wiping the base of her neck where sweat soaked into the cloth of her choli. 'This is simply not possible.'

'Why? All you have to do is ask. Why do you not ask?'

'Beta, there are many reasons why. Reasons I cannot explain to you. You are too young—'

'I am not young anymore, Mama,' Ladli said bitterly. 'I am seventeen, the same age you were when you married my father. Arjumand was betrothed at fifteen; she would have been married then if things had progressed as they should have. If you could arrange for Arjumand's marriage, why not mine? Do you love her more than me?'

Mehrunnisa rose and came over to Ladli. She tried to put her arms around her daughter, but Ladli jumped off the rock and stood to one side, her hand raised to block her mother. 'You know you can do this.'

'Ladli,' Mehrunnisa said as firmly as she could. 'You must forget Khurram. There will be no marriage with him. Is that clear?'

All the fight fled from Ladli. She moved away on feet that were old and tired. Her shoulders hunched into her. 'Only too clear, Mama.'

When she left, Mehrunnisa went back to her work and dug furiously in the soil, uprooting a few vines, slicing her spade through the thick, fleshy meat of near-ripe gourds. She was deeply angry, not with Ladli but with Khurram. He had made her daughter fall in love with him. He was responsible for this. He would go to the Deccan as soon as she could manage it and take Arjumand with him. He would leave his three sons at the royal court as a surety against any rebellion. As for Ladli, only one thing would cure her—marriage to someone else. Khusrau may have said no to Mehrunnisa as Khurram had. This time, she was determined that yet another royal prince would not deny her.

Khurram strode the length of his apartments. When he reached the end of the long room, an arrow of sunshine touched the diamonds on his turban and his cummerbund. He turned and marched up to the divan where Arjumand sat.

'I will not go to the Deccan!'

Arjumand looked up from her embroidery. Khurram had stormed into their apartments half an hour ago. This was the first time he had spoken to her, but Arjumand knew her husband well. When he was in a rage, it was better to let him work things out for himself. So she had kept silent.

'Who says you are to go, my lord?' she asked now.

'The Emperor ordered me to the Deccan, but it is obvious where the orders come from.'

'Softly, my lord. It is said she has spies even in our palace.'

Khurram looked around and then twisted his young face to hers. Jahangir had sent for him early in the morning. Ambar Malik had rebelled again, and Parviz was a poor leader. So Khurram had to go and relieve him of his command.

'What did you say?'

'What could I say? I had to agree.' Khurram ran his fingers through his hair worriedly. 'Why does she want to send me away?'

Arjumand frowned. 'Why indeed? Is there some real danger to the empire from Ambar Malik?'

'I do not think so. The lands he has stolen from us were ones we took from him. He has gone no further, but he is too close now.' Khurram sat down on the divan and hunched forward, hands resting on his knees. 'Why should I have to go, Arjumand?'

She smoothed the hair on his nape, and Khurram leaned into her hand. 'Because there is no commander like you, my lord. You must go, if you obey the Emperor in this, and return victorious, as I am sure you will, his Majesty's approval will fall upon us again. Then, no one can shake it, not even the Empress.'

'Do you think that is all there is to this order? The Deccan is a long way off, Arjumand, and will be farther still when his Majesty returns to Agra.'

'What do you worry about, my lord?'

'You,' he said, taking her hand and placing it on his chest.

'I will come with you,' Arjumand said with a laugh. 'This time, I will come. And no one will be able to stop me.'

'Are you sure?' Khurram asked anxiously. 'It is not comfortable on campaign.'

'I will come.' Arjumand's back grew rigid. 'I will come,' she said again.

Khurram rubbed her hand over the silk brocade of his nadiri. Upon his return from Mewar, the Emperor had gifted him this coat in the Diwan-i-am. It was a sign of imperial favour, favour he knew Mehrunnisa would dearly like to tear off his back. So he wore it every day—once the coat was bestowed the wearer could have many more sewn. Khurram had three hundred nadiris.

Arjumand said he must go to the Deccan; as she spoke more of it now, Khurram saw that it would be to his advantage indeed. He would return to court and be showered with gifts, perhaps even a new title. His succession would be secure. He had stayed by the Emperor's side all this while, watching Mehrunnisa at court with a thick sense of dread. She flaunted rules, flirted with conventions, but her hold on his father was as strong as ever. She could do no wrong, and so Khurram worried if he had done the right thing in refusing Ladli. He could no longer go to Mehrunnisa and ask for the alliance again—it would be like asking for forgiveness. Another thought rose to disturb him.

'I cannot leave Khusrau here,' he said suddenly, interrupting Arjumand. 'If I do, the Empress will make him marry Ladli.'

She sat up and turned his face to her. 'Then take him with you, my lord.'

'Take him...' Khurram smiled at her in delight. 'Yes, I will take him with me. He will be safer with me than with the Empress.' He kissed her on her mouth. 'You are brilliant, Arjumand.'

The next day Khurram approached his father after the afternoon Diwan-i-am session and walked back with him to the zenana apartments. He would go, he said, if he could have Khusrau's company during the journey. Why, the Emperor asked? Where had this sudden brotherly affection come from? Khurram protested that he had always had that affection. Khusrau was blind, a burden on his Majesty, surely a trip away would benefit all of them? Jahangir let Khurram trail beside him as he went on. Any liking he had had for these two sons had vanished. They had insulted Mehrunnisa, and in doing so, had insulted him. In the end, he agreed to Khurram's request.

So Khurram left Mandu for the Deccan to enormous fanfare. He rode out in a copy of the English coach Roe had given Jahangir; a new jewel-studded sword worth one hundred thousand rupees hung from his belt, and tucked into his cummerbund was a short dagger worth forty thousand rupees. The coach had two copies, one for Mehrunnisa and one for Prince Khurram. The original had been dismantled and reupholstered in brocade and jewelled silks. Brass nails had been replaced with silver nails, and the floor of the coach had been covered in beaten silver sheets.

Khurram's entourage was not ten days on its journey when Empress Jagat Gosini died. The illness came upon her suddenly, a fever one night, delirium the next, a coma the following morning from which she never woke. After Mahabat Khan, her one ally, was banished to Kabul, Jagat Gosini was crushed into obscurity. Even Khurram was lost to her—lost, really almost from the first year of his life, given to Ruqayya, and then to Arjumand. The woman who merely gave birth to him had little place in his affections, and this Jagat Gosini realized at last. That Ruqayya had defeated her.

There might have been some solace in the news that came to Mandu just before Jagat Gosini's passing, but she died without hearing it. At Agra, a month before, Ruqayya Sultan Begam had died too. She had chosen not to travel to Ajmer and Mandu with the royal court. And one day, in the zenana palaces of the Agra Fort, Ruqayya saw the dreaded rat flee shrieking through her apartments to dash its head against the wall. The bubonic plague took her. But Ruqayya died as she had lived, greatly daring, a woman of substance.

Mehrunnisa mourned Ruqayya's passing with a depth she had not expected. It was not a daily grief, for Ruqayya had been at Agra these past few years, and so there had not been a daily connection. But she had always been there, someone Mehrunnisa could ask for advice, someone to talk with, even through the written word... now no more.

Parviz was still, in his desultory fashion, living in the Deccan. Only Prince Shahryar was at court. Khurram went on his new campaign with a lightened heart, sure that he had taken out yet another arrow from Mehrunnisa's arsenal. But he forgot that his youngest brother was seventeen, born the same year as Ladli.

Shahryar was old enough to be married.

Chapter Twenty-one

The King's revenue of his Crown-land, is fifty Crou of
Rupias; every Crou one hundred Leckes, and every Lecke
a hundred thousand Rupias; all which in our money is fifty
millions of pounds;* a summe incredible, and exceeding
that which is said of China.

* The amount must indeed have seemed enormous to our
author, as the regular revenue of England at that time could
scarcely have exceeded a single million.

—J. TALBOYS WHEELER, ED.,
Early Travels in India, Sixteenth and
Seventeenth Centuries

SIR THOMAS ROE HAD BEEN IN INDIA FOR TWO YEARS NOW, AND HE WAS
wretched. He was no closer to a treaty than when he had first come
to the Emperor's court. The fevers that had caught him upon his
arrival never really let go—they came and went with a frightening
regularity, leaving Roe feeling sick most of the time. He had taken
no trouble to learn the local languages; Roe knew just a smattering
of Persian, with which he haltingly communicated with Emperor
Jahangir. When it came to the treaty itself, or any talk of it, Roe
had to let his interpreters do the talking. It was frustrating to not
know whether the formality of his language and his respectful tone
and manner had been communicated. He could only watch Emperor

Jahangir's reactions, and as always, Jahangir kept a bland face and always gave Roe a polite reply. Diplomacy was a tedious, time-consuming, temper-keeping process, and Roe was running out of both time and temper.

His royal hosts were very kind, though. Almost every day, fresh kill from the Emperor's hunt—boars, wild pigs, nilgai, venison and partridge meat—found its way to Roe's kitchens. Mehrunnisa sent him slave girls for his use too, which Roe returned with a respectful thanks, but his was a bachelor establishment, your Majesty—he explained—women had little place in it. She gifted him golden and luscious musk melons that she had grown in the zenana gardens—Roe found these irresistible and cool in the heat of the summer months.

Roe doggedly reciprocated to each of the offerings with something of his own. The Company sent huge cargoes of gifts of all kinds to India, hoping to buy their way into the country. But Roe could not match Mehrunnisa and Jahangir's generosity—their pockets ran deep into the imperial treasury itself.

The imperial couple dithered, their quills never quite hovering over Roe's much desired treaty, though always open in courtesy to Roe. The Empress had what she wanted from the ambassador—protection from the Portuguese for her ships in the Arabian Sea. Her ships, somewhat incongruously, also carried the Portuguese cartaz. Roe woke from one of his illnesses to find the Jesuit priests re-established at court and a special new envoy from the Viceroy a pace away. Mehrunnisa had acquired a double indemnity of sorts. Both the English and the Portuguese patrolled the shipping routes, both of them guarded her ships, both wished the other to damnation, and neither knew how to achieve it.

Roe said nothing, knowing he had been cleverly finessed. He still hopped around the topic of the treaty, of course. For her part, Mehrunnisa did not ask Roe, *what* trade with England?

It was not a ridiculous question. What was it England had to offer in trade for all they wanted from the empire?

There was literally *nothing* from the English markets that would sell in Indian markets in large enough quantities to own the title of trade. The English offered broadcloth; in the beginning it was a curiosity, but so impractical in the end, too thick and heavy and unsuitable to the searing heat of India. The advantages lay with the empire. Roe was here not merely as the first official ambassador from England but very much as the chief representative of the East India Company. He had orders to buy a number of items such as gum resin, copper, brass, silver, cotton, indigo, saltpetre, opium, and spices like pepper, turmeric and saffron. The two most important were indigo and cotton.

Indigo was a dark blue vat dye used to colour silks, wools and cottons. It came from a plant that grew in the brackish water in places like Bayana, southwest of Agra. The dye was precious, named *neel*, or 'blue', in India, though Roe called it as all others did: indigo, or 'the colour of India'. The leaves of the plant were soaked in huge vats of water for two days until the blue dye seeped out. The water was then drained, and the indigo sank to the bottom of the vat. This was allowed to dry and then rolled into balls and stored in clay jars for shipment. The warehouses that housed these precious indigo balls were huge buildings, lit by the sun through ceiling skylights, with massive shelves reaching to the roof, each stacked with jars of indigo.

The English were vying with the Portuguese and the recently arrived Dutch for most of the Indian goods. As a result, the price of indigo fluctuated wildly, depending upon the demand for the dye or the supply, which in turn depended upon the indigo harvest. Roe was almost daily in touch with news from Bayana about the price of indigo, and when it fell, he bought large amounts to store in their factories for the next ship to England.

Not having a very favourable balance of trade, having nothing to offer in return for what they were taking out of the empire, the English were pouring gold and silver coins into India for the goods they bought. England's coffers were slowly depleted, and the Mughal imperial treasury grew fat with gold and silver. As soon as the English coins came to the treasury, they were promptly melted down and re-coined with the Emperor's stamp.

Roe wrote numerous letters to the East India Company warning them of the consequences of pouring too much silver into India. The imperial treasury was so surfeit that the silver deposits in the empire lay unmined, the miners off in search of a new trade. When the empire needed silver, the English practically *gave* it to the Mughal treasury, to melt and export as the need arose. So with all his worries about diplomacy and courtly behaviour, Roe had this other added headache. Finally, the Company decided to trade with their imports.

Porcelain came from Macao, camphor from Borneo, spices from Achin and Bantim, raw silk and lignum aloes from Thailand, ivory and amber from Africa, and silver from Japan. The markets at Agra were lavish with all these curiosities from so many countries around the world that no Indian merchant had ever set foot upon.

So Roe plodded on in India, executing his duties as conscientiously as he could, and all the while yearning for the cool dampness of England. One afternoon, Roe was lying in a hammock strung in his gardens when an attendant brought news that Jahangir's entourage was passing by. The ambassador hurried out to pay his respects. When Jahangir was abreast of him, Roe bowed from the waist. The Emperor reined in his horse.

'How are you, Ambassador?'

'I am doing well, your Majesty.'

'What do you have for me?' Jahangir asked, looking curiously at the book that Roe held.

Since it was etiquette to never appear before the Emperor without a gift, Roe had hurried out of his house with the latest edition of Mercator's atlas. The ambassador had nothing else in his house to give to the Emperor; he was still waiting for the latest shipment from England. Upon arriving in India, Roe, comparing Mercator with the local maps, saw that the atlas wrongly showed the Indus River emptying into the Gulf of Cambay instead of the Sind. Lahore was nowhere near the Ravi, and of Agra, the capital of the empire, there was no mention.

He offered the atlas. 'Since you are emperor of so vast an empire, your Majesty, please accept this book of maps. I give to a mighty king the world.'

'Everything that comes from you, big or small, is greatly welcome, Sir Thomas.' Jahangir laid his hand on his chest as he spoke. 'Tell me, has your latest shipment arrived?'

'I expect it any day, your Majesty.'

'Where do you live?' Jahangir looked around. Roe pointed to the ruined mosque that was his home.

'That is very fine,' the Emperor said gallantly, as he signalled his attendants to move on. Roe bowed and waited until Jahangir was out of sight.

A few days later, news was brought to Roe that the English ship had docked at Surat. Among the gifts it carried for Jahangir were two mastiffs. Edwards had first brought the Emperor a mastiff as a present. That dog had gone to the hunt ferociously and killed a leopard and a boar, while the dogs from Persia had snivelled in fear. Impressed, Jahangir had demanded more dogs from Roe. Six mastiffs had left England, and only two had survived the journey.

Jahangir ordered that the two mastiffs were to always travel with him, borne along in gold and silver palanquins. Each dog was to have four attendants specially assigned to its care, and a pair of gold tongs was fashioned so that Jahangir could feed the dogs pieces of meat himself, without having his hands bitten off.

The shipment also brought the requisite hats, coats and paintings that the Emperor was so fond of. After looking at them, Jahangir and Mehrunnisa chose the paintings that they liked the most, and these were sent to the royal ateliers, where the empire's painters copied them in every exact detail. The paintings were given out to zenana ladies and courtiers as signs of favour. So English hunting scenes, battle scenes, pictures of the ladies of James's court all adorned the palaces of the harem and the homes of the nobles at Mandu.

A few days later, Jahangir summoned Roe to his presence and showed him one of the paintings. It was of Venus and the Satyr, showing the Satyr with his horns and swarthy skin.

'You must remain silent, Roe,' Jahangir said. 'I shall ask the nobles in the court for an interpretation of this wonderful painting you have brought for us from England.'

The Emperor turned to the assembled courtiers.

They eagerly gave their explanations, but Jahangir was not satisfied.

'No, none of you is right,' the Emperor said when the last person finished speaking. 'You tell us what it means, Reverend,' Jahangir said to Reverend Terry, Roe's companion and chaplain.

'Your Majesty,' Roe said. 'The reverend is a preacher, a man of God. He knows very little of such matters.'

'Very well then, Sir Thomas, give me your explanation.'

Roe hesitated. Something was wrong, but what? 'Your Majesty, the artist simply intends to show his skill, but the interpretation escapes me. I have not seen this painting before,' Roe said cautiously.

'I will accept your excuse and give you an explanation myself,' Jahangir said. His tone was as gracious as ever, but the words were not. 'The moral of this picture is this: the painter scorns Asians.

This is evident from the fact that the naked Satyr represents us, with his swarthy skin. See here,' Jahangir pointed, 'Satyr is being held captive by the nose by Venus, who is a white woman. The painter means to show contempt for all Asians by portraying them as captives of the white people.'

'Most certainly not, your Majesty,' Roe said hurriedly. 'I beg pardon if the artist has somehow offended you. There has been some misunderstanding.'

'Never mind.' Jahangir waved a hand. 'I shall accept the gift nonetheless. You may go now, Ambassador.'

Roe bowed.

'By the way, take Mercator's atlas back with you.' Jahangir handed Roe the book of maps. 'I have shown it to the mullas at court, and none of them can understand it. I could not rob you of such a jewel.'

Roe bowed and cursed under his breath. He had made two mistakes, and both had not been directly of his doing. He rushed home and wrote a furious letter to the East India Company detailing the incident with the painting and cautioning them against sending any more allegorical pictures for fear of offending the Emperor.

Giving the atlas to Jahangir had been his own mistake, but only for the lack of anything else to give. Mercator showed the Mughal Empire to be but a paltry piece of land on the earth. There were other vast countries, some explored, some not. The Emperor had called himself 'World Conqueror' upon his ascension—according to Mercator he was no such thing. Roe had insulted Jahangir.

The Emperor made no further reference to the painting; his point had been made—it was a diplomatic glitch, and if the English wished to remain longer in India they would not make such a blunder again. The oils and watercolours that came from England were now of benign and happy scenes, pleasing to the eye, not even remotely reprehensible to the sensibility.

And so time passed. The plague waned and finally came to its death in northern India. Another winter came, it was awaited with terror, but no, Agra, Delhi and Lahore survived. Jahangir and Mehrunnisa decided to return to Agra, and from there go to Kashmir for the first time since they had been married.

The Emperor made Roe the same offer he had made William Hawkins—if he wished to stay on in India and quit the East India Company, he only had to say so. The imperial treasury would give him a huge salary, one much bigger than what the Company was paying him now; he would be a legitimate mansabdar of the empire, a commander of a thousand horses, and finally, he would get the title of Khan. Sir Thomas Roe Khan. Or Khan Thomas Roe. Any way he wanted it.

Roe wrote one final letter to the East India Company directors, resigning his duties. He advised against another 'official' ambassador to take his place. It was useless, he said, to try and wrangle a treaty from the Emperor—his Majesty was too canny to lose the tremendous advantage he had, that of playing the English and the Portuguese off each other.

On 17 February 1619, a fleet of ships put to sea from the bar off Surat, headed for England. Sir Thomas Roe was aboard the *Anne*.

He wanted to go home.

Chapter Twenty-two

*In a single empire there was no room for two such
masterful spirits as Nur Jahan and Shah Jahan. Each had
known the other too well to be under any delusion. The
issue was perfectly clear—Nur Jahan must either soon
retire from public life or supersede Shah Jahan by a more
pliable instrument. With characteristic daring and ambition,
she preferred the latter course. The difficulties were great
but she was not the person to be deterred by any difficulties.*

—BENI PRASAD,
History of Jahangir

THIS YEAR THE MONSOONS CAME TO AGRA IN THEIR SEASON. TURQUOISE
clouds turned indigo, indigo deepened into a plum purple, etched
with the brilliant silver of the sun behind them. The heat dwindled,
and the sky was no longer a burned white glaze at midday. The
Yamuna slowed and waited. Deliciously cool breezes swirled through
the city, lifting silk ghagaras with their fingers, caressing heat-worn
faces, raising spirits and bringing smiles.

The city was decked out in its best finery. The streets had been
swept with palm-leaf brooms, and the cobbled stones shone with
washing. Houses were newly whitewashed, the blight and smell of
the plague ostracized, rooms, courtyards and gardens fumigated.
The bazaars of Agra thronged with well and healthy people. There
were no more furtive looks to see whether the man shivering

nearby carried the dreaded plague, no fleeing at the sight of red and angry boils on an arm or a leg oozing pus, no rushing through the bazaar with noses and mouths hidden in the long folds of turbans. The plague had departed. Agra could live again. And the city had more reason to live—after five long years away, Emperor Jahangir was returning to the capital of the empire.

On the afternoon of the royal procession into Agra, the monsoon clouds opened their arms and let fall their burden of rain. It was a warm, soothing rain. Faces were raised to the sky above, mouths opened to let the water come in. It was a benign rain, one that would bring life to the city and the fields around it. It was a welcomed rain, one that would wash away memories of the plague, of the terrible deaths when entire families had been extinguished, with no one even left to perform the rituals of the cremations. Emperor Jahangir had commanded the rains to Agra. He thought it fit to return, so the monsoons came to receive him.

The streets were jammed with people along the route of the procession, soldiers standing shoulder to shoulder to keep them from stumbling under the path of the imperial elephants and horses. When the imperial elephant turned the corner into the main street of Agra, the people yelled.

'*Padshah Salamat!*' All hail the King!

Eager hands threw jasmine and marigold flowers in front of the elephant and showered rose petals from upstairs balconies. Jahangir and Mehrunnisa sat on a gold-and-silver-plated howdah atop the elephant. As it lumbered over the cobbled street, its huge feet crushing the flowers, they dipped into embroidered bags and flung masses of silver rupees into the crowds.

Mehrunnisa laughed at the crowds, laughed with them, suddenly so happy to be back at Agra. Her veil clung to the lines of her face, she was as wet from the showers as the people below, drops of water drenched the silk of her choli and her ghagara, but she did not care. The men shouted praises of her too. They welcomed her back with as much love as they did the Emperor. It was good to be home, and Agra was home.

When they entered the palaces, nothing had changed. In the gardens a few trees had sickened and died and so had been cut down. In the zenana apartments, divans and carpets had been burned after the plague. But nothing much else had changed. The marble floors shone mirror-like with polishing. The heavily pleasant smell of musk perfumed the hallways and apartments. The carpets, newly woven in Agra workshops, gleamed in a myriad of colours. The once deserted gardens and corridors echoed with voices filled with delight as the women who had stayed back ran out to welcome Jahangir and Mehrunnisa. They met as many of the zenana women as they could, paid their respects to the elders, and went to their rooms. There, Mehrunnisa started planning for Ladli's wedding.

The usual formalities of a wedding were skipped over for Ladli. Normally, marriages began with a call to the marriage broker. These were women usually of many years, their faces cracked with wrinkles, grey, thinning hair showing patches of brown skull, teeth yellowed from chewing tobacco and paan leaves. Marriage brokering was a prosperous business; *everyone* got married at some time or another, so the women were in much demand. Almost from the announcement of a new birth, they would visit the homes in their neighbourhoods, watching over the children with the fussing of a maternal hen. *How was he doing in his studies with the mulla? Or had she learned her embroidery well, were the stitches like seed pearls?* If not, a scolding was bestowed upon the tyrant. *Do you not want to marry well?* So when the time came, when the parents looked around for a prospective bride for their sons, they would approach the marriage broker.

Mehrunnisa had a long time to think about Ladli's marriage

after Prince Khurram left for the Deccan. He sent news every now and then of minor victories. Pockets of land were conquered, Ambar Malik's men were captured or driven away, and the imperial army rested before beginning a fresh onslaught. Months had passed since Khurram was gone, and Mehrunnisa watched Ladli grow still and quiet. Now she knew. And suddenly the years seemed to grow on her. Ladli no longer ran flitting through the corridors, her laugh no longer burst upon Mehrunnisa's consciousness while she prepared farmans, and there was a dullness in her eyes.

It was then, as Mehrunnisa wrestled with Roe's demands for the treaty and Ladli's sudden loss of interest in everything, that Emperor Jahangir fell ill again. It was much like the last time. His asthma came upon him, and Mehrunnisa spent hours by his bedside, wishing that she could somehow breathe for him, listening to his lungs tiredly inflating and deflating. She read when he wanted to hear the sound of her voice, she slept sitting on the floor, leaning against his divan, his hand near her head. He only had to touch her or move and she would awaken. Ladli came to be with Jahangir too, through those long and by now familiar hours of nursing. She did not say anything about Khurram, but when news came of him, or from him, she left the room.

So Mehrunnisa stood between a beloved husband and a beloved daughter, holding the weight of the empire in her hands. She was the one who went to the jharoka each morning, there were no darbars at either the Diwan-i-am or the Diwan-i-khas; all the empire's business took place in the courtyard below her jharoka balcony. She moved tiredly through the days. Jahangir recovered soon, much sooner than she expected, but his breathing still troubled him greatly. He gave her a gift when he was well.

The Emperor allowed her to mint coins in her name. It was an immense privilege; all through Mughal rule in India, no woman had had her likeness or name on the currency of the empire. Now

Mehrunnisa did. She had a set of coins minted in the imperial workshops in gold and silver with the twelve signs of the zodiac upon them on one side, and on the other, written in Persian, were the words 'by the order of the King Jahangir, the gold got a hundred ostentations added to it, by getting impressed on it the name of Nur Jahan, the Queen'. The minting of coins gave her a solid place within the empire's structure. Mehrunnisa was now a sovereign too. She sat at the jharoka; she had coins with her imprint upon them; she was Emperor in all but name.

And this was literally so. There were three badges of sovereignty in Mughal India—the ability to sign on farmans, the imprinting of coins with a name or likeness, and the *khutba*. Mehrunnisa had the first two. The third was the calling out of the Emperor's name in the vast and flung-out Mughal lands, where many would live and die with just his name upon their hearts—no sight of him, no other news, really, of him. The khutba said this: *All hail Jahangir Padshah, Light of the Faith, Conqueror of the World, Lord Most Mighty*. Every Friday before the midday prayers, the muezzins in every mosque around the empire sang out Emperor Jahangir's name. Yet, as the last soft echo of their tuneful voices faded, another, unborn voice whispered Mehrunnisa's name.

The empire began to see that Jahangir and she were one entity. Gone were speculations on why or how Mehrunnisa had found her place in the Emperor's heart—she was there, to him as important as his life. He did not care about any filthy insinuations upon his manhood or virility in allowing a woman to run what had essentially been a man's business. He was man enough not to care about it. Jahangir could trust no one but Mehrunnisa, and he let his courtiers, his nobles, his commanders know of this.

As Mehrunnisa saw her own power grow, she watched Ladli waste away, a wraith who haunted her mother's apartments, always at hand, rarely speaking. She lost flesh from her bones, her eyes stood huge in her face. Ladli still smiled though, and each time she did, it broke Mehrunnisa's heart. And it hardened her towards Khurram, for he had toyed with Ladli, almost deliberately.

A few days before leaving on their long journey back to Agra from Mandu, Mehrunnisa went to Ladli's apartments. She found her painting by the light from the windows. Ladli was seated on the floor, her feet wedged under a divan, the easel propped on her raised knees. Clay saucers of paint were arrayed around her on the stone floor. Some red pigment had spilled from a saucer, and gleamed like blood on the slabs. Ladli looked up, her face flushed from the heat, tendrils of hair escaping from her plait.

Mehrunnisa sat down next to her daughter. 'What are you painting, beta?'

'The view from this window.' Ladli pointed with her brush. Her fingers were smeared with greens and blues. Mehrunnisa saw the outline of mango trees, the thick and dark green of their leaves, and an owl seated stoically on a lower branch. She kissed the side of Ladli's forehead.

'You have some time, Mama?' Ladli turned to her expectantly.

'Only a little, beta. And then I have to go.'

Ladli dipped her brush into a pot of water, shook it vigorously, and pinched the wet bristles to clean the green paint. Then she squeezed the tip to a pinpoint and dipped it lightly into the streak of red on the floor. The owl's eyes glowed.

'This is a night colour,' Mehrunnisa said, looking over her daughter's shoulder. 'An owl's eyes are brown and yellow in the daylight.'

Ladli smiled. 'It is all perspective, is it not? To me, an owl, either in the light or the darkness, has these glowing eyes. The mullas tell me it cannot see when the sun is out—I am giving it vision.' She turned to her mother, her gaze serious. 'Which one is it going to be, Mama? Parviz or Shahryar?'

Mehrunnisa put her arm around her daughter's thin waist and leaned her head on Ladli's shoulder. She was growing old too. Perhaps not in years yet, but the constant battling to keep the empire on an even keel was fatiguing her. Ladli had become a young woman away from Mehrunnisa. Where had she got this gentle understanding? It had always been there, even before the whole Khurram episode. Only then, it had been hidden under her playfulness and a lively spirit that was now already weighed with sadness. Ladli was asking which of the royal princes she would marry. Somehow she had heard about Khusrau's refusal. Her face buried in the cool skin of her daughter's shoulder, Mehrunnisa prayed that she had not heard of Khurram's.

'Shahryar,' she said finally. 'Parviz is a weakling, beta.'

A little rumble of laughter rose in Ladli's chest. 'The choice is rather sparse, is it not, Mama? Parviz may be a weakling, but Shahryar is called *nashudani*. A good-for-nothing.' She stroked her mother's face and pulled her closer into her. 'Has he... said yes?' Only in that question was there a brief stumbling over the words. Ladli held herself rigid.

'Yes.' Mehrunnisa did not say that Shahryar always said yes. He had few opinions of his own, and what they were, no one knew, for the prince took care not to voice them. What an unsatisfactory alliance this was going to be. But what other choice was left for her now? It had to be Parviz or Shahryar. Parviz was a drunkard, and this was all Mehrunnisa knew of him, for she had not seen him in too many years. At least Shahryar grew up around the court... his absurdities were understood—he was the lesser evil.

'When is the wedding to be?'

'When we return to Agra,' Mehrunnisa said. She put her other arm around Ladli, who turned to her. And so sitting side by side, their arms around each other, Mehrunnisa and Ladli rested for a few long moments.

Over Ladli's shoulder, Mehrunnisa saw the maroon leather-bound book embossed with gold leaf writing. She picked it up from the carpet. Firdausi's poems. Little flecks of gold dust smeared on her fingers.

'You like Firdausi, Ladli?' she asked.

Ladli smiled gently, without reproach. 'I always have, Mama.' She held her hand out for the book.

'But you did not like poetry once, beta,' Mehrunnisa said.

'Once.' Ladli inclined her head. 'A long time ago.' She set her brush down on the edge of a saucer of paint. 'Can I have it back, Mama?'

'Yes, of course.' Mehrunnisa held the spine of the book in the palm of her hand and extended it to Ladli. The gold-tipped pages fell open to somewhere in the middle, and Mehrunnisa saw why. Pressed against the page was a dried flower. It slid into Mehrunnisa's hand, and she held it up to the light by its stem. It was a rosebud, at the cusp of unfurling, frozen now forever thus, its petals still with their exquisite form but washed of all colour.

A little piece flaked off the edge and went flitting down to the carpet.

Ladli's hand shot forward to grip her mother's wrist. 'I... can I have that, Mama?'

Mehrunnisa let the dried rose fall into Ladli's other hand, surprised at the vehemence of her touch. 'Do you press flowers, beta?' she asked.

Ladli shook her head, cupping the flower carefully in her hand. 'Just... this one.'

Why? Mehrunnisa wanted to ask, why this one? But her daughter was suddenly unreadable, as though she were miles away on some forgotten frontier of the empire. The sweet aroma of the rose swirled from the pages of the book. There was no mistaking it—this was a Persian musk rose, the one used to make attar. Its value lay in the heaviness of its perfume. But musk roses were precious, Mehrunnisa thought, grown in the imperial gardens only for the attar, and for little other pleasure. Yet, at Ajmer, in Khurram's apartments, one bush thronged over the courtyard walls, branches laden with clusters of white musk roses, pearls in the moonlight. And only... in Khurram's apartments.

She wanted desperately to ask if this rose was so cherished because Khurram had given it to Ladli. And why? Under what circumstances?

Instead, Mehrunnisa held Ladli's face in her hands and kissed it, touching the skin on her forehead, her cheeks, her chin and her nose with her lips. 'It will be all right, beta.'

Ladli nodded. 'Yes, it will. I know I have to marry some time. And there are few of us who are fortunate enough to choose that person.' The words were philosophic, worthy of an old seer, not one as young as Ladli. At her age, Mehrunnisa would have raged, at least inside herself, and shown it in brief glimpses to people around her, Bapa, Abul, her mother. But Ladli had a cultivated sense of self-command, a thin sheath of protection she raised in front of everyone, even Mehrunnisa.

She kissed Ladli again softly on the forehead and rose to leave. Mehrunnisa stopped at the door at the sound of Ladli's voice. She turned, but her daughter's head was bent towards the stiff Persian musk rose in her hands.

'Mama, did you ever ask Khurram?'

The wedding took place in April of 1621, after the royal party returned to Agra. Shahryar sent Ladli a thick gold band set with a hundred tiny, perfectly faceted diamonds as a promise to marry her. She returned to him five leaves of paan—betel—with a small ball of jaggery, betel nuts and sugar cubes, wrapped in a red silk handkerchief. *Let me sweeten your mouth, my lord, upon the occasion of your betrothal.* Music parties were arranged on the lawns under the chenar trees, the malis worked hard in trimming rose-bushes of thorns so no silk veils would catch as the women danced by. On the morning of the wedding, they rose early to pluck marigolds and lilies for garlands at the first blush of dawn. Gifts went from the zenana apartments to the mardana where Shahryar lived—silks, jewels, emerald-studded saddles, Arabian horses of immaculate bloodlines, sweets from the imperial kitchens, gold and silver jugs of wine, and farmans from Mehrunnisa for the prince. His mansab was raised and his income was doubled. Shahryar now was a commander in the army, with a mansab of eight thousand cavalry and four thousand infantry—almost as much as Khurram. Mehrunnisa signed the farmans herself. The royal princes were wealthy men, but none had as much wealth as their father's favourite wife—Mehrunnisa's income was equal to that of a commander of thirty thousand horses, only there was no commander in the empire who could put his name to that amount of money each year.

As the ceremony progressed, Mehrunnisa sat behind the curtain that separated the women of the imperial zenana, watching and listening. She heard the qazi ask Shahryar if he would take Ladli as his wife. His reply was weak, almost disinterested. He slouched on the divan, in looks a magnificent prince—fingers thronging with diamonds and emeralds from his dowry, his silk qaba embroidered with the finest gold zari, shimmering as he turned this way and that, the turban on his head sporting a ruby and diamond aigrette; but there seemed no spine in his back.

The qazi turned to Ladli and asked the same question.

'Yes, I will.' Her reply was quiet, but stronger. And when she spoke, her voice did not waver, and Shahryar turned to look at the woman who was to be his wife. She sat by Mehrunnisa, thickly veiled in red chiffon, behind the zenana curtain.

He had not seen her in many years. Though they had both grown up in the same palaces, they could well have lived miles apart, for Ladli had been with Mehrunnisa and Jahangir, Shahryar, in some corner with his myriad nurses.

The qazi called them all to prayer, and they prayed, heads bent, voices following his command. Ladli began to tremble, violently, and Mehrunnisa clasped her daughter's hand and brought it to her heart, suddenly harshly angry. This was all because of Khurram. They would not be here at Ghias Beg's house, inaugurating a sham marriage, if not for Khurram. Mehrunnisa had *wanted* Khurram to be her son-in-law. She did not like him any more, but Ladli did... Ladli did, and that was enough. He would have treated her well, this Mehrunnisa knew. And for Ladli, his very kindness, perhaps a visit every now and then when Arjumand was unwell, would have sufficed. She had not her mother's ambition.

Mehrunnisa kissed Ladli's hand and put it against her cheek. The prayer was over, and the men and women rose on both sides of the curtain, calling out congratulations and best wishes, hugging each other. Ladli sat still, her head bowed under the wedding veil. To Mehrunnisa most voices were strained, even her own. She smiled and laughed, tried not to look at her daughter when she spoke of her happiness. She sent slaves to carry news of the ceremony to Asmat, who was ill and in bed. That in itself was an omen, one Mehrunnisa would not think about, that Ladli's grandmother had not been here to witness the wedding.

On the other side, Ghias Beg went to his son and held out his arms. Abul and he embraced.

'Congratulations, Bapa,' Abul said.

'And to you too, Abul, your niece has been married,' Ghias replied.

Then they fell silent and glanced at Mehrunnisa. She nodded to them, watchful of their expressions. Ghias looked tired, and old.

This was an occasion of joy, yet neither was happy. Abul would write to Khurram of this marriage. But where did *his* affections lie? With her or with his son-in-law? Their junta had perished now; this marriage was the final break between them.

The rooms were cleared and food was brought in for the wedding party. Mehrunnisa ate slowly, without tasting the golden naans, the bread freshly peeled from the walls of the tandoor oven and brought to her plate. Ladli did not eat, her plate was returned to the kitchens as it was, heaped with the naans and curries of lamb and goat. She was crying, but softly, tears running down her face.

Mehrunnisa pushed away her plate, wishing she could gather Ladli in her arms as she had when she was a child and tell her everything was going to be all right. This was a wretched beginning, and for the first time in a long time, she doubted whether she had done right. But what other alternative did she have?

A few weeks later, Jahangir's hacking cough returned, and he fell ill again. Mehrunnisa decided that they should go to Kashmir, perhaps the clean air of the mountains would help.

In the Deccan, the first place Khurram reconquered was Burhanpur, where Parviz had ruled, and where he had met Roe and indulged in the finest English brandy the East India Company could muster. From there, the prince pounded south into Khirki, the capital of Ahmadnagar, and set fire to it, determined that Khirki would never call itself a city again. The houses were forlorn blackened skeletons, men, women and children were locked inside and burned with them, and the wells and reservoirs were filled in with sand and rocks. The stench and stumps of charred oxen and cows smouldered in the streets. Khurram then pursued Ambar Malik to Daulatabad, cornered him, and waited patiently for Malik to die or surrender. And it was here the letter found Khurram.

Sitting outside his tent on a rock, Prince Khurram read the

news of Ladli's marriage. He tossed it into the fire in disgust. How could anyone want to marry that nashudani? Ladli deserved someone like him, Khurram—a prince worthy of the title, a warrior, the man who would be Emperor... He remembered how she had always been an enchanting child. He remembered too how she had suddenly grown into a graceful woman, with a light step, with smiles that bespoke secrets. After that night at Ajmer, Khurram had not seen much of Ladli. She still came to their apartments, but much less than before, shyer with him than she had ever been. The temptation to take Ladli, to marry her and bring her into his harem, had been almost crushing in its intensity. But he had not... and she had to marry someone. But nashudani?

This changed everything. He had taken Khusrau away with him so Mehrunnisa would not have a chance of forcing him to marry Ladli. But he had taken away the wrong prince. She must have been planning this marriage even as he had left for the Deccan.

He pulled so hard at his hair that some of it came away in his hands, and Khurram threw it into the fire. A sour smell rose. Khurram bent over, coughing, and turned away. What was he to do now? Jahangir was ill again, if he died... Shahryar would become emperor, and he, Khurram, was too far away to be effective. Besides, Ambar Malik was at the edge of surrender here; if he left now, all these months of fighting would come to naught. And if he was victorious, and his father survived, he could claw his way back to the Emperor's good graces. So through the night, as the camp slept around him, as the fire dwindled to a few glowing embers, Khurram sat outside under the stars and thought.

When morning came, he wrote to Abul Hasan. It was a plain and direct letter. He knew his father-in-law's loyalties lay with him, not with his sister. If Jahangir died, Abul was to secure the throne for Khurram. The prince watched the runner leave his camp. It was easy for him to command this of Abul. But the logistics were terrifyingly complex. How was Abul to keep a crown safe on an empty *gaddi* when Shahryar was right there to sit on it? Khurram needed to return to Agra.

As though on cue, Ambar Malik was vanquished in less than a week's waiting, starved into submission. The negotiations for peace took longer—treaties were drawn up, terms agreed upon, much talking and drinking and celebrations indulged in. Impatient, Khurram decided to give the kingdoms of Bijapur, Golconda and Ahmadnagar easy terms; five million rupees were to be sent to Emperor Jahangir.

He rushed back to Burhanpur and wrote a long letter to his father. Khurram embellished details of the siege on Ambar Malik, giving himself more consequence than he deserved, desperate to return to court. And he waited for a reply.

It came, but there was no invitation to the imperial court. The Emperor thanked him, Mehrunnisa thanked him for his efforts on behalf of the empire; he was a brave son indeed, and perhaps... the air at Burhanpur suited him well enough?

Khurram ranted to Arjumand, to anyone who would listen, went on hunts and drinking binges until he had to be carried to bed each night. He would not be feted again at court, he was no longer the victorious and triumphant prince returning to a father's benign gaze. Shahryar, that good-for-nothing, had replaced him.

A month later, Khurram sobered up. Shahryar he would deal with later. But if he wanted the throne for himself, *any* other man within shouting range who had royal blood in his veins was a danger too. His head keen and unclouded without liquor or opium, Khurram began to think again. He had asked to be Khusrau's guard for more than one reason. Half-blind and half-mad, Khusrau was still the eldest son, still the prince who was hailed as the next heir to the throne. He was a threat.

Emperor Jahangir had once said that kingship knew no kinship.

Prince Khurram was about to prove him right.

Chapter Twenty-three

Shaw Jehan, for some time, affected to treat the unfortunate Chusero with attention and respect... He disregarded the mandates of the court of Agra: and... assumed, soon after, the Imperial titles; laying the foundation of his throne in a brother's blood.

—ALEXANDER DOW,
The History of Hindostan

KHURRAM WATCHED AS THE COMMANDERS OF HIS ARMY CAME INTO THE outer reception hall of the zenana. Each man stopped at the doorway, performed the konish, and walked up to the prince, where he bowed again. Abdur Rahim came in last. Khurram had insisted that the commander-in-chief of the Mughal army join him in this Deccan campaign—it had been one of the conditions he had placed before the Emperor. So Abdur Rahim had left Parviz's side, where he had been stuck for so many years, and joined Khurram's army. He too bowed to the prince. When he straightened his back to look at Khurram, his face was a vacant mask. All the nobles were tense, vigilant. They had been called here to be part of a momentous decision, they knew, for Khurram had invited them into the zenana itself. This reception hall was one rarely visited by men not belonging to the imperial family. The prince was showing them favour, but why? What was he going to ask in return?

Khurram sat down on his divan at the head of the hall and waved his hand. 'Please sit.'

The nobles glanced at each other briefly. Another privilege— only in camp, at the battlefield, were such courtesies dispensed of with the royals. But they were no longer at war, and they had to treat Prince Khurram as they would the Emperor himself. They hesitated, and then sank on shaky knees to the carpets, sitting on their heels, toes flat out, hands resting on their thighs.

'You are all sworn to secrecy. Not a word of what is said here today must pass to any other ear.'

The men nodded.

'I have received news that the Emperor is dying,' Khurram said. The men looked on the ground, stealing glances at each other. They had only heard of Jahangir's illness, and that he was recovered now. The prince said softly, 'His Majesty Emperor Akbar had a great fondness for me. He wished the throne to be mine...'

Abdur Rahim, to Khurram's right, spoke. 'Prince Shahryar is with the Emperor, your Highness. It is generally believed that he has both his Majesty's and her Majesty's support.'

'But that would go against Emperor Akbar's wishes,' Khurram said, watching the old soldier. Rahim sat with difficulty, his arthritic knees gave him distress, but if he was in pain, it did not show either in his face or in his voice. If any trouble came to change his plans, Khurram thought, Rahim would be the man to start it.

'As you say, your Highness,' Rahim said now, 'his Majesty wished for you to shoulder the burden of the empire. But that was a long time ago.'

'Who else is there, Rahim?' Khurram flared.

'Now that is an interesting question, your Highness,' the soldier replied. He met the prince's eyes without flinching. Abdur Rahim had lived too long to fear anything. His entire life had been spent at the helm of a marauding army; he was not to be cowed by a prince's petulance. 'You are but one of four princes.'

'Parviz and Shahryar? Tell me what their value is?' Khurram demanded.

Abdur Rahim smiled. 'But little.'

'Khusrau?' Khurram's tone was contemptuous. 'He is mad.'

Abdur Rahim nodded. 'The prince is unfortunately circumstanced.'

'Do you still support him, Abdur Rahim?' Khurram said, referring to the role Rahim had played in Khusrau's rebellion against Jahangir. 'If you do, it is best you leave now. What I am about to say is not for you.'

Rahim spread his hands out. It was a placatory gesture. 'Slowly, your Highness. You must act slowly and with discretion. I merely pointed out that as much as we may swear fealty to you here, there are others in the empire whose loyalties sway towards the other princes. Prince Khusrau did not live up to his early promise...'

He let the words hang between them. Khurram picked at the sash of his cummerbund with unsteady fingers. *This* was what he had wanted. This why he had taken the chance of bringing Abdur Rahim to the conference. Once his advocacy of Khurram was so readily evident, the rest of the commanders would follow Khurram's lead.

Khurram spoke then of what he wanted to do. There were no voices raised in protest, no murmurs even. They all knew that when Khurram became Emperor, he would remember who had been in this room. The men rose from their places and, one by one, knelt and kissed the ground in front of the prince. When they departed, Khurram called for his slave Raza.

A few days later, Khusrau was laid up in bed with colic pains. Khurram solicitously sent the royal physicians to attend to him. The hakims looked at the prince's white, pain-wrought face, ran their fingers over the thin pulse on his wrist, and clucked to each other in one corner of the room. They did not dare effect a cure—there was no cure against the determination of one brother to kill the other. This had merely been a rumour for so long. When Khurram had demanded to take Khusrau with him, Jahangir had been plagued with wailings from the zenana ladies. Why did Khurram request this? He must have some devious plan in progress. The Emperor had listened to all the women, but in the end, only one woman's voice had prevailed, Mehrunnisa's. She had said Khusrau must go. If he would not marry Ladli, it did not matter whether he was at court or with Khurram. Mehrunnisa did not suspect that Khurram would try to murder Khusrau—that thought did not cross her mind, for it was one so incredible. Khurram would be a fool if he followed through with this. His brother was in his care, and if he died in obviously suspicious circumstances, royal blood or not, Khurram's head would roll.

The hakims hung around in the room, as far as possible from the prince, trying not to hear Khalifa's mumblings as she knelt by Khusrau's bed. The princess was praying. Every now and then she would touch her husband's hand, but he was in too much pain to react. He did not know she was there.

One of the hakims split from the group and went down on his knees beside Khalifa. He raised his hands as if to pray and, still looking ahead, said in a whisper, 'Your Highness, what has the prince been eating?'

Khalifa turned to him in surprise. 'What he normally eats, why do you ask?'

'Please,' the hakim said hurriedly, 'please do not look at me when I talk.'

'All right.'

'Perhaps...,' the hakim paused, 'it would be better if you personally oversaw his meals.'

'Poison!' Khalifa's voice rose. 'You suspect poison.'

The hakim stumbled to his feet. 'I have already said too much, your Highness. I have to leave.'

He almost ran out of the room, leaving a dazed Khalifa staring after him. That evening, the princess commanded a mud and brick chula to be built outside their rooms. She inspected every piece of meat and vegetable, washed each thoroughly before she cooked the food on the chula, and tasted the dishes before she put anything in Khusrau's mouth. She watched over him for the next few weeks thus, and slowly the pains lessened, Khusrau's stomach felt less raw, he became stronger. He recovered.

The dark night lodged over Burhanpur, smothering the city with a warm and humid coat of velvet. A few hours passed, and all the lamps were extinguished one by one as the city went to sleep. A thick silence settled in the streets, and the night watchman's tapping stick rang out on the cobbled stones, accompanied by his voice singing out the hour. The moon in the skies was a broken half melon, with enough light to paint black and silver shadows under the mango and tamarind trees.

Within the fort all was quiet. Khusrau's palace was at the southern end, where the sun seared through the very walls during the day. The guards outside the palace were asleep, sprawled against the front walls, their spears slung over their laps.

Two shadows detached themselves from behind a tree and crept up to the gates. They pushed the gate open and froze as it creaked. The guards did not move. The men slipped silently into the courtyard, pulling the gate shut behind them.

'Why didn't the guards awaken?' one man whispered to the other.

Raza Bahadur turned to his accomplice. 'They have been drugged. We can dance on their stomachs and they would sleep on.' He grinned, his teeth gleaming in the light from the moon. 'However, be careful, perhaps someone is still awake.'

The men ran up the stairs to the prince's apartments. Their feet were bare and made no sound on the stones. Raza wiped his sweating face on his sleeve. At the top, they leaned against the door to Khusrau's bedroom. The door was of solid and heavy wood, embellished with brass fittings. It did not give way. As they stood there, a lamp came flickering towards them in the darkness of the corridor.

'Who goes there? Identify yourself,' the guard shouted, raising his lantern in front of him.

'It is I, Raza Bahadur. I have a gift for Prince Khusrau from the Emperor,' Raza replied, whipping his turban off his head.

'What is it?' the man asked. Raza watched as the man stumbled along the stone floor. He was drugged but had somehow managed to keep awake. He did not ask why they were here so late, why the gift couldn't wait until daylight. The man swayed from one side to the other along the corridor.

The guard groggily accepted the parcel from Raza and bent his head to look at it. Raza moved behind him. His dagger gleamed briefly in the light before he jerked the man's head up and sliced his throat. The guard crumpled to the floor, dead before he hit the ground. His lantern crashed and the light went out, leaving a thick darkness. The smell of fresh blood swirled upward, and Raza's accomplice gagged.

'Was that really necessary?' he gasped, leaning against the wall to fight off nausea.

'Yes. We must not be identified. Now let us find a way to get into the prince's room,' Raza said curtly.

'Wait a minute, Raza. Is the princess in the room? I will not be responsible for her death.'

Raza dragged him to the parapet, where the moonlight lit up

their faces. 'We have a duty to perform and we will, irrespective of whom we have to kill. If Princess Khalifa is sleeping with her husband we may have to dispose of her also. But set your mind at rest, I hear that she is back in her apartments tonight.' Raza strode back to Khusrau's door, his feet squelching in the pool of blood.

Inside the room, Khusrau was asleep. He woke at the knocking and instinctively reached under his pillow for his dagger. 'Who is it?'

'Your Highness, it is I, Raza Bahadur. I have come from his gracious Majesty, Emperor Jahangir.'

'What do you want?' Khusrau asked irritably. 'What is so important for you to wake me in the middle of the night?'

'Your Highness, the Emperor has sent you a robe of honour.'

'Leave it with the guards.'

'Your Highness, I was asked to deliver it to you personally,' Raza argued. 'Please open the door so that I can give it to you.'

'Go away!' Khusrau yelled. 'Guards, take this madman out of here.'

'The guards are asleep, your Highness,' Raza replied. 'It will be better if you open the door, or we will have to force our way in.'

Prince Khusrau flung himself backward into the wall, pulling at the sheets for cover. 'Go away!' he shouted again. What was going on? Where were the guards, and who was this man? Why did he come like this, in the darkness of the night? Khusrau began trembling and shivering. He pressed into the stone behind him. He could hear a loud thump. The door groaned. Another thud. And another one.

Khusrau clutched his dagger close to him and rose from the bed. The men were working in darkness, that much he could tell. If they had no light, he could still fight them. He knew every divan and carpet in the room, could walk in it without hitting anything.

The prince ran to the side of the door and stood against the wall, his heart banging. The door creaked on its hinges one last time and then toppled on to the floor in a rush of air and sound.

The men crashed into the room and stood for a minute trying to get their bearings. Before they could realize that Khusrau was not in his bed, the prince jumped on Raza's accomplice. His dagger went cleanly into the man's shoulder. The man shouted in pain and Khusrau saw a blur of motion, then a fist smacked into his chin. As he staggered back, stunned, the two men grabbed his arms and lifted him off the floor.

He yelled and screamed. *Help. Help me. Who are you?* But there was no one to hear him. Raza held Khusrau down, his knee crunching into the prince's thin chest. His accomplice looped a sheet over a broad beam on the ceiling. Khusrau was hauled upright and dragged to the centre of the room. They knotted the sheet around his neck and yanked hard at the other end. Khusrau went bellowing and flailing into the air. His fingers grappled with the tightening cloth around his neck, and then they fell to his waist and to his thighs. His body twitched, life slowly ebbed away.

In silence the two men let go of their end of the sheet until Khusrau slumped on the ground. They carried him to the bed, laid him on the mattress, and arranged the wrinkled sheet around him. In the light of the moon that came into the room through one of its windows, the prince looked as though he were asleep. As though he was, at last, at peace.

Khalifa awoke with a start and stared with bewilderment at the ceiling. Where was she? She involuntarily reached out a hand for Khusrau but hit only empty space. Khusrau had insisted that she return to her chamber for the night. His mutterings and dreams kept her awake, so just this one night, he had said, so she could rest finally after all these past weeks spent nursing him. The princess got up and went to the outside verandah, shivering in the cool morning air. The sky was pinkening with dawn, birds had started their busy chirping, and the air was fresh and delicious. She glanced down at the front courtyard, looked back toward the rising sun, and then looked down again. Something was wrong... the front gates were open. Why?

Khalifa turned from the verandah and ran back into her bedroom. In a few minutes, she was flying down the corridor. As she turned the corner, the princess stepped into something wet and sticky. She stopped and put a hand to her bare feet. Her fingers came away stained with a thick fluid that looked suspiciously like blood. It streaked red and thick along the floor. Khalifa ran to Khusrau's room. She saw the dead guard lying across the doorway, his head hanging grotesquely at right angles from his torso. She jumped over his body and fled inside.

Khusrau was on the bed, his face turned away from her. Khalifa bent over him, praying aloud. Her fingers slipped on cold, stone smooth skin.

'Khusrau! Get up!' she screamed.

Khalifa tried to pull his face towards her, but his neck was rigid and unmoving. She put her cheek on his chest, there was no sound, no comforting beating of a heart. 'Khusrau,' she said, her voice breaking and subdued. 'Wake up, my dear lord. Wake up.'

Khurram was away hunting in the forests near Burhanpur. The message reached him two days after Khusrau's death. The runner came upon him, sweat-stained and weary, as the prince was raising his musket to his shoulder to aim at a placidly grazing nilgai. At the sound of the runner's footsteps, the nilgai scampered off, and Khurram turned irritably. 'What is it?'

The runner proffered the letter, he could not talk, he could barely breathe for the panting, and he had not stopped to rest even once, his feet flying as though on fire.

Khurram handed his musket to the Mir Shikar and unrolled the letter. 'Prince Khusrau has died suddenly in Burhanpur.' He glanced up at his commanders. The men did not meet his gaze. They looked down at their feet, at the barrels of their muskets.

'I must go to my brother.' Khurram ran to his horse and jumped into the saddle. As he kicked his heels into the horse's flanks, the whole hunting party scrambled for their mounts. They rode away from the hunting grounds and headed directly for Burhanpur. They stopped only to eat and change horses at the sarais along the way, and so, tired and drooping in their saddles, the prince and his commanders rode into Burhanpur. People thronged the streets, wailing and crying, their wails louder when they saw Khurram. He nodded to them, tears on his face. Dismounting in the outer courtyard of the fort, he ran to Khusrau's apartments. The prince's body lay on a huge slab of ice, melting wetly onto the floor. Khalifa sat on the ground in one corner, staring at her hands. She did not look up when Khurram entered, and would not listen to him when he knelt by her side and kissed her hands.

The next morning, Khusrau was buried in the gardens of the fort. Khurram was one of the pall-bearers; he took his brother's body to its grave and watched as mud was thrown over the coffin and a large marble slab pushed over the top. Then he went to his rooms to write to his father. When he finished the letter, he called his commanders to him and read out the contents. Khusrau had died of colic; he had been suffering for the past month. Khurram could not send his body to Agra for a proper burial because it had already decomposed in the heat.

Matab Nuruddin Quli stood apart from the group crowded around the prince. Quli had been present at the first conference when Khurram had invited the commanders to the zenana reception hall. Nothing had been said outright about killing Khusrau, but all the men knew that they were complicit in this. Yet something gave way inside Quli. Khusrau had been a royal prince, and this was murder. Quli had gone into Khusrau's bedchamber in the middle of the night to look at the prince's body. He had stepped into the water melting from the ice and loosened Khusrau's collar. The angry red gashes around his throat had told their own story, and an unmistakable one at that. Then Quli had looked towards the princess. Khalifa had fallen asleep, alone in the room with its one flickering oil lamp and her husband's body. She had been sleeping as she sat, her head plunged into her neck, tears dried on her cheek. She had not heard Quli come in.

The noble had buttoned Khusrau's collar again and stood in the semi-darkness looking at the princess for a long while. Then he had gone home, but not to sleep.

Prince Khurram sealed his letter and called for the runners.

That night, two runners set off for Agra. Mehrunnisa and Jahangir were on their way back to the capital after their stay at Kashmir. Both runners were carrying a letter for the Emperor.

Chapter Twenty-four

She communicated her suspicions to Jehangire: she told him, that Shaw Jehan must be curbed; that he manifestly aspired to the throne; that all his actions tended to gain popularity; that his apparent virtues were hypocrisy, and not the offspring of a generous and honest mind; that he waited but for a convenient opportunity to throw off the mask of deceitful duty and feigned allegiance.

—ALEXANDER DOW,
The History of Hindostan

THE SERVANTS WAITED IN A ROW AT THE VERY FRONT OF THE CAMPSITE, peering anxiously into the west, but there was no sign of their Majesties. Tiny hills, childlike compared to the Himalayas they had just left behind, rolled and swayed in the path of the dying sun. The royal entourage was camped at Bahlwan on their way back to Agra from Kashmir. Early that morning, Jahangir and Mehrunnisa had left on a hunt in the neighbouring forests.

The men stood, their eyes upon the cusp of two gently sloping hills, and finally saw a little cloud of dust smearing the golden light of the western horizon. One of them broke away from the line and trotted steadily towards the royal party, some two miles away.

Mehrunnisa and Jahangir rode together ahead of the others. They were both tired, and gloriously so. It wasn't just the exhilaration from the hunt, the scent of the prey, the smooth shots from their muskets, but also the freedom from being confined to a jogging palanquin on the journey south to Agra. Mehrunnisa glanced at the Emperor and smiled. She did this so often that he finally turned to her.

'What is it?'

'You are well today, your Majesty.' And he did look well after all the months of illness. The air of Kashmir, pure, heady and clear, cut through by the Himalayan mountains, had been beneficial to all of them, especially to Jahangir. Without the dust of the lower plains to clog his lungs, his asthma had cleared and his cough had vanished.

Jahangir smiled at her. 'I feel as though I were young again.'

'But you are.'

'You flatter me, Mehrunnisa,' he said, laughing. 'Look at the grey in my hair.' He patted his comfortable stomach. 'Look, my cummerbunds have been growing larger and larger; one day the workshops will send a message that there is not enough cloth in the empire!'

She reached out a hand to him, and he held it, looking into her face. Mehrunnisa was unveiled, it was too hot to cover her face, she had said, her breath stopped under the muslin in all the dust. So she had taken it off and laid it about her shoulders. And they had ridden ahead of the rest; all that could be seen of her was that slender back, straight upon the saddle, the legs looped over the horse, the neck rising from the shrouds of the veil, and a small glimpse of her profile as she turned to Jahangir.

'You are as lovely to me as the first day I saw you, Mehrunnisa,' the Emperor said.

Little lines of worry patterned her forehead. 'Have I done nothing to disappoint you, your Majesty?'

'Why? ...Because of Ladli?'

Mehrunnisa nodded her eyes troubled. 'I still wonder...'

'It cannot be wrong,' Jahangir said, 'I hear there is to be a child.'

'Perhaps; it is too early yet, but perhaps.'

'Then why are you so tense, my dear?' He leaned over to rub her back. Their horses bumped into one another and then shied away. 'I miss Asmat too. She was truly a mother to me.'

Mehrunnisa allowed her horse to amble a few yards to the right and yanked at the left rein when she saw he was straying. She did not speak, just listened as the Emperor talked about her mother. Asmat had died last October, six months after Ladli's wedding. She had been too ill to attend the ceremony, but none of them had realized that she would never rise from her bed again. And after Ladli's wedding, Mehrunnisa had been so occupied with watching her daughter to see if she was happy, content, or at least merely not distressed that she had not watched over her mother. Asmat had died as she had lived, gently, not staining the lives of those around her with evil or malice. She had been a quiet presence for many years, and had gone just as quietly.

Mehrunnisa had not even been able to cry, for too many people had needed her. Ladli had been sad, Jahangir had fallen ill, Abul had come to her weeping, Ghias had broken away from his own life, a shallow shell of what he had been, lost without his wife. So Mehrunnisa had looked after them all. She had brought Ghias to Kashmir with them, but he had barely lifted his head to enjoy the spring cherry blossoms lading the trees with their frothy pinks and whites, or eaten the first strawberries, or sat outside in the gentle sunshine of the early mornings. He had stayed in his apartments, coming out when she had insisted, conversing with her, but without heart.

'Someone comes,' Jahangir said, pointing towards the camp with his riding whip.

'Bapa!' Mehrunnisa jammed her heels into the horse's flanks and sped down the dusty plain, her veil unwinding from around her neck to swirl through the air to the ground. She could hear Jahangir a few paces behind.

'What news?' she yelled, pulling up near the man.

'The diwan ails, your Majesty,' the slave said, his eyes fixed at the level of her diamond-studded sandals.

She leaned down to shout in his ear. 'He ailed this morning. Is he worse now?'

The slave did not move as Mehrunnisa and Jahangir cantered around him, and he would not answer.

Mehrunnisa looked up at the Emperor.

'Come,' he said, and turned his horse to pound towards the camp.

They came racing through the soldiers on the outside, past the makeshift Diwan-i-am, past the workshops and ateliers, and went to the tents in the very centre of the camp.

Mehrunnisa swung off her horse and ran into the tent where her father lay. Inside, it was cool and glowing, the white canvas of the tent providing shelter from the sun, and in this light, she saw Ghias as she had left him in the morning, on the divan in the centre of the tent. Abul knelt near him. He turned when he heard Mehrunnisa and put a finger to his lips.

'Is Bapa?...' Mehrunnisa said in a whisper. Was he dead? For she could see no rise and fall in his chest, just that deathly stillness. Ghias stretched out on the divan, the white of his hair melting into the satin pillow under his head, a sheet over his body, tucked under his arms. His hands, thin now from his self-imposed fast after Asmat's passing, lay crossed over his stomach.

Abul shook his head. He could not speak either. Tears came down his cheeks into his beard, and he put out his arms. Mehrunnisa knelt by her brother and hugged him fiercely, and he started to cry into her neck. Neither heard Emperor Jahangir come into the tent. He went to sit on a stool at one corner, his back to the canvas.

Ghias moved, mumbling to himself, and Mehrunnisa and Abul looked up. She rushed over to the other side of the divan, and each held one of Ghias's hands.

'Bapa,' Mehrunnisa said softly. 'Are you all right? Rest now, I am here.'

They sat thus for the next few hours, hanging over Ghias, watching him, waiting for him to open his eyes and speak to them. They both rested their heads on the divan, hands still firmly clasping their father's. The sun set, a slave padded in quietly to light the lamps around the tent and to hang a lantern from the central pole. He started and bowed copiously when, in the light from the lantern, he finally saw the man seated away from the others. The slave began to speak, but Jahangir waved him away with an impatient gesture.

Mehrunnisa felt Abul's hand touch her head.

'How much longer, Nisa?'

She looked up at him and felt that sudden rush of affection she always felt when he called her by her childhood nickname. It had been so long since he had done so. Too much had come between them. Marriages, other responsibilities... yet Abul had been, was, her most cherished brother.

'He will not last the night, Abul.' Her voice was clear and unbroken. With her hands on her father, she felt that he would not live long. At least she, they, could be here with him. Ghias would go knowing that his children were together, by his side.

'Nisa...'

'What?'

Abul hesitated and moved away from the divan, imperceptibly. Seeing this, Mehrunnisa waited, the affection in her dying away. What did he want?

'Prince Khurram should be at court, Nisa,' Abul said in a rush. 'He would want to be present at our father's funeral.'

Mehrunnisa raised herself and sat up straight. 'That is not possible, Abul. Khurram has other responsibilities in the Deccan. He has to make sure Ambar Malik does not rebel again.'

'Arjumand should be here for her grandfather's funeral, Nisa,' Abul said doggedly.

'Why? Her place is with her husband. And where Khurram is, she must be.'

Abul was quiet for a while, picking at the embroidery, on the coverlet. 'When is Khurram to return to court?'

'I do not know.'

'But you do know, Nisa,' Abul said, raising his voice. 'You are the one keeping him from the Emperor.'

In his corner, behind Abul, Jahangir moved, and Mehrunnisa's gaze swung to her husband for a few minutes. He did not rise but settled more comfortably on his stool, and she nodded. She moved her eyes back to her brother. Abul now enjoyed the title of Asaf Khan, the fourth in their family to bear that name. His mansab was at twelve thousand horses, a grade shy of the royal princes, and he was merely her brother, or merely father-in-law to Khurram. He had no royal blood, would never have any, yet he held a lofty title and an impressive salary. Abul did not stop to think where this munificence came from—from her, because of her, because he was her brother. She had asked for these honours from Jahangir over the years for Ghias and Abul. Now, forgetting this, he dared to shout at her.

'Khurram is a fool, Abul,' she said quietly.

'Why?' he flared. 'Because he would not marry Ladli?'

And so finally, things were to be said between them that had remained unsaid and festering for so long, Mehrunnisa thought. Now she would know where Abul's loyalties lay. Their father would die tonight, and the calming influence, the voice of reason that had held them together, would be gone.

'Yes, that,' Mehrunnisa said finally. 'Khurram should have married Ladli. You know this, Abul.' When he opened his mouth, she held up a hand. 'Don't give me that nonsensical story about him loving Arjumand too much to ally himself with another woman. He loves other women too. Your son-in-law enjoys his harem, he always will. And Ladli is no mere alliance; she is *my* daughter.'

Abul's black eyes glittered at her. 'I was not going to say this, Mehrunnisa, but I will now. Khurram is a man; it is a man's privilege to enjoy his harem, and for Arjumand not to resist this. My daughter knows her place. She does not interfere with either Khurram's pleasures or his work.'

'She does not?' Mehrunnisa said, almost shouting at him. '*She* was the one who made sure Khurram did not marry Ladli, Abul. You are a fool if you think otherwise. What had Khurram not to gain from an alliance with Ladli? Tell me this!'

'You are an evil woman, Mehrunnisa,' Abul shouted back at her. 'Think what you like, but Khurram will be the next Emperor.'

They had both risen on their knees now and glowered at each other over their dying father. Abul held the blue fire in Mehrunnisa's eyes with his own until he could no longer. She was right, he knew this. For many months he had tried to convince Arjumand and Khurram that he should marry Ladli. But Arjumand was jealous, whimsical, overwrought from all her pregnancies, terribly frightened that Khurram would love Ladli more. He had tried to tell her that Khurram could never love any woman as much as he loved her, but she would not listen. That marriage would have brought them together as a family, as they should have been. Now... with Ladli married to Shahryar, everything was changed.

'Do not fight.' Ghias's voice, reedy and raspy, rose between the two, and their heads swung down to his. They both subsided by his side again, arms reaching over his thin shoulders, kissing his hands, speaking at once.

'Did you speak, Bapa?' and 'How are you, Bapa?' and 'Oh, Bapa, talk again. What is it you want to say?'

But Mehrunnisa and Abul had also heard Ghias admonish them as he once had when they were children and would squabble with each other. Shame came to flood over them, but the anger did not subside—they still simmered on either side of the divan, pointedly not looking at each other.

'Where is the Emperor?' Ghias said, softly this time, almost in a whisper.

Jahangir rose from his stool and touched Abul on the shoulder. When he moved away, the Emperor knelt by Ghias's side and held his hand.

For the next twenty minutes, Ghias talked, with Jahangir leaning in to listen. He would not speak to either of his children; he had nothing more to say to them. But Jahangir he thanked, over and over again, remembering, at this moment of his death, all the generosity he had enjoyed from Akbar and Jahangir over his lifetime. He had been a Persian refugee to India, adopted by this country as her own. But none of this—his daughter married to the Emperor, his granddaughter to a prince, he himself treasurer of the empire—would have happened if not for his Majesty. So Ghias said to Jahangir, comforted by his monarch, for he could not be comforted by his children.

He died thus, in mid-sentence, the breath in his chest stopped, halting the flow of his words. His eyes were still open; it was Jahangir's hand that closed them. Angry, sad and bitter at the same time, Mehrunnisa and Abul stayed where they were, she by her father, he standing at the back of the tent, where he had been relegated when Jahangir had taken his place at the divan. Jahangir rose to call the slaves to prepare the diwan's body for its last rites.

Then he led a stunned Mehrunnisa away to his tent. Abul, he did not even glance at once.

Following the rule of escheat, Ghias Beg's estate, which was considerable, reverted back to the Emperor. The law of escheat was an old law—there was no personal property in the empire, nothing that did not belong to the Emperor. It kept prospective coups in check; where there was no private fortune, there could be no rebellion. If Jahangir decided, and he usually did so, he could donate the estate to the eldest son after making sure that the widow and other children had their allowances. The Emperor's magnanimity towards the dead man's family depended upon his relationship with the Emperor during his life. If it had been good, his family was well provided for, if not, they were given the barest sustenance.

So Ghias's estate should devolve upon Abul Hasan, as the eldest surviving son. A few weeks after the minister's death, Emperor Jahangir and Mehrunnisa lay in their apartments. Above them the punkah creaked steadily on slick hinges, back and forth, a long rope leading from it to the hands of the eunuch seated outside the room.

'Are you all right, Mehrunnisa?' Jahangir said, pulling her closer. He reached around her to touch her face, and felt the tears. Jahangir wiped the wetness from her skin and kissed her shoulder. A few stray jasmines, wilted now and brown with age, were caught in her hair. The Emperor pulled them out gently, without tugging at her hair, and threw them over the edge of the divan. In the light from the lantern, the grey in Mehrunnisa's hair glinted silver. Her hair was still thick, still to her waist, just as he liked it. But age had come to her as it had to him. Lines had formed on her face in two arched bows on either side of her mouth, they creased outward from her eyes and below them, they spread horizontally over her forehead. Jahangir knew every line, he watched her as she slept, waking early in the morning in the first glow of dawn before the jharoka to lean over his wife. He watched her while she read, when she was animated with laughter, when she was furious with anger—he never seemed to tire of this.

But he did not know what to say when she cried as she did now, with deep sobs from within her somewhere. He had worried when Mehrunnisa had refused to cry at Asmat's death. And Mehrunnisa had not cried for a long time, her face hard, her eyes dry, until tonight. He was sad too at Ghias and Asmat's deaths so close to each other.

He rubbed her arm in slow circles. Mehrunnisa's breathing evened, and Jahangir turned on his back to look up at the punkah. He thought about Ghias's estate, which had passed on to him. By law—well, by an unwritten law that he himself followed at all times—it should go to Abul. But Abul had made his feelings clear in Ghias's tent, by brawling so shamefully with Mehrunnisa. She had not forgiven her brother; Jahangir could not do so.

Bitterness filled him. Runners from Burhanpur brought news that Khurram was playing at being Emperor in the Deccan. Jahangir had given him the title of Shah Jahan, King of the World, and now he acted as though he really was that, within his father's dominions. Khurram was a *bidaulat*, a wretch, Jahangir thought. He moved closer to Mehrunnisa's back and went to sleep. Heat hung inside the apartment, the punkah did little but spin the air around the room, but Jahangir could only close his eyes when some part of him was against her. They would each wake many times at night to find sweat thickly matted between their skins, but half-asleep they would wipe it away, find another position in which to lay their bodies, another place in which they made contact. An arm, a leg flung across, a shoulder lodged against a hip, even fingers touching, it did not matter, touch they had to.

The next morning, when Mehrunnisa came back to the palace from her jharoka appearance, she found Jahangir kneeling on his prayer rug facing towards Mecca.

'What is it, your Majesty?' she asked. 'Did you not go to the jharoka?' She had left him on his way there.

He turned to her, stunned and in a daze. 'A letter arrived... I could not go. Khusrau is dead.'

For a few minutes, Mehrunnisa was silent, then she held out her hand for the letter. Another death. How had Khusrau died? And why? He had been demented, but he had been healthy. Surely Khurram would not have dared... or had he? Jahangir gave her the letter he had been clutching to him, and she read it. Colic, she thought. Colic was a convenient excuse for unexplained death.

As they sat there, Hoshiyar knocked on the door and bowed.'Your Majesty, a runner has come from Burhanpur with a message from Matab Nuruddin Quli. He insists upon seeing you.'

'Later, Hoshiyar,' Mehrunnisa said.

'Now, your Majesty,' the eunuch said as he shifted on his feet. There was some important news.

Jahangir rose wearily from his knees and went to the reception hall. The runner, a young lad of eighteen or nineteen years, was sleekly muscled from his occupation. He was saturated in sweat; his kurta stuck to his chest, his pyjamas to his shins. The boy quaked as he performed the konish and then knelt in front of the Emperor, proffering the letter above his head. He simply brought the mail to its destination, but Quli had been very specific in his instructions— the letter was to be placed in the Emperor's hands.

'What is this?'

'Your Majesty,' the boy's voice shook. 'You are to read this.'

'Go to the imperial kitchens,' Jahangir said, placing his hand on the boy's shoulder. 'Get something to eat and drink. And rest before you leave again.'

The runner bent to the carpet and put his forehead on the floor. When he heard the sound of Jahangir's footsteps fade away, he rose from his knees, his body trembling, and put his palm on his right shoulder. Still clutching the place where the Emperor had touched him, he found his way to the kitchens.

Jahangir walked back to his apartments, turning the letter over to look at Quli's seal. The news would be unpalatable. But what could it be? He entered to see Mehrunnisa still on the floor. The Emperor slit open the letter and sat down next to her. They read it together. Khusrau had not died of colic; he had been murdered, his own brother's hand had taken his life.

Jahangir shouted to Hoshiyar to bring him his writing materials, and sitting there, on the carpet, hardly able to hold the quill steady, he filled two pages of a letter to Khurram. His son was to order Khusrau's body exhumed and sent to Allahabad, where he was to be buried next to his mother. And what of Khalifa and her two sons? Why were they still at Burhanpur? Send them to Lahore to live in the palaces of the fort there. Was there any truth in these dreadful accusations? Had Khurram really dared to kill his own brother? He had to leave Burhanpur *immediately*, upon receipt of this letter, and come to Agra to answer Quli's charges.

Jahangir later commanded the new diwan to his presence and ordered that Khalifa and the boys were to have a large and steady income for the rest of their lives, and use of any of the imperial palaces whenever they wanted.

Mehrunnisa looked over Jahangir's shoulder as he wrote. Stupid, stupid Khurram, she thought, to take away his brother's life thus. Did he think he would be answerable to no one? Did he think he could flee from his father's rage? Did he think his actions made the throne more secure for him?

Khurram read his father's letter in Burhanpur. Most of his commanders had melted away from the fort, on their way now to visit Jahangir and tell him of their part in Khusrau's death. The prince fretted for days, wondering how he was going to stand in front of his father and defend himself. He could not go to the Emperor. He had been witness to the punishment meted out to an insurgent Khusrau fifteen years ago, and that had been only for a simple rebellion—how would Jahangir react to murder?

So the prince wrote to the Emperor, explaining himself as best he could. He denied everything. Khusrau had died of colic pains, pure and simple. And he was unfortunately unable to leave the Deccan, Khurram said, the imperial armies had need of a commander.

The Emperor was furious. He wrote to Khurram again, demanding his presence at court, and if he did not come, the prince could consider himself without a family and without a father. Jahangir then gave all of Ghias Beg's huge estate to Mehrunnisa. Abul would not have it, he decided, lest the minister chose to use that wealth to support that bidaulat. He also ordered that Mehrunnisa's orchestra and drums be played at court after his own. She would not be visible, hidden behind the marble screen of the zenana balcony, but the nobles would have to acknowledge her presence nonetheless.

Those of Khurram's courtiers who had chosen to stay with him also fled for the imperial court now. They knew the prince was in trouble. He had no intention of returning to his father's presence, where he once desperately begged to be allowed. Mehrunnisa, with Ghias's estate added to her own large income, was now frighteningly wealthy and massively powerful with this heaping of favours upon her. And the courtiers knew that she disliked Khurram. They came to plead for their lives, to protest that they had not had any actual intentions to be complicit in Khusrau's death. Khurram's courtiers had a long journey ahead of them, for Mehrunnisa and Jahangir were on their way back to Kashmir.

And while the imperial court was at Kashmir, trouble began to breed in Qandahar.

Ever since the first Persian siege on Qandahar in 1606, it had been quiet on the north-western front. For the last ten years, there had been a Persian ambassador at the Mughal court, bringing with him lavish gifts and assurances of brotherly affection from Shah Abbas to Jahangir. So constant was Persian presence at court that permanent apartments, richly appointed, were built for the ambassadors.

When Mehrunnisa and Jahangir were at Rawalpindi, on their way back from Kashmir, they first heard the news of another Persian invasion in Qandahar.

The Qandahar problem went back two generations to the time of Humayun, father of Akbar and the second Mughal Emperor of India. When Humayun became Emperor, four years after his father conquered India, he found a country discontented with its conquerors and hoping to oust them. He was defeated by Sher Shah Suri in the battles at Chausa and Kanauj and expelled from India.

The Emperor took refuge with Shah Tahmasp Safavi in Persia and with his help drove the Afghan king out of Qandahar. Using the city as a base, Humayun conquered Kabul and finally marched back into India victorious, to set up the empire again. Humayun and Shah Tahmasp had a tacit understanding that once India was conquered, Qandahar would be given to Persia. But this had not happened. Humayun did not give it away, Akbar did not give it away, and by Jahangir's time, it had become part of the Mughal Empire.

The 1606 siege, if it could even be called by that name, had been a simple raising of war standards and flags outside the city. Now there was no doubt about the Shah's intentions. He wrote to Jahangir, reminding him of the promise once given by his grandfather. Jahangir wrote back, asking why the Shah was so interested in a petty village when he had a mighty empire himself. Both letters were written in phrases of honey and sugar, and neither the Shah nor Jahangir was fooled by the other. The Shah would invade Qandahar; Jahangir had to defend it.

Another piece of gossip had found its way to the royal court, riding on the official news of the invasion of Qandahar. The Shah had ordered his eldest son killed by a slave. It was done in a terrible fashion, the prince was stabbed one rainy evening in the local bazaar, and his body lay in the slush of the streets for two days before it was dragged away to be buried. Why, Jahangir wondered, and how, could a father order his son's death? The Shah was mad; this was why he was plaguing him now. Shah Abbas had to be stopped. And the only person who could command a victorious army was Prince Khurram. The Emperor wrote to his son in the Deccan yet again. He was to head north and handle the Qandahar problem. If he did, he would be forgiven.

Khurram did not go. The monsoons had arrived in full flood; he could not possibly cart an entire army on this long journey and hope to arrive there with his cavalry and infantry in decent enough shape to meet the Shah's men. He would stay here until the rains subsided.

Jahangir sent him a bitter letter. *Come to the royal court at once!*

This the prince would absolutely not do. His father was furious with him, and he was no fool to present himself to be burned in the flames of Jahangir's wrath.

Khurram was right about the Emperor's temper. Jahangir was ailing, his asthma flared, headaches beset him; everything irritated him now. If the prince came to Jahangir's court, his head would soon part company with his shoulders. This Jahangir was determined about. The empire was to belong to Shahryar.

After all, a precedent had been set. If one king could order his son's death, why not another?

Chapter Twenty-five

The soothsayers named an auspicious day on which the treasure of gold and silver was to be brought out and, in accordance with the King's command, to be handed over to Asaf Khan... Itibar Khan who was bringing out the royal treasure, took it back to the fort and Asaf Khan went away empty-handed.

——B. NARAIN, TRANS., AND S. SHARMA, ED.,
A Dutch Chronicle of Mughal India

WINTER CAME SLOWLY TO THE SRINAGAR VALLEY IN 1623. THE POPLAR trees turned a fiery orange and deep maroon along the edges of Dal Lake. Reeds and rushes yellowed and stooped towards the lily pads. The last pumpkins ripened and sprawled over the eastern edge of Dal Lake in their floating gardens, which were large chunks of soil cut away from the banks and tethered to the bottom. The sun rode lower in the sky, in an arc barely skimming over the mighty foreheads of the Himalayas. A chill caught the air, and little fires burned in the bazaars, fanned by the wind. As November approached, the streets grew deserted, shops closed earlier; at the first hint of darkness, shopkeepers and patrons hurried home to warm dinners and cups of chai.

The Hari Parbat hill surged upward almost apologetically from the western bank of Dal Lake, a tiny anthill compared to its stupendous neighbours. But the view from the hill was magnificent nonetheless. The lake stretched blue and green below, the wooden houses of Srinagar arranged around it, the majestic Himalayas cutting into the heavens above and in jagged reflection in the waters below. It was here Emperor Akbar had built a fort with walls curving up and down the hillside, and wood and stone palaces. December came and the snows fell, covering the pass into the Srinagar valley with ten-foot-deep piles of snow. The city was now cut off from the outside and would be until the roads were cleared. This did not happen normally, the residents merely waited in their snowbound, still world until the spring thaw, but in the winter of 1623 things were not normal. Emperor Jahangir had decided to stay on in Kashmir and not travel back to Agra.

Mehrunnisa stood at the window to the balcony in her apartments in Hari Parbat Fort. It was snowing outside, a light and flaky snow, settling amply, though, on the smooth surface of the lake, and drifting over the steeply sloped roofs of the houses. She put her face against the cold glass pane of the window. Behind her, the room was lushly covered with thick carpets, edge to edge, without an inch of the stone floor showing. It was warm too, the air heated by coal braziers dispersed around the room. Mehrunnisa turned to her daughter.

Ladli was sitting on a divan, her feet pulled under her. A minute later, she shifted and leaned back, but even that was uncomfortable, so she sat up again and rubbed at the bottom of her spine.

'Shall I do that for you, beta?' Mehrunnisa asked.

Ladli patted the divan. Mehrunnisa went and sat next to her. She put her hand on Ladli's back and massaged the muscles there. Ladli put her head on Mehrunnisa's shoulder. 'That feels better, Mama.'

Mehrunnisa touched Ladli's stomach lightly. 'It will be a boy, I know. He gives you so much trouble already.'

'I do not want a boy, Mama. She will be a girl.'

'Why?' Mehrunnisa asked, smiling.

Ladli raised her head. 'So there will be no question of her fighting for the throne. I will not have a child for the empire.'

Mehrunnisa got up and moved away. 'This is stupid thinking, Ladli. What use will a girl be? You *must* have an heir.'

Ladli poked at the coals in the brazier near her with a pair of silver tongs. The embers hissed and crackled in response. She reached into a brocade bag and spread the sandalwood shavings over the coals. The bits of wood caught fire, and an aromatic, swirling smoke journeyed around the room. 'What use will a girl be, Mama?' Her tone was wry. 'You and I were girls once. Were we worthless?'

Mehrunnisa sighed and sat down again, this time near the little table in a corner. Farmans lay piled on it, their parchment gleaming softly in the lamplight. She had to read through them and decide which ones to sign, which to throw away. 'You know what I mean, beta,' she said, leaning against the wall behind her. 'When Shahryar becomes Emperor, he must have a son to give the empire to.'

'It will NOT be a boy!' Ladli sat up on the edge of her divan, her face contorted. Little drops of sweat gathered on her forehead, and she wiped them with the back of her hand.

Mehrunnisa looked at her daughter from across the room. impending motherhood had brought a fretfulness to her. As her body grew, her emotions plumped up too, skittering out wildly with every sentence. But she was still lovely. Her skin glowed golden and clear, her eyes had lost their constant sadness, and she moved with a grace Mehrunnisa had not seen in many women in this stage. The child brought happiness to Ladli, and an undeniable contentment to her mother. Now the marriage to Shahryar had some value, Mehrunnisa thought, now, finally, she had done right by Ladli.

Ladli muttered to herself, tucked her hair back into her plait, and subsided on the divan. She breathed heavily, as though she had run for a distance. 'I do not want my child to be caught in all this fighting, Mama. I do not want you to use him for the throne.'

'You do not want to be mother to an Emperor, Ladli?' Mehrunnisa said, her gaze a hard, deep blue. Ladli shook her head and bent to wrap her arms around her stomach, the fingertips meeting at the bottom, as though she was carrying something heavy in front of her. 'You do not want to sit in the zenana balcony at court and look out at your son's back while the most powerful amirs and nobles pay their respects to him? Tell me,' the Empress leaned forward, hands on her knees, 'tell me you do not want that. You can have what I do not, Ladli. A child who will wear the crown, whose name will live on for posterity to remember, and because of him your name will live on.'

Mehrunnisa rose and went to stand over her daughter. She looked down at her daughter's dark head, with a little sliver of skin where her thick hair was parted. She touched her head, but Ladli moved away as fast as her ponderous body would allow her. Mehrunnisa turned and went to the pile of velvet cloaks in one corner of the apartment. Swathing two over her head and shoulders, she went out into the balcony.

It was as bright as daylight outside; the falling snow caught the light from the houses and the street lamps and spread it thinly orange over all of Srinagar. The air was clear, washed with ice, with a sharp edge of cleanness to it. Mehrunnisa leaned out over the parapet and breathed deeply. Why was Ladli thinking like this? Everything she did, she did for her daughter. Surely she knew that? Shahryar was a fool, to be sure, but he had the empire's blood in his veins, worth ten times any lode of gold. The child she was carrying would have that value too. Ladli did not remember, because she did not know, that they were but refugees to India.

Ghias had come here with little in his pockets, and less on his back. And half of Ladli was given by her father, who was but a soldier and, before that, a table attendant to the Shah of Persia. Within her, she now bore a future Emperor. Why was she not grateful?

Mehrunnisa swept the snow off the edge of the parapet with a sharp gesture. It turned her palm cold and blue, and she rubbed her hand against her side. Ladli still blamed her for not asking Khurram. But she had asked, and Ladli did not know this, for Mehrunnisa would never tell her. Still... Ladli blamed her. What was Khurram's worth now, in any case?

A few days ago, before the snow had started falling, Mehrunnisa had had another reason to be upset with Khurram. She had given one of her jagirs to Shahryar as a gift and had petitioned the diwan to turn over the papers to her son-in-law. Khurram had also sent a formal petition to the diwan for the same jagir, but of course, it had gone to Shahryar. However, Khurram, always in a hurry and sure that he would get the jagir of Dholpur, had sent his men there to set up offices. Khurram's servants had met Shahryar's servants, and a bloody fight had followed, in which four men had been killed. Mehrunnisa had demanded that Dholpur be returned to Shahryar, but she was sure Khurram would refuse, just as he had refused to go to Qandahar.

And as time passed in all their plentiful letter writing and demands, the fort at Qandahar fell to the Shah of Persia's army. Although Jahangir had called it a petty village, it was of strategic importance to the empire for trade and defence. Now it had been cut away from the north-western edge. Khurram, despite all his excuses, was quite clearly intent on staying on at Burhanpur, so Mehrunnisa ordered Shahryar to go instead. He was sent away in the autumn from Srinagar, with much fanfare, but even his mother-in-law had little hopes in his military prowess. Giving Shahryar the command of the imperial army was to tell the court that he was now the favoured son. The most Shahryar would do, Mehrunnisa knew, would be to loll around the outskirts of Qandahar, send out a few half-hearted sorties, and then return home. But there was to be a child. The boy would be the next Emperor. He gave Mehrunnisa hope. There would be a boy, *please Allah*, wouldn't there?

The snowflakes settled on the top of Mehrunnisa's head, clung to her eyelashes, and tucked themselves into the folds of her cloak. But she still stood in the balcony. Only her feet were cold, slowly numbing as the snow melted and seeped in through the leather of her shoes. She liked being outside in this impossibly white world covering all the sins and dirt of Srinagar. It was densely silent and peaceful. Here, she was no longer Empress, no longer anything, not even a mother or a soon-to-be grandmother. Here she was not even a wife, although as she stood, her head slanted to the doorway on her right where Jahangir slept. He coughed, and Mehrunnisa closed her eyes and listened. He would cough three times, one low, one so shallow as to come from his mouth, one from deep within his lungs. They had stayed on in Srinagar hoping that the Emperor's asthma would leave in the clean and crisp air of the valley. It had abated somewhat, but as Mehrunnisa heard the dreaded cough from within, she knew that it would never go.

Jahangir was a dying man. Maybe not for a few years more, but his body would not be able to put up with this punishment for much longer. Mehrunnisa saw this with a clarity and calmness that frightened her. Ever since that one terrible illness when Jahangir had almost died, Mehrunnisa had been preparing herself for his death. At that time, the thought had terrified her, but so many years had passed, and time had a way of making oft-pondered ideas if not appealing, at least bearable.

The cold finally seeped into her bones and left her teeth chattering. She had thrown herself into the work; every farman went out with her signature, she took the jharoka audiences, she ran the empire while Jahangir rested. Mehrunnisa was the one who had sent Shahryar away. If Khurram refused to give up Dholpur, the jagir he had so officiously taken over, she would confiscate all his estates in the northern part of the empire. Let him rot in the south, she thought. Let his entire family, his wife, his sons, his father-in-law... but no, Abul was here with them. They were adrift from each other finally, thoroughly ashamed that Ghias had died while they had fought. But Abul had not left the imperial court to seek out Khurram.

Huddled under the warm fur of her cloak, Mehrunnisa gripped her arms about her waist. Should she send Abul away? On what pretext, and how would the courtiers react? The nobles had been strained, skittish, in her jharoka audiences lately. This was due to many things—the Qandahar problem, the so-obvious switch in imperial favour from Khurram to Shahryar, Jahangir's constant illnesses. They were unsure, Mehrunnisa was too, not really seeing Shahryar as Emperor or seeing him hold the throne for long. But now, with the child, if he could just rule for a *little* while... That, though, would come later. And whatever Mehrunnisa did about her brother Abul, she had to do this with the approval of the nobles at court. She thought then, her head hunched into her chest. An idea came as she stood there; Abul had to be pushed into the open.

The sound of another series of coughs startled her. She listened, but now she heard a fourth cough, and this was loud and coarse. Mehrunnisa plowed through the drifting snow down the balcony into Jahangir's apartments.

'You want me to do what?' Abul's voice was filled with disbelief.

'Bring the treasury to Lahore,' Mehrunnisa repeated patiently. She put a hand to one of the palanquin's pillars to steady herself. They sat close to each other in the enclosed space, their knees drawn up and touching. The curtains, of a sheer green silk, were closed. The sun filtered through them, filling the palanquin with a liquid green light.

Abul looked at his sister. He had trouble sitting like this, his thighs ached, but he would not let her know that. The royal entourage was on its way to Lahore after the winter in Srinagar. It was spring; well, the snows had melted in patches from the ground, but it was still cold and slippery outside. At the last stop, Mehrunnisa had asked for him to ride with her. Abul had had to brace himself as the eight bearers had lifted the palanquin onto their shoulders and set off in a steady trot.

'You want to move the *entire* treasury, Mehrunnisa? Do you know what that entails?' Abul rubbed his chin and felt the bristle of a spot of hair that his barber's razor had not touched that morning. 'And why?'

Mehrunnisa's eyes gleamed. 'It will be safer where the Emperor is, Abul.'

Abul shook his head. 'Yes, but...'

'You do not wish to do this?' Her voice was sharp.

'No, of course, if this is the Emperor's command, I will... but what does safer mean? Who would dare to lay siege on the treasury of the empire, Mehrunnisa? It is safe enough at Agra.'

'Khurram.' Mehrunnisa said this quietly. Abul glanced at her and then away at the blurred green images of the soldiers outside. Their horses marched in unison, or so it sounded to him, with a steadfast rhythm. This is what Mehrunnisa saw during those long hours of travel when she chose to journey by palanquin.

'What has Khurram done now?' he asked carefully. What *had* he done? Abul had heard nothing of their plans from Arjumand the last time she had written. But she rarely told him anything in writing, there were too many eyes eager to read, too many hands that would willingly put her letters under Mehrunnisa's gaze.

'We are too far away from Agra, Abul.' His sister's voice had taken on that resigned tone again, as though she were talking to a child. 'The Emperor wishes to return to Kashmir when state duties allow him to do so; the court will not visit the capital for some time. If we are to be so far north, the treasury will not be safe from Khurram.'

'He would not capture the treasury, Mehrunnisa.'

'Oh?' She leaned forward and caught one of his hands. 'How do you know this?'

Abul pulled his hand away and backed into the wood wall of the palanquin. 'I know nothing. I have had no contact with Prince Khurram in many years.' Only with his daughter, but he was not going to tell Mehrunnisa this.

'You are to leave the entourage tomorrow. Itibar Khan has orders to give you the treasury, along with an army to guard it. Look after it well, Abul.'

'I will,' he mumbled.

Mehrunnisa rapped on one of the pillars with the back of her fan. The bearers stopped and Abul climbed out, jumping to the ground. The palanquin swayed to adjust to the loss of his weight and then went on again. The soldiers passed him, some bowing from their saddles. Abul Hasan waited until his own horse was led up to him. He mounted it and let it follow the entourage. The green and gold coverings of Mehrunnisa's palanquin glittered in the bright sunlight. Abul bent his head. What was she up to? Why order *him* of all people to bring the treasury to Lahore? Did she not know that he would never let his Arjumand down?

Abul had said nothing when their father's estate had been given to Mehrunnisa. What could he have said, anyway? He could not have protested; no one questioned the Emperor's commands. But hatred and jealousy and greed had seared their way inside him. It was *his* money, and in giving it to Mehrunnisa, the Emperor and she had made Abul into a eunuch. The amirs at court had snickered, some openly, asking if he suddenly found himself poor, if a loan would not be amiss. Even as they travelled to Lahore, the stonemasons and architects were hard at work in Agra, building Ghias Beg's tomb. Abul had seen the plans for it when Mehrunnisa had held them out in front of him excitedly.

Look, Abul. So Abul had looked, holding the paper in his hands. A jewel of a building on a raised and decorated platform. It was to be square with four octagonal towers and sharp and thick eaves along the top. Silk thin marble latticework for the main chamber where Ghias and Asmat would lie. A garden around, with long lawns, shade and fruit trees, water in channels. The tomb was to be of marble, unblemished and pure as newly fallen snow. And into each surface was cut a pietra dura inlay. What was that, Abul had asked. And Mehrunnisa had mimicked the stonemasons, digging out inch-thick slivers of marble from a sheet of stone and filling the spaces with jasper, cornelian, topaz, onyx, lapis lazuli, all polished to show their grain to the greatest advantage. The whole would then be smoothed down until it would look like, and feel like, one piece.

'When you lay your hand on it and close your eyes, you will not be able tell that there even is an inlay, Abul,' Mehrunnisa had said.

'It sounds expensive,' Abul had said. The plans showed that *every* surface of the tomb was to be covered with this work— interlocking circles and hexagons, tulips on slender stems, betel leaves.

Mehrunnisa had laughed. 'I wanted them to build the outer walls of silver, the architects persuaded me that marble would endure longer. So the cost is but little, Abul. And the money means nothing to me. I have so much.'

He had felt impotent that day. His father's tomb was *his* to build; *he* was the oldest son. Now Mehrunnisa's name would be over it. She would be the one commended and lauded for its beauty. She was the one who had the resources to pay for its construction. Abul had gone back home trembling with anger. He knew that only royalty had the right to leave their mark on the face of the empire's soil. He knew that in marrying Emperor Jahangir, Mehrunnisa had become royal.

He could never be royal. In being born a man, and being born into a family with no imperial pretensions, he could never change his status. At best though, Abul thought, yanking at the reins when his horse veered off course, he could be father-in-law to the next Emperor.

Before he left with a small army to Agra the next morning, he wrote to Khurram.

Prince Khurram read his father-in-law's letter and made his plans quickly. He sent out word among his nobles that he was going into the forests for a month-long hunt. As the preparations for the hunt commenced, his army was ordered to ready itself for a march. Khurram left the city, headed south to the hunting grounds, and when his army of seventy thousand cavalry joined him, they moved up north towards Agra.

There was an irony in this plan of Khurram's—once, about twenty years ago, Jahangir had done this same thing, leaving his futile war in Mewar to storm the treasury at Agra, hoping that with the money he would vanquish Akbar and grab the crown that was his anyway. Jahangir had not succeeded in this quest, but the empire was his now. Prince Khurram, riding through the long and hard days and nights towards Agra, knew that he had little chance for the throne of the empire... he *had* to do this, or Shahryar would be Emperor.

Abul Hasan reached his mansion in Agra at nightfall. He forced himself to wait through the night, and ended up lying in bed staring at the flapping punkah. Long before dawn broke, Abul was up and ready. He ate little at breakfast, a cup of chai, half a chappati with duck eggs scrambled with onions, ginger and cumin seeds. Abul entered Itibar Khan's offices with slow and measured steps. Soon, he thought, very soon he would be guardian of the richest treasure in the world. Once Khurram came, they would have the empire too. Emperor Jahangir could never compete with the wealth of the treasury, it would buy them armies by the thousands, entire towns and villages, fealty from every noble at court. Abul had had a long time to think about all of this during his ride to Agra, travelling with only a small group of soldiers.

The moment his letter to Khurram left his door, Abul knew he had cut ties with his sister. Mehrunnisa had been very stupid, he thought, in giving him the guardianship of the treasury after insulting him so constantly since their father's death. There were brief moments of fright, of course, always what if... his venture were not successful, if Khurram did not come, if something went wrong. If his letter to Khurram went elsewhere, and in doing so, found its way to Mehrunnisa. But he had left the entourage, ridden to Lahore, then to Agra, and nothing had happened.

Itibar Khan met him at the door and bowed. '*Al-Salam alekum*, Mirza Abul Hasan. To what do I owe this pleasure?'

In the Mughal Empire, where *every* man's shoulders supported his head only by the Emperor's whimsy, Itibar Khan had enjoyed a relatively long reign as the warden of the imperial treasury at Agra, for some thirty years. It had been Itibar then, who, standing outside the fort at Agra, arms crossed over his chest, cannons and soldiers lined up behind him, had turned Emperor Jahangir away from the treasury that had not been his yet.

'*Walekum-al-Salam*,' Abul replied. 'I have come from the Emperor to escort the treasury to Lahore.'

'Certainly. But if I may have some proof...,' Itibar said and then added, 'please, do not misunderstand me, I require a letter for the files.'

'Of course not.' Abul Hasan handed the royal farman to Itibar Khan.

The treasurer read the farman slowly. It clearly ordered him to release the contents of the treasury. Abul fidgeted on his feet. He wanted to lean over and shake the old man. Khurram would have left Burhanpur by now, and if he was travelling with an army, it would not be long before news of that reached every corner of the empire.

'The entire treasury!' Itibar spread out his hands. 'The inventory will take weeks.'

'That is not possible. I have to leave in five days,' Abul said quickly. 'The Emperor wishes it.'

'He says nothing in this farman about that.' Itibar pointed at the writing with one finger. 'I cannot send you on your way in five days.'

'Please, his Majesty may not have mentioned anything about the time, but he told me that he wants the treasury at Lahore as soon as possible,' Abul said.

'Certainly, his Majesty must not be kept waiting.' Itibar put an arm around Abul's shoulders and led him to a divan. 'In the meantime, perhaps you will enjoy our hospitality?'

Abul sat down. He did not wish to sit. He wanted to be in the treasury vaults hanging over the huge chests of gold and silver coins, the strings of pea-sized and grape-shaped pearls, the diamonds and emeralds, the rubies set in gold. But he said nothing.

'I shall give orders immediately to start the inventory, Mirza Hasan.'

For the next two weeks, Abul Hasan watched as the treasurer counted the gold mohurs personally. New leather bags were ordered to carry the coins. Copious notes were made of every item in the treasury in ledgers. The gemstones were counted, restrung and then sealed in silk pouches.

At the end of the second week, Abul Hasan insisted that he would take the treasury as it was and answer personally for any losses to the Emperor. Itibar Khan was shocked at the suggestion. It was unthinkable that he would be so derelict in his duties. Abul retreated into apologies and returned to his smooth diplomatic talk. He could do nothing until Khurram arrived, and there was no news of the prince. At least that was heartening. If he had heard nothing, chances were that Itibar had heard nothing too. Praying that this was so, Abul waited through the immeasurably long days.

Finally, the day arrived when Abul Hasan was to get the treasury from Itibar Khan. His attendants had already packed his belongings; as soon as the treasury was handed over, he would leave Agra. He wanted to put as much distance between him and the city as he could before Prince Khurram arrived, for Agra was well armed against invasion.

A fanfare of trumpets and drums greeted him at the main gateway of the fort. Abul Hasan felt a little prickle of apprehension when he saw cannons wheeled to the ramparts of the fort. What was Itibar Khan up to? A small contingent of soldiers came out to escort Abul into the fort. In the main courtyard, two divans had been set up under a canopy of gold cloth.

Itibar and Abul sat back on their knees on the divans, facing each other. The treasurer began to speak about the rituals involved in moving the treasury.

'Why all the formality?' Abul asked impatiently. 'Just give me the treasury and I will be on my way.'

Itibar Khan shook his greying head in outrage. 'My dear friend, there is a protocol for everything,' he said. 'If we, as officers of the court, forget etiquette, how shall we answer to his Majesty?'

'You are right,' Abul mumbled. He was on edge, shifting his weight about. He had not slept in quite a few nights, wondering whether this moment would ever come. Itibar Khan was an old man, one stuck in ritual and formality, and in this lay his entire life. How could a few minutes' delay affect his plans? Abul settled down, composing his face to the same gravity he saw in Itibar. The ceremony took a few hours.

Finally a long procession of servants came out, weighed down with heavy leather bags, caskets and wood trunks. Abul watched as the treasure was piled onto elephants, camels and bullock carts. Itibar showed Abul the ledgers and inventory books. Abul Hasan brushed them aside, bowed to the treasurer and swung up on his horse.

As he dug his heels into the horse's flanks, Itibar called out, 'Mirza Hasan, you have forgotten something.'

Abul turned back slowly. What now?

'You have to sign the letter of release,' Itibar said. Abul grabbed the letter and scrawled his name on it. Then, without another bow to the treasurer, he pounded out of the courtyard. The elephants, camels and carts followed at a slower pace. They rode through the fort to the Hathi Pol on the western side. Abul's heart thumped heavily in his chest. A few more steps and they would be outside. A few hours and they would be on the outskirts of Agra. A few days and the imperial army would never catch up with him.

As he approached the gateway he realized that it was very dark in the entrance, and with good reason. The drawbridge was being cranked up slowly, swallowing the sunlight outside. Abul raced to the soldiers at the doorway.

'What is going on?' he yelled. 'Let me through. I am on my way to the Emperor.'

One of the soldiers shrugged. 'The treasurer's orders. The treasury is not to leave the fort.'

'What? Let down the drawbridge!'

The men looked away from him. Abul turned his horse around and rode wildly past the treasury, dodging the guards and carts. Itibar was waiting for him, standing alone in the centre of the courtyard.

'What is this?' Abul shouted, jumping off his horse and running up to the man.

'The treasury will not leave the fort, Mirza Hasan,' Itibar said. 'Prince Khurram is on his way to Agra.'

'So what?' Abul shook Itibar by the shoulders. When he stopped, the old man peeled Abul's fingers away without difficulty. He was no longer smiling, no more the courteous treasurer.

'But... but... I have orders from the Emperor,' Abul spluttered. 'He will have your head for this.'

'Doubtless his Majesty would have me beheaded if I let the treasury fall into the prince's hands,' Itibar agreed. 'But I should have an opportunity to defend it.'

'It will be better for the treasury to be away from Agra. Don't you see, if the prince is on his way here, then it should be taken away.'

'I cannot agree with that,' Itibar replied. 'The fort is invincible. The treasury will be safer here than on its way to the Emperor.' He turned to an attendant. 'Send a message to the Emperor informing him of the prince's movements. Assure him the treasury is still at Agra and it is being well guarded.'

Abul watched as the treasury was unloaded and taken back to the cellars and vaults. Itibar kindly provided Abul with an armed escort to his mansion. Abul could not even step out of his house without being followed by a guard. He was constantly watched, could send no message to Khurram. He knew then that Mehrunnisa had devised all of this. Abul had been fooled by the sister he thought a fool.

Indu Sundaresan

He had drawn Khurram out from the safety of his fort at Burhanpur on this mad errand. Mehrunnisa and Jahangir were on their way to Agra from Lahore. Outside the walls of his gardens, Abul could hear the imperial army being put through their training. Thousands of feet marched past his house, armours and mail clanked, and all the while, Khurram neared Agra.

Chapter Twenty-six

The tree that is bitter in nature
If you plant it in the garden of Paradise,
And water it from the eternal stream thereof,
If you pour on its root pure honey,
In the end it shows its natural quality,
And it bears the same bitter fruit.

—A. ROGERS, TRANS., AND H. BEVERIDGE, ED.,
The Tuzuk-i-Jahangiri

'IT'S NO GOOD, YOUR HIGHNESS.'

'No one will offer us hospitality? Not one person?'

Raja Bikramjit, commander-in-chief of Khurram's forces, shook his head. Both men turned to look down the deserted street of the village three miles from Agra. The shop fronts were shuttered and bolted, all the houses were locked from the inside. They had spent two hours first knocking on doors, then banging against them. *Koi hai?* Is someone there? It was as though the village had just emptied, as though people had fled from a plague. There was *nothing* outside, no dogs or cats or hens picking in the dust, no cows lounging fatly in the way of traffic. A thick silence stood around them.

'How did they hear of our arrival? We left Burhanpur in the greatest secrecy.'

Raja Bikramjit grimaced. 'Bad news travels fast, your Highness.'

Like the prince's, Bikramjit's face had a thin coating of dirt. They were both a fine sight, Khurram thought, as were his men. They had sped through the breadth of the empire, pausing for two, sometimes three, hours a night. They had changed horses at the sarais for travellers, but the last few days they had travelled on the same mounts. As they had neared Agra, they had met with a wall of silence, backs turned upon them, eyes cold with hatred. Khurram had not paid much attention to this, he had been too tired to pay attention. But now as he stood in the village street, he knew that his father must be on his way to meet him.

'What shall we do?' Khurram asked. Where was the village well? They were near the main square, but if there was a well dug into the ground, it was cleverly hidden. 'The soldiers need food and water. Shall we go to Agra?

Bikramjit shook his head. 'Agra is prepared for our arrival also.'

'Why didn't I hear of this from Abul Hasan?' Khurram demanded.

'He is under house arrest, your Highness. Itibar Khan has locked up the treasury in the vaults.'

Khurram squinted into the darkness. Even the lamps were not lit on the street. The village had died rather than welcome him. He leaned against his saddle, thinking. They had to go on, he could not come this far and turn back. He could not return defeated to Arjumand. 'We must march on to Agra and try to take the fort and the royal treasury.'

'I would not recommend it, your Highness. The soldiers are tired.'

'I cannot turn back now,' Khurram said stubbornly. He put one foot in the stirrup and dragged himself up into the saddle. 'Command the soldiers to move on to Agra.'

But Itibar Khan had been hard at work. The battlements of the fort were strengthened with plaster and stone. The main gates were bricked up, there was no sign of wood anywhere. Cannons stood guard on the ramparts, gaping blackly at Khurram's army, and soldiers in full armour stood behind.

Khurram and his men loaded their muskets and shot at the soldiers, but the cannons answered, extinguishing vast pockets of his army in flares of explosion. They uprooted a tree and used it as a battering ram, but the brick would not give way. Finally, late into the night, as fires burned in the fields beyond the fort, as the smell of charring human and horse flesh rose into the air, as most of his men lay broken, crying and dying on the earth, Khurram whipped his horse around and led the remaining army away.

He could barely keep upright in his saddle; a bullet had winged its way through the skin of his arm, and a tourniquet of cotton was tied around to staunch the flow of blood. Khurram was exhausted, as were his men, holding onto their horses' necks as they pounded away from the fort. They went into hiding north of Agra. The fort at Delhi would be next assaulted. Khurram would not flee to the Deccan without something to show for his journey. But he did not know that his father's entourage, along with the bulk of the imperial army, had already arrived at Delhi.

Abul was brought into Mehrunnisa's apartments in shackles, chains binding his wrists together and swinging down to encircle his ankles.

'What is this, Mehrunnisa?' he yelled. 'What is this outrage? Why am I treated like a criminal?'

Mehrunnisa was making paan. She did not look up at her brother, and Abul did not come nearer. When he moved the first time, Hoshiyar's firm hand descended upon his nape in an unfriendly manner. 'Stay here, Mirza Hasan.'

She sat on her divan, the silver plates of betel leaves, betel nuts, lime, raisins and sultanas in front of her. Mehrunnisa dipped a heart-shaped betel leaf into a bowl of water, rinsed it, wiped it dry, and piled the centre with the contents of the plates. Then she meticulously folded it into a square parcel, tightly bound, and kept the folding in place with a clove stuck in.

Abul shivered in his place. His wrists were on fire, the iron cuffs chafing against his skin. What was Mehrunnisa going to do to him?

'Mehrunnisa,' he said pleadingly, and this time she looked up. There was no expression on her face, no anger or hatred, nothing. She opened her mouth, put the paan in and chewed, and she did not take her eyes away from her brother. It was Abul whose gaze dropped.

'Who told Khurram about the moving of the treasury, Hoshiyar?'

Abul's head whipped up. 'I did not, Mehrunnisa. You have to believe me.'

'How did he know then?'

'I do not know.' Abul said this without flinching. He started to tremble again though, setting the chains clanking.

'Take those off, Hoshiyar,' Mehrunnisa said, leaning back on the cushions. She cleared the plates away and put them on the carpets. 'Come here and sit, Abul.'

Abul massaged his wrists, bent down and rubbed his ankles, and hobbled over to sit by his sister. 'Do you believe me? Mehrunnisa, Khurram is on his way to sack Delhi. You must let the Emperor know.'

Mehrunnisa raised an eyebrow at him. 'Is this true?'

'Yes. I heard of it yesterday.'

'Then will you command one of the armies against Khurram, Abul?'

He did not hesitate for even a second. As soon as she finished her question, Abul Hasan said yes. He looked her in the eye when he said this. He thought she believed him.

Mehrunnisa sent him away. He stumbled out of the room. No harm was done, she thought, in bringing him to her like a prisoner. Now she knew that Abul would never be at her side, only at Khurram's. He would battle his son-in-law, though, and if Abul gave any sign of fleeing to Khurram, she would leave orders with the commanders that he must be killed before he was even halfway there. The prince was on his way to Delhi, Abul had told her this as though it were something new, something to take away her suspicions of him. But Mehrunnisa already knew, of course. Not just what his plans were, but where he was right now.

She called Shahryar away from Qandahar. Abul would command yet another army. Who would lead the third? Khurram had two men with him whom Mehrunnisa would have dearly liked to see at the helm of the imperial army—Raja Bikramjit and the Khan-i-khanan. She thought for a while and then remembered the man who had stood up against her time and again in those early days of her marriage. The man who had boldly gone to Jahangir to complain about her. He had shown courage and, in some ways, a loyalty to the Emperor few other men had.

Mehrunnisa wrote a letter to Mahabat Khan at Kabul, offering him release from the governorship there if he would come and join the imperial army. She wrote as though she asked a request, but it was a command. There was no question of Mahabat having a choice. So Mahabat Khan accepted. Actually, he desperately grabbed at the chance. He had spent ten years away from the imperial court and had aged twenty in that time. There had been nothing to spend his energy on, his duties in Kabul had been light. But here finally was the opportunity to return.

The three imperial armies headed by Mahabat, Shahryar and Abul met Khurram's army south of Delhi. The conclusion was preordained—there was no way Khurram's men could stand up to the might of the imperial forces. The prince fled to his home in the Deccan by nightfall and Raja Bikramjit was dead. His head was cut off, stuffed with grass and hay, and hung on an upturned spear on the ramparts of the Delhi Fort. The Raja's family had had in their possession, through many generations, a pair of perfectly matched pearls the size of small cherries. These Bikramjit had worn in his ears. When his head adorned the spear, it was without its ears, which had been sliced off for the family heirlooms.

Khurram ran away to the Deccan, but of course he was not to be allowed to go away so easily. Mehrunnisa gave out gifts to all the nobles who had participated in the battle, and she left out Abul. He was to stay with her at court, though; she could not trust him anywhere but near her. She sent a message to Prince Parviz, pulling him out of his life of drink and sloth. He was to come to Delhi, and from there pursue Khurram in the Deccan.

Mehrunnisa gave Mahabat Khan charge of the campaign along with Parviz. The Emperor had taken to his bed with yet another illness; he could not rise to give the orders himself, but he listened when she talked with him. Jahangir suggested that they travel to Ajmer and wait for news of Mahabat Khan and Parviz's pursuit of Khurram.

So the royal entourage moved to Ajmer. Once Mehrunnisa and Jahangir had come here to support Khurram's siege on Mewar. Now they came here hoping to hear of his demise.

Khurram fought Parviz's army outside of Burhanpur, or rather he fought Mahabat Khan's command. He was easily defeated, and the prince fled again, heading south to the Tapti River. This time he took Arjumand and their sons with him. The party that left with him was sadly depleted—Mahabat, exercising his diplomatic skills to the utmost, had sent secret letters to the nobles of Khurram's court, promising them amnesty from Jahangir's wrath if they defected to the imperial side.

The rain spewed down steadily and in torrents. The crash of the downpour was thunderous; it blotted out every other sound. Lightning forked across the sky and lit up the caravan trudging slowly down the muddy hillside.

Khurram rode at the head of the procession, wiping the streaming rain from his face. He could not even look up; the water lashed into his eyes if he did, so he bent down over his horse's neck, praying that it was surefooted. The horse plunged into the mud on its hind legs, lifting Khurram in the air, and then it painfully extricated itself from the sludge and moved on. Khurram looked back at the lead palanquin and wondered how Arjumand was doing. She must be drenched through also, he thought. The palanquin cover and curtains had been ripped to pieces in the monsoon winds, modesty was thrown away, and Arjumand clung to the skeleton frame of the conveyance, her veil bunched and wet around her neck. Khurram cursed under his breath. Here he was, a royal prince, forced to flee like a common fugitive. Suddenly someone shouted out aloud, and Khurram reined in his horse.

One of the elephants had dropped into the soft mud, the ground not being able to support its weight. The animal struggled wildly to extricate itself, trumpeting in fear as it sank deeper.

An attendant rode up to the prince. 'We shall have to leave the animal, your Highness,' he said, leaning into Khurram's ear.

'Do so, and quickly,' Khurram shouted, lifting his voice over the clamour of the rain. He watched as the baggage strapped onto the elephant's back was unloaded and distributed to the other already sorely burdened horses and elephants. Khurram looked away into the wet darkness as a shot rang out. The elephant's cry stopped in mid-trumpet, and it fell back on the ground with a thud.

It was two days since Khurram and his party had forded the Tapti. The river was swollen with rainwaters, and the crossing had almost been a disaster. Entire barges with their belongings had been rushed away down the angry Tapti; they had just barely made it to the other side. The monsoons had begun just as Khurram had left Burhanpur, but he could not have waited for the rains to subside, he had had no time. Even now, as they struggled towards the southern frontier of the Mughal Empire, the imperial army was but a two-day march behind them.

They moved forward again, the animals protesting against the extra weight and lack of food or rest. Khurram was determined, at all costs, not to be taken prisoner by the Emperor. He had witnessed Khusrau's fate and knew his own would be worse. He raised his hand and pointed south. 'Let us go!' he yelled.

Arjumand huddled in one corner of the palanquin, seeking shelter and warmth from the pouring rain. She was feeling nauseous. It was a familiar feeling, and the princess's heart plummeted as she realized that she was pregnant again. What sort of a life would this child have. Born to fugitive parents who were fleeing from the wrath of the Emperor? For that matter, what sort of a life would all her children have? At one time, it had seemed certain that Khurram would be Emperor, but now...

There were no more mishaps that night, and by afternoon, Khurram and Arjumand slipped over the southern border into the kingdom of Golconda. Once, Khurram thought, he had led an army to fight the Golconda king. Would he be given shelter here?

Behind Khurram, Mahabat Khan moved doggedly through the blinding rain. He had been drenching wet for three days now. His barge had turned over in the Tapti, throwing Parviz and him into the shallow end on the other side. They had clung to some tree roots until the rest of the army had been able to pull them out of the water. Mahabat was weary too. He was no longer young, no longer able to ride on campaign for the hours and days it took to achieve victory. But Jahangir had commanded this of him.

Mahabat Khan lifted his balding head to the rain and opened his mouth to drink the sweet water. When he captured Prince Khurram, he would be celebrated as a hero. Jahangir would give him his place in court again, next to Sharif. They would be friends and companions again, as they once were. He dreamed thus in his saddle, his horse stumbling through the wet and dark night. The same lightning that flashed to show Khurram's party lit the skies above Mahabat. He saw his army clearly defined in that light, soaked and miserable, cold from the constant dampness, their lungs clogged, coughs racking their thin bodies. Mahabat let his mind wander again. Sharif and he had written letters to each other, fewer as the years had passed, for Mahabat had burned with jealousy at all Sharif's accounts. The garden parties, the festivals, the imperial weighings on birthdays. He had seen all of these in tremendous detail, reading through Sharif's casual sentences. The Amir-ul-umra had kept his place in court because he could, and did, keep his mouth shut. Mahabat knew he would not have been this complacent at Mehrunnisa's jharoka audiences, at the effortless way in which she, from behind the veil, nudged and bullied the nobles and princes into doing what she wanted. Reading Sharif's letters, Mahabat had often thought he was better at Kabul, away from the temptation to fight with Mehrunnisa, rather than at court resisting it every minute of every day. But his place was with the Emperor. And surely, he could return now!

Mahabat's horse trudged through the rain. He kept his head bowed, seeing glory for himself in the dark wetness. The shivers that beset his body, the ache in his thighs from so long in the saddle, the constant hunger for sleep, none of these mattered.

His army followed the path Prince Khurram had taken; they stumbled upon the dead elephant drowning in the rains upon the hillside, then came to the edge of the empire. Here the tracks from

Khurram's entourage moved into Golconda. Mahabat and his army rode around the perimeter looking for further marks, hoping that the original tracks were false, and that Khurram had moved off the road in another direction. But no, he had gone into the enemy kingdom with his wife, his children and his army.

Mahabat stayed at the border for two more days, and then turned back to Burhanpur, dragging the ever-complaining Prince Parviz with him. It was a victory of sorts. Khurram would not be a threat anymore—and so he wrote to Mehrunnisa and Jahangir in a letter sent by runner immediately upon his arrival at Burhanpur. And there, between the lines, he implored to return to court to give a personal accounting of his campaign.

A few months later, Khurram sent his father a letter begging pardon. He did not want to live in exile anymore, though the Golconda king had been welcoming, even generous, to an old enemy. But Golconda was not home; the empire was.

From Lahore, Mehrunnisa set harsh terms for his surrender.

Khurram had to send a million rupees to the imperial treasury. Two of his sons were to be escorted to the imperial court as security against further rebellion. Khurram had to give up any claims on the forts of Asir and Rohtas. The prince agreed and took his family to Nasik on the Arabian Sea. He was officially in exile, although still on the empire's soil.

News of Mahabat's defeat of Prince Khurram spread all over the empire. Mahabat Khan was fifty-five years old and had routed a prince about half his age. He was a brave soldier. Once, when Jahangir had first come to the throne, people could not take the Emperor's name without saying Mahabat and Sharif's too in the same breath. Mehrunnisa had changed all that. Now Jahangir was synonymous only with his twentieth and most powerful wife.

A grey, ghostly dawn chiselled at the edges of night on the eastern horizon over Lahore. In this thin light, the city sweepers began their work, washing down the cobbled stones with water, using thick jute brooms to swirl the dirt away. Milkmen brought their cows to doorsteps to rouse sleepy maids, and they gushed sweet, frothing, warm milk into earthenware jugs. An hour later, the lamplighters would arrive to douse and clean the street lamps.

The many palaces of Lahore Fort slumbered densely in the cool of the early morning. Lights flickered here and there, in verandah arches, in niches set in the sandstone walls, at the western entrance to the fort, the Hathi Pol, and along the ramparts.

In one palace, the sesame oil lamps had been lit early the previous evening and still burned fervently, fed through the long and tiring night.

Ladli wailed, the cry drawn from deep within her. The sound curled through the lushly appointed apartment, bounced off the mirrorwork-embellished walls, and flew out the open windows into the coming dawn. Blood rushed to her face as she gripped her eyes shut, breath knocked out of her lungs, her lower body straining. Then she sank back on the divan. 'Mama.'

'I am here, beta.' Mehrunnisa leaned over her daughter and rubbed her face gently.

Ladli clutched at her hand, grinding her fingers in a tight vise. 'It hurts, Mama. It hurts.'

'I know, beta,' Mehrunnisa said. She put her head against Ladli's, wishing she could take away this pain. Sweat drenched Ladli's skin and lay her hair in strands across her skull. If it had cooled during the night, neither noticed, for the room was fetid with the smell of perspiration and the blood that soaked through the white satin sheets of the divan under Ladli. The birthing had started hours ago, so many hours ago now, Mehrunnisa thought. At first it had been almost easy, a deepening ache in Ladli's lower back, and the happy anticipation of the child who was to come. They had talked and laughed, *who would he look like? How much hair would be on his head?* There was going to be a new life, one that would belong to them. In these early hours, Mehrunnisa felt the crushing weight of the past few months rise from her. Khurram was forgotten, the empire even forgotten, although the worrying letters from Burhanpur lay on her lap.

Ladli ate ghee-roasted cashews, pistachios and sultanas by the handful, drank new milk from a water buffalo, all to help her keep her strength. Midwives flitted in and out of the chambers, and Hoshiyar stood in one corner, so proud and upright that he might have been the expectant father. Mehrunnisa remembered Ladli's birth, how hurried and frightening that had been, how much she had ached with yearning to see her child after all those miscarriages. How fierce that want had been. Some of that yearning returned now, but it was pleasurably so, for a boy was to be born. A prince, a future Emperor.

And then Ladli's pains started to come faster, nearer each other. Mehrunnisa put down the letters from Burhanpur and sat by her daughter. She shouted at the midwives huddling around the bottom of the divan. What was happening? It is all the process of birth, your Majesty, nothing to worry about. The night progressed, and Ladli screamed, over and over again, drowning out Jahangir's coughs in the nearby apartment, until Mehrunnisa could only hear her voice, could not think of Burhanpur, or the hacking, terrible sound of her husband's lungs.

Another contraction came ripping through, and Ladli jerked off the divan to sit upright, knees pulled against her chest. She shouted with pain, almost into Mehrunnisa's ear, unwilling to let go of her mother's hand.

Above her screams, Mehrunnisa yelled at the midwife, 'Do something!'

The woman cowered but found voice enough to say, 'It is not for me to do something, your Majesty. The princess has to push, the baby is stuck.' She reached between Ladli's legs, her fingers slipping over the smooth black head showing there. Why would the child not come out? It should have been relatively simple at this stage. A few pushes and the baby should be out. But the head stayed where it was, and Ladli's belly swelled and ebbed as her body strained to release the child.

Another plume of blood gushed out and blossomed on the sheets. The midwife, old and grey from this lifelong work, stupidly raised her bloodied hands in the air.

'I cannot get my fingers around the child, your Majesty,' she said, trembling at the fire in Mehrunnisa's eyes. 'Please ask the princess to remain seated, it will help bring him out.'

Mehrunnisa lunged over Ladli at the midwife, waving wildly to tell her to put away her hands, but it was too late. Ladli had seen the blood. She started to cry, in huge sobs. 'Oh, Mama, I am going to die. Look, I am going to die.'

'Get her out,' Mehrunnisa said to Hoshiyar, and he unceremoniously dragged the midwife from the room. Another midwife took her place; she was younger, but with a wise face.

'What are we to do?' Mehrunnisa said to the midwife.

'The princess must sit, your Majesty. But in a moment...' She bent to prod and pull against Ladli, then with her hands still down, she looked up and nodded.

Mehrunnisa and Hoshiyar hoisted Ladli up and put a few cushions under her back. When the next contraction started to blight her face, Mehrunnisa put an arm around Ladli, leaned close to her ear, and said, 'Now, beta. Try as hard as you can. I am here. So is Hoshiyar, nothing will happen to you. All right?'

Ladli nodded, looking only at her mother, and heaved inside. Through the pain and wrenching of her body, she could feel the child's shoulders slip through, and then the torso, and then, finally and with relief, the legs.

The midwife expertly cut the umbilical cord and cleaned the child while Ladli lay back, breathing heavily.

Mehrunnisa turned to the midwife. 'Is the child alive?'

'Yes, your Majesty,' the woman mumbled, still swabbing at the baby. She held it upside down, away from Mehrunnisa, and slapped it lightly on the back. A massive, healthy bawl filled the room. Hoshiyar shouted with laughter, his bushy moustache swinging up to his ears. Ladli clung to Mehrunnisa, one arm around the eunuch, tears flowing from her to wet her mother's choli. They put their heads together and prayed, laughing and crying at the same time.

'Thank you, Allah,' Mehrunnisa said. 'Thank you for that glorious sound.' Then, she said, 'Bring him here, so we can see him.'

The midwife wrapped the child in the red, cotton cloth offered by another slave, and held the child up. Her arms trembled. 'It is a girl, your Majesty.'

For the next few minutes, no one spoke. Ladli, still sobbing with happiness, had not heard, but Mehrunnisa and Hoshiyar were still. The midwife shivered, holding in her arms the child no one reached out for yet. The baby was well swaddled, her dark and lush hair visible above the cloth, her cries stopped.

And so long moments passed. This was a trick, Mehrunnisa thought, she had misunderstood the midwife, or she had not seen the child properly... but no, the midwife would not dare make such a mistake, not when her life depended on it. It was a trick though; fate had tricked her out of a male grandchild.

'I want the child.' Ladli put her arms out.

Mehrunnisa watched as Ladli touched the child's face with wonder, her fingers light and questing over a perfectly formed ear, over the sweep of hair still wet from the womb, the thinly traced eyebrows, the pink mouth, and a funnily stubborn chin. The baby's eyes were a dark blue—she had Mehrunnisa's eyes. One little hand, fingernails long, clutched the end of the cloth, and when Ladli uncurled the fingers, they wrapped around hers. She laughed with delight.

'Look, Mama,' she said, her face lit from inside with such joy that Mehrunnisa could not help laughing with her. As she did, tension drained from the room, let out through the windows into the now golden glow of the morning. Ladli unwrapped the child carefully, and then smiled again. 'A beautiful little girl. I shall call her Arzani. What do you think, Mama?'

'A lovely name, beta. A lovely name.' Suddenly exhausted, Mehrunnisa kissed her daughter on the cheek and laid her lips against the soft skin of the baby's feet. She then rose and went from the room, Hoshiyar following her out to Emperor Jahangir's apartments.

Mehrunnisa crawled into bed next to her husband and put her head against his chest. With her ear so close to his lungs, she could hear his breath march in and out in loud, rhythmic rasps. But at least sleep had come to rest his body and his mind. Mehrunnisa did not sleep, though. So much hope had lain with that child. Every dream of hers, every wish for the empire, for her life... now none of those would come true.

For Shahryar too, of course. Shahryar had little importance on his own. He had gone to Qandahar and tried to regain the city, but the Shah of Persia now had a strong foot in it and was not shaken off. If the Emperor died now, or soon, no one would turn to the nashudani. Now there was no male heir to give Shahryar prestige.

'They are still young, Mehrunnisa.'

She looked up at Jahangir, her vision blurred. She knew it was stupid to cry for this, but the wanting had made her weak, she could not help herself.

He rubbed away the tears from her face. 'There will be other children,' he said.

'How did you know...'

'The slaves came to me,' he said. 'But there will be other children, and soon, a son for Ladli and Shahryar.'

'Yes, your Majesty.' Jahangir was right. Now her hopes must rest on future children.

'Did you read the letters from Burhanpur?' he asked.

Missives had come from the southern border of the empire, one after another. Most were filled with praises for Mahabat Khan's victory over Prince Khurram. Even here, at Lahore, Hoshiyar bent time and again to fill Jahangir and Mehrunnisa's ears with tales of what was being said of Mahabat Khan.

Mehrunnisa wondered whether bringing Mahabat back had been such a good idea after all. Most disturbing was a letter from an obscure commander at Burhanpur. Mahabat and Prince Parviz, who was nominally at the head of this last campaign, had become... close. Parviz, for all his ineffectualness, his drinking, his dependence—or perhaps *because* of these qualities—had the astonishing ability to attract the benevolence of powerful ministers. First, the Khan-i-khanan, Abdur Rahim, and now, strangely, Mahabat Khan. Neglected at court, Parviz invariably found champions in his guardians. Mahabat was too friendly with Prince Parviz, the letter said, perhaps he was grooming him for the empire.

Being so recently rid of Khurram, Mehrunnisa and Jahangir had never considered Parviz to be a threat to Shahryar's claim on the throne.

'I find it hard to believe this letter, your Majesty,' Mehrunnisa said slowly.

Jahangir laughed, the sound of his voice rumbling into her ear. 'Mehrunnisa, where the crown is concerned, *every* rumour, however flimsy its source, must be heeded. Mahabat can no longer stay in the Deccan with Parviz. Together, they will grow too strong. Prepare a farman commanding him here to court.'

'But we did not ask for him to come before, your Majesty, when he begged for permission. What excuse can we give now?'

The Emperor rubbed his chin. 'Hoshiyar, call for the barber,' he said, raising his voice. Then he said to Mehrunnisa, 'Any excuse... did the letter not mention infractions of some sort?'

'Yes...,' Mehrunnisa said. She rose from the bed and knotted her hair at the nape of her neck, smiling at her husband. 'Are you feeling well today?'

'Yes,' he said, rising too. 'After a long time. Where is Hoshiyar?'

'Gone to do your bidding, your Majesty.' She kissed him on the cheek, lightly, her lips scraping against the day-old stubble. 'I must go write to Mirza Mahabat Khan.'

Then Mehrunnisa ran out of the apartment to her writing table. She paused for a moment to look into the little mirror on her thumb ring. Held so close, she could see sections of her face—an eyebrow, the dark circles under her eyes that bespoke a night not slept, the curving lines around her mouth. She was a grandmother today, blessed with a healthy grandchild, and a happy and content child. A husband who adored her. And finally, an empire at her command.

She wrote to Mahabat Khan. She had heard that Mahabat misappropriated funds for the Deccan campaign to line his own coffers. And that he kept the captured war elephants for his own stables. Was this true?

So Mahabat had an invitation to come to court finally, couched in phrases of insult and disrespect.

But both Mehrunnisa and Jahangir had forgotten that Mahabat Khan loathed her for various indignities, real and imagined, for being, quite simply, a woman with power in a man's world. As much as Mahabat wanted to come to court, as much as he had languished in boredom during his ten years at Kabul, his pride had not broken. And neither had his hatred for Mehrunnisa.

Chapter Twenty-seven

*Mohabet had a great many enemies: his sovereign had but
little firmness. The abilities of the former had raised envy;
and nature had given to the latter a disposition too easy
and pliant, to be proof against misrepresentation.*

—ALEXANDER DOW,
The History of Hindostan

IN MARCH OF 1626, MEHRUNNISA AND JAHANGIR DECIDED TO LEAVE
Lahore for Kabul. Summer was upon them, and they retreated to
the cool and verdant gardens of Kabul this time, instead of Kashmir.
Before Kashmir was conquered, Kabul had been the summer resort
of the Mughal kings, and Babur, the first Mughal Emperor and
Jahangir's great-grandfather, was buried there. The royal entourage
was encamped on the eastern bank of the Jhelum River when news
of Mahabat's arrival in the area reached them. The minister came
to pay his respects to the Emperor with an army of five hundred
Rajput soldiers and two hundred war elephants.

Jahangir was outraged at this show of force. He sent Mahabat
a message—he was to leave his army behind. If the charges against
him were false, that could be easily proved; the truth would defend
him.

Mahabat consented to the Emperor's demands, anxious to
clear himself. He sent his son-in-law Khwaja Barkhurdar as an

emissary, along with his two hundred elephants, to the Emperor's camp on the Jhelum. He was willing to even hand over his wives and children as a pledge of his loyalty, but he would not allow himself to be dragged in front of the Emperor like a common criminal.

Khwaja Barkhurdar was ushered in to see Jahangir and Mehrunnisa. He bent low in the taslim and, still with his head bowed, presented Mahabat Khan's letter. The elephants were arrayed in the outer courtyard of the camp, standing in a solid line of grey, their tails twitching in the heat to whip at the throng of flies.

The Emperor read the letter. 'Why is Mahabat not here, Barkhurdar?'

'He will be, your Majesty,' the young man replied. He kept his gaze pinned on the carpets below, not daring to look at Mehrunnisa, though she was veiled. 'When you have forgiven him.'

'This is a strange way to ask for forgiveness.' Mehrunnisa's voice was sharp. It had taken them six months to get Mahabat Khan from Burhanpur. He had disobeyed her orders the first time, or rather, Parviz had written and requested that Mahabat stay with him. He had grown used to Mahabat's guardianship, the prince had said.

And all through these six months of waiting for Mahabat to present himself, Mehrunnisa had had spies send her daily missives of Mahabat's doings in Burhanpur. The reports had worried her, he was clearly procrastinating. But why? Finally, she had sent Parviz another guardian because he could not be without one, he had said, and she had commanded Mahabat to leave Burhanpur immediately.

'Your Majesty,' Mehrunnisa said quickly, putting a hand on Jahangir's arm. 'Before you decide anything in Mahabat Khan's favour, you should know who his emissary is.'

Jahangir turned in surprise to her. 'Who is he?'

Mehrunnisa told him. Abul stood behind her and filled in what she did not know about Mahabat's son-in-law. Who his father was, what his position was at court, and other details about their jagirs and holdings in the empire. Abul Hasan was with Mehrunnisa at this meeting because she had called him here. She knew that Abul disliked Mahabat Khan, and that this dislike went back to the early years of her marriage to Jahangir. For as her power had grown at court, so had Abul's. He was her brother and had been part of the junta that had taken away Mahabat and Sharif's importance. As much as Khurram drove them apart, Mahabat brought them together.

'A fine young man,' the Emperor commented. 'The two families are fortunate in the relationship.'

Barkhurdar was nervous. He tried to hold himself still as etiquette demanded, but he could not. Something was not right, he thought, but what?

'No doubt, your Majesty, but...' Mehrunnisa hesitated. 'The marriage was not sanctioned by you.'

'Is that right?'

It was a Mughal custom that all courtiers had to get royal permission to contract any marriages in their families. Consent was perfunctory but nonetheless required, for ritual had to be followed. Mahabat Khan, left to languish at Kabul, so far from the imperial court, had forgotten to ask Jahangir for permission before he married his daughter to Khwaja Barkhurdar.

'Your Majesty, Mahabat Khan insults you by sending this man as an emissary, knowing well that you did not consent to the marriage,' Abul said, bending to Jahangir's ear.

'Throw him in prison,' Jahangir said. Whether Mahabat meant it as an insult or not, the Emperor could not, after having been made aware of Barkhurdar, react any other way.

Barkhurdar moved suddenly, his hand on his dagger, but the Ahadis pounced on him and dragged him away. The young man's property, especially the dowry he received on his marriage, was confiscated and added to the imperial treasury.

In his encampment, a few miles upstream, Mahabat Khan paced restlessly up and down the thick Persian rug. He went to the main flap of the tent, lifted it and gazed out. There was no sign of his son-in-law.

Mahabat let the flap fall back. What was taking Barkhurdar so long? He could have talked to the Emperor twenty times by now. Horse hooves came clipping up the riverbank. Mahabat ran out of his tent and waited there with his soldiers. The rider was too far away, awash in a cloud of dust. When he neared, they saw that it was one of the imperial mahouts.

'What happened?' Mahabat demanded, even before the tired man could dismount.

'My lord, the Emperor has imprisoned your son-in-law,' the mahout said as he fell out of the saddle. He was not used to the discomfort of a horse's back.

'Why?'

'You... you did not request permission for the marriage. The Emperor has confiscated all his property.'

'Is he safe?'

The mahout nodded, still gasping. 'Safe enough. He tried to fight, but they put him in irons. He is alive, though. I saw him.'

Mahabat turned away, enraged. He would have to see the Emperor personally and explain all of this. It was a misunderstanding. But he needed to see Jahangir alone, not with Mehrunnisa present. And where she was, her hated brother would be too.

'I will go to the Emperor immediately,' he said. 'Saddle my horse.'

'No, my lord. That would not be judicious. The Ahadis have been ordered to arrest you on sight,' the mahout said. 'And most of the camp moves today to the west side of the Jhelum, my lord.'

'Where will the Emperor be?' Mahabat asked, with a glimmer of hope in his voice.

'Here, on the eastern side, with the Empress. He is too unwell to travel tonight.'

If most of the camp moved, the imperial guards would move too. Mahabat turned to his soldiers, plotting in his head, and they listened when he spoke.

The soft, dark night stole upon the Jhelum River, turning its waters indigo. The advance camp was just settling down on the western bank under Abul Hasan's supervision. Earlier in the day, he had escorted the royal zenana, the officers of the court, the baggage, the arsenal, and the imperial treasury across the bridge. The treasury resided with the camp now; after Khurram's attempts at storming it, it had been commanded from Agra to the Emperor. A few hundred Ahadis and Rajput soldiers were left on the eastern bank to guard the Emperor and Mehrunnisa.

When the last of the sun died, lights glimmered on both banks of the river as the camps prepared dinner. The aroma of roasting venison from the day's hunt and thick gravied curries mingled with the smoke from the cooking fires. The night was clear, with a cool edge in the air. Stars littered the clear sky.

Horse hooves, muffled in cotton cloth, pounded up the eastern riverbank to the Emperor's tent.

'We are almost there,' Mahabat Khan said softly to one of his commanders. 'Take two hundred soldiers and go to the bridge on the Jhelum. Make sure that no one is allowed to cross from the western bank. If they attempt to, burn the bridge.'

The commander nodded silently and signalled to his troops. They rode off into the night. Mahabat and his men waited in silence for an hour. The bridge would be secure by now. He then yanked at his reins and rode to the entrance of Jahangir's tent.

The royal guards were drowsy, sleep heavy upon their eyelids. They had eaten well at the night's meal, and drunk many goblets of wine. There was no threat to the Emperor, so a short nap would surely not be amiss. The men woke to see sword tips pointed at their throats. They dropped their spears, muskets and daggers to the ground and raised their arms.

From within the royal enclosure, an attendant wandered out to smoke a beedi. He saw Mahabat and yelled, 'Mahabat Khan is here! Inform the Emperor!'

As he fled back into the tent, a soldier flung a dagger at him. It hissed quietly through the air and caught him between his neck and his shoulders. The attendant fell, and the soldiers trampled over his body into the tent. The Ahadis had scarcely heard the shout; they had moved, hands to sword hilts, but the Rajput soldiers were in front of them. It was too late to fight.

Jahangir was asleep when Mahabat Khan entered. He woke to his minister's touch. 'Mahabat,' he said, opening his eyes. Then he sprang up. 'What are you doing here?' Mahabat's Rajput soldiers stood around his divan. 'What is the meaning of this?'

'Your Majesty, I have come to answer the charges against me.'

'Why could you not come during the day?' The Emperor sank back into the cushions.

'You must come with me to my camp, your Majesty,' Mahabat said. He still held his unsheathed dagger in his hand.

'It was not necessary to force your way here, Mahabat,' Jahangir replied. 'I would willingly have granted you an audience.'

'Now, your Majesty,' Mahabat said. 'Please rise or I shall have to help you do so.'

Jahangir rose from the divan. What was going on? Where were his Ahadis? How had they allowed Mahabat to come so far into the royal tent without resistance? And where was Mehrunnisa? At this thought, the Emperor shuddered. He hoped she was safe, that she would not fight with Mahabat—there was no telling what Mehrunnisa would do if she was in a rage.

He thought quickly. 'I will not go unless I ride on my favourite Arabian.'

'As you wish, your Majesty,' Mahabat replied. He signalled to a royal attendant.

'My lord, the steed has been taken to the western bank. I could ride over to bring it,' the attendant said.

'No, that is not possible,' Mahabat said. He bowed to Jahangir. 'Your Majesty, perhaps another horse could be found for you. Any of my soldiers would willingly give up his mount.'

'I want my Arabian steed,' Jahangir insisted. 'I cannot ride out without the steed.'

'Please reconsider, your Majesty,' Mahabat said in desperation. Any moment now, the army on the western bank would be alerted of his presence. How long would his soldiers be able to stave off an attack? He had to get the Emperor to his own camp or he would not be safe.

They argued for the next ten minutes, and finally, with great reluctance, Jahangir gave in to his minister. The Emperor climbed into a howdah atop a royal elephant. Mahabat Khan's Rajput soldiers formed a circle around the elephant, and the Ahadis watched as Jahangir was taken out of the camp. Jahangir looked around him, but he could see no sign of Mehrunnisa. Perhaps she had fled already? If she had, she would lead an army against Mahabat. He talked loudly, of trivial things, and mostly of Mahabat and his early friendship, the days they had spent together as children, the games they had played, their most successful hunts. Mahabat began to smile and laugh at the memories, and his expression softened. At least his mind was now elsewhere, Jahangir thought.

They reached Mahabat's camp without incident. As he was helping Jahangir dismount, Mahabat remembered Mehrunnisa. He pushed the Emperor back into the howdah, and they left for the royal encampment. Jahangir complained, making his voice as querulous as possible; he knew Mahabat would not dare injure him, but he would Mehrunnisa. But Mahabat was firm too. He could not leave Jahangir even at his own camp, for it was possible that the Empress might have already rounded up an army to rescue the Emperor.

As Mahabat Khan was riding back to the royal camp, an old woman and her son approached the Rajput guards on the eastern bank of the Jhelum. One of the guards ran forward and pointed his spear at them. 'Who are you?' he shouted.

'It is I, Saliha, and my son, Sharif,' the woman's voice trembled.

'No one is to cross the Jhelum,' the guard said harshly. 'Go back, old woman.'

'But I have to get to the other bank, Sahib,' the woman begged. 'I sell fresh fruit for the zenana ladies' breakfast.' She showed him a basket full of apples and pears.

The guard brought up his lantern to peer into her basket. As the light fell upon the woman's face, he recoiled and stumbled back. She was ugly, with deep wrinkles on her skin, but more frightening were the purple and red sores on her forehead and cheek. Were those signs of the plague?

'Stay away from me, you wretch,' the guard yelled, raising his spear again.

'Let me go, Sahib,' the woman wheedled. 'I have to earn my livelihood.'

The guard thought quickly. If this woman carried the plague, then she would infect all of them. It was better to allow her to go to the western bank, as far away as possible.

'Go then.' He stepped back further and called out to his comrades.

As the word passed through the Rajput soldiers that the woman was infected, they shrank back to allow them to cross the bridge. She hobbled across, leaning heavily on her son's shoulder.

As soon as she was on the other side, the woman's limp vanished, her back straightened, and she strode swiftly to the advance camp, dragging her son along with her.

Mehrunnisa threw the basket of fruit on the side of the road and smiled at the man next to her. 'See how easy that was, Shahryar?'

Mehrunnisa ran to Abul's tent. At first, he would not let her in, then she spoke to him and he recognized his sister under the putrid sores on her face.

'Why are you dressed like this?' Abul asked as Mehrunnisa called for water to wash her face. She told him, rubbing the make-up from her skin with a vigorous hand.

'Call for the nobles, Abul. You are responsible for this, and now I have to make it right.'

Abul's face grew hard. 'How was I responsible, Mehrunnisa?

She turned to him, dabbing at her face with the end of her veil. 'You were in charge of the advance camp, Abul, and you have brought most of the imperial army over here with you. There were too few men left to guard the Emperor.'

The nobles staggered in, woken from their sleep. The old woman in rags, her ghagara and choli ripped in places, the skin on her hands a dark, crumpled brown, began to speak. Their mouths gaped. What was the Empress doing dressed like this? When they heard what Mehrunnisa had to say, they became serious, alert. They were not to try and go over to the other side, Mehrunnisa said. Mahabat had left two hundred Rajputs on the eastern end who would set fire to the bridge when they saw the army crossing.

The army was woken up. Lights blazed on the western bank of the Jhelum, and the shouts of the men carried across the dark waters as Mehrunnisa prepared the men for battle.

On the eastern shore, Jahangir stood watching the flurry of activity. He knew Mehrunnisa would lead the army herself if she got a chance. He sent her a letter with his signet ring, telling her not to prepare the regiments. Mahabat meant no harm. But Jahangir also knew that she would not listen. After the messenger crossed over to Mahabat's camp, his men set fire to the bridge.

At the first light of day, a huge army led by Abul Hasan started from the advance camp towards the Jhelum. When they reached the bank, scouts were sent out to find fords along the river that were passable. After some searching, a ford was identified by the boat commander.

But the choice was a poor one; that ford was filled with deep and unexpected pits. The soldiers found the soft mud giving way no matter where they put their feet. And across the river, on the other bank, Mahabat's men stood waiting for them, patiently, armed with spears and swords. Abul's soldiers retreated, already exhausted before the fight, to flop on the warm stones on the western bank.

Mehrunnisa, seeing the imperial soldiers scatter from their formations, urged her elephant into the river from her howdah. Ladli, Arzani, and the child's nurse were with her—she did not want to leave them in the camp alone, in case Mahabat's men found their way there. Seeing Mehrunnisa's elephant plunge into the Jhelum, the imperial soldiers rallied and tried to cross again. A few made it to the other side, only to be welcomed by a volley of arrows and spears from Mahabat's soldiers. Other fords were found downstream, and small bands of the imperial army crossed on them to the eastern bank.

With her elephant in the water up to its stomach, Mehrunnisa looked around her. A few hundred yards away, Mutamid Khan stood on a little patch of dry land between two branches of the river. Why were they not moving? Was this a picnic?

Mehrunnisa turned and shouted to Hoshiyar. 'Hoshiyar, send a man to Mutamid and find out what he is doing. Tell him to go across.'

She watched as a eunuch swam to Mutamid. He bowed in her direction, and his men jumped into the river again. But the imperial army was too scattered to be effective. Here and there, a few men found their way to the eastern bank and were easily killed by Mahabat's men. Abul's horse was swept away by the current, and he seemed to give up; the other commanders plunged forward heedlessly and ended up killing half their men in the water before they could even get across.

'Mama,' Ladli said, pulling her down when an arrow whizzed past the howdah. 'Do not do anything silly; let the men fight.'

Mehrunnisa thrust her daughter's hand away. 'But we must, beta. Keep Arzani on the floor.'

Ladli laid the child down and piled cushions on her. Arzani squirmed and started to wail. 'Hush,' she said, looking at Arzani's nurse in exasperation. This was her job, what was she doing, shaking like that? The nurse was hanging over the edge of the howdah, little whimpers coming from her mouth.

'Look after the child,' Ladli yelled, pulling the nurse from the howdah edge and placing her hands on the baby. 'This is what you are paid to do.'

'Here.' Mehrunnisa thrust a loaded musket into Ladli's hands and fit an arrow into her bow. The two women brought up the ends of their veils and knotted the cloth behind their necks, wearing their veils like masks. As the elephant lumbered slowly to the eastern bank, Ladli and Mehrunnisa loaded the musket and the bow over and over again and shot at Mahabat's army. Suddenly, an arrow came hurtling through and pierced the nurse in her arm. She began blubbering incoherently, prayers and moans mixed with her wails. Arzani began to cry too, and their voices mingled with the shouts from the men, the trumpeting of the elephants, the booms of musket shots.

Mehrunnisa put her bow down, tore her veil off her face, and used the cloth as a tourniquet, tying it tight around the nurse's arm.

'Keep quiet,' she commanded. 'It's only a scratch.'

She turned back to the battle and found that Ladli had not been able to keep the Rajput soldiers away with just her musket. A few floated dead in the waters of the Jhelum, but most of them were already close to the imperial elephant. Mehrunnisa let a few more arrows fly. The Rajputs surrounded her elephant, treading water. 'Please surrender, your Majesty!'

Mehrunnisa hesitated. Ladli's face was flushed, and gunpowder smudged her fingers and cheeks. Arzani cried again. She pushed the cushions off herself and leaned over the edge of the howdah, her hair falling in curls over her eyes.

Mehrunnisa threw down the bow and grabbed the waist of her granddaughter's ghagara. She turned to Ladli, whose eyes flickered to her mother just briefly, the Rajput soldiers held steadily in the musket's sight. 'Whatever you wish, Mama,' she said quietly.

With Arzani struggling in her grasp, the nurse still sobbing softly in one corner, Mehrunnisa called out, 'We surrender.'

One of the soldiers climbed up the trunk of the elephant, knocked the mahout into the water, and guided it towards Mahabat's camp.

But the fighting went on all day. By evening, as the sun was setting, the waters of the Jhelum ran red with blood. Bodies of the imperial soldiers lay in the shallow ends of the banks or against sandbars in the middle of the river. Horses and elephants caught in mud struggled in fear and pain, their neighs and trumpets added to human cries, until a benevolent shot from Mahabat's soldiers cut those short. Two thousand imperial soldiers had died trying to cross the Jhelum, another two thousand had been massacred by Mahabat.

Abul had fled from the Jhelum long before the end of the battle. He had watched Mehrunnisa goad her elephant into the waters, and then he had mounted his horse and ridden away to his estates nearby, without lifting his matchlock once to his shoulder. Mahabat Khan went in pursuit of Abul and brought him back in chains. Now he had Jahangir, Mehrunnisa, Shahryar, Ladli and Khusrau's son Bulaqi as his prisoners.

He took them to Kabul, as originally planned. On the way, Mahabat finally realized what he had done. All he had wanted was a moment to talk with Jahangir, and now he had overthrown the Mughal government. If only Mehrunnisa had not decided to fight his soldiers, he thought. If only she had stayed in the zenana apartments as a woman should. He would have had the time to beg an audience with his Emperor, and all would be right. And now...

Now Mahabat Khan *was* the Mughal government. Unwillingly and unwittingly, as matters had spiralled out of his control, Mahabat Khan had effected a coup.

Chapter Twenty-eight

But Nur Jahan Begum was beginning to recover her courage. She recruited large number of men every day and was conferring with the secret enemies of Mahabat Khan with the object of devising the best means of destroying him...

—B. NARAIN, TRANS., AND S. SHARMA, ED.,
A Dutch Chronicle of Mughal India

AT KABUL, THE COURT WENT ABOUT ITS NORMAL BUSINESS. MAHABAT KEPT Mehrunnisa away from Jahangir as much as possible, determined that she would not interfere in the administration of the empire. He did not allow her to sit at the jharoka, insisted that the Emperor agree to all of his decisions, and acted the despot as much as he could. But his heart was not entirely in this. All Mahabat wanted was for Jahangir to forgive him for imagined faults. But the Emperor, ailing now and sick in his bed most of the time, would not even listen to Mahabat. He turned his face away when the minister entered his apartments, looked at the walls, would not pay any attention to him. Jahangir signed the farmans presented to him and asked for Mehrunnisa.

'She is busy, your Majesty,' Mahabat said.

Jahangir threw a cushion in his direction. It missed and went tumbling onto the carpets. 'I want to see the Empress.'

And so he kept saying to Mahabat. *I want the Empress.* The minister tried to pacify Jahangir. He tried to tell him that Prince Khurram was the best choice of heir. Shahryar was a weakling; how could he rule?

While they were at Kabul, Parviz had died at Burhanpur, and Mahabat had found his loyalties shifting to Khurram, the prince he had hounded to the southern rim of the empire. Shahryar, the nashudani, the good-for-nothing prince he would not support, for he was Mehrunnisa's son-in-law. But Khurram was a bidaulat, a wretch, Jahangir said. *Bring the Empress to me.*

But Mahabat was adamant. *He* refused to see Mehrunnisa too, although she commanded him many times. The only person Mahabat would see, on Mehrunnisa's behalf, was her brother Abul. So Abul ferried phrases of curses and disrespect between the two, back and forth, for Mahabat would not allow Mehrunnisa out of her apartments.

She sweated there, literally, confined within four walls. If she ever stepped out, Mahabat said—and he sent his Rajput soldiers to make good his word—she must be heavily veiled. Not the flimsy covering of chiffon that showed her teeth and her smile or even the blue of her eyes, but a thick, black cotton under which she would be faceless. She must not raise her voice in public; a Mughal woman's voice must never be heard. What Mahabat once demanded of Jahangir all those years ago—that Mehrunnisa be subdued, that it must not be her hand that ruled the empire—he now made true. He made her pay for his ten years at Kabul, for the years he had aged while there.

So Mehrunnisa paced the carpets in her apartments threadbare, fury simmering inside her. Mahabat had taken from her every duty, little and big, and each day the irritation grew. On the other side of this anger was a deepening hurt. She missed Jahangir desperately, the bed beside her an ocean of emptiness every night. She fretted about him——was he well, had his cough come back, did he eat properly, was he smoking too much opium, drinking too much wine?

Mahabat allowed just one meeting, at which he was present.

Mehrunnisa stood at the door to Emperor Jahangir's rooms, shock rendering her immobile and silent. Jahangir had suddenly grown old in the time she had not seen him. He could no longer breathe without gasping, and she could hear the air scraping against his tired lungs. He cried when he saw her, she did too, kneeling by his bed, his trembling hands cradling her face. They talked, heads close to one another, indifferent to Mahabat Khan standing at the door.

'Let me stay here, Mahabat. His Majesty is unwell,' Mehrunnisa said, despising the timbre of pleading in her tone.

'That is simply not possible, your Majesty.'

A eunuch came to lift her from her knees and take her out of the room. Mehrunnisa paused in front of Mahabat long enough to say in a quietly furious voice, 'If his Majesty dies in your care, Mahabat, I will have your skin cut in strips from your body while you still live.'

He did not answer, merely turned away, eyebrows arched. But for a brief moment, Mehrunnisa saw a quiver of uncertainty around Mahabat's lips.

Back in her rooms, she was only furious. No longer frustrated, or debilitated by Mahabat, or even apprehensive, but quite simply in a rage. Jahangir was dying, and she could not be with him. She would demolish Mahabat Khan. He did not allow her to step out of her apartments, so she would decimate him from within.

'Hoshiyar,' Mehrunnisa said.

The eunuch rose from his place at the door and came to her. He led her to her bed, and Mehrunnisa leaned into him. To the guards at the door, it seemed like her Majesty was too tired; she needed Hoshiyar's help. They did not see—for Mehrunnisa's back was to them—that with her head on the eunuch's shoulder, her lips moved softly.

A week later, in the very middle of the night, as the city of Kabul lay hushed and silent, wreathed in dreams, the Ahadis, the imperial bodyguards, stormed the camp of Mahabat Khan's Rajput soldiers.

Before the soldiers could even awaken or take a breath of air, throats were slashed, chests perforated, heads hammered against stones. The Ahadis proceeded to massacre them methodically. At the end of three hours, the soldiers' cries had stilled, along with the life from their bodies. Those who were fortunate enough to keep their lives—having hidden in rice bins, or under piles of sheets and clothes, or inside trunks—were yanked out and sold as slaves in the Kabul markets, clad in iron chains and led away like cattle by their new owners.

When Mahabat heard the news the next morning, he was at breakfast with Muhammad Sharif. The ten years apart had changed the views and behaviour of the two former friends; they no longer were one in thought and deed. At Mehrunnisa and Jahangir's first command to come to court to answer the charges against him, Mahabat had written to Sharif, asking for help. *Go to the Emperor, Sharif,* he had said, *make his Majesty see reason. If anyone can do this on my behalf, you can, dear friend.*

But Sharif had not sent him a reply, only months of silence. And this morning, as they sat together, Sharif said, 'You have done wrong, Mahabat.'

Mahabat flared up, his brown face set in clean lines of anger, eyes afire. 'And what is it you have done, Sharif? Lived at court like a pig in a pen, content with your meals, wallowing in a sty filled with stink and sloth. Fed by a woman's hand. The whole empire has rotted thus.'

But Sharif would not rise to meet Mahabat's words. He said again, shaking his head with the disapproval of a strict mulla, 'You have done wrong. You are not Emperor, Mahabat. This is not your place. Allah Himself has ordained who is to be king and who a subject—one blood cannot mix with the other.'

Mahabat was fighting panic at Sharif's words when an attendant bent to tell him of the slaughter at the Rajput camp. Mehrunnisa was responsible, of this he had no doubt. How could she have managed to mobilize the entire contingent of the imperial bodyguards from behind her prison walls?

He turned to his friend, tears swamping his face. 'Sharif...'

But Muhammad Sharif merely rose from his seat, bowed to Mahabat, and left his house. He no longer wanted a part of this. He left his unspoken accusations behind: *if these men died, it is because of you. It is because you chose to stomp on the normal order of things, Mahabat.*

Mahabat Khan wiped his face and raced to Emperor Jahangir's apartments. He put up as much of a bluster as he could, complaining about the behaviour of the Ahadis, demanding retribution.

Jahangir, propped up against the divan's pillows so his breathing could be easier, did not budge. He even smiled at the quaking minister. His body had weakened, but nothing would take away the dignity of royalty. The Emperor gave Mahabat two Ahadis, who were said to be the leaders.

'If you speak anymore, Mahabat, of *anyone* else complicit in this, I will have your tongue cut out,' Jahangir said. He then banished Mahabat from his presence. 'If your soldiers cannot defend themselves, perhaps they should look for another leader.'

At the end of that summer, in September of 1626, the imperial court set out from Kabul with Mahabat Khan still nominally in the lead. They were one day's march from Rohtas when Mehrunnisa decided that the minister had weakened enough. She stole into Jahangir's tent one night, cutting a slit through the canvas and slipping in. So lax was the guard around her that though the soldiers had seen her leave, not one hand had dared to raise itself to block her way. With the Rajput camp massacre, the balance of power had shifted, for Mahabat had had charge of those men, and he had not been able to defend them.

The next morning, Abul went to Mahabat Khan's camp to inform him of Jahangir's wishes. 'The Emperor wishes to delay his march to Rohtas,' Abul said.

'Why?' Mahabat asked suspiciously.

'He wishes to stay back at camp to review her Majesty's cavalry. You are to proceed to Rohtas.'

Mahabat listened to his new orders. He had been by the Emperor's side for the last three months, knowing that if he left, he would lose everything. But he wanted to be gone. This was not the life for him. Mahabat did not want Jahangir's hatred, and that was all he had now. He was tired of playing king. He had not wanted this coup, or the power that came along with it. Once... many years ago, when he had been younger, he could have seen it through. He also knew that Sharif was right—there was no royal blood within him, and the crown could only belong to those so blessed by Allah. He *had* done wrong.

Mahabat gathered his few remaining Rajput soldiers and fled as far away from Rohtas as possible.

For Mehrunnisa, Mahabat's defeat was but a small victory. There was too much still to be done. Jahangir was going to die... and soon. Shahryar had to be groomed for his new position as Emperor, and this would not be easy. In the last few months the prince had cowered in his apartments, done what Mahabat had told him to do, played at marching and wars with his mock armies. And, more worryingly for Mehrunnisa, Shahryar had been falling ill too often lately, with strange and sudden fevers that came and went, rashes that blossomed in patches on his face and hands.

But there was one result of Mahabat's coup Mehrunnisa had not yet come to fully recognize. With Mehrunnisa confined to her apartments, Abul had been her voice to the outside world, carrying her commands to the court and the nobles. The courtiers had not seen her at the jharoka, and without this sight of her, without the sound of her voice, they had lost their faith in her. Mahabat's coup, ineffective as it ultimately was, had injured Mehrunnisa too.

If Jahangir died soon, it would be Abul they would turn to, not the woman who had directed their lives for the last sixteen years.

And if they turned to Abul, they would turn to Prince Khurram.

Chapter Twenty-nine

On becoming king, Jahangir was at first very severe. He meted out strict justice to all evil-doers, for which he was called Adil Padshah, or the 'Just' king. This lasted until he got into the clutches of this woman, who has ruined his fair name.

—B. NARAIN, TRANS., AND S. SHARMA, ED.,
A Dutch Chronicle of Mughal India

THE YEAR TURNED INTO ANOTHER WHILE THE IMPERIAL COURT WAS AT Lahore. But these were not a quiet few months for Mehrunnisa. Jahangir sickened steadily during the months of Mahabat Khan's coup. It was an enormous effort to keep his composure while Mahabat badgered him into signing farmans, exhausting to read every single one of them, to argue against estates bestowed on Mahabat's relatives and friends. Over the years, Mehrunnisa had taken so much of this burden from him. She was the only person he trusted absolutely—Mahabat could not take her place.

And the nights were lonely and frightening, especially when he could not breathe and stayed awake coaxing air into his lungs. Jahangir wanted Mehrunnisa by his side desperately, he wanted to curl up against her, to hear her say that he would become better.

So it took Emperor Jahangir a long time to recover after Mahabat Khan fled. He would not allow Mehrunnisa out of his presence, and he was too sick to go to the jharoka or the Diwan-i-khas for the daily audiences. When she saw how much Jahangir had been undermined, Mehrunnisa sent her brother after Mahabat Khan. Abul was to bring him back alive, and she would decide Mahabat's punishment personally. Abul left, and he raced behind the man who had so ignominiously captured him a few months ago. They flew through districts and jagirs along the north-western edge of the empire, but Mahabat was always a day's ride ahead, and Abul soon tired.

He returned to confess failure to his sister—Mahabat Khan was not to be caught. Mehrunnisa took her revenge in other ways then. She confiscated all of Mahabat's lands, posted imperial guards over his fields and estates, and raided any caravans that travelled under his name. She made Mahabat Khan a fugitive.

There was, of course, yet another dissident in the empire, one of long standing now—Prince Khurram. Quiet at first in exile in Nasik, Khurram gathered an army and rushed north upon hearing of Mahabat's coup. What it was he had in mind was not clear, least of all to the prince himself. He only knew that Mehrunnisa had somehow been vanquished by Mahabat, the crown floundered, perhaps if he stormed the treasury at Lahore... or he attacked the court itself... or he could snatch the imperial turban from his father's head. So, filled with these fanciful ideas, Khurram came roaring up north, laying siege on towns and villages, asking for fidelity from the vassal kings he met on the way. Some agreed to support him, some did not.

Then the coup ended, and Khurram fled back to Nasik and from there to the Deccan kingdoms again. He roamed the southern border of the empire, straining to set foot upon Mughal land again, detesting the inactivity, hating to be such a coward. But he could not take too many chances. Arjumand was pregnant again, and they had their little children with them. Also, Khurram kept falling sick with fever. But he wanted the empire. He still wanted the crown.

And this was when Mahabat Khan wrote to him from his place of hiding, offering to support Khurram in whatever he wanted to do. Neither thought it ironical that they should form an alliance— in Mughal India, with so much power and so much money at stake, loyalties shifted thus, from one person to another, as though born of lifelong friendships. Mansabs, jagirs, titles, gold mohurs and robes of honour more than made up for enmities and hatreds.

Mehrunnisa spent long hours by Jahangir's bed, keeping as many troubles from him as she could. So she did not tell him when news came to her that Mahabat Khan and Prince Khurram were now collaborators. But she kept herself informed of their every movement—whether it was to rise, or brush their teeth, or shout, or fight. She knew where they laid their heads at night, with whom, and why. She knew their thoughts before they did.

A week into February in 1627, Mehrunnisa held a hugely lavish party in her gardens at the Lahore Fort. She gave Shahryar a raised mansab, and every single noble at court of any significance was invited to this party. From behind a screen, she watched as the men bowed in front of Shahryar in the konish and backed out slowly with their spines still bent. This was her way of making sure the courtiers gave their hearts and minds to the man who would next be Emperor.

In March, Jahangir's asthma worsened and they left for Kashmir again, hoping the clean, cool air of the mountains would relieve the pain in his chest.

The attendant timidly brought forth the mirror and held it in front of Shahryar.

He plunged back into the pillows and buried his head. 'What has happened to me?'

Shahryar peeped over the embroidered edge of the sheet and

yanked the small mirror towards his face again. A white, unblemished monkey stared back at him. His head was smooth as a shaven coconut, gleaming with oil. He had *no* hair—where his eyebrows had been, there was only the slight puckering of pink skin; his cheeks were clean of sideburns; his chin and upper lip were slick with sweat and nothing else. Even his eyes were little black holes ringed by lashless lids. Pale patches splotched uglily over his nose and neck.

'What is this?' he yelled. 'Who is this in the mirror? What has happened?'

The royal hakims stood in a row at the bottom of his bed, their gazes downward. Finally, one bent in the taslim. With his back still bowed, he said, 'Your Highness, it is a form of leprosy.'

Shahryar let the mirror fall. Leprosy! That dreaded, incurable affliction that ate away at extremities. He held a shuddering hand to his face and counted his fingers. Five, the nails were still wedged firmly under his skin, still pink with health, with little white half-moons. No, they had not vanished... yet. Shahryar dug his hands under his armpits, as though to keep them away from the disease. He did not want his arms and legs to become mere stumps. The prince moaned, drew his knees to his chest, wrapped his arms around himself, and started to rock. He wanted to cry, wanted to shout against the fate that had brought him to this. Out of the corner of his eyes, Shahryar saw the eunuchs and slaves step back a pace or two. Hands flew stealthily to noses, as if the very air he breathed was poisonous to them.

He looked up at the hakims. Now they met his gaze. At least they did not fear being so near him, he thought. 'Do something.' It was a plea, not a command.

The hakims bowed again. 'We have done everything we could, your Highness. Nothing seems to work.'

'Nothing? Absolutely nothing?'

The physicians shook their heads. They could try, of course, and would try, a few brave ones spending hours at the prince's bedside, but they had given Shahryar the best treatment imperial money could buy. Yet his hair had fallen out, the leprosy had spread.

An attendant entered the room. 'Her Majesty has come to visit.'

Shahryar pulled the sheet over his nose and wrapped one edge around his head like a turban. 'I cannot see her. Tell her to go away.'

'She insists, your Highness—' the eunuch started.

'I do,' Mehrunnisa interrupted the man and swept into the room, followed by Hoshiyar. 'What has happened to you, Shahryar? What sort of illness is this? You have not shown yourself at court since May. Is this the behaviour worthy of a future Emperor?'

At her entrance, the hakims sank to their knees, eyes fastened to the ground. One or two glanced up, this was a chance not to be missed, to be this close to the Empress, to perhaps see her face— surely, she was not veiled. But as gazes rose, Hoshiyar's heavy hand came down upon their shoulders. He said softly, 'It would be better if no man looked upon her Majesty.' After that, no one dared.

Shahryar had by now covered himself completely with his sheet.

'Go away,' he mumbled. 'I cannot see you now.'

Mehrunnisa yanked at the sheet and froze when she saw the denuded creature. Her first thought was whether Ladli had seen him like this. Her second was, This is the man Ladli married? She flinched and let the sheet fall.

Shahryar laughed, his teeth salt-white against his mottled, diseased skin. 'Are you afraid, your Majesty?'

Mehrunnisa ignored the jibe in his tone and turned instead to the hakims.

'What happened to him? Why didn't anyone inform me?' she asked sharply.

'Your Majesty, the prince specifically asked that you should not be told.'

'What is it, though?'

The men did not speak. From the bed, Shahryar laughed again. There was just a hint of madness in that laugh, thin, from the edge of his mouth. 'Leprosy, your Majesty. Your daughter's husband has leprosy. Look'——he held up his hands, and Mehrunnisa's gaze attached to them—'your daughter will be touched by these hands. Pray Allah it does not come to her.'

She turned away, forcing herself to do so, disgust beginning to rise in her. Why was she to be cursed with this behaviour from every prince? Shahryar, the once malleable idiot, had turned, over the years, as stubborn as an ass. All this had come from her—if he was a commander of a lofty mansab, one just below hers, it was because she had raised his mansab; if he owned lands in the empire, it was she who had gifted them to him. And in doing this, she had raised his consequence, given him prestige. Like Khurram and Khusrau, he too chose to trample on her. What fools these boys were, she thought.

'Will the prince be able to take up his state duties?' she asked.

'His Highness is perfectly healthy, your Majesty. There is nothing wrong with his mind.'

Shahryar glared at his mother-in-law. 'I am not going out in public like this.'

'You have to, Shahryar,' Mehrunnisa replied. 'The Emperor is unwell and the people are getting restless. They must see the heir to the throne. You can wear a wig and some false eyebrows if necessary.'

'No,' Shahryar said mutinously. 'I will not go out of my apartments. You cannot force me. Go away.'

Mehrunnisa stared at him in exasperation. What were a few hairs compared to an empire? Why did he not see what was at stake? Shahryar wanted the throne, he had said so many times, but did he think it would come to him without effort, a gift for his taking? 'We will talk of this tomorrow.' She turned and left the room.

The next day, Shahryar sent a message to his father asking permission to return to Lahore. He hoped that the warm weather would bring some cure. Jahangir agreed and persuaded Mehrunnisa to let the prince go. She did not allow Ladli and Arzani to leave her, though.

So Shahryar set out with his retinue to Lahore, and a few days later Mehrunnisa and Jahangir followed—they could not risk being too far from the prince.

Camp was pitched at Bairam Kala, a favourite hunting spot. The town lay snug against the foothills of the Himalayas, lush and heady pine forests smothering the slopes behind it. It was the gateway to India—called thus when Kashmir and the mountains had been foreign territory. Even thirty years after the conquest of Kashmir, when Mehrunnisa and Jahangir stopped at Bairam Kala, they still felt as if they were stepping on Indian soil for the first time. The Emperor, too weak to ride a horse, opened his eyes as the palanquin came to a stop.

'Where are we?' he asked.

'Bairam Kala, your Majesty,' Mehrunnisa replied.

'Ah...' Jahangir fell back on his cushions. 'I used to hunt here. Those were good days...'

'They were indeed good days,' Mehrunnisa said gently. 'If you rest, you will regain your health and we can return here to hunt.'

'I wish to hunt today.'

'Not today, your Majesty.' Mehrunnisa shook her head. 'Some other time, when you are better.'

'Will you deny me this last pleasure?' Jahangir asked.

'Hush, you must not speak thus of last pleasures.' She crawled forward on her knees until she lay beside him in the palanquin. It was mid-afternoon, the sun hung steadily overhead. Mehrunnisa leaned her head against Jahangir's shoulder, and he touched her face with his hand. They both gazed out of the thin ochre netting into the shimmering waves of heat over the mountains. The pine trees swam in a sea of green, the air redolent of crushed pine needles.

'This is the end, Mehrunnisa,' he said softly. 'Will you be all right?'

'Yes,' she said after a long time. 'I will miss you, your Majesty.'

'Let me hunt.'

Mehrunnisa summoned the Mir Shikar and ordered him to round up game. Attendants went into the nearby forests and drove deer and other game to the hunting grounds. Jahangir was brought to the grounds in a chair carried on the shoulders of four bearers. They set the Emperor down and handed him his musket. He was too weak even to lift the musket or to sit up straight in his chair.

Nonetheless, he hoisted it to his shoulder and pointed at the stag standing in front of him. He hit it in its right hind leg, and the stag stumbled away.

'Go after it!' Jahangir yelled, his eyes feverish with excitement.

An attendant ran behind the stag. As he passed the nearby cliff his foot slipped. He seemed to hesitate there, aslant in the air for a moment, and then he plunged over the cliff into the ravine. His thin, keening wail of distress came rising up to them.

'Rescue the man,' Mehrunnisa cried.

A few servants ran to the edge of the cliff and looked down. They turned back to the royal couple and shook their heads.

Jahangir started shivering. 'This means I am to die now, Mehrunnisa.'

'It was an accident,' Mehrunnisa said. She signalled to the attendants, and they lifted the chair and took Jahangir back to camp. On the way there, she laughed and talked, a little too much, turning his face to hers with an insistent hand. She did not allow him to dwell on the omen. *It meant nothing, your Majesty. You will become better, and then we can return here for another hunt.* Mehrunnisa gave him wine to drink, but Jahangir could barely keep it in his mouth, let alone let it slide down his throat. An hour later, a fever came to catch him, and he became delirious.

That night, as Mehrunnisa sat by his side, Jahangir said one lucid word. 'Water.'

She poured some water into a goblet and held it to his lips. He drank and fell back. Jahangir slept, his breathing no longer harsh, and Mehrunnisa stayed by him. She watched his face in the light from the lamps. Memories came to her then, and through the long night. She remembered them both young, that first kiss outside Ruqayya's apartments when he had shattered her heart with wanting. Their wedding, a quiet one upon her insistence. Their fights, some torridly physical; their coming together after those fights as though no one else mattered. And no one else had, Mehrunnisa thought. Her whole self was vested in this man. After him... well, even before him, there had been nobody else.

In the early hours, attendants flitted around the tent with messages, but Mehrunnisa allowed no one inside. Outside the Emperor's tent, the imperial court gathered. The nobles came to stand there in clothes of white, for mourning. They were silent. They watched the flap of the tent. They could not hear Jahangir's voice anymore.

As the night fled to give way to a pale grey dawn, Jahangir took one more deep breath. His body jerked, his lungs fought for air, and he put out his hand with his eyes still closed and let it fall upon Mehrunnisa's. His fingers closed upon hers.

Emperor Jahangir did not breathe again.

It was 28 October 1627. He was fifty-eight years old that year.

Chapter Thirty

The will of Jehangire had been opened immediately upon his demise. He had, at the instigation of the Sultana, named his fourth son Shariar, as his successor in the throne; but that prince had, some weeks before, set out for Lahore.

—ALEXANDER DOW,
The History of Hindostan

MEHRUNNISA SAT THERE AS JAHANGIR'S HAND GREW COLD IN HERS. HIS fingers were still wrapped around hers, the ring with the areca-nut-sized ruby rubbing chill against her palm. Akbar gave him this, she thought, when he passed the crown on to his son. She bent to gently put her face against his. *Wake, my lord. Wake and speak to me. Who will I talk with now?* She could not bear this massive hollowness inside her. This body lying here was her husband of sixteen years, the man she had loved beyond all else for much longer, since she was eight. How would she now live without him?

She put her arms around his cold neck and laid her head on his chest. The embroidery on his white kurta's front scratched against her cheek. It was strange to lie like this and not hear the familiar heartbeat, or the rasping of air in his asthmatic lungs. If only he would talk once more, Allah, just once more, that was all she asked. Mehrunnisa lifted her head and smoothed the hair from

Jahangir's forehead. When had his hairline receded so far over his head? When did this intense white come to catch his sideburns? Without life in his body—in his smile, his eyes, his ability to touch her—all this suddenly became so visible to her. She touched the pearls he wore in his ears that had become such a fashion now, which he had first donned after an illness. There was so much about him that people must not forget. Jahangir had been a just Emperor, he had been kind and generous to his people, more willing to listen to them than any other before, even his father. This... no one must forget.

Mehrunnisa raised herself tiredly. She did not cry, she could not cry, something inside her took away that relief. She turned his hand over, traced a line over the nails, the hair on the back, the imperial ruby ring that was Akbar's, then Jahangir's, and now... She looked away. She must get to Shahryar, and send him a message soon. He had to be crowned as soon as possible. Mehrunnisa kissed her husband's hand a last time and rose from her place. She grabbed one corner of the blue chiffon veil lying on the divan near her and flung it into the air and over her head. She lingered by the tent flap, willing strength to come back into her again. Her voice must not shatter, her back must be straight, her chin high, all these if she was to convince the court outside that Shahryar must be heir. Then she went out of the tent.

A low mist hung over the camp, touching every face, turban and chest with dampness, but all the nobles still tarried around Emperor Jahangir's tent. They stood waiting as though they were in the Diwan-i-am, their arms folded across, fingertips splayed just right on elbows. Etiquette was followed here too—the nobles were arranged according to ranks, titles and mansabs, the more common ones falling to the very back, so far from the tent that only

Emperor Jahangir's red and gold flag, with its crouching lion in front of a rising sun, was visible.

Hoshiyar Khan cleared a path for Mehrunnisa. She faltered for just a moment, and as he had so many years ago, he said to her so no one else could hear, 'Courage, your Majesty.'

She stepped out then into the morning mist. Coolness came to cover her gently, welcome after the stifling warmth inside fed by coal braziers. The courtiers were all dressed in white kurtas and pyjamas, their heads were bare; in that dim light they looked like silent ghosts. Around them, the night torches still burned, though low now, wisping blue smoke upward. Mehrunnisa stood in front of the men, her hands clasped at her waist, under her veil. Somewhere in the distance a horse whinnied, and she waited for it to quiet.

'The Emperor has departed from this world to the abode of paradise.'

The men sighed. In the morning hush, it was like a breath of errant wind, here now, gone in an instant. Some eyes filled with tears, but no one dared to raise their hands and wipe their faces. Seeing those tears, Mehrunnisa felt the beginnings of a sob catch inside her, and she stifled it. Did she give them confidence, she wondered, standing here in front of these men who towered over her, who had fought battles without fear for anything, least of all their lives, who would give those very lives to Emperor Jahangir if he so much as hinted it? Would they do this for her?

She spoke again, her voice clear and resonant. 'His Majesty wished for Prince Shahryar to be crowned Emperor. I am here to ask for your fealty on behalf of his Majesty.'

Still not one person moved. At her first sentence, there had been a little flutter, an almost imperceptible shake of heads, but she rushed on to say that this was what Jahangir wanted. What were they thinking? She looked at them intently, but faces were shuttered to her. Mehrunnisa knew she was asking for something difficult—Shahryar had not, could never, inspire confidence as an Emperor. But she would help him. He would have her strength, her power behind him. Mehrunnisa met each gaze without flinching. These amirs were all warriors, as all nobles in the empire had to be, but bereft of their swords, daggers, muskets and bows, they were now statesmen. She turned finally to the man standing closest to her.

'Abul,' she said, 'will you come within the tent with me?'

Abul Hasan bowed. 'Yes, your Majesty.'

He came up to her, and Mehrunnisa allowed herself to lean on his arm as they went into the tent. She wanted the nobles to see her thus too—as a woman wanting support in this time of need, when it was not just Emperor Jahangir who had died, but her husband.

Hoshiyar Khan let the flap of the tent fall down behind them and stood guard outside. For a few minutes, the nobles stayed where they were, then hands moved to brush away tears, and they glanced at one another. It was at this time the empire was most unstable, their lives had no direction, they did not know to whom they were to bow their heads. They looked towards Hoshiyar, but the eunuch's face was impassive.

Mehrunnisa led Abul to Jahangir. There, he touched his forehead to Jahangir's bare feet.

'His Majesty is at peace now, Mehrunnisa,' he said.

She drew the veil from her face. 'Abul, we must leave here for Lahore as soon as possible. Shahryar must wear the crown before the week has passed. I want you to make the preparations.'

'Of course,' he said quickly, almost too quickly for Mehrunnisa. 'Leave the arrangements to me, Mehrunnisa. You should stay here, by the Emperor, while the body is prepared for interment. This is the role you must play now.'

Mehrunnisa nodded. In the brief minutes she had been outside, she had realized this too. The nobles paid heed to her words, but she felt them move away somehow. It was as though her voice had no strength if it did not call out from behind the Emperor. Abul was right, a grieving widow who kept her mouth shut and face concealed from the outside world was who she should be now. Ah, if only Shahryar were here and not at Lahore. He was only a two-day journey from his dead father, but it might well have been a thousand miles. And of all the people, she had to turn to Abul, to use his man's voice to give her countenance. Abul, who had constantly betrayed her with Khurram. Thankfully Khurram was more than a thousand miles away now. Before he could be anything close to menacing, the imperial turban would reside on Shahryar's head. Still...

'Will you betray me, Abul?' she asked.

He shook his greying head, his eyes meeting hers without fear. 'I will not, Mehrunnisa. You and I, we are of the same blood, I will not betray you.'

Mehrunnisa went to the wooden trunk in one corner of the room, unlocked it, and took out a palm-sized cloth bag. She pulled loose the drawstrings that held the bag together, and took out two mud-coloured seeds.

'Promise me on the datura, Abul,' she said, holding the deadly seeds out to him.

'All right,' he said. Then, in a repetition of what she had once said to him fifteen years ago, 'Is this wise? We could die, and all your plans would be frittered away.'

She dug around along the bottom of the trunk and took out a

mortar and pestle. 'It will be worthwhile even so, for now I want your fidelity, Abul, not the crown. If I have your loyalty, we will not die.'

'All right,' he said again. He watched as she pounded the seeds to a thin white powder.

And so, standing there, across Emperor Jahangir's body, they each wet their right index finger, dipped it in the datura powder, and filled their mouths with the thickly bitter taste of the datura.

'Thank you, Abul,' Mehrunnisa said as he turned to go.

Within the tent, Mehrunnisa retched uncontrollably into a silver bowl, kneeling by Emperor Jahangir. She laid her sweating face against her husband's cold hand. 'It will be as you wanted it, your Majesty.'

But she did not know that though Abul had dipped his index finger into the datura, it was his middle finger that had gone into his mouth and come out clean for her to see.

Outside, Abul called his attendant, Iradat Khan, and ordered a guard around Mehrunnisa. She was not to be allowed to talk to anyone or send messages to Shahryar—if she did, the twenty men around her tent would not live to see another day.

Abul walked away, wiping the datura on the silk of his kurta. There was no question of giving Shahryar the crown, and it was to his advantage that the prince was not here at Bairam Kala; if he had been, Abul would have found it difficult to stop him. This bought him some time.

He called for his swiftest runner and sent him to the Deccan with a message by mouth—Emperor Jahangir was dead, Khurram was to head for Lahore immediately.

But how could he keep the throne empty for three months?

The empire would disintegrate in a civil war. Abul thought hard about the other claimants to the throne. Bulaqi, Khusrau's eldest son, was also in line for the crown, and Bulaqi was here, in the royal encampment. So were Khurram's eldest sons, of course—he had sent them as surety against his rebelling many years ago. But Abul would not put either of Khurram's sons on the throne; they would have to wait their time, after his death. It had to be Bulaqi.

The day passed into night. Attendants bowed their way into the tent to carry out Jahangir's body to prepare it for the burial. Mehrunnisa let them. She did not ask for Ladli to come to her, wanting to be alone for a while to think. She did not allow herself to doubt Abul, and this took a tremendous amount of will power, for everything inside her said that her brother was untrustworthy, but she had no other option. Their father was dead; with Shahryar in Lahore, there was no other man she could turn to. And in this world of hers, when kings died or were born or crowned, men were the most visible, most involved in every public ritual, so she must stay hidden for now.

As night came, she rose exhausted from her divan to go outside. Abul should have brought her news about Shahryar by now. Where was he? She lifted the tent flap and stepped outside. The twenty men around her tent jerked upright and formed a tight circle of guard.

'What is this?'

One man stepped ahead, his spear held across his chest. 'Please go inside, your Majesty. You are not allowed outside your tent.'

'On whose orders?' Mehrunnisa asked.

'On Mirza Abul Hasan's orders. Please go inside now, or we will be forced to carry you in.'

Ah, Abul, Mehrunnisa thought, *so you are a traitor. A base, cowardly man who pledged upon blood and poison not to betray your sister and then did.* She saw then that she should not have taken the time to mourn, not allowed Abul or the other nobles at court or the priests to preach to her about a woman's duties. Cursing Abul would not help now. She beckoned to one of the guards at the back row. He was really still a boy, his face untouched by the barber's razor, little wisps of hair on his upper lip.

When he moved, the first guard came between them. 'You are to talk to no one, your Majesty.'

Mehrunnisa tilted her head upward and met his eyes. 'I want to send a message through this guard to my brother. Be careful of how you talk to me, or your life will be worth little.'

The guard hesitated and then allowed the boy to follow the Empress into her tent. Mehrunnisa took off three rings. The soft golden light from the diyas and braziers set fire to the diamonds, rubies and emeralds in the palm of her hand.

'Take a message to Prince Shahryar at Lahore.'

The youth moved back. 'Your Majesty, I cannot. Mirza Hasan will have my head if he finds out.'

'And I shall have it if Shahryar becomes Emperor,' Mehrunnisa said harshly. 'Be reasonable. Do you really think Mirza Hasan will win? Prince Khurram is miles from here. Before he gets to Lahore, Prince Shahryar will be on the throne. But I cannot do that without your help.'

The boy demurred, his eyes lighting greedily upon the rings.

'Think about it,' Mehrunnisa continued. 'You will be instrumental in putting Prince Shahryar on the throne. Think of the mansabs and jagirs—'

The guard cut into her words. 'I will do it, your Majesty,' he said. 'What do you want me to say to Prince Shahryar?'

Mehrunnisa scribbled a letter in two minutes, for she did not want to keep the boy in her tent longer than was necessary. But her orders to Shahryar were explicit. The prince was to secure the fort at Lahore and gather an army to fight Abul Hasan. More importantly, Shahryar was to write to Qasim Khan, the governor of Agra, and warn him of what was happening. A large chunk of the imperial treasury had been moved back to Agra a few years ago, and Qasim Khan was in charge of it. They needed to be sure that the treasury was secure from Khurram—without the weight of it behind them, the throne, the crown, the imperial turban, were all worthless.

When the boy left, Mehrunnisa sat down to think. Who else could she appeal to? Which nobles would help her, which had she given prominence to during the past few years?

As the night wore on, she prayed too, slipping down to her knees, facing west towards Mecca. *Allah, let Shahryar prove that he has a spine, and if he does, he will be truly worthy of the crown. Let the letter reach him at Lahore.*

The guards watched their Empress's figure through the cloth of the tent, highlighted by lamps. They watched her pray, they watched her pace. They had their orders to keep her confined, but they felt that though she might be physically here, Empress Nur Jahan had a reach that went beyond a mere mortal's ability.

The next day, last rites were performed for Emperor Jahangir. This was an important step in the succession, for until the last rites were performed, Jahangir's reign was not officially at a close. Abul commanded the Emperor's body taken to Lahore for burial. Mehrunnisa, still under heavy guard, followed the bier. But they left a day after Abul and Bulaqi. To Abul's surprise, Mehrunnisa did not protest, or even try to send him a message through the guards.

Worried now, Abul crowned Prince Bulaqi Emperor of Mughal India at Bhimbar as soon as the last prayer was completed over Emperor Jahangir's body. The khutba was read in his name, officially pronouncing him sovereign of his grandfather's empire. It was 29 October 1627, one day after Jahangir's death.

At Lahore, Shahryar paced excitedly in his apartments. He glanced at the letter in his hand. The Emperor was dead and Mehrunnisa had called upon him to gather an army and defend his rights. Shahryar skipped around the edges of the carpets, his feet barely touching the cool stone floors. He would be Emperor soon. He was already Emperor of Hindustan! That would make everyone take notice of him. They had called him nashudani, and ever since the onset of the leprosy, Shahryar had felt even more incompetent. But not anymore... his wig fell over his eyes as Shahryar danced around the room, and he set it straight on his head. Not anymore. He shouted for his attendants.

'Inform the city of the Emperor's demise,' he said. 'Further, send a proclamation that I am Emperor now.'

He then called for his guards and ordered them to seize the royal treasury still at Lahore and all the wealth of the state of Lahore kept under guard at the fort. An army was prepared to meet Abul Hasan. In order to guarantee the support of his army, Shahryar distributed the royal treasury among his soldiers, buying their loyalty. The army was then sent to the Ravi River to prepare for battle with Abul Hasan.

Abul Hasan and his soldiers moved swiftly from Bhimbar to Lahore. His army met Shahryar's army three miles outside the city.

They had hardly begun the battle when Shahryar's men, faced with the might of the imperial army, took fright and fled, leaving Abul to march victorious towards the fort at Lahore.

When Shahryar heard news of the defeat, he ran back to the fort and barricaded himself inside with two thousand of his infantry. The next morning, many of Shahryar's nobles defected to Abul Hasan and allowed the minister access to the fort. He went searching for the prince, who was hiding in the zenana apartments, literally under the skirts of the women of his harem. Abul dragged Shahryar in front of Bulaqi and made him pay homage to his new Emperor. Then, he had the prince blinded and thrown into prison.

All this transpired before Mehrunnisa arrived at Lahore with the funeral cortege. She was ordered confined to her apartments. Every meal she ate, every breath she took, every word that came from her lips—these were all reported to Abul. She tried to see Shahryar, to find out what had happened, how this could have happened. She tried to call for Abul, but he would not take her messages or even acknowledge them.

A few days later, Emperor Jahangir was interred in the Dilkusha gardens on the banks of the Ravi. Abul did not give Mehrunnisa permission to attend the burial.

For three months, Mehrunnisa plotted in her rooms, but she could not buy a single person's loyalty. The empire had its Emperor—she was now merely a Dowager Empress. And all this while Khurram sped towards Agra from the Deccan.

As he neared, he sent a message to his father-in-law. Abul was still at Lahore, keeping sharp watch over Bulaqi and Mehrunnisa. Early in January 1628, Abul entered Bulaqi's apartments, wrenched the imperial turban off his head, and threw him into prison. The muezzins' voices rose over the city of Lahore later that day, still haunting in their sweetness, but calling out another Emperor's name. *All hail Emperor Shah Jahan, Lord of the Mughal Empire.*

Abul had received Khurram's message. On 23 January 1628, the sun woke to witness a mass execution in the grand courtyard of the Lahore Fort. Four men, blindfolded, hands tied behind their backs, stood against the far wall of the courtyard. Abul was to one side, near the two neat rows of archers. The soldiers fitted solid silver arrows into their bows, drew the bowstrings taut, and waited. Abul shivered in the quiet and cold of the early morning, but his hand did not waver as it lifted into the air. The arrows flew straight and strong through the courtyard, taking with them the lives of Bulaqi, Shahryar, and two of Khurram's cousins.

The khutba had been read three times in the last three months since Emperor Jahangir's death. First calling out Bulaqi's name, then Shahryar's, albeit for one short day, and now Khurram's. A bewildered empire struggled to find a home for its loyalties. Who was Emperor? Towards whom should their heads bow?

But as news of the royal princes' deaths spread around the empire, the doubts were banished. There were no claimants to the throne left who could not link their bloodlines directly to Khurram and Arjumand.

And so Khurram came riding into Agra, triumphant and assured that the crown was his. As the royal party progressed down the main street of Agra, up the sheer and blind-cornered ramps of the fort constructed to confuse enemies, and into the thronging Diwan-i-am, Arjumand leaned out of her howdah, one hand clutching a pillar to steady herself, and flung out silver rupees into the crowd. Finally, their life of exile was over. They would no more be hounded around the empire like fugitives, no more living with mere canvas cloth for a roof, no more packing and fleeing in a few hours' time when bad news came. Khurram was Emperor, as he should be, as was his due.

Abul Hasan had met them outside Agra. Arjumand tugged at the sleeve of her father's qaba. 'Bapa, the Empress—'

'You are Empress now, beta,' he said gently. 'You must become used to this title.'

'Is she under guard, Bapa?'

Abul caught her by the shoulders. 'She is. And this is not for you to worry about, Arju. Let us... let the men think of the safety of the empire.'

She melted back into the confines of her howdah then, yanking the curtains shut. She was Empress because of Khurram and because of her father, nothing in her own right. At least her aunt was no longer a threat. But this hard-won, hard-fought-for victory over Mehrunnisa would not stay with Arjumand for very long. Even as she sat behind Khurram, pride overwhelming her at the sight of the heron's feather in his turban, death came stalking.

For Arjumand Banu Begam, newly styled Empress Mumtaz Mahal, would die in four years—four years during which if she dared something innovative, something outside the zenana, she was stifled with kind words by everyone around her. *This is not for you, your Majesty,* or *this is too much like the Dowager Empress. Do what you do best and be content.* So Arjumand did just that. Her income was enormous, and she used it for charity, for jewels and clothes. She kept the royal seal and the title of Padshah Begam of Khurram's harem. She gave him more children, almost one for each remaining year she had left. And then her fourteenth child came into the world, and with its coming, took away Arjumand's life.

Mehrunnisa lived though, for quite long after Arjumand's death, banished to her mansion at Lahore, and though still on the empire's soil, officially in exile.

Arjumand did not know that Khurram would build the Taj Mahal in her memory. Or that the Taj would come to symbolize this land her grandfather had adopted as his own. Or that as much as she had envied that feast of roses Emperor Jahangir had laid out for her aunt, posterity would remember *her*, Empress for four short years, two, three, even five hundred years from now.

Epilogue

ON 18 DECEMBER 1645, THE TAJ MAHAL WAS VERY NEAR COMPLETION.
Arjumand died in 1631 at Burhanpur, but she would reside forever
in Agra. Her body was disinterred and moved there, to a plot of
land along the banks of the Yamuna that Khurram bought from a
vassal raja. Twenty thousand men and women were employed in
the building of the Taj. An entire city of tents—Mumtazabad—was
erected around the building site, and here masons, stone-cutters,
bullock drivers, silver and gold craftsmen, engineers, architects and
lay labourers lived for years, rearing children into adulthood in the
shadow of the Taj. The money spent on the mausoleum was
enormous, for the work was at a lavish scale. Khurram had hills
levelled, the ground flattened, and trees cut down, all to improve
the views of the Taj Mahal. Even the Yamuna was carved away
from her original, millennia-old path to curve gently past the Taj.
There were gold wall panels inside the tomb, the main doors were
solid carved silver, a gold railing surrounded the sarcophagus, the
lamp fixtures were of gold, and a velvet canopy with pearls,
diamonds, rubies and emeralds would cover the sleeping Arjumand.

For the outside and inside walls, marble was carted, slab by
slab, to Agra from Jodhpur, a hundred miles away. And each was
carefully inlaid with semi-precious stones. Turquoise came from
Tibet, jasper from Cambay, malachite from Russia, lapis lazuli

from Ceylon, carnelian from the bazaars of Baghdad, along with jade, black marble, amethyst and quartz.

Khurram dedicated the first anniversary of Arju's death with a sumptuous, extravagant party, wine flowing in fountains, alms given in millions to the poor, verses from the Quran chanted day and night by the muezzins until the air was ripe with them. And he bowed his head in front of the Taj Mahal.

Mehrunnisa laughed. In the silence of her apartments, with just the fire in the coal brazier hissing softly in one corner, and Hoshiyar's gentle snores in another, the sound was like the rippling of water over pebbles. Each day that Khurram bowed his head in front of the Taj Mahal, he bowed it in front of Mehrunnisa, for in the design and construction of the Taj, Khurram had copied her own style. She had not seen the Taj, of course—Khurram kept her at Lahore, here she was in exile from him and his court, and he was too afraid of her to let her live freely elsewhere. But Mehrunnisa heard about this marvellous pietra dura inlay of fantastically coloured semi-precious stones in the marble from Jodhpur—how long it took for that inlay to be set into the stone, how hard the work was, how exquisite the final effect. How much like her father's tomb that stood across the Yamuna River...

Hoshiyar stirred, harrumphed in his sleep, his white head nodding over his chest, and Mehrunnisa shut off the sound of her laughter, smiling instead into her pillow. The pietra dura inlay was *her* idea—if the Taj was going to be magnificent at all, it would be because of the woman its builder had hounded from the empire!

The wooden door to her apartments swung open, and Ladli put her head around it. She smiled when she saw Mehrunnisa's bright eyes turned towards her.

'Are you awake, Mama?'

Mehrunnisa beckoned. 'Come here, beta. Where is Arzani?'

'With me,' Ladli said, still softly so as not to awaken Hoshiyar Khan.

They came into the room on bare feet, and Mehrunnisa watched them approach her bed. In these last eighteen years, Ladli had aged immeasurably it seemed. Like Mehrunnisa, lines now took hold of the skin of her face, her walk was slower, her voice less assured. But she had that same gentleness within her, that same tenacity of will nothing could shake. After Shahryar's death in 1628, offers of marriage had come in abundance for Ladli, but she would agree to none, not even when the man was a minister at court, one possessed of vast mansabs and jagirs, willing to defy Khurram's wrath. She did not want to be married anymore, it was as simple as that, she said. The first time, it was her duty, now no longer. She had her mother and her daughter and Hoshiyar. And for Ladli, they were enough.

Mehrunnisa glanced at her granddaughter, and for a moment it was as though she were looking at herself in the mirror forty years ago. Arzani had the blue of her eyes, the same straight back, the thick mass of hair to her waist, but none of her quickness. Where at Arzani's age Mehrunnisa had been forever restless, forever wanting something, Arzani had her mother's quietness. What joy this child brought her, Mehrunnisa thought. She remembered how once she had so desperately wanted Arzani to be a boy... but if she had been... she would have died along with Shahryar. The only reason Khurram allowed Arzani to live was because she posed no threat to him. She was twenty-one this year, should have been married long ago, but, like Ladli, she found no one to interest her enough. The interest would come after the marriage, Mehrunnisa almost scolded her granddaughter. But she had neither the heart nor the strength to press for a match.

She reached out to them, and they came to kneel on either side of her bed on the white and gold Persian carpets. Ladli's eyes were red from weeping, but she smiled, not willing to bring her grief into her mother's chamber.

'Will you be all right, beta?' Mehrunnisa asked, cupping Ladli's chin with her palm.

'Of course.' Ladli's voice did not falter. 'Are you comfortable, Mama? Shall I change the sheets? The pillows?'

'No,' Mehrunnisa said. In her mind, she was deeply grateful that she could face death so easily, awake to her child and grandchild, able to talk with them. She listened while Arzani told her a story—some gossip from the neighbour's house, a child who looked little like his father and too much like his uncle, whose vastly different looks bespoke the fact that the two men were stepsiblings.

Ladli settled the cotton *razai* over her mother, tucking the top ends under her arms. They must be cold though, Mehrunnisa thought, for winter had laid hold of Lahore outside. She laughed at Arzani's story, thinking how stupid the woman was to have made a child with a man who looked so different from her husband, how much easier if they looked just a little alike.

This was peaceful, to lie here with her most beloved people around her, to not want anything anymore. It was time to go—not because she was unwell but because she had no will to live any longer. She had completed Emperor Jahangir's tomb and her own, fighting Khurram for payment on every invoice, for he had frozen her vast wealth in the imperial treasury. Abul had died too, four years ago; he was buried here at Lahore, but Mehrunnisa had not gone to his tomb, or sent condolences to his other children.

Only in the last year had some calmness come over Mehrunnisa. She rose each day with a simple joy within her. She finally understood how the Jain monk Siddhicandra felt, what he had talked about when he had said that peace came from a lack of want. Siddhicandra had found this when he had been little more than twenty; it had taken Mehrunnisa a lifetime.

And yet, even with this knowledge, she could not help wondering about her life, about those last moments after Emperor Jahangir's death, if she could have changed anything. What if Ladli *had* married Khurram? What if Arjumand had approved of this? That was where she had made a mistake, Mehrunnisa thought. She should have asked *Arjumand* instead of Khurram. But Mehrunnisa had never asked for help, for advice, from any one woman within the zenana—except for Ruqayya—in the early years. She had simply never turned to a woman for support, always the men. Bapa, Abul, Khurram, Hoshiyar, and, of course, she had had Emperor Jahangir's benevolence, without which none of the others would have meant anything. Perhaps that was where she had strayed, Mehrunnisa thought, in not consolidating her power among the women, in the women's world in which she lived.

'I wish I could live my life again.'

Ladli kissed her mother's hand, and that was when Mehrunnisa realized she had spoken aloud. 'You have lived enough lives for ten women, Mama,' Ladli said.

And then she started to cry, her arms around her mother's waist, hiding her tears in the cotton of the razai.

Mehrunnisa closed her eyes at the sound, remembering how she had not been able to cry when Jahangir had died. How the tears had come for years afterward with the laying of each slab of marble of his mausoleum, when she had lit the diyas inside the tomb each night, when she had knelt in prayer by his sarcophagus. *I will be with you soon, your Majesty.*

An hour later, Ladli dried her tears and whipped her head to the corner where Hoshiyar sat, his head still curved into his chest. The sound of his snoring had stopped, and he was too still, how his neck must hurt at that angle, Ladli thought. And then she realized that he could no longer feel any pain, for his chest did not rise and fall with breath. She rose to go to the man who had been a beloved uncle, a cherished father to her for so many years, and as she did, her hand brushed against her mother's.

The room had grown cold as the coal braziers had died down, they needed to be fed, Mama must feel the chill, she must put her hand inside the razai. Ladli picked up her mother's hand and dropped it again. When she looked into Mehrunnisa's face, there was the same stillness, that same loss of breath.

Empress Nur Jahan, too, had died.

Afterword

MEHRUNNISA IS, OF COURSE, KNOWN MORE CONTEMPORARILY AS EMPRESS
Nur Jahan. Jahangir first bestowed on her the title of Nur Mahal,
'Light of the Palace', and later, sometime in 1616, changed it to
Nur Jahan, or 'Light of the World'. In Mughal India, titles were (as
they were in the Europe of that time) marks of imperial favour and
blessing. The nobles of the court and the women of the zenana,
being closest to the Emperor, were all beneficiaries of this favour,
in some cases posthumously.

The word *nur*, signifying 'light', had its antecedents in Emperor
Akbar's time—he was known as a devotee of the sun, even
conceiving a new religion that had at its basis the worship of the
sun. When Jahangir ascended the throne, he used this sun imagery
in his own title, calling himself Nuruddin Muhammad Jahangir
Padshah Ghazi, the first of which was to denote 'Light of the Faith'.
So it was only natural for him to give Mehrunnisa this lofty title
too, calling her the Light of the World, of the imperial world—she
was the one in whom was lodged his well-being and comfort.

I chose to retain the name Mehrunnisa—the name she was
born with—for various reasons. Primary among these was the fact
that it was a name *I* was comfortable with, having lived with her
through *The Twentieth Wife* (Penguin Books India, 2002), which
tells the story of her life before she married Jahangir. I also

believe that both she and Jahangir would have, in private, thought of her as such—Mehrunnisa. The title of Nur Jahan was one for the more public world.

If the other characters in the book are unfamiliar upon reading *The Feast of Roses*, it may be because they too are better known by their later titles. Ghias Beg, Mehrunnisa's father, is known as Itimadaddaula, a title given to him by Emperor Jahangir. And his tomb at Agra, diagonally across from the Taj Mahal (and, in my belief, the early ancestor of the Taj, with its prominent and lavish use of pietra dura inlay of semi-precious stones in marble), is called Itimadaddaula's tomb. Mehrunnisa's first husband, Ali Quli Khan Istajlu, is known by his title of Sher Afghan. Her brother Abul Hasan is known as Asaf Khan IV. Her niece, Arjumand, is Mumtaz Mahal—the woman for whom the Taj was built, the woman from whose title of Mumtaz Mahal the very name of the Taj Mahal comes. Khurram is Emperor Shah Jahan; he is very little known as Khurram.

The Feast of Roses is a fictional account of Mehrunnisa's life as Empress Nur Jahan. But it is, in the main, historically accurate. Mehrunnisa did form a junta of sorts with her father Ghias, her brother Abul, and Prince Khurram. It was evident, to courtiers and travellers alike, that from behind the veil it was Mehrunnisa's voice that commanded the actions of these three men. But only to a point, since the rift in the junta also became obvious about halfway through her reign as Empress.

There is documentation on Mehrunnisa's attempts to marry Ladli to Khusrau, and to Khurram, although the latter is sometimes regarded as false by contemporary historians. I chose to believe both accounts, for the arguments put forward against Khurram's marrying Ladli were mostly these—that Khurram was so in love with Arjumand that he would not countenance marrying again, and that to Arjumand's cousin. Khurram undoubtedly adored Arjumand; he demonstrated that by building the world's greatest monument to love, the Taj Mahal, in her memory. But he did marry again, about five years after he married Arjumand. More importantly, why would Mehrunnisa not ask Khurram *first*, before she asked Khusrau? Khurram was the prince she was so clearly schooling to be the next Emperor, why search elsewhere for a suitable groom for her daughter? Especially Khusrau, half-blind, half-demented, blessed only by his father's disfavour. Shahryar was almost certainly a last choice, for the prince sported, even in his lifetime, the unflattering nickname of nashudani—good-for-nothing.

Sir Thomas Roe mentions Mehrunnisa copiously in his memoirs, realizing, quite soon after his arrival in India, that the 'beloved wife' was the real power behind Jahangir's throne. He is, naturally, an excellent source for Anglo-Indian relations during Jahangir's rule, and an interesting witness of court politics and the junta's infighting.

Mahabat Khan's coup is also based on historical record. Mehrunnisa was about fifty years old when this happened, had been Empress for sixteen years, and was at the very pinnacle of her reign. The coup hurt her in more ways than one, leading to her swift downfall after Emperor Jahangir's death.

Other incidents—the lion hunt with Jagat Gosini, the public brawl between Mehrunnisa and Jahangir where they slap each other, Mehrunnisa killing the intruder into the imperial zenana—are also documented, though whether they are accurate or the stuff of legend, myth or gossip is in some doubt.

I have taken some liberties with historical facts. The ship *Rahimi*, which indirectly caused so much trouble for the Portuguese

Viceroy, and by association for the entire Portuguese embassy in India, belonged to Jahangir's birth mother, Maryam Muzzamani—not Empress Ruqayya Sultan Begam. Ruqayya did own trading ships, as did Mehrunnisa, but I 'gave' the *Rahimi* to Ruqayya to suit the purposes of my story.

Also, Khurram receives his title of Shah Jahan from his father after the Deccan wars (which he went to more than once), and not the Mewar campaign. But there is little doubt of his complicity either in his brother Prince Khusrau's death or in the wholesale massacre, just before he ascended the throne, of the men connected to the royal family who had any claim at all to the empire.

And since you have reached this far, thanks must go to you, dear reader, for accompanying me on this journey into India's past. *The Feast of Roses* ends Mehrunnisa's story. I do hope you have enjoyed both this story and *The Twentieth Wife* as much as I have enjoyed narrating them.

Indu Sundaresan
October 2002

Acknowledgements

THANKS GO, AGAIN AND ALWAYS, TO THE MEMBERS OF MY CRITIQUE groups, and especially to those who so kindly put aside their own work and speed-read through the manuscript: Louise Christensen Zak, Laura Hartman, Joyce O'Keefe, Julie Jindal, and Janet Lee Carey.

I believe everyone should have a literary agent in his or her life, and quite preferably someone like mine, Sandra Dijkstra. She is a joy to work with, and very engaged in all aspects of my writing, from early reading of drafts to marketing and championing the book through all of its stages. I am also grateful for the effort Sandy's entire agency puts into my work.

The Feast of Roses is thrice blessed at Atria Books. My publisher, Judith Curr, continues to be enormously supportive and friendly, and still willing to put her faith in me. Then there are my two editors: Rosemary Ahern, who worked through the early drafts of the novel and whose vision shaped the final story; and Malaika Adero, who willingly adopted this child of mine and lavishes her care upon it. I am deeply thankful to all three of them.

A disclaimer: I do not play chess. If the chess scene in *The Feast of Roses* is authentic at all, it is due to these people: Santosh Zachariah, who 'found' the game for me, given strict restrictions on number of moves and ease of comprehension; David Hendricks of the Microsoft Chess Club, who, one afternoon, laid out a chess board on a table in the cafeteria and painstakingly took me through the moves and explained the motivations of the players; and my brilliant nephews Gautam and Karthik, who whisked through the game and had to be begged to slow down to a pace more understandable by their doddering old aunt. If, despite all their efforts, there are still mistakes in the game, I readily claim them as mine.

I could not do without the three women who constantly give me love and strength and form my family: Amma, Anu and Jaya.

And finally, I must acknowledge the libraries of the King County Library System and the University of Washington Suzzallo and Allen Libraries for their treasure trove of literature on Mughal India—letters, documents, memoirs, books and maps, which have allowed me to travel through time and distance without leaving home.